Zach drew her slowly toward him.

He smiled, so tenderly it caught at her like a strong vine, so possessively, it terrified and dominated her.

"Oh, Rosita, my little rose, my adored. I know what you are, a lovely little girl, a more lovely woman, all grown up now, ready for love, and marriage. Aren't you, aren't you?"

He held her, his gaze flashing over her, over her slimness and lovely form. His warm mouth closed over her lips, possessed them, hurt them with his hard passion before he became gentle. He pushed back her head so he could kiss her chin, her throat, down to her rounded breasts just revealed by the top of her maillot. She felt stinging heat there, as though he branded her with his lips, made her his, marked her as the belonging of Zach, his thing, his woman, his to flame up, burn up, go to ashes at his will . . .

Also by Janet Louise Roberts

Golden Lotus
Silver Jasmine

Published by
WARNER BOOKS

Flamenco
Rose

Janet Louise Roberts

WARNER BOOKS

A Warner Communications Company

WARNER BOOKS EDITION

Copyright © 1981 by Janet Louise Roberts, Inc. All rights reserved.

Cover art by Elaine Duillo

Warner Books, Inc., 75 Rockefeller Plaza, New York, N.Y. 10019

A Warner Communications Company

Printed in the United States of America

First Printing: July, 1981

10 9 8 7 6 5 4 3 2 1

Flamenco Rose

Chapter 1

Rosita Dominguez stood in the chilly hallway at the end of the line of her brothers and sisters. She would come in last of the dancers. Following her would be the two guitarists, her brother Oliverio and brother-in-law Jacinto.

She smoothed the sharp-frilled skirts of her red dress and tried a little tap of her black shoes. Her hand went to her head, and made sure the braids were fastened securely. Her sister Cristina sometimes fastened hers so lightly that they came loose during the performance and her hair flew about her shoulders. She said it looked more sensuous like that.

At twelve years of age, Rosita did not worry about looking sensuous. She had a trim little body; she was only four feet ten now, and she felt that all she could contribute was a good dance that would not disgrace papa's training.

When the dancing went well, the proprietor of the nightclub paid them better. When it went poorly, he bawled out Rosita's father and reproached him; that made them all sad.

Gypsies seemed to go up and down, Rosita thought. Sometimes she was gay and happy without cause other than that the sun was shining and she had seen a beautiful garden of flowers. Other times she was brooding and silent, depressed equally without cause. Her small face was usually solemn, for she was a thoughtful child, and life was hard in San Juan, Puerto Rico, for Spanish Gypsies who did not always dance as passionately as their audiences expected.

Over the heads of his brood, Papa Pascual Dominguez glanced back critically, to the young Rosita. His inquiring look lingered on her; she nodded quickly to show she was ready. His face softened, his proud look gentled. He mouthed, "My baby," fondly, and she understood.

She squared her shoulders, and listened. The announcer was saying, "And now we have the honor to present to you—Spanish flamenco dancers. They come from a long line of Gypsies—have given Spanish performances—" and finally the words, "the Dominguez dancers!"

There was only a light spattering of applause. It sounded like a small audience tonight. But sometimes there were tourists, and they did not clap much until they were sure they were going to get a good show.

The dancers ran out, followed by two guitarists, who quietly took their places at the back in two chairs. Rosita stood on the end. She was not nervous; she did not look at the audience.

Marcos, next to her in line, whispered, "The Hamiltons are here! Did you hear that?"

She was clapping her hands sharply in rhythm. She frowned. The Hamiltons? Of the big rum family? That must be what he meant.

She glanced at the audience then, and could not avoid seeing the large, round table of guests near the stage. From the array of bottles and plates, it appeared they had been feasting. She saw two red-haired men, one young and the other middle-aged, and some beautiful ladies.

Then she forgot them. The encouraging shouts of her family came to her. *"Ay, ay, ay, Rosita! Rosita! Ay, gitana!"*

She moved forward to the rhythm of the guitars and the clapping hands. Slowly, gracefully at first, she began to dance. Her small feet moved in and out of the patterns she had begun learning when she was scarcely able to walk. There was music in her bones, her father had said approvingly as the tiny Rosita had swayed to their music at home.

She stamped her feet to increase the beat, and the clapping of hands increased. Someone yelled, "*La Soledad! La Soledad! Hola, gitana!*"

Rosita heard it, but could not soften the grave solemnity that made her seem so remote. Her sisters tried to encourage her to smile as she danced, but she could not. It was a serious thing to dance, to be caught up gradually in the ecstasy of movement, in the final wild whirling and oblivion of the music.

The small form moved in and out of the pattern, her grace and quick movements catching the attention of the evening crowd. She lifted her hands over her head, and clapped sharply faster, a signal to the family that she wished to increase her tempo. Her father caught up the rhythm, and the line of dancers picked it up after him. The guitars sang, strumming the melody she liked.

Her feet beat on the wooden floor in ever quickening pattern. Her small, thin arms moved about her in graceful movement, her fingers curling and clicking castanets. She picked up her skirts with one hand, fanned them against her legs swiftly, then went ever faster into the dance.

Not fast enough. Impatiently her hands clapped sharply. Pascual looked proudly at his youngest daughter. He clapped with her, increasing the beat until she nodded her smooth black head, and went into the wild movements, whirling around and around. The crowd murmured, then began to cry out to her encouragingly.

"*Hola*, Rosita! *Hola, gitana! Aya*, Rosita! *La Soledad!*" They caught up the nickname for her. "*La Soledad!*" The little solemn one, the serious one with the lovely grave face that never smiled, though she shone in ecstasy when she danced.

She spun round and round on one foot, her red skirts frilling about her legs. She did not hear anything but a vague blur of sound, only the sharp rhythm of the guitars. Oh, the excitement and pleasure of dancing! Oh, the happiness and joy when it went well, and she felt the music strumming through her small body!

From one end of the stage to the other, she spun, and back again. The crowd cheered, but she scarcely heard. She was so happy; the music burned in her as her small arms flung out again, again, again, in the turns. Then she came to an abrupt, dramatic halt, and with a final click of her heels bent into a low bow.

How they cheered! The waves of applause came up to her, fanning her flushed, perspiring body. She bowed again, curtsyed with her frilled skirts held out. Then demurely she returned to her place on the end beside Marcos.

The music did not stop. The guitars hummed, and Marcos stepped out in his light dancing step, his handsome face serious for once. He took his dancing as seriously as Rosita. The crowd hushed to hear him.

Rosita waited until he had started, then quietly slipped out the side door to her mother. Margarita hugged her baby, then wiped her shoulders and arms with the towel. Rosita took the tissue held out to her and carefully blotted her face, to keep her makeup from smearing.

"It went well, *pequeña*," whispered Margarita. "The Hamiltons applauded much. Your papa will be proud."

"Hamilton Rums?" murmured Rosita, giving her arms a final wipe with the towel.

"*Sí*. Many of the family are ballet dancers. They are critical. I hope they like us all."

Rosita nodded, and waited at the steps, half-hidden from the audience until Marcos was finishing. As his steps increased to a rapid fire of tattoos, and the audience began to applaud in excitement, Rosita slipped up to the stage and stood at the end of the line again, clapping with the dancers to the rhythm.

Marcos finished to applause, bowed several times, and returned to his place. At fifteen, he was almost as good as Tadeo, and had a good feel for music in dancing and the guitar.

Luisa danced next. She was plump, like a cow, Cristina accused, but her pretty face glowed and she was all smiles and had a nice form in the blue full-skirted dress. The men liked her and applauded her as she came forward, with her skirts held out in her plump fingers. Rosita was relieved when she received a good hand. Some nights there were critical people in the audience, who did not like her nice sister. Luisa had such a good heart, she was not like Cristina, who was selfish and vain.

Cristina nodded and came out next to the sharp claps. *"Hola, Cristina,"* Rosita called mechanically. She watched critically as her nineteen-year-old sister began to move to the dance. Her slim hips swayed coyly in the green dress; she had insisted on its being more low cut than the others, so the tops of her breasts showed almost too much.

She danced well, and eyed everyone over the top of her black lace fan. The men liked that, oh, *mucho,* as Marcos muttered to Rosita. They could say quite a bit between their encouraging shouts of *"Ay, gitana! aya!"*

There was a brief break from the dancing. This was the spot for Jacinto and Oliverio, playing their guitars as the dancers stood back on either side of the stage. The spotlights shone on their faces and hands, as the guitars sang. Jacinto was a quiet man, devoted to their eldest sister, Elena, and their three young children. He was a good guitarist, content to be in the background.

Oliverio was quick, high-strung, nerves on edge all the time. Mama said it was because he smoked too much. Rosita thought it was because he felt the music too much. He could play like an angel or a demon, he could compose and music came to his head like flashing lightning. Jacinto usually played the background, and Oliverio made up tunes when he felt like it, changing the beat, the accent, improvising on the melody.

The audience held their breaths. Rosita glanced out once, and saw the people at the Hamilton table leaning forward, watching intently, listening as though they cared. Some listened to the music, but stared at her. One tall red-haired girl with a proud face stared frankly at Rosita for a long moment, before turning her attention back to Oliverio. The tall young red-haired man was staring at her also. His look did not waver as she stared back at him.

She had to drag her gaze from his. It was a disturbing sensation, and she did not much like it. Sometimes men stared, she shrugged them off, she was small and only twelve. Mama kept men away from them all, and her brothers were big enough that few men came to pester.

But the stares. Rosita never got used to them. That was why she tried to pretend nobody was out there. She could not look at the audience. She always imagined they were just rehearsing, having fun, and dancing because they loved to dance, and the music sang in them.

Oliverio was having a very good night. He bent over his guitar lovingly, and he was improvising on the melody, playing with it, drawing it out, lifting it up, creating new sounds while Jacinto carried the tune. He played a long sizzling crescendo rising up and up and up, until he finished, high, triumphant. His hand stroked the strings in a finale, then he leaned back in the chair to smile at the audience. He had a shy sweet smile when he was not cross and unhappy. Tonight he was happy, he knew he had played well.

Some men jumped up, and shouted, "Bravo! Bravo, Oliverio!"

Rosita clapped with them, she was so proud of him. She stole one shy look at the Hamiltons, and saw the two red-haired men and one with black hair standing, shouting and clapping with the rest. That made her feel very good.

The audience calmed down and the dancers moved back in place. Papa Pascual led them all in a gay foot-stomping rhythm. Then Tadeo and Inez performed their duet. They were very much in love and had been married but three years. Inez was lovely, pretty, flirtatious, and she made serious Tadeo look good as he circled around her. Her pale blue skirts flirted about his long black-clad legs. He bent her over across his arm, and kissed her lips in the finale of their love-duet.

Elena was next and although she could not dance as fast as the rest, she gave a beautiful, slow, dignified dance, that went well. Tonight the crowd was determined to be pleased.

Mama Margarita came out on stage and sang two songs.

She sang like the Gypsy she was, plaintive wild songs, with feeling and deep emotion. Tonight they loved her. Rosita was so proud! Papa Pascual danced his special dance, and the audience clapped and cheered.

The finale included all the dancers; it was a special one papa had created. They had half the audience on their feet by the ending, and pranced out gaily into the hallway.

"Encore," papa ordered, and led the way back in. One more quick dance, then they made way for the next act waiting in the wings: a blond dancer from the United States and her pianist. They were smiling and applauding also as the Dominguez dancers came out for the last time.

"Very good, very good," she was saying generously.

Rosita wiped her arms and shoulders in the large dressing room, and flung the towel across a chair. She put on her shawl, and settled down with her history book at the circular table. Cristina was being spiteful to Luisa. She was really jealous of Inez but dared say nothing because Tadeo would have slapped her. "Great cow," she mocked. "I wonder that you can move. Why don't you lose weight?"

Luisa was flushed and hurt, as she sat down beside Rosita. Marcos, bringing over his chemistry book, said it for her. "We cannot all live on vinegar!" he said innocently, and winked at Rosita.

Cristina tossed her head at his double meaning. She did have a vinegar temper. She sat down at the dressing bench, and peered into the mirror. She picked up an eyeliner pencil; she loved to fool around with making her eyes look larger and darker.

Papa Pascual came back into the room. "The Hamiltons wish to speak with Rosita," he said, looking troubled.

Mama looked up alertly, Rosita raised her head slowly.

"With me? Why?"

Mama was mending a small tear in Inez's dress as the girl stood next to her. "Elena, you must go out with her then," she said, biting the end of the thread. Elena nodded, and held out her plump hand to Rosita.

Rosita took it, and hesitated. "My shawl?"

"Take it off, it will look better," Elena advised. The shawl was old and faded, but warmer than any other she had.

The two went out into the brightly lit nightclub. The blond dancer was kicking up her heels to the delight of the crowd. As she showed her white panties, they clapped and catcalled.

Elena made her way through the close-set tables, and Rosita followed her closely, nervously. Why would they want to talk to her? They should congratulate Papa Pascual.

The men stood up as Elena came to the table. She curtsyed, as did Rosita, imitating her sister. The women smiled at the child. The young red-haired man was staring keenly at her.

The oldest woman there leaned forward across the table. "Child, you dance well," she said, with an accent Rosita could not place. She had a beautiful face like a proud cameo, clear and pink and her hair was snowy white.

Another woman with graying brown hair and delicate features murmured, "Such fire, such grace. And so young." Her blue eyes were gentle as she looked at Rosita.

"Thank you, señoras," said Rosita, clearly, though she was embarrassed by their words. She curtsyed again, her red frilled skirts dipping gracefully.

'You have good movements, you dance with the music," said the oldest woman, with a fluid wave of her fingers. Rosita's eyes followed the woman's hands in fascination. Perhaps she was the one who had been a great ballerina. The woman confirmed Rosita's thought as she added, "When I danced in Moscow, long ago, I could guess which dancers would one day be great. For they all had music in them, pretty bodies or no, lovely faces or no. Their bones would tell."

There was a young lady, sitting erect and proud at the table, and her hair was fiery red gold. She was staring critically at Rosita, not smiling. Rosita thought she would say something nasty, perhaps like Cristina, but the girl surprised her.

"You dance well, child," she said. "Rosita—is that your name?"

"*Sí*, señorita, I am Rosita."

"Have you ever considered becoming a ballerina? Do you take ballet lessons?"

Rosita stared. What a curious question! She was a Gypsy flamenco dancer, she went to school five days a week, danced seven nights a week. When would she study ballet? "No, señorita," she murmured.

"Why not?" came the crisp question.

"Really, Isolde—" the elder woman admonished.

"Because I am a Gypsy," Rosita said finally.

"Oh." Isolde shrugged her beautiful white shoulders in the low-cut crystal white gown, and turned away indifferently.

There was an awkward pause. Elena said, "We must return now. You have been most kind." She turned to leave. She was always sensitive to atmosphere.

"I will escort you," the tall young man offered. He reached out naturally for Rosita's cold hand, and took it in his. He smiled down at her as they followed Elena. "I am Zach Hamilton," he said.

She gazed up at him with wide, dark eyes. How handsome he was, tanned and smiling, with his white teeth flashing. How graceful he appeared in his white jacket and black tie, with legs that moved like a dancer's among the crowded tables.

He took them to the doorway of their dressing room, and paused.

"*Gracias*, señor," said Elena, and turned to go inside.

His hand moved so quickly and smoothly to his lapel and back that Rosita scarcely caught the motion. "You are a little Spanish rose," he said, with a smile, and pressed the rose from his lapel into her hand. He bowed, and left her dazzled.

For some reason, Rosita held her hand down behind her so that her full skirts hid the rose in it.

"What did they say?" asked Cristina, swinging around from the table. "Did they tip you?"

"Oh, you always think of money," Elena said placidly. "They complimented Rosita, said she was very graceful and danced well. That is all."

"Pooh. I should have gone out. They would have taken

more notice of me!'' said Cristina. ''No matter how bright the lights are, I can always see the handsome men! And they see me, I make sure of that!''

''It is because the lights are in your eyes that you think all the men are handsome!'' said Marcos, with a laugh.

''What did you say about me?'' snapped Cristina, pettishly.

''Silencio, todos!'' commanded Margarita, taking up her crocheting. She was making a blanket for Elena's youngest. When she spoke so, they all became quiet. Cristina sulked at the mirror. Inez sat drinking coffee with Tadeo.

Oliverio went out into the hallway to smoke. Pascual followed him, to talk softly about the music. Luisa studied her civics book, a slight frown between her brows as she concentrated. Marcos became absorbed in his chemistry. Rosita returned to her history book.

She reached into her book bag for a pad of paper and a ball-point pen. Furtively she put the rose inside, peeping at it. Yes, it was red.

She drew out the paper, and contemplated it. She could not think about the history. She would write her essay for English class.

She wrote neatly at the top of the page. ''By the Seashore. Rosita Dominguez,'' and became absorbed in the description for the essay, about a trip to the sea—the beach, the shells she had found with Marcos.

They always danced from eight to nine, then from ten-thirty to eleven-thirty. Then the three younger ones went home, to be put to bed by their grandmother Alejandra, who also took care of the small babies of Elena and the one of Inez. The others remained for the late show, from one to two.

At about ten-thirty, Rosita had completed her essay roughly, and was reading the American history lesson. The proprietor of the nightclub came to the door, Pascual went to meet him. The man was grinning and happy. He was not always happy with them; it was good to see him smiling.

''All goes well,'' he announced. ''The Hamiltons are remaining for the second show! I hope you dance as well as the first time!'' His hand went into Pascual's, leaving a bank note.

Pascual said, ''Thank you, señor, very much. We will do our best, as always.''

''Good, good,'' and he went away. The family lined up, Margarita inspected their dresses and suits critically. She frowned at Cristina's heavy eye makeup, but said nothing. When Cristina sulked, she made her displeasure felt to the farthest table. Mama would speak to her tomorrow, Rosita thought.

They went in to the music of the previous band as it concluded its number. The band members departed as the dancers took their places. Rosita gave a quick glance to the Hamiltons' table; yes, they were in place. The oldest lady was gone, and one of the men, but the others had stayed.

She was a little tired now, it was Friday, and the week had been busy as always. But tomorrow she could sleep until noon, it was Saturday, and they all slept, then they went out to the beach for several hours to relax and play. Ah, it would be a good day. They would have more food than usual, papa had more money. Mama would laugh and sing, Oliverio would give Marcos more lessons on the guitar, which the boy enjoyed so much.

Rosita would dance barefoot on the sand, and dream of their trip to Spain next winter. They went every year. Usually they remained for two months, visiting relatives, dancing in nightclubs, renewing old friendships. The children were given permission to take their work with them, to make up examinations after they returned. Once an older Spanish lady had gone with them, a teacher in high school, and supervised their studies while she studied at the university. That had been a good year, a fine year, and nobody had gotten behind in their schoolwork. Rosita might get a new dress made this year, she had grown two inches taller since last year. She would like a rose-colored dress next, she thought; it would be made in Seville.

Rosita joined in the clapping, looking down, concentrating on getting into her dance. She brooded, thinking, remembering the first steps, moving into the mood of it.

When she was ready, she moved out onto the stage, and began to dance. She forgot her tiredness, and tossed her small head back, letting the music carry her little feet into a drumbeat of rhythm.

She heard someone call. *"La Soledad!* Rosita, *ay, ay, ay!"* It was a new voice with a laugh behind it. Was it that man, Zach Hamilton? She did not look toward the audience.

She danced faster, her hands clicking the castanets. She felt inspired tonight. Was it the praise? It had been sweet to hear the words. Then she forgot them and lost herself in the dance; nobody mattered but Papa Pascual watching her alertly, ready to increase the beat.

She clapped her hands sharply, faster and faster. Papa caught it up, adding his sharp distinct clap. The beat increased, and Oliverio's guitar went into the melody line more quickly, excitingly, as she whirled about. She whirled again, again, again, from one side of the stage and back, turning about again and yet again, until her skirts swished about her slim ankles.

Her heels beat faster and faster, stamping their quickened rhythm on the wooden floor. She was in the melody, she *was* the music, she was dance itself, whirling about in her red white-dotted frilled dress. Her small fingers clicked, her breath caught, her cheeks were flushed brighter and brighter.

And her dark eyes sparkled with the emotion that only dance brought to her.

Chapter 2

For the first time in her young life, Rosita and her family did not go to Spain the winter of 1973–1974. She knew money was very short; however, she had not thought it would mean remaining in Puerto Rico all the winter, and not seeing their relatives and friends.

Rosita sat at the end of the dressing table, taking out her book bag and her cosmetics to get ready for the eight o'clock show. It was not so large a room as usual, they were crowded here, and the nightclub was not so large, either. But it had a good reputation. If they could only do well . . .

Elena was expecting another child. She remained home now with all the babies. Mama Margarita had to go on the stage and dance as well as sing. It was hard on her, she was almost fifty, but she was a trouper. Grandmother Alejandra stayed backstage, alert in spite of her seventy-three years, and prepared their costumes, sewed tears and buttons, and prepared coffee for when they returned from the stage, hot and weary.

Rosita leaned toward the mirror and applied rouge carefully. At fourteen, she was two inches taller, now five feet tall. She had a rose dress with white lace and white frills, and the usual black slippers.

Janet Louise Roberts

Cristina was gone. She had married a widower with three grown children. He was a pharmacist who owned his own shop. She had been proud to leave home, a married woman, and bragged of how happy she was in her new house, the pet of her older husband. But last week she had come weeping. When asked what was wrong, she had sobbed, "I am pregnant!" and was so upset that both mama and papa had scolded her vigorously. How she had sulked!

But they missed her in the dancing. No Elena. No Cristina. And Luisa at nineteen was more plump and not quick-moving and flirtatious. That left mama and Rosita, one too old to attract the eyes of men, and the other too young.

One had to be practical, thought Rosita. The men stared at women dancers not because they could dance beautifully and place their feet correctly but because they liked to see a pretty woman wiggling her hips, at least that was what Cristina said, and Rosita thought she was right. The Dominguez family was not so popular now, and they took in much less money.

"Next year when Marcos has finished school," said Pascual, "he may stay for the third performance. That will improve our line. Now if one of my sons might marry a lovely Gypsy dancer like our beautiful Inez—"

Inez preened. Oliverio stared down at his guitar. He was shy around women, he had no steady girl.

Marcos blurted out, "But I want to go to the university, papa!"

There was an ominous silence. Finally papa said, "Why, my son? What university can teach you more about flamenco dancing than your father? And who can teach you more about playing the guitar than your brother?"

Marcos was pale under his tan. He applied eye shadow deftly, and his hand did not shake, Rosita noticed from her place next to him at the long lighted mirror.

"I wish to study chemistry, papa. It is very interesting. And a chemist can make money." He said it bravely. He had confided his dreams to Rosita, who had shaken her head, worried that he could not have what he wanted.

Pascual was silent. His mother Alejandra was not. In a

shrill tone she inquired, "Chemistry? What is that? A profession for stupid ones who cannot dance! We are the Dominguez! We are Gypsies, of a long line of fine dancers! Who can do the flamenco better than us? I ask you! And he says he wishes to study the chemistry! Pah!"

"It is your heritage," said Pascual slowly, looking troubled.

"I should not have spoken now. I am sorry, papa," said Marcos. He finished his makeup, his face grave for his seventeen years.

"*Sí*. We will speak later," said Pascual. He raised his hands in a helpless gesture. "There is the music."

Rosita hated to see him look beaten. Her proud, confident, handsome papa! She ran to him, put her hand in his arm, and leaned her head against his shoulder. She could feel the tautness and nervous tension in him. He laid his hand on her smooth braided head.

"My baby," he murmured. "You are ready, *sí?*"

"*Sí*, my papa," she whispered. She would have done anything to console him. She adored her father; he was the best, kindest, most considerate father in the world. *And* the best flamenco dancer!

They lined up—Pascual, and Margarita, then Tadeo and Inez, Luisa, Marcos and Rosita. Behind her came Jacinto and Oliverio with their guitars. Pascual gave them his usual long critical look, nodded sharply, and they ran out gaily, feet tapping and skirts swirling.

As the youngest, Rosita always danced first. It helped her to concentrate if she paid no attention to the audience, just the music. Oliverio was good about that. He always started her music as soon as they went out, and during the clapping and whistling from the audience he would play it firmly, giving her the beat.

She moved out, fingers clicking to the rhythm. Someone cried out, as they often did now, "*La Soledad! La Soledad! gitana, ay, gitana!* Flamenco Rosita! Flamenco Rose! Flamenco Rosita! *La Soledad!*" Others took it up, her dancing had become more popular, she had even been mentioned in the newspapers on several occasions when critics came to watch.

21

"The new young Dominguez dancer, the littlest one—watch her, she has potential. She has music in her body—watch her—" She had been so proud when her father had praised her and given her a dollar to spend.

She deliberately forgot all the troubling words that had passed between her parents and Marcos and concentrated on the dance. She would wipe it all from her mind. She was dancing, and she loved to dance.

Her feet tapped more sharply, she clapped her hands to increase the beat. Papa Pascual caught it up, clapped sharply faster and faster until she nodded.

Behind her, Oliverio was playing wildly. He did that sometimes when he was troubled. He strummed the guitar in heavy, exciting beats.

Rosita caught it up. She forgot everything for the exciting Gypsy music of her elder brother. Her feet flew. She tapped and swirled, and her skirts whirled about her slim legs. The audience grew quiet, watching.

Tadeo jumped forward, excited also. He picked her up as she whirled before him, tossed her into the air the way he did Inez sometimes. Rosita flung up high, flung her arms up, and landed softly in his arms. Someone yelled, she heard that.

Oliverio strummed faster, the music was wild Gypsy music. Her mother began to sing to it, swaying, her high notes soaring. Pascual clapped more quickly.

Rosita danced from one end of the stage to the other, whirling back to where Tadeo was stamping out the beat. He picked her up again, laughing down into her small face. He tossed her up almost to the ceiling! Then he caught her, and swooped her down into a dramatic curve.

They were making up the dance, they were creating, and everyone knew it in the line. It was tremendously exciting for them, when the music caught them up like that. It did not often happen during performances, Pascual drilled them to do as he said. But tonight, his face perspiring, Pascual nodded to go on, and on.

Sometimes Rosita had danced with Tadeo on the beach, barefoot, not caring if she fell because the sand was soft. But tonight they danced, inspired, as though they were Gypsies dancing in the caves of Spain, for their own kind, offering it up for their gods, showing their passion and desires and sensuous natures.

Rosita whirled one more time, again, again, and came to a dramatic halt as Tadeo flung her high up in the air, and caught her on his shoulder. She held out her arms, her grave face shining, her dark eyes sparkling.

The audience went wild. They were on their feet, stamping, clapping, calling, yelling, screaming! *"Brava! brava!* Rosita! *La Soledad! La Soledad!* Rosita! Rosita!"

It was heady wine to the young girl. She could have danced forever. Tadeo let her slip down, bowed behind her, holding out his hand proudly to indicate his sister, miming, "There she is, Rosita. Is she not magnificent?"

They applauded more as she curtsyed and went back to her place. Pascual shook his head as they demanded another dance, his baby was tired, panting. Marcos came out, and he could do no wrong. He tapped his feet, drumming them faster and faster, his proud lean form sideways to them, showing his fine figure, his tapping heels.

Rosita then slipped away, down the three stairs to the hallway, where Grandmother Alejandra waited with a towel. Her grandmother caught her to herself passionately. "My *gitana* baby! My little Gypsy flower! How you danced!"

"*Gracias, abuela,* they clapped so much!" Rosita patted her face carefully, mopped at her shoulders and arms. Her grandmother adjusted the dress, the shoulders had slipped sideways on her thin arms. She tucked a pin in the hair, surveyed her baby critically, then nodded.

Rosita slid back up to the stage and into line. She was thinking about Marcos, and how well he danced, when an insistent look drew her gaze. She felt a shock running through her as she saw the round table nearest the stage.

The Hamiltons were there! A man was staring at her; it was young red-haired Zach Hamilton, smiling at her. Beside him the tall, proud Isolde, with flaming hair and a vivid green dress tonight, was also staring at her, not smiling, but intense,

thoughtful. Rosita dragged her gaze from them, back to the
stage. She dared not lose concentration.

The others danced, their mother sang, Oliverio played to
applause. But it was not enough, they needed more pretty
girls. Rosita sighed as the dancing ended to a spatter of light
applause. It was dying down even as they left the stage. No
encore tonight, after the magnificent beginning.

Pascual kissed her in the dressing room, solemnly. "My
baby, you did very well tonight."

"Thank you, papa," she smiled at him gently, and went
to her place. She put the shawl about her shoulders, and opened
her book bag.

She always concentrated on one thing at a time. Now she
must study home economics. She opened the textbook, and
was absorbed before Marcos had taken his place with his advanced chemistry textbook.

Alejandra was preparing coffee, the smell of the rich mixture filling the air of the small room. The door opened, and two
handsome young people stood there.

Rosita glanced up, absently, as the cold draft swirled
about her warm legs, causing her to curl them under herself.
She stared, so did all the others.

Isolde Hamilton came in, followed by her lean brother,
Zach Hamilton. They shut the door after themselves.

"I must speak to you," said Isolde imperiously, without
even saying good evening. Her bright blue eyes glittered with
excitement. The green dress had glitter on it also, thought
Rosita, and the swaying earrings in her pretty ears. She looked
like a dancer, but she was so tall, so very tall! She stood on her
high green heels, and she was as tall as Papa Pascual next to
her.

Pascual offered her his chair, she seated herself slowly, in
a dignified manner, like a dancer. She had appeared in the
newspapers, they spoke of her brilliant future in New York
City. Rosita gazed at her, entranced. How graceful she was,
how very beautiful!

Zach shook his head as Oliverio offered his chair. There
were not enough chairs in the room; usually the men went out

and smoked in the hallway, or took a walk. Zach leaned against the wall, his face was sober, his eyes intent, as blue as those of his sister. He was glancing toward Rosita, constantly; she warily met his gaze, hers puzzled.

"Rosita is very talented," said Isolde.

Pascual's face lit up. Rosita knew what he thought—a special performance for which they would receive money—perhaps a benefit, for charity, that always drew a good crowd, and paid well, and it would be mentioned in the social columns. "She is a good little dancer," he said soberly. "All my children learn well."

"Rosita is more than a good dancer," said Isolde. "She can become great! She has the basics, a good body, good head, good proportions. And she moves well, she has grace and precision. She feels the music. I want to train her for ballet."

There was a silence in the room, as of breath suspended. Alejandra's hand paused in pouring coffee. Pascual's hand was halfway to his chin. Marcos choked on his words, saying only, "But—Rosita—"

"Rosita—a ballerina?" Margarita whispered. "No, no, she is a Gypsy! She dances flamenco!" She looked worriedly at her husband.

"Yes, she is a Gypsy," said Pascual, in relief. "You do not understand us, Miss Hamilton. We are Gypsies. Rosita is one of us. She dances like us, she thinks as we do."

"She is young, she can change," Isolde said flatly. "I have seen her dance, she has a strong spirit in her. She can dance flamenco, but those moves tonight—they were ballet moves! By instinct, and no training, right?"

Pascual nodded slowly.

"And I think that dance with her brother was spontaneous, not rehearsed? It was crude, but she responded so well most of the audience knew no differently," said Isolde, with such force that Rosita blinked. "I knew because I have danced for years. Just the slightest of hesitations, just the least look from one to the other, to see what was going to happen. That was the only clue that it had not been rehearsed. But that child, that young child, only—how old, Rosita?"

"Fourteen," murmured Rosita, still dazed. She knew this could not be happening, it was a strange dream. But the grave blue eyes of Zach were studying her face intently.

"Fourteen," groaned Isolde. "And no ballet training! But does she learn quickly? I'll bet she does—"

"She learns quickly," said Pascual. "But señorita, you do not understand. I am sorry, she must remain. We have no money to train our child in ballet. And we need her in the troupe. You see, Cristina has married and left us, Elena expects another child. The women in our family—" His eloquent hands told his dismay. "We cannot lose our Rosita. We need her."

"I will train her, you need not worry about that. I will pay all her expenses, her clothes, her shoes, her schooling. My sister Delphine is fifteen, she is training with us. The two girls will live together in my apartment. I will chaperon them, supervise their schooling and their ballet training." The tossing red head was imperious, she was confident of her ability.

"It is kind of you, but we cannot do it, we need our Rosita," said Pascual, though he was troubled. His gaze sought Rosita. She kept her face sober, not showing her fear that this girl would sweep away all their objections. Was she crazy? To think of training a Gypsy girl for the ballet!

Isolde hesitated. Zach said, "The girl has tremendous talent. However, she probably wishes to remain with her family."

"Yes," said Rosita, in a low voice. "I wish to remain here."

Isolde shook her head. "No! You must listen to me. I know what I am doing. I am too tall to be a good ballerina in the way they wish it today. I cannot go on deceiving myself. I must find a way to make my training pay, though I myself cannot become famous." A faint bitterness tinged her words. "Rosita is a perfect size, she will probably grow another inch or two. The size of her head in proportion to her neck, her body, her legs, all are perfect." The critical gaze ran over Rosita as over a colt.

"It still does not mean she can go," said Pascual. "We

need our Rosita—in another three years she will be a young lady," he added anxiously.

"Those three years are terribly important, Mr. Dominguez! In those years she can train for ballet, make her debut in important parts. She can be a star! She can become famous! She can earn tremendous amounts of money! But she can't wait any longer."

Pascual looked politely dubious, as though he had heard such promises before, the reckless promises of a promoter. "You are most kind to say so—"

"I *know* so," said Isolde with arrogant confidence. "With her looks and talent, with my schooling and contacts, she will make it. I promise you! To show my confidence in this, I will send you money twice a year for her, against her future earnings. We can set on the amount you think best—"

Pascual went out into the hallway with Isolde, Zach, and Margarita. They talked a while, then returned. Pascual looked set, Margarita bewildered.

Pascual went over to Rosita. "They will pay much money for you, my baby," he said, wearily. "Twice a year they will pay money, against your earnings. It will—help much. But if you do not wish to go—"

Rosita stared at him. She had tried to concentrate on her homework while they talked, conscious of Marcos's tension beside her, conscious of the low murmur of voices in the hall. But she had never thought they would agree . . .

She would be away from her family, cut off from the warm, happy companionship. Living in New York City, that dangerous place where killings took place daily. Learning a new kind of dancing . . .

"You—want me to go, papa?" she faltered.

His eyes could not meet hers, and she realized how much the money would mean for them, while Elena had her baby, while times were tight, while Marcos finished high school . . .

Tears began to run down her cheeks. She did not realize it until Zach uttered a low exclamation and came over to her. He handed her a handkerchief, she shook her head and reached for a tissue, and carefully blotted her rouged cheeks.

"You don't have to," he said, half-angrily. "Look, Isolde, she is too young for this—"

His sister exclaimed in her anger, "She is almost too old! Fourteen! I should have taken her two years ago, when I first had the idea! A ballerina starting at fifteen, or fourteen, it is ridiculous. It may be too late—"

Rosita felt a momentary hope, but it was quashed as the talk continued. She was intensely conscious of Zach leaning against the wall behind her. And she heard the music starting up. Margarita stood. "She must think about this. And we must go on. They are almost ready for us."

She was calm, dignified. Zach straightened, as though to leave.

Isolde said pettishly, firmly, "I want to know tonight! I want Rosita to move in with us tomorrow, so I can start her training, get her some proper shoes, and take her with us to New York next week. I have to get back—we must leave on Thursday at the latest."

Rosita clasped her cold hands, she looked at her father, at her mother. Leave them? Leave her family? She looked at Marcos, he was standing now beside her as she had stood to shake out the ruffles of her dress. She gazed at him long, he gave a short nod.

"It would be good for you, Rosita," he said. He touched her cheek gently. "Go, Rosita. God go with you."

Because she knew and loved her brother, whom she was closest to, she knew why he said this. He himself wanted to break with tradition, and become something no one in their family had become, a chemist. If he could not—well, Rosita could be the one to break away. A sort of quiet rebellion.

But she did not want to rebel. She did, however, want to help her family. And the money would mean the difference to them—this next year of living on a desperate margin—or being well fed, able to plan ahead, go to Spain again, being happy and confident.

"I will go, papa, if you wish," she said steadily, leaving it to him.

"Very well, my child. You will go, and we will be proud of you always, for your talent and your obedience."

The door opened, the proprietor of the nightclub said impatiently, "They are ready for you—what is going on?"

The Dominguez family lined up, the Hamiltons stood out of the way as they prepared to go on. Isolde looked triumphant. "I will come for you in the car tomorrow," she said to Rosita, as they began to march out.

"Yes, Miss Hamilton," Rosita said faintly. This was the last time she would go on—the last time with her family—she could not believe it. This must be a nightmare, a terrible dream from which she would wake in the bed beside Luisa, in their tiny attic room.

A long silver Lincoln Continental arrived to fetch Rosita at noon the next day. Rosita was ready. She and Elena had packed her clothes in boxes and a suitcase battered from much use. A tear had fallen onto every dress and shoe as they packed.

She had kissed all the babies good-bye. They did not understand and beamed and patted her cheek when she hugged them. Then she kissed everyone in the family: papa, mama, Cristina and her husband, Tadeo and Inez, all of them whom she would not see until next summer. Isolde had said carelessly they would return then.

It was a long time away, from January to summer. But she must endure it. Perhaps she would disappoint the arrogant Miss Hamilton, and would be sent home in disgrace. She surprised herself with that willful thought.

A chauffeur, a Spaniard with a dour face, came to help put the boxes in the car. Isolde came to the door, and smiled at everyone like a great queen; indeed, she looked like a queen as she towered over them in stilt heels of silver. She wore a magnificent dress of silver blue, and a white fur cape about her shoulders on that cool day. She swished Rosita away with her, saying, "I understand you are sorrowful. But it will be exciting, Rosita. Wait until you see New York!"

Rosita could not reply. Her throat felt tight with tears and terror. New York! She might be killed! What was she doing here? She must be mad. Why had she consented to this dreadful plan? It was insane—she was not great—she was a fourteen-year-old girl who could dance flamenco with the encouragement of her beloved family.

She had no time to think. The automobile was sliding smoothly through the narrow streets of Old San Juan, and up a cobblestoned hill. Over to the left she could see the creamy Cathedral of San Juan shining in the sunlight. Isolde was chatting, kindly trying to put her at ease.

"We are in the old section," she explained. "The house was built more than a hundred fifty years ago. The Hamiltons came to San Juan to build a new refinery for their rums. You do know about our rums? We have islands of sugarcane plantations. After the cane is crushed there, it is brought here where the rums are made, bottled . . ."

The pleasant voice ran on and on. The car did too, so silently and smoothly, not like the cranky one that took them to the beach. They had gone every Saturday except today, and the days when it rained. Today it did not rain, the sun shone, but Rosita felt it raining inside herself, dark and cloudy and ominously stormy.

The car came to a halt. Only a narrow sidewalk separated them from the tall stone house with black wrought iron balconies outside the tall windows. Carved wooden doors with a large *H* insignia on them swung open.

Servants came out, and took the boxes, their faces too well trained to show any amazement over the crude array. They carried them inside, and Isolde followed with her hand in Rosita's arm. Did she worry that the girl would run away?

The hallway was cool and dim. Beyond, at the end, was a glimpse of a bright sun-filled patio with a fountain in the center. They did not go toward that, however, they went past carved wooden chests, coat stands, tables with porcelain vases and fresh flowers, and turned left into a beautiful huge drawing room.

Rosita blinked at the golden curtains, the gold taffeta-covered sofas and in a slightly different pattern, the chairs and hassocks. A beautiful chandelier hung from the ceiling on a ruby velvet pull. Mirrors reflected her shy self in the rose cotton dress and plain cardigan sweater. Two men rose, awaited her. Other ladies sat on the sofas.

"Here she is," Isolde said, and smiled all around, as though she had pulled off something smart. "This is my father, Rosita. Mr. Thomas Hamilton."

Rosita curtsyed to the graying red-haired man. His smile was kind, but she thought that his face showed many lines of worry and weariness. He shook her hand kindly. "Welcome, Rosita," he said.

"And you know my brother Zach. This is my brother Kevin." A brief shy look showed a young man, maybe about Marcos's age. Zach came forward and shook her hand, Kevin bowed.

"How do you do?"

"And you remember my mother, Mrs. Hamilton. Isabeau was a ballerina in Paris when father met her!"

Rosita gave her a curious look. The delicate porcelain face smiled at her kindly, as it had in the nightclub. "I am happy to meet you again, my dear Rosita," she said in a delicious accent. "Do not let Isolde bully you, she is quite capable of it!"

"Mother!" Isolde said impatiently. "Don't talk like that. Pay no attention, Rosita. This is granny—my grandmother, Mrs. Sonia Lothaire. She was a ballerina in Moscow."

"A long time ago," completed the older woman, with a slight smile. She was so tiny, she seemed to melt into the thick golden cushions, except that her back was so erect and her feet firmly planted on the soft-hued carpet. She took Rosita's hand in a firm manner. With her thick white hair coiled on top of her head she looked as though she could be a queen mother with ease, Rosita thought.

A girl stepped forward from behind granny. "And I am Delphine," the girl said, and gave her a sunny, mischievous smile. Her red gold hair was a softer shade than her sister's, and she was much smaller, only a bit taller than Rosita. She was like a sugar doll in the candy store, all pink and white with blue eyes and a pretty blue sundress. "I wanted you to room with me here, but you have a room to yourself, Isolde says. But in New York, we can room together, and tell each other secrets!''

Isolde sighed in affectionate exasperation, her mother laughed softly. Rosita melted toward Delphine; she was not haughty or arrogant.

Rosita sat down where she was told, and the talk ran over her head, all about the coming journey to New York, the apartment to be made ready, a governess chosen for the girls.

Finally Mrs. Hamilton looked at the two younger ones. ''Delphine, show Rosita to her room, and the practice room, also, if you wish,'' she said, with her gentle smile. ''Luncheon will be served at one. You have time to get acquainted, then come down in time, will you?''

''Yes, mother.'' Delphine jumped up. She held out her hand to Rosita in a confident gesture. ''You'll like your room, I helped choose it, and we put red in it, because Zach said it was your color, and I want to show you my room also, which is gold, and—''

Soft laughter followed the girls from the room. Zach held the door for them, and he was grinning, but somehow Rosita did not mind. They were warm, not cold to her, and Delphine was sweet.

Delphine took her up the winding stairs. She said, ''There are more stairs, up from the patio. Isolde uses them, Zach, too, when they come back late and don't want mama and papa to know. They are outdoors, and when it rains they are too slippery to use, but I like them, and when I date and want to come in late, I'll use them too—''

She never seemed to run out of breath or words. Silent Rosita listened solemnly, amazed at her. They came to the second floor, and Delphine pointed out, ''That's mother's room, and father's. They have the master suite. Granny has that other corner.'' She led the way along the inner hallway, protected by large windows closed now against the breeze. Looking through them, Rosita could see a narrow balcony surrounding the inside patio, and the fountains, and frail vines covered with purple flowers, bougainvillea and wisteria. Pots of scarlet geraniums stood at intervals on the balcony.

On the north wing, Delphine pointed the first room to Rosita as, "Isolde's, and the next one is mine." She pushed open the door, and showed her the lovely room. The tall gold bed was of brass covered with gold paint, and the pure white counterpane was of embroidered silk.

The dressing table caught her eye. It was of dark red wood, with a skirt of frivolous blue and white silk. It was a girl's dream, covered with cosmetics in gold and glass jars and bottles, golden mirrors and gold-backed brushes. A ballet doll in a pink dress sagged beside the mirror. "That is my doll, Emily," said Delphine. "Zach gave her to me when I was six."

They went out again, along the polished hallway, past the stairs that led up from the patio clear to the fourth floor.

Delphine pointed to the corner room next to hers. "That is Zach's. Want to see it?"

"Oh, no," said Rosita, horrified.

"I guess not, he would be mad," said Delphine cheerfully. "Come on, we'll take the outside stairs." She opened the long French windows, and went outside onto the balcony lined with black lace iron.

She started up the winding stairs, Rosita following her, glancing down into the beautiful tiled patio. White iron chairs were set about, and tables, and more plants in red pots.

They went up to the next floor, Delphine leading the way inside, and along the hallway to the room above Zach's. "This is yours," she said, pushing open the door.

Rosita recognized her boxes and suitcase, nothing else. She gasped as Delphine tugged her impatiently inside the doorway.

"Do you like it? Do you like it?" the older girl asked eagerly. "Zach chose the furniture from storage, he said you would like Spanish furniture. I like it, it looks old and cool and dignified, and settled, you know what I mean?"

Rosita gazed at it. It looked like the furniture in the home of one of her wealthy uncles in Spain. The bed was a huge four-poster of carved dark wood, with a brief canopy of scarlet silk over it, and a matching coverpane of red silk. The dresser was of matching wood, with a pretty white lamp on it. There was a tall dark wardrobe for her clothes, a chair of dark wood and plump cushions of creamy silk in one corner, and a dresser stool covered with an embroidered tapestry in a design of flowers, roses and vines.

"It is too grand for me," she whispered. At home she had an attic room which had been shared by the three youngest girls until Cristina had married. Her house was small, the other bedrooms were occupied by the couples, with the unmarried men in the other attic bedroom. Everything was cramped, with their wet stockings hanging from hangers on nails, their clothes for performances carefully given the best space on the wall hooks. This—this was bigger than their drawing room at home!

"I hope you enjoy it," said Delphine cheerfully. "Now come upstairs and see the practice room. Mama fitted it out for Isolde, and Zach planned it. He is very clever."

They went outside again, up another flight of wrought iron stairs, to the top floor. Delphine pushed open a door and inside, to Rosita's dazzled gaze, was a ballroom.

The floor was not polished, but it was huge, and mirrored on three sides. Along three walls were long bars of polished wood, and in the center were free-standing *barres,* as Delphine called them. Delphine went over to stand beside one. She rested her hand lightly on the wood, and posed.

"See? Like this?" Slowly her free leg came up, into a graceful movement, and then curled around behind her back. "I can stand *en pointe* for much of my lesson now!"

It was another language to Rosita. She stood in silence, then went over to the end window, drawn by the glitter of blue sea. She gasped. She could see out all over Old San Juan, from the center of it to the Atlantic Ocean.

Delphine came to stand beside her, slipping her arm naturally about Rosita's waist. "You can see the whole city," she said softly. "I love this view. When I'm in dusty, dirty, hot New York, I close my eyes, and pretend I am standing here, looking out to the cool blue ocean. Look at the roofs, all brown and red contrasting with the creamy buildings, and you can see the old church, and over there from the front window you can see El Morro—''

As she looked, Rosita had a quiet, comfortable feeling. This was not some strange place she was. It was San Juan, her home, and the ocean she swam in, and the cathedral, and the old fort where she and Marcos had run around on the grass.

Delphine giggled a little, breaking into Rosita's thoughts. "I'm going to tell you my first secret, my most important secret!" she said, with mischievous intentness. "Rosita, guess what!"

"I cannot guess," said Rosita, turning reluctantly from gazing at the blue Atlantic. She could endure it here, this was home, for a while. And Delphine was sweet and natural, and she could see her family whenever they came home. The view from here was so glorious . . . it was her San Juan, her home!

"I'm never going to be a great ballerina!" Delphine said, her pink mouth curved in an impish grin. "Isolde is too tall to be in star parts, like Odette and Odile and Sleeping Beauty. But I'm not going to, either!" She nodded triumphantly. "I'm going to get married and have babies, lots of babies! I'm not going to be tough and harsh-tongued like Isolde. I've been dancing in ballet since I was six, because Isolde wanted it, and mother wanted it. But I am tired of being dedicated and not dating boys and not eating all the ice cream I want! So there!"

Rosita stared at the pretty girl beside her. Laughter welled up in her, and joy, because the girl understood, and she could talk to her. "Oh, Delphine!" she said, and began to giggle. Delphine hugged her, and laughed with her. "Oh, Delphine, I think you will do what you want! And you will be a beautiful mother for your babies, just like my sister Elena!"

"Tell me about her! Tell me about your family," Delphine urged.

The two girls talked and talked, discovering much that was alike and thrilling to how much was different about them. When a soft bell chimed for them to go down for luncheon, they were fast friends.

Chapter 3

Zachariah Lothaire Hamilton was wealthy and spoiled, his grandmother Sonia told him severely, many a time. But she helped spoil him.

His father would add quietly, "But he has sense, and intelligence, and he works very hard."

Zach grinned absently as he thought about his family. He had a good life, he had a wonderful family. Not like his best friend, Jeronimo Oviedo. No wonder Jeronimo got heavy and lazy, and complained more about working in the sun. He, too, was wealthy and spoiled, but there was no love from his family to him. His father was a playboy, with many mistresses. All of them went through money in that family, like a knife through warm butter, as Sonia would say. Jeronimo had all the money and girls he wanted, but no direction except from the Hamilton Rum Company.

Zach glanced up at the sky, from the wheel of the yacht he was steering deftly into its harbor among the yachts just outside San Juan. A storm was coming up, and it would be one of those heavy rain and thunderstorms that frequently arrived about this time of year. Good thing they were returning home. He would hate to be out at sea in this yacht, sturdy though it was.

"Hey, Jeronimo, get the rope!" he yelled down to the

deck where his friend lay prone and half-asleep on the towel he had brought out. Jeronimo lifted a hand, and forced himself to his feet. His tanned oil-covered body was getting plump, his waist had expanded several inches the past year.

Zach frowned a little, thinking about the two weeks' journey. Jeronimo had grumped and groaned about being out in the midday sun, he had slept every afternoon for a couple of hours, he had complained about counting barrels or inspecting the machinery. Zach had ended up doing most of the work. He had finally left Jeronimo on one island to complete the inspection there, and had gone alone to Elysia. Zach liked Elysia, it was his favorite island; it was there his ancestors had first come from England to grow sugarcane and make rum. He did not want disruptive elements there.

Well, this trip was over. He would be glad to get home, and tackle the work in his office. His father looked so tired. Kevin was working part-time, between his freshman studies at the university. He was a big help, but he could not be there all the time, and he was just learning. He could not make the company decisions—even if the uncles would let him.

The yacht was tied up by two blacks he employed on the yacht and he left it in their care as he jumped down to the dock.

"Hey, I'll give you a lift," he said to Jeronimo, as he saw the chauffeur in their cream Cadillac driving up to the pier.

"Not on your life," grinned Jeronimo. "I'll bet you're going to the office, right?"

"Sure," said Zach, hands on his hips, studying his friend. "It is only midday."

He wore neat white linens today, donned this morning so he could go right to the rum works. Jeronimo still had on oily shorts and his hairy chest was bare.

"I've got a ride," said Jeronimo, peering beyond Zach to the parking lot. He waved, grinning. "You can work all you like Zach, but there are other things in life, and one of them is right over there!" He laughed as he walked over to the waiting car. Zach caught a glimpse of smooth shiny dark hair, a pouting red mouth, and the girl leaned out to receive Jeronimo's kiss.

She slid over for him to take the wheel. Zach shrugged, put his suitcase into the car, and sat beside the chauffeur.

"To the works. All okay at home?"

"Yes, I think so, Señor Zach. Your mother sings, your grandmother scolds, and Mr. Hamilton goes daily to the office."

Zach's grin met his, they laughed a little, then settled down for the drive through San Juan around the bay to where the silvery buildings of the distillery and offices were set in a grassy plain beside the bay. Zach's critical gaze went over it as the chauffeur drove in around the circle where crimson and yellow hibiscus bushes surrounded the simple stone marker with the name "Hamilton Rums" on it.

He jumped out, said, "Pick us up at six, will you?" and ran into the building. The coolness surrounded him like a blessing; he slowed down and inhaled deeply.

On the way to the offices he peered at the great vats of fermenting molasses, and nodded to the control man at the computer. Then he took the elevator up to the top floor and stepped off onto white tile.

He strode down the hallway to his father's office at the front, and tapped lightly, then went in. Thomas Hamilton glanced up from his mahogany desk, and smiled with pleasure.

"Zach. Right on the dot. I sent the chauffeur."

"He met me. I have some good reports, dad. The cane looks just great, some have started to harvest." He dropped down into the chair opposite his father's desk, and told him concisely what he had seen.

Subconsciously he noted that his father kept rubbing his chest, the jacket was open, and the white shirt showed sweat stains.

He broke off what he was saying about Elysia. "Are you ill, Dad? Anything wrong?"

"Me? No. Why do you ask?"

His father's face seemed pale and weary, the lines graven deeply along the forehead and around his mouth.

"You are rubbing your chest. Any pain?"

"No, it just feels a bit heavy. Something I ate, I expect."

They talked about the cane, and how soon some would be arriving from Elysia. Zach got up to leave.

"Are you going to be in for dinner?" Thomas asked, as he picked up the telephone.

Zach grinned. "I thought I might see Helena—but mother will rant and rave if I don't come home the first night."

"Not rant and rave, but look sorrowful," Thomas laughed. "So Helena is the current girl?"

Zach shrugged. He liked Helena, he had liked other girls. She had a luscious mouth, and a firm body that he liked to caress. She had permitted him many liberties—which had promptly removed her from the possible candidates for matrimony. It was unfair, but that was the way it was. Many girls would like to marry Hamilton Rums, Zach had known that since young boyhood.

Thomas kept his hand on the telephone, he had not dialed. "You will be in charge of Hamilton's one day, Zach," he said, unexpectedly. "I hope you will find the right girl by then, a fine woman like your mother, devoted and loving. This is a tough job. You don't want to go home to trouble, as so many men do. Find a girl who will be as devoted to you as you will be to her. Faithfulness, love. There's no time for playing around and wrecking a marriage, it doesn't work out."

Zach smiled tenderly at his father. "If I can find a girl like mother, I'll be very happy indeed. Giving up her career, devoting herself to you and to us—giving us all the love and attention we wanted—and remaining happy and cheerful. But do they make girls like that anymore?"

"Thank God, yes," said Thomas slowly. "Keep looking until you find one. When you are president of Hamilton's, you will have enough trouble in the works, you won't need any at home. I am training you for this post, it will be yours one day. When you are sitting in this chair, Zach, you will know you have not just money at stake but the lives of more than three thousand workers and their families. That responsibility cannot possibly be light."

"I know, dad."

His father sighed. "You cannot possibly know," he said, with a humorous twist of his lips. "But, bless you, you'll find out one day! And God keep you then!"

Zach laughed. "I'm not going to stay up nights worrying about that! Well, I'll go to my office, and see what trouble awaits me. I expect the mail is stacked high—"

He turned to the door, opened it. Then he heard a curious sound. He turned back, saw the telephone receiver falling to the desk. His father was bent over, his free hand at his chest.

"Dad? Dad?" Zach raced around the desk, put his hand on his father's shoulder.

"Father, what is it?"

"Chest," he managed to say.

Zach hit the buttons on the square base of the telephone. He got the clinic receptionist. "Zach here. Prepare for my father—possible heart attack. Make sure the doctor is there. Send up a stretcher right away!"

He heard the gasp. "Oh, yes, sir. Right away!"

He hung up, held his father gently back against him. Thomas said feebly, "I'm sorry, it's probably just indigestion. I can't remember what I ate."

Zach hung on and prayed. He was dazed. It could not be happening. The cool air conditioning seemed suddenly cold and chilly. He turned it down. Thomas was shivering violently, then leaned back, wearily.

"My chest . . . feels heavy . . . odd . . ."

The elevator pinged softly. Two men in white carrying a stretcher entered the office. Thomas tried to get up.

"Just stay quiet, Mr. Hamilton," one orderly said crisply. His dark skin contrasted with the starched white of his uniform. "We'll put you on the stretcher ourselves, don't move a muscle yourself. Let us do it, sir."

Grumbling a little, Thomas stretched out self-consciously on the stretcher, and they carried him away. Zach followed closely. They walked down the long hall, into the waiting elevator, were whizzed to another floor, through the door to the cool white clinic.

It was well equipped, Thomas Hamilton had seen to that.

His workers should have the best. It was ironic that he should be carried here, thought Zach, as the stretcher was carried through to the examining room. The doctor was there.

"You wait outside," he said firmly to Zach. They were already stripping Thomas, attaching monitors.

He went out into the receptionist area, motioned to use the telephone. He telephoned home, and got his mother. "Mother, it's Zach!"

"Oh, darling, you are home, how lovely," said his mother. "When are you coming—"

"Listen, mother, and don't panic. Dad is rather sick, we have him in the clinic. Can you come right away? Get one of the men to drive you."

She gave a soft gasp. "Zach, is it . . ."

"Maybe heart, I don't know. But do come, will you?"

The next hours were thankfully blurred in his memory. His mother came, Kevin came from his lab. The uncles gathered, and Aunt Hortense, crisply efficient. His aunt was a highly qualified chemist, she lived for her work, but she was also a sensible warm human being. Her strength supported his mother until the end came. Thomas was conscious for a time, and held his wife's hand.

Then he began to slip away. They sent the family out, and worked desperately to try to revive him. No equipment or human skill could work. They learned later he had had a massive coronary, the heart had just burst inside him.

Zach went home in a complete daze. But he could not remain in his room to agonize and weep. Someone had to plan, notify everyone. Kevin took over the telephone, quietly sensible, making suggestions in a practical tone. Sonia wept, then dried her tears to take care of her daughter Isabeau, who was in a state of collapse.

A message had been left for Isolde. She telephoned that night when she returned from the ballet. "My God, Zach, it can't be!" she cried. "He was never sick—tell me I'm having a nightmare!"

"I'm sorry, my dear," said Zach wearily. "It is true; he had a massive heart attack. If—if he had lived, he would have been a complete invalid. It is a terrible shock for us, but a blessing for him, he would have hated that."

"Yes, yes, I know, but I—" Strong Isolde was crying, and he felt a warm sympathy for her. She had leaned on their father, as they all had, for comfort, advice, aid.

He comforted her as well as he could. She said they would fly back at once.

"Oh, no, Isolde, you cannot do that," he told her quickly. "We have heavy rains, the airport is closed. Uncle Samuel was to fly from Ponce, and he cannot even do that. Don't try to come."

"Don't tell me that!" she cried. "I must come. I must see father for the last time—and mother—I must be with mother."

"The airport is closed," he repeated patiently. "I'll let you know if it reopens, but I don't think it will for a couple of days. The rains are very heavy, the roads are flooded, and it is still coming down. You know how it is this time of year."

Reluctantly, Isolde agreed to wait. Then Delphine wanted to talk to him. "Oh, Zach, oh, I am so—so—" Her voice was thick with tears.

"I know, my dear. Father loved you so much, you were always his beautiful baby."

Delphine sobbed uncontrollably. Zach soothed her, then asked to speak to Rosita.

The girl came on the line. Her voice was soft, slightly accented, but clear.

"Rosita, how are you?"

"Fine, Mr. Hamilton."

"Zach," he said. "Call me Zach. Listen, I want to ask you a favor."

"Oh, anything—Zach," she said. "What can I do?"

"You are close to Delphine. Let her cry a while, then tomorrow take her to church. Is there a Catholic church near you?"

"Yes. There is one next to the convent where we go to school."

"Oh, I remember." Isolde had been delighted to find a fine Catholic school for girls just two blocks from them, and a

43

church next door. She had sent them there, instead of hiring a governess. "Yes, go there with her, and comfort her. Have the priest talk to her, if she grieves too much."

"I will, Zach. And—and I am so sorry—"

"I know. Thank you. It is difficult—"

"I wish we could all be there with you," she said quietly.

Her voice was like a cool hand laid on his forehead. "I wish you could, also. But it is best not. The storms are very bad, especially in the mountains."

He talked to Isolde again, then hung up. So many details, and he was so tired—and shocked— But the responsibility was his, as his father had predicted. He began to wonder if his father had had some premonition, that he had spoken so just before he died. Of course, his father had said these things before, yet . . .

Zach worked hard with Kevin helping him. Aunt Hortense was a pillar of strength; he had never appreciated the sensible spinster so much. She had an apartment of her own with her cats, in an old part of San Juan, just blocks from them, but somehow they had never visited much, except on holidays. Now she was in and out, always with practical advice, and suggestions about things he had not thought about.

The funeral was held on a dark rainy day, it poured all during the service. The Dominguez family all attended, sitting in the back of the church, in two pews, at the cathedral which was the family church of the Hamiltons, and had been for one and a half centuries. Zach shook hands with them, thanked them for coming.

"I talked to Rosita the other night, when my sister phoned. She is doing well, I am happy to say."

Their dark, tanned faces lit up, they all strained to hear what he said about their Rosita. How close they all were, Zach thought, and how handsome. They all had beautiful expressive features and grace.

Few followed to the cemetery, the ladies were taken home, because the chill wind was intense. They walked in mud to the grave site, all the more grievous because the skies seemed to weep with them.

Zach felt like collapsing when it was all over. He sat in the study, having changed to dry clothes, and put his slippered feet on the fender before the roaring fire. Only Kevin was here, the other relatives had gone home earlier. His mother had gone to bed, and so had his grandmother. The house seemed suddenly empty. He kept looking to the door, waiting for his father to enter. It was incredible that his father would never enter that door again.

"Well, you will have the problems of the company now," said Kevin. "That is—if you become president."

"If?" asked Zach idly, yawning. "What do you mean? Father wanted that."

Kevin was silent for a short time. Zach turned his head to gaze at his younger brother. Only a freshman in college, he seemed so much more mature than he had been a few months ago. "Aunt Hortense and I were talking. I think I had better tell you what they are all saying."

"What is that?" Zach asked sharply, frowning. Did they think he was incapable of handling the company? He was only twenty-two, he would be twenty-three this August. However, he had been part of the company since he was fourteen, when he started going to the works, when he had gone with his father to visit the islands and see the cane.

Kevin said slowly, deliberately, "I went to the works yesterday, needed some papers. I was in the hallway outside father's office, his secretary was in the outer office. I saw Steve, and stopped to talk to him."

Steve was their cousin, Uncle Morgan's eldest son. He had just finished college, and come into the firm, as a chemist, like his father.

"What did he want?"

"Nothing much. While we were talking, Uncle Morgan came along. He went right into father's office, past the secretary, and he said to Steve to come along, they had a lot of work to do. While I was standing with my mouth open—figuratively speaking—he sat down at father's desk, and messed around with the papers on it. I looked at father's secretary, she looked at me, and lifted her shoulders."

"My God, the gall of him!"

"He means to be president," said Kevin slowly. "Aunt Hortense heard Uncle William talking. He was angry, he thought as vice-president of sales he should be president, he says Uncle Morgan doesn't know anything but lab work."

"Whew," Zach said.

"So I thought you better count the stock," said Kevin. He reached into his pocket, pulled out a paper with neat figures on it. "I started counting—there's me, and you, Isolde—she will probably vote her stock for you. There's mother and her vote with Delphine's stock. Father left her his share, of course. Does granny have any?"

"No, father put her money into other things, along with some money he inherited from his father."

Zach reached for the paper, Kevin handed it to him. "I think Aunt Hortense will vote for you, but you had better ask her. She is independent, you know."

"I will. And Uncle Samuel—"

"Better bag him early, before Uncle Morgan reaches him with some promise about being head of the United States outlets."

Zach stared at his brother again. "That much of a hurry, huh?"

Kevin nodded. Zach, sighing, went to the telephone, and began to call. First, Isolde in New York. They exchanged news, he asked for her proxy, and she promised to send it. Then Aunt Hortense, they talked for a time, he told her frankly what he thought about their future.

"We are going to have to do something about the United States sales, they have gone down so far."

"I have some ideas about that," said the clear voice. "Let's talk about it this week. If you can have a meeting of all stockholders, and have some practical ideas to present about our slipping sales—"

He totaled up the amounts of stock he would have if all his immediate family and Aunt Hortense voted for him. He was still worried about that, when the will was read the next day.

His father had left him half the shares he owned, and the

other half to Isabeau and Delphine. Isolde and Kevin had been given their shares on maturity, reaching the age of eighteen. Zach was now the main stockholder, having thirty percent of the shares, given him at eighteen and twenty-one.

He counted up.

> Zach—thirty percent
> Kevin—five percent
> Isolde—five percent
> Mother and Delphine—ten percent
> Aunt Hortense—ten percent

That made sixty percent. It would be enough, and a little more; with the important exception of the issues that required a two-thirds vote. He phoned around. Uncle Morgan was set on becoming president, Uncle William also wanted the presidency. Uncle Samuel would vote for whichever man would give him the vice-presidency in charge of United States sales, based in Atlanta. "No way," thought Zach. Uncle Samuel was inclined to imbibing too much of their own product. So far from home, nobody would have control over him.

A bare ten percent were held by outside stockholders. But they were worried about the firm. The value and sales had gone down since World War II, when rum sales had fallen off so drastically during the war. Poor quality of rum, ruthless distributors who had substituted watered rum for the good—all had contributed to their slide.

They had the job of trying to build up the reputation of rums, and their own brand. And trying to find new markets among people who preferred Scotch or wines.

Since Thomas Hamilton had died, the stockholders were all the more worried about the fate of the firm. Zach ordered his broker to watch like a hawk for any stocks of Hamilton Rums going on the market, and buy at once.

They soon phoned him back. All ten percent were on the market, but offers had come in from San Juan. Could he put down enough to hold them?

He phoned his bank, obtained a loan on the stock he had in other companies, and bought the stocks of Hamilton's. All this before his uncles could jump in and buy, with a firm offer. They were furious.

"You've got forty percent now," they grumbled at the meeting to elect a new president. "What do you want with so much? You are sure gambling on the future of the company, to put most of your money in Hamilton stock!"

"I believe in it," he said ironically. "And I want to leave it to my children one day."

"You must expect a large family!" sneered Uncle Morgan. "Fine talk for someone not even married yet!"

"I can wait. And yes, I do expect to have a good-sized family," said Zach thoughtfully. "Sounds like a nice idea, thank you, Uncle Morgan."

His uncle snorted, red with rage. The vote was held, only a formality now, thanks to Kevin and Aunt Hortense. If he had gone in innocently and unprepared—Zach shuddered to think what might have happened.

"Well now, Mr. Director, what do you intend to do, to build up the firm?" Uncle William snapped. "I'll tell you sales are far down what they were once!"

"I want a full report on that," Zach said. "Prepare one, will you, Uncle William, and have it on my desk in a week. At that time, we will meet and discuss our potential. I think we should come up with fresh advertising ideas, and new products. Aunt Hortense had suggested a new white rum, a light one for the States. She says women like the light rums better than the heavier dark ones."

"Women! Who cares what they drink?" snapped Uncle Morgan. They were all pettish and cross today. "They don't drink anything but their fruit-filled drinks!"

Aunt Hortense glared at him through her horn-rimmed glasses. "Women are more than fifty percent of the population. And if they want fruit-filled drinks, we will persuade them to make their drinks with rum! Planter's punch is a most highly thought of drink. And all those phony Polynesian drinks—"

They argued about that for a time, Zach taking notes mentally, and thinking about it. Aunt Hortense had a strong point. Women liked their drinks light, but they did want a form of liquor in them. Why not try for an even lighter rum than they now produced, and appeal to the women?

And mixed with—yes. Mixed with lime, with lemon, with coconut and orange, all the tropical fruits. Perhaps a bottled drink combination to add to rum and have the drink all ready to pour over ice cubes.

By the next morning, he had looked over the sales figures and had his suggestions ready. They fought it, all the men, half because they did not want to listen to Zach, half because they rebelled at preparing a drink for women. Zach insisted on trying it, and told the lab to prepare one-fourth the year's barrels for a lighter rum, silver white, and less than eighty proof. Only Aunt Hortense had faith in the project. She turned all her skilled abilities to working out the formula using the secret formulas of the Hamiltons worked out over the years. She consulted with Zach regularly about her results, and Kevin was appointed as her assistant.

When it was about ready to approve, Zach asked them what to name it. The men were scowling. He turned to Aunt Hortense.

"Since it is your idea, and your formula, Aunt Hortense, I think you should have the honor of naming our new rum."

She flushed, pleased. "I did have a name ready," she admitted. "I thought of Hamilton's Silver. And a logo, of a silver flower on the label. Perhaps a silver rose, I do like roses."

The men scoffed, Zach waited until they had calmed down, then said, "I think it is a splendid idea. We'll go ahead on that," he said to the head of advertising.

By remaining calm, by calmly enforcing his ideas, and preparing in advance heavily for all meetings, he was able to keep one or two steps ahead of his uncles, and keep the reins in his control.

But it meant working night and day, weekends in the study at home, nights in the study and days in the works, walking around, watching whatever happened. Kevin was an excellent assistant, but he had his college courses. He must complete college, perhaps go on to MIT or Wharton School of Business in the States. The times ahead would be all the more complex, business never became simpler in the complex world of international money. They would all have to work hard to bring Hamilton's back to its pre-World War II position. And not just come back, Zach determined; he meant to make Hamilton's a world leader in rums. They could do it. They had the modern equipment in a fine up-to-date factory in San Juan. They had islands of sugarcane, the best, most carefully grown in the Caribbean. They had the reputation of one hundred fifty years of experience in world markets, and another fifty from the island of Elysia.

Rums had gone out from Hamilton's since the first Thomas Hamilton had come from the States, a Loyalist deprived of his plantation, determined to make a new start on his beautiful island. Morgan Hamilton and his wife Tess had continued the tradition, and further generations had carried it on.

It would not stop here, Zach vowed. He would work like the devil—or like a red-haired Scotsman, part French, part Russian, but all American, and make this work.

Chapter 4

The girls came home from New York City early in June. Rosita thought at once how tired Zach looked, and how many years older than his age. He was working such long hours, no wonder.

He sat now at the head of the table at dinner in the evening, looking more mature, self-controlled, not laughing so much. He seemed absorbed in his thoughts, much of the time scarcely hearing the conversation.

Rosita went to see her family on Sunday, and spent the day with them. The babies had grown so much, the younger ones did not even know her. And Elena's new baby had arrived, a tiny adorable boy with a frizz of black hair.

Cristina seemed more cheerful, reconciled to having a baby. Her husband was ecstatic, and showered her with presents. That probably helped her mood, for she was plump and heavy with the child, probably a boy, said granny, the way she carried him low.

Rosita got a chance to talk to Marcos alone. "How does it go, tell me truthfully, Marcos," she begged.

He pinched her cheek affectionately. "We manage. Did you think we could not manage without you, little one?' he teased.

She looked him right in the eye, and he sobered.

"We do not have such good jobs now, without you," he admitted. "Elena is back dancing. And Luisa is learning more, father spends more time with her. Inez and Tadeo have improved their act, it goes over well. But the money—" He shrugged, "It is not good. The money from Isolde came in just the other day, thank God. Father banked it, and we will draw on it more cautiously. Elena's bills were high, that took all we had in the bank."

"Oh, Marcos. I wish I could help more."

"The money helps so much, you could not help more," he said baldly. "These are bad years for us. Two other companies are opening in San Juan, and they have fewer dancers than we do, but several pretty and young girls. So—" His hands lifted expressively.

"And about you, Marcos. Has father agreed—"

"He is allowing me to go part-time to the university here. I take two classes a week, and with the dancing it takes all my time. The homework—whew—and the lab time—it really cuts into my playtime with girls!" And he laughed. But he seemed satisfied, and she was pleased. Marcos would have the chemistry courses he craved, and might one day work in a pharmacy, and he could dance nights. A compromise, but all life seemed to be a compromise, between what one wanted and what one could have.

"How long will you be in San Juan?" Marcos asked presently, stretched out like a great dark cat on the sands. His black curly hair was covered with sand; playfully she trickled more sand on him.

"I don't know. Isolde did not say. I think maybe a month, not the summer. She is restless. She spoke of a summer festival to which we might be invited. It would be good experience, she said."

"I thought you would have the summer off." He rolled over to peer up at her.

She grimaced. "We practice five hours every day!" she laughed.

"A slave driver!"

"Well, she knows what she wants. She says I have learned very quickly, she is generous in her praise. But I have much to learn, so does Delphine."

He asked about the company they were in, she told him about the New York Festival Ballet Company, the people in it, the choreographers. "One is the famous Russian man, the one who defected about 1963," she told him. "Dimitre Kerenski. He is a fine dancer, but is also doing some choreography. He looked at me one day, and asked about my training in flamenco. I think he wants to use me in a ballet. Isolde was very excited."

"What about boys?" asked Marcos. "Are you dating anybody special?"

"Me?" her voice squeaked in her surprise. "Me? I am too young and skinny," and she laughed.

"Are they all—homos?"

"No, I think not. Some are, Delphine says. They all cluster about her, so she knows which one is, and which one is not. But I don't know anything about that."

"Father worried about you. I told him Isolde would look after you."

"Yes, she does. She watches us like a hawk, even when she is dancing a good part. After rehearsal, we go right home with her. And on Sundays—Delphine and I go to the museums with one of the maids! Oh, they are so nice." She told him about them.

Maria and Madelena were Puerto Rican women, both widowed, sisters, with grown children. They lived in at the huge Hamilton apartment on the East Side in the Sixties. They were fond of the Hamiltons, but were even closer to Rosita, and often chattered with her in Spanish. Their brothers, Pedro and Lorenzo, tough and burly, were on standby to chauffeur the girls wherever they wished to go. They were silent, competent, dependable.

"Father was glad when you wrote about them," said Marcos. Their father wandered over to them, and dropped down on the sand beside them.

"May a poor papa listen to his daughter's adventures?"

53

he asked. Rosita sat up to lean against his strong chest. She had missed so much the warmth and closeness of her family, kind though the Hamiltons were.

"Oh, I missed you, papa," she whispered.

"And I missed my lovely baby," he said, his cheek on her hair.

They talked all the day, laughter rising from the sand. Rosita hugged all the babies, and played with them happily. How sweet to see their sturdy brown forms tumbling about on the sand, clutching at their parents' legs as they went swimming.

Marcos and Tadeo drove her home to the Hamiltons.

Tadeo asked quietly, "Is there a chance you could come to dance with us nights when you are home? Will they let you?"

Rosita thought. Delphine had a heavy cold, and retired early. Isolde spent much of the evening with her grieved mother. Zach was often at the office or in the study, with Kevin.

"Yes, I think so," she said slowly.

"I could come and wait at the gate at seven-thirty," Marcos offered. "If you can leave, come out and meet me. If you cannot come, I will drive to work. But come when you can, it would help."

"Yes, I will. Ask Luisa to bring my dress and shoes, and my headbands. When I can come, I will. I would like to dance with you again."

Marcos asked, "It would not interfere with the ballet lessons, will it? I mean, it is not so different to dance—"

"It is different, yes, but it is all dancing," said Rosita.

They drove up to the door, the guard came out from beside the house. He stared keenly at the brothers. They got out of the car. Rosita introduced them.

"Jaime, this is my brother Tadeo, and this is my brother Marcos," she said. "They will often drive me home. It is all right for them to come to the door, is it not?"

She waited for them to stare at and recognize each other, and Jaime said, "It is better for them to drive around to the back, where other guards are, and it is safer for you, Rosita.

Out on the street, it is no good. Come inside, around to the garage entrance, and you can enter by the patio. We will always be there.''

She thanked him, so did her brothers, and she went around to the back with Jaime. ''I may go out nights with my brothers,'' she said carefully. ''Marcos will come for me, but I will go out by the back way, so I do not disturb the Hamiltons.''

''Sí, comprende,'' said the guard, with a quick nod. She thought he understood more than he said, that she was not one of the family really, that she wished to be apart from them and live her own life.

On Monday, Isolde kept them working until midafternoon, with only a brief stop for luncheon. Delphine grumbled, she felt miserable with her cold. She went to lie down at three-thirty, when they finished. Rosita went to her lovely room on the third floor, and also slept. She wanted to be fresh for the evening.

She had said nothing about her plans. It was not their concern if she went to her family. She was grateful to Isolde for the financial help. But her family needed her in the night-club act, she understood that, and Isolde was very possessive about Rosita's time. If Rosita could help the act this summer, and they were better paid, it would help them through the winter. Her dancing had improved, especially her hand movements. The graceful movements and gestures and mime of the hands were very important in ballet as well as in the flamenco.

Delphine ate supper in bed, and went back to sleep. Zach was out. Kevin left supper early, to work. Isolde and Isabeau were talking, when the mother began to weep silently. She retired from the table, and Isolde went with her.

Grandmother Sonia Lothaire sighed, and glanced at Rosita, sitting across from her. ''This is a sad household, I am sorry for you, child,'' she said kindly.

''It is nothing, madame, I understand,'' said Rosita.

''How does your ballet go?''

''Isolde is pleased with me—at times,'' said Rosita carefully.

A smile crinkled the elderly beautiful cameo face. ''She is

difficult, no? Tell me about New York. Tell me how you dance. You are in the *corps de ballet?''*

"Yes, madame." Because the woman seemed lonely and sad, Rosita talked to her about the ballet company, the members. Cathy and how catty she was. Tall Melinda who was so graceful. Dreamy Amy, and her beauty. Denise, and how her mother pushed.

"Ah, I know the type. She will run away and get married, or something terrible, one day," nodded Sonia.

"Bernadine is so ambitious. She hates it when anyone gets a good part, and she does not. She cannot refrain from sniffing and making remarks under her voice. When Lupe noticed me, and asked to have me for her understudy—"

"Her understudy—ah, tell me about that, child!"

So Rosita told her about beautiful Lupe, a prima ballerina and thirty-six, who was so skillful. "She does this Spanish dance, she is also Spanish, and she wished me to learn the part if she gets sick. I was so thrilled—and Isolde was very excited, but she said unfortunately Lupe is very healthy. And so she was. But I would have been terrified to try to do the part. Not yet. I am not ready."

Sonia nodded. "I understand. It is thrilling, but scary also," and she told about how she had had to take a part at the last minute, at fifteen, in Moscow, and how scared she was. "But I did well, and they forgave me for being young, and many men came around to my dressing room and stared at me. How excited I was, not smart enough to be scared out of my wits! All those young Russian officers, so handsome and so devilish, with their flashing eyes," and she smiled and sighed, and fluttered her Spanish fan.

After supper, Sonia excused herself. "I have enjoyed our little talk. Tomorrow, maybe, after luncheon we will talk a while, and I will show you more about hands, okay?" American slang dotted her speech like polka dots on silk cloth, odd, yet attractive.

"I would like that, madame. You are most kind."

Rosita skipped happily up to her room. It was quarter past seven, time enough to pick up her makeup and purse, primp a minute, then rush down to meet Marcos. Nobody was about, the halls were silent. She slipped down the back way, and spotted Jaime.

"Your brother Marcos waits for you, Rosita," he said, and walked beside her to the rattly car, tall and sturdy and polite. She felt safer with him there, he was so big and tough.

Marcos grinned on seeing her. "Oh, great! We'll make the floor stamp tonight!" he said happily.

They went off in the car, and the excitement was rising in her. To dance with her family again! The warmth, the thrill of flamenco, the music of guitars—

Her father greeted her with a beam and a hug. "Marcos said you might come! My baby! How good to have you with us!"

Her mother hugged her, and her grandmother. Cristina and her husband were sitting with the babies. All the rest of the family had gathered in the small dressing room.

The men left the room and stood in the hallway silently while Luisa and Elena helped Rosita dress. Margarita looked over Rosita after she was ready, then tucked a fresh red rose in her hair, in among the dark shiny braids.

The music was starting. They lined up, Papa Pascual looking back over the line, his dark eyes shining with joy that Rosita was with them. She beamed back at him, and nodded, her usual sharp confident nod that said "I am ready."

It seemed years since she had last danced with them, that fateful night when Isolde Hamilton had come backstage and asked—no, told them that Rosita must come with her. Less than six months—but so much had happened—

They ran out on stage, prancing and smiling. Rosita drew a deep excited breath, then calmed herself. She would be first, Marcos had told her, and said that Oliverio would be ready with her special music. There had been no time to practice anything new.

Oliverio and Jacinto sat down, cradled their guitars, began the strumming and the music. Rosita clapped briskly, head bent, getting into the rhythm. She thought of her first steps. Did she dare put in some of the ballet moves she had practiced so much this winter, under Isolde's keen eye and direction? Perhaps a *pirouette en dehors*, in quarter turns, something simple she knew she could do well. And the jumps, the *échappés sautés changés.* She could do those.

She heard the claps increase, jumped forward to the center of the stage. She did not see the audience; it was light she knew by their sounds of stirring, the clink of glass and china.

But someone remembered her. She heard the call, *"La Soledad! La Soledad!"* from some masculine voice. It was vaguely familiar, over the sound of the guitars. Absorbed, she paid little attention.

Someone else took it up, from the other side of the room. *"La Soledad! La Soledad!* Flamenco Rosita! Flamenco Rose! Flamenco Rosita! *Brava!"*

Nice to be remembered, she thought, as she went into the first light steps. Click, click, click, her heels were out of practice from dancing so much on her toes and feet in the ballet. But they remembered, from the years of practice. And sometimes she danced a bit in the kitchen for Maria and Madelena as they clapped in rhythm, broad brown faces beaming at the show.

She flung herself into a *pirouette,* again, again, the moves came even more easily. Vaguely she heard the cheers of excitement.

She did other moves to the Spanish guitar music. Oliverio was watching her closely, following her, anticipating what she would do somehow, because of his closeness to her, his musical senses. The music lifted her, then Tadeo was there, clasping her waist, lifting her into the air in the beats. He was grinning and happy, pleased.

She went up into the air with the help of Tadeo, and beat her feet lightly against each other, forward, back, forward. He let her down again, she ran to the other side of the stage, heels clicking, fingers rapidly clattering the castanets. When she ran back again, she flung herself into his arms, he bent with her, and she swooped almost to the floor. Wild cheers, shouts of *"Brava!"*

When she ran back to the other side of the stage, this time

58

Marcos was there! He was ready to catch her, hold her and help her twirl about, swinging her frilled skirts. She gazed up at him, and he grinned down at her, his strong arms muscular as he turned her about. They danced closer to Tadeo, Marcos picked her up, tossed her lightly to Tadeo, she landed in the older brother's arms. The men were standing cheering, she heard some shrill feminine cries of pleasure.

From Tadeo back to Marcos, then on her own, dancing, whirling, in control, her breathing good because of Isolde's training. The flamenco moves, a ballet step in place, then feet fluttering as she jumped in the air. Her arms circling, fingers clicking. If only she did not have the castanets in her hands, she would be able to mime better, she vaguely remembered thinking. But this was flamenco—and she concluded with those steps, faster, faster, as Papa Pascual clapped vigorously. Ending in a whirl of skirts, she sank to the ground gracefully.

Wild cheers, shouts. *"La Soledad!* Rosita! *La Soledad!* Rosita! Flamenco Rosita!"

She bowed, curtsyed, again, and again, dancing back into the line, so that Oliverio could start the music for Marcos. When he was well into his dance, she slipped down the stairs, reached for the towel her grandmother held.

"Better than ever, my *gitana!"* whispered Granny Alejandra hoarsely, her wrinkled face even more creased with pleasure. She gave Rosita a long hug.

Rosita grinned at her, mischievously. Her grandmother had not approved her leaving them for New York, not for that foreign ballet stuff. "A ballet dancer is not so bad, eh?"

"Go on with you!"

Rosita patted her face dry, then went back on stage. Marcos's dancing was inspired. She watched him, then having caught her breath, she clapped for him vigorously. He was coming back into the line when she caught sight of a man clapping, at a table toward the back. He had leaned forward to applaud, and the candlelight on the table caught the red gleam of his bright hair.

She caught her breath audibly. Zach Hamilton. Of all the luck! He would tell Isolde—she would complain in her possessive way, and forbid Rosita to dance here—oh, why had he chosen this nightclub to take his girl to? She saw the girl sitting so close to Zach, a girl with dark hair and a luscious red mouth smiling at him. Tall girl, beautiful, with a dress cut down to the point of indecency, scarlet red dress, jewels glittering— So that was Helena, his current girl, as Delphine had said.

Rosita felt an odd pang, something like fury, something like sadness. Funny feeling, hurting in the chest and throat. Probably because Zach would tell his sister, and Rosita would have to fight to be with her family again.

She deliberately turned her gaze from him, back to the stage. Luisa was dancing, trying to be coy, but it did not suit her. She was simple, honest, with a sweet smile, and gentle shy ways. Mutters from the crowd. But the girl danced better. If only her hands were better. Rosita could help her now with hands, if only she had the chance.

The others went on, and on. Sometimes the applause was good, sometimes light. They finished, and went backstage.

The talk backstage was good. Rosita seized the chance to talk to Luisa about her hands, and Elena came over and then Inez, and listened and watched, and imitated her.

"You see, the miming is important. This way," circling her face, "means I am pretty. Pointing to the heart, means to love. Arms out like this, the fingers shaking and hands up and down, is to fly. The hands can move with the fingers curling up gracefully—" She showed them how Isolde wanted her to hold her fingers, in the most graceful position, moving them around in a circle, hands moving, then back to herself.

The girls learned quickly. They could use some of the moves in their dancing. Most important was the pretty position of the hands, to make them look the most beautiful.

They went on in the second evening performance. Zach had left with his pretty peach, thought Rosita savagely. She could imagine where they had gone. Zach was attractive, wealthy, popular. She felt her teeth grit. She would be fifteen in September—but he was so much older, and so was that girl!

She found it hard to concentrate.

She danced again, forgetting everything in the dance.

Tadeo and Marcos danced again with her. After the act, back-stage, her father sent her home.

"No, you must get your rest. You practice in the morning, until midafternoon, you said. You must get your sleep. The ballet is most important. Will you come back tomorrow night?"

All eyes were on her, eagerly. "I hope so," she said soberly. "If any guests come, Isolde says I must remain. When it is just the family, I think I can slip away, it is all right."

"Well, I'll come each evening and wait for you, just in case," said Marcos, cheerfully. He and Tadeo took her home quickly, and left her with Jaime to see her inside. She went in the back way, into the patio, and up the outside steps, to the third floor, her steps light on the iron rungs.

Rosita felt guilty. She had said it about Isolde, as though the girl knew she had left the house. Isolde had only said she wished Rosita to come to dinner when there were guests, so that Rosita would become acquainted with important people. And she must learn to be at ease with anybody, of any status. Rosita had quietly offered to remain from the table when they had guests, as she was not one of the family. Delphine had protested, Isolde said of course she must come.

The lights on the second floor were dimmed, Delphine must be asleep, Zach was probably still out. She went on up to the third floor, stepped inside to the hallway, and tiptoed to her room. She opened the door cautiously, closed it before switching on the light.

She took off her shawl, and hung it on a chair, then turned to the mirror. Her cheeks were flushed, her eyes bright from excitement. Then she stopped; there was something different about her dressing table.

Her hand reached out for the crystal glass vase, a bud vase. Had it been there today, and she had not noticed? No, she would surely have noticed when she dressed for dinner, or when she gathered up her makeup to leave.

It was a beautiful glittering crystal vase. And in it was a single lush, romantic red rose. Just opening, it breathed a heavy crimson fragrance.

Who could have put it there? Delphine? No, she had gone to bed early, cross and flushed with fever from her cold. Isolde? No, she had been absorbed in her mother's and her own grief over her father.

She scarcely knew kind Kevin, nice as he was, absorbed in his studies. Madame Sonia? Perhaps. She was pleasant, she knew how Rosita felt in this household of strangers.

Yet somehow she guessed, it must be Zach. Her heart beat rapidly as she bent to inhale the fragrance of the rose. Why had he done it? To tease her, to say he knew she had been dancing tonight, playing hooky? To be nice, to say he would not give her away? Or to say he had liked her dancing, to say this was her rose, the rose for Rosita? A tribute to her performance?

She went to sleep with a strange sensation in her chest. A happy warm feeling, a little excited, with the fragrance of the single rose filling her beautiful room.

Zach did not tell. He said not a word about seeing her. He gave her a smile at dinner that next evening, but said nothing. When she slipped away, he said nothing again.

Delphine soon caught on that Rosita was going to her family. She would not tell, she said. But she wished she could come! If only she did not have this horrid cold—

Of course, as Rosita went out almost every night, Isolde finally caught on, about the end of the second week. She was very cross, and scolded Rosita.

Sonia protested, "Why should the child not go to her family? She longs to dance with them, why not? Let her alone!"

Isabeau did not pay much attention, she was lost in her grief. Zach came home, to hear the scolding continuing at dinner. He listened, then said, "Let her alone. Rosita must have some fun."

"Fun!" echoed Isolde, waving her graceful hands. "If she has so much energy, she can practice evenings! She will ruin her feet! I don't want her to dance flamenco any longer! It must be ballet, ballet!"

"You are too possessive," he said, frowning. "Rosita has not been with her family since January. Rosita, you continue to go out as you wish. Only do what you want, do not drive yourself. You are too young to work from morning to night. Sleep in tomorrow.''

"Sleep in!" cried Isolde, outraged. "I want her to practice every day! How can you say—Zach, you have nothing to do with her training!"

"I have something to do with everybody in this household," he said, losing his smile. "I am in charge now, and don't forget it! Father left me in charge!"

They looked like they were going to have a big fight over her. Rosita spoke up hastily, flushing. "Please, Isolde. Mr. Hamilton—"

"Zach," he said firmly. "What is it, child?"

"I only wanted to say—I do not get tired, I get plenty of sleep. I will practice every day, as Isolde wishes. And my feet will not be ruined by flamenco, I talked to Lupe about that. She still does both, and she is much older than I.''

"Well, I'll look at your feet tomorrow," said Isolde, somewhat appeased. "I'll let you know then."

Zach winked at Rosita, and she smiled at him, her face lighting up. "You are most kind to me," she murmured, so only he could hear her, and his grandmother, seated at his right, next to Rosita.

"I have to protect my own," he grinned back at her. "And you are under my roof, Rosita!" He glanced at his watch. "Seven-fifteen, do you want to be excused, child?"

"Yes, please, if I may," she said, relieved. She slipped from the table, though Isolde looked cross, and sped away. At the dancing that night, she felt curiously light and terribly happy. She was not quite sure why.

It might have been the echo of Zach's pleasant voice saying, "I have to protect my own."

Chapter 5

It was November in New York City. The summer sun of San Juan was a faded memory. Isolde went through the warm-ups at the *barre* a little mechanically this morning.

A bright summer, but a grieving summer. How difficult to realize her father was dead. Such a kind, generous man, gone. All the security of knowing he would back her up, encourage her, advise her, scold her if she went astray—all gone. Zach was in charge. But he was only two years older than Isolde.

How her mother had wept. It had been hard to comfort her. Then had come a sort of stoic resignation that had been even more difficult and worrisome. Her mother had lost for a time her will to live, and that was dangerous. Isolde felt frightened about it, but what could she do? She was but twenty-one and this was outside her experience.

How gray the November days. Cold and rainy and chilly. And the winter season was coming. In two weeks they would all be frantically busy. Well, she would welcome that. Six weeks of performances at the New York Arts Center.

Her company, the New York Festival Ballet Company, had been formed only three years ago. It was relatively large already, a classical ballet company, popular in New York and in their guest appearances around the United States. Rumor had it that they might go to Europe next season, perhaps even in the spring.

They would give within a six-weeks' period a dozen performances of *Swan Lake* and of *Giselle*, and over a half-dozen new ballets created by their own choreographers. Add to that fifteen ballets of previous seasons and of other companies, borrowed by permission. That made a formidable and exciting program for them all.

Bend—stretch—slowly—slowly—her right foot moved through the round motions of warming up. *Demi-plié. Demi-plié. Demi-seconde* of the arms. *Ronds de jambe à terre. And one and* two *and* three . . .

Pause while the ballet mistress outlined the next exercise. They all took class and then went into rehearsals. The younger ones were at the side, and did most of the exercises under the keen eye of the assistant to the ballet mistress. Isolde glanced at her sister Delphine. She was earnest this morning, concentrating well. Rosita as always was sober and exact in her movements. Her heart-shaped face shone. She loved the moves.

There were forty of them in the company. It made for a large class, and the ballet mistress, Madame Olga Lenski, took her duties very seriously. Madame Olga had a soft, firm voice that carried well over the precise music of the piano. Now in her fifties, she had been in ballet in Moscow, then in Paris, then in New York.

The chief choreographer, Alan Landis, was in the corner conferring with the director, Eleanor Stanton. At sixty, Miss Stanton was brisk, keen. Smartly gowned in gray silk, she was wealthy in her own right, or she could never have formed this company. Her previous company had taken off, gone under someone else's direction, and she had shrugged and formed a new one. Her pearls shimmered in the bright lights of the studio. Her pink cheeks glowed as her hands waved gracefully, making a point to Alan.

Planning the season, and its publicity, thought Isolde, as they studied sketches, glanced at the company, and back again at their pages. Most of it was ready. Photos had been taken last week, and studied intently on the bulletin board. Many would be used in a publicity brochure on sale at the performances.

Dimitre Kerenski was at the last *barre* in back. He was so tall that he and Isolde usually took the last positions. She felt so self-conscious about her height, five feet ten. Only Dimitre was near her height when she went up *sur les pointes*. She gained five inches. It was so humiliating—if only she were small like Delphine, or better yet like Rosita. It was a terrible effort not to be jealous of Rosita. The girl was so perfect in form, a dainty trim figure, softly rounded breasts, small hips, long slim legs, and only five feet one and a half now! She would probably go to five three, Demi thought. And Delphine would not be much taller.

All her hopes of becoming a prima ballerina had gone up in smoke. The classical ballet demanded so many ballerinas to be of a petite build, small head, long neck, trim figure, and short. Short. Short. And Isolde was so very tall. She had just grown and grown and grown, and Grandmother Sonia had sighed deeply, and shaken her head.

She was the Lilac Fairy and the mother and the Goddess of Spring. Rarely with a partner, usually on her own, looming grandly over the little fairies. How bitter. And she was not as graceful and as dainty as the others—how could she be? Her long, long legs, her big build, her wide shoulders—it was all impossible. Madame Olga had talked to her last year, gently, about going into contemporary dance. "There is a chance there for you, Isolde," she had said. "Your height will not count against you, at least, not so much. Had you considered modern dance?"

Isolde had shaken her red gold head stubbornly. She was almost in tears, but she would not cry. "No, I am a classical dancer, madame. My heart is here."

"Very well, dear, very well. I understand. *Je comprends. Naturellement*. Nature dictates what we are able to accomplish. We must work within our limits, stretching them as we may. We shall continue as we have."

She dismissed the subject. But Isolde, on returning to the company, found herself more and more in the background.

The class finished. They had one hour of rehearsal, then broke after completing the first act of *Swan Lake*.

They scattered then to the large lunchroom, and sat down at tables. Isolde saw that Delphine and Rosita were settled with a couple of their young friends, chattering away. It had been interesting to watch Rosita. At first, she had been silent, big-eyed, quiet, aloof. Delphine had drawn her into her circle of friends, laughing, giggling, gossiping. Gradually Rosita had opened up, talked, smiled. Her words were listened to. When she showed a girl how to move her hands, or how to accomplish a step that had troubled the girl, she was watched, listened to respectfully. They knew by instinct, those children, which ones were doing right.

Isolde sat at a table by herself, hoping. She spread out her luncheon from the lunchbox. Madelena always prepared them well. Thermoses of milk for the girls, of milk and tea for Isolde. Sandwiches of peanut butter, stuffed celery with cheese, pieces of raw carrot and peppers, an apple or orange.

Since September she had asked Madelena to prepare enough for two persons. The maid had silently done as she asked, curiosity in her gaze.

Today she was rewarded. Dimitre strode into the lunchroom, looked about, saw her, and came over. He sank down into the chair; he was always as graceful as a large cat, a leopard.

"May I?" He reached for a piece of celery. She smiled, nodded, suddenly radiantly happy. He crunched with her. She poured a cup of hot tea for him, yellow with milk, the way he liked it, and she had learned to like it, full of honey. "Thank you." He looked at her, smiled, their glances meeting. He knew she had prepared for him, she blushed and was silent.

"It went well," she said.

He nodded, his gaze focusing on the wall. "The prince is coming along well. Giselle is inspiring sometimes. Today she did well."

Lupe, small and graceful, was Giselle. They had worked in the small room while the rest of the company worked on the *Swan Lake*. Isolde had managed to go from one to the other rooms, watching, listening. Rosita was in the crowd of peasants who danced with Giselle and the disguised prince. Later she was in the long line of Wilis, the spirits of dead girls who had been betrayed in love.

She pushed the sandwiches to him. He munched on peanut butter. "I have a mania for peanut butter," he said somberly. "It is dreadful. Never did I think I would come to eat such."

She smiled. "It is good for you, full of protein."

He had a large mouth, sensuous, shaped square like a faun's. She watched it move as he spoke, fascinated, and watched his cheekbones, high and like a Tartar that he was. His eyebrows were so well defined, his hands so expressive, his head so large and splendid. He looked like the parts he usually played—the cavalier, the prince, the hero.

"I have something very serious to discuss with you, Isolde," he said finally. "I am thinking of my dancing future, and of yours. There is much to think about. No?"

She felt weak. Could he mean marriage? No, perhaps not. He never spoke of it. He had played around when he first came to New York. Rumors of a wife in the background had been played up in the newspapers when he had first defected in 1963. Then there was no more talk, no questions, for he would never answer them. She thought he was divorced, but he never said. He wore no rings. He lived alone in a large bachelor apartment not far from hers on the East Side.

"Yes, I have been thinking also. I will never be a great star," she added bitterly.

"Perhaps not. But you could be other in the dance world. Let us discuss it. Say, on Sunday, my place?"

She nodded, little thrilling chills going up her spine.

"Say about twelve o'clock?" he added, with a smile. "I will prepare luncheon for us. Borscht and stuffed cabbage balls, your favorites, eh?" He was teasing her, laughter in his vivid blue eyes. He knew she hated them.

"Sorry, I cannot come, I just remembered a previous important engagement at a museum."

"Ah, you disappoint me. Perhaps if I offered steak and salad?"

"Accepted," she said, and they both laughed softly.

The rest of her day and week were lit with radiance. Nothing could go wrong. She danced all the day, and sang in the apartment in the evening, to the music played on the complex stereo set that Zach had helped install. Delphine and Rosita danced on the piano-shaped stage under the winding stairs that led to the mezzanine where their bedrooms were set. They had the top floor of the apartment building, an elegant duplex. The first floor of the apartment was open completely, even the kitchen set off only by a low brick wall. The rest of the room was all carpet of off white, wide windows open to the skies except on the worst days, plump sofas, cushions on the floor, huge armchairs, bookcases, incidental tables, and a grand piano near the door. In one area near the kitchen was a huge round table that sat twelve. When they entertained more, it was buffet.

The quarters up on the mezzanine were set around the open staircase, a balcony running clear around the stairs. Isolde had her own bedroom and bath. The girls shared a large room to the back, with their own bath. Maria and Madelena shared the matching room on the other side. There were two guest rooms and baths also on the floor. It was perfect; the Hamiltons could all fit in when they came. And they could be separate from each other, when Isolde needed to read and think on her own. When the girls had homework and had to concentrate, and go to bed early. When Isolde had guests until late at night, and the girls must be in bed early.

Isolde watched the girls dancing, dreamily, Rosita leading, and Delphine following. It was that way now. The older girl had become the devotee, Rosita the inspired leader.

When they tired, they went to their rooms and worked on homework. The nuns at the convent, understanding, had arranged that most of their classes were taken together. Rosita was ahead of herself in English, history, mathematics, oddly enough. She had a keen head for many subjects, and shifted easily into the advanced grades. The girls were happier if they could go to class together, study together, write essays with each other's approval.

Delphine had done much better work this year, the nuns told Isolde. "It is amazing how much a friend can help. And dear little Rosita is so good and studious. She has been trained well."

It was a relief to Isolde that Delphine was happy and contented. She was determined that her sister should be the fine ballerina she could not be. And Rosita— Isolde tapped her finger on her lip. She was anxious to hear what Dimitre said on Sunday. As well as what he might do. She leaned her red gold head back on the creamy sofa, and closed her eyes, to dream.

On Sunday, she saw the girls off to a museum with Maria, and went on her own way. At twelve promptly she was at Dimitre's door, knocking. Her heart seemed to be pounding as though she had climbed the stairs instead of taking the elevator to the tenth floor.

He opened the door at once, managing not to look ridiculous in jeans, T-shirt and a long dark blue apron. He grinned down at her. How marvelous, for a man to be taller than she was! She had defiantly worn high heels, with her trim scarlet wool suit and mink jacket.

"You look too gorgeous," he said. "I thought I had acquired a cook's helper."

She smiled, leaned up and kissed his chin, casually, as though she not thought about this touch for hours. She went past him into his large neat apartment, into the living room, shed her scarlet jacket with the black braid, draped her mink over a chair back and said "I'm ready. Salad?"

She liked his apartment as well as her own. She liked the colors, of amber and brown with touch of bittersweet red. She liked the long casual sofas, the huge chairs for large people, the battered piano, upright in the corner. She liked the bare floor, where he sometimes tried out dances, the bar on the end, and the *barre* at the other side. The magazines scattered over the tables, news magazines, and *New York* and *Dance,* and sections of the *New York Times*.

"I'm ready," she said, and followed him out to the kitchen. The steaks were on a chopping board; he was pounding

71

them. She took out lettuce, tomatoes, carrots, peppers, cucumbers, olives, and began to fix the salad. She knew what he liked now.

She paused to set the kettle on for hot tea. He was talking about the dancing on Friday. "It looks like it will never be in shape, then suddenly all at once it begins to come together. No? I felt it on Friday, felt it in my bones, it was coming alive."

"It looked it. It felt it," said Isolde carefully, hiding her jealousy that he was dancing with a good ballerina, a small perfectly formed woman.

"I was watching your little charge, the girl Rosita. In the peasant dance, she must hold back not to overshadow—is that how you say it? Overshade? Overshadow?"

"Overshadow, yes. She must hold back, I noticed that also," said Isolde, chopping green pepper with care. He liked small, neat pieces. He was a very neat cook, very precise. "Rosita has improved so rapidly I cannot believe it. Madame Olga is looking at her; I think she will be using her before long in something big."

"That is something I wished to discuss with you," he said. "We both know that you have charge of both girls, your Delphine and Rosita. Yes, they are in the *corps de ballet*, but we feel you wish to direct their careers."

He glanced over at her. She nodded, made a grimace. "Yes, I want that. I will never be a prima ballerina." She was amazed that she could say this calmly, this hurt inside her. "My own career is limited by my height. I do not want modern dance, that is not me. but directing others, perhaps a company of my own one day—"

He nodded, slowly. "Yes, I can see that would be good. You are young, but decisive. You can direct, teach, you are listened to. You can see the whole picture, you know what is needed. It is not everything to dance oneself."

She kept her gaze on the dressing. She mixed oil, measured vinegar, a touch of Dijon mustard, shook in herbs from the jars. She fastened the cap on the mixing jar and shook it vigorously. "I wanted to dance so much. It was—painful when I realized I could never achieve my ambition."

He was close behind her. He bent over and touched his lips to the nape of her neck, where the smooth red gold hair was fastened up. The thrill went right through her. "You are brave, my darling," he said. She felt as though someone had just pinned a medal on her. "I have not been so brave."

"You? You?" She asked it in amazement, turning to face him to look up into his shadowed face. "But you—you are the best—everyone raves—"

"But the years catch up. You know my plans last summer. I went to Australia to dance, and was injured—my leg muscles. All the summer wasted," he said, without bitterness, but with resignation. "It made me feel that I am thirty-four."

"Thirty-four. That is nothing!"

"In six years I will be forty. In ten more years, fifty. Do you think, do you imagine, I will still be dancing? Oh, no, the dancer's life is limited. Men of my age are thinking of retirement, of starting a dance school, of going into life insurance business! Yes, Jack told me the other day. His father wishes him to return to Wisconsin, to the family insurance business. He says he will go if he is injured once more this year."

He took the steaks off the fire, set them on plates, warmed in the oven. She had put the salad in bowls, and they sat down at his bittersweet red lacquered kitchen table to eat. Sitting opposite him, talking with him intimately, was such a sweet pain to Isolde. She wished—she wished they were closer, that she did not have to go home at the end of the day.

"So—" They were so attuned now, she knew what he was thinking. "So you are thinking about what you wish to do when you retire from active dancing."

He nodded his head, the blond straight hair falling over his forehead. He pushed back the lock, glanced at her, holding the fork of steak poised, forgotten. "So, yes. I wish to learn more about choreography, that is the first step. To plan the dances, to plan background, sets, music, publicity, photogra-

phy, directing, financing, all that, that is next. And I think I
will work with Rosita, if you permit.''

''Ah, I see.'' Her mind worked at that, keenly. Rosita.
Young, pliant, with possibility in her. ''Yes, I see. She is
good, potentially great.''

''I think so. What are your plans for her?''

Isolde shook her gleaming head slowly. ''I have not planned.
I thought only to see my sister and Rosita through their schooling, into better parts, then plan. I was busy thinking about my
own career—but that is—'' She shrugged.

''That is not what you had dreamed.''

''Yes, not what I had dreamed, hoped for.'' She forked
the salad over, absently, ate another bite. ''I also should plan
ahead. I have gone almost as far as I can go. The next years
will only see me in these same parts, the queen mother, the
second lead for the quartet, and so on.''

He nodded. ''And I will grow older,'' he said whimsically.
''My gray locks will appear, my steps will be less agile, and
others will defect from Russia and push ahead of me in the
headlines. Well, I have had my publicity. In the early years, I
saved my money, I could not believe it would continue like
that. Of course it would not. I have money in the bank, and I
wish to invest it in my future, in our future.''

She held her breath, but he did not speak of love or
marriage. He went on about directing, learning more, perhaps
forming a company one day.

''You have money,'' he said presently. ''Would you invest in a company?''

She nodded. ''I talked to Zach about it, my brother. He
said I can do what I wish, so long as I do not sell company
stock. I have other stock. But I think he did not listen to me
very much. He has other worries on his mind just now.''

''Well, that is all in the future. But with money cautiously
used, an aim, a direction—we must consider what kind of
company. It should be unique, different.'' He frowned. ''The
dance world becomes crowded, we must be different.''

They washed the dishes, then took their mugs of pale tea

into the drawing room, and stretched out, casually, legs up on hassocks, talking, and talking.

"I would like you to see Rosita dance flamenco," said Isolde. "I have a small platform at home in the apartment, and guitar music. You must come sometime and watch her. She comes to life then, and dances like the gypsy she is."

"Gypsy? She is a Spanish Gypsy?" He twisted sideways to study her face.

"Yes. Her family are the Dominguez family, Spanish Gypsies who dance in their own troupe in San Juan. I have watched them, they are the authentic ones. Rosita is already well known in San Juan. When she dances on, and comes forward, and the clapping rises, they shout *'La Soledad! La Soledad!* Flamenco Rosita!' She dances with that sober little enchanted face, and her feet going like castanets, her skirts swirling about her." She smiled at the pleasant memory. "She is a very exciting dancer. It is surprising when one just looks at her, so quiet and still, to think how much fire is in her."

"Ah—fire. What is this *La Soledad?*"

She frowned, trying to think. Spanish was so a part of her life, she took it for granted.

"Well, *La Soledad* means—the solitary one. Solitude, seclusion, loneliness. Rosita's face is so solemn, her eyes so big and grave. It has a connotation of—sadness, wistfulness— you know, in a world alone, bemused. You want to rush up and hug her, and make a fuss over her."

He nodded, intent. "So. I understand, seeing her. I should like to see her dance like that. Perhaps next Sunday?"

He had never come to her apartment. They had begun an affair last year, it had remained tentative, careful, infrequent meetings. She wanted him to see her setting, to understand her, to want to be with her more often.

"Yes, do come at noon. I will feed you some of Madelena's cooking, Spanish and sometimes a bit hot! And Spanish wine, or better yet, some of our Hamilton Rum!"

"Oh, of course! I must try some of your rum, that will be good. Shall I taste sunshine and sugarcane, coconut and limes?"

"Yes, naturally! And hibiscus flowers, bougainvillea, hot beaches in the sunshine also."

"That sounds very good to me. I will come next Sunday, then, and see *La Soledad* dance. Then perhaps I may make up a ballet for her," he said more seriously. "Madame Olga and I spoke of this. It would be good for me and for her. She is now fifteen, you said?"

They had finished their hot tea, set aside their cups. She kicked off her high heels, lazily stretched on the sofa. She was aware of Dimitre watching her, aware of her. Excitement was building in her.

He leaned over to her, kissed her neck where the red gold hair was piled high, leaving her throat vulnerable. She turned to him, met his lips. His large sensuous mouth was open. She pressed her lips to his, shyly, closing her eyes.

He put his arms about her, drew her to him. They clung, kissed, then he bent her back into the cushions. He leaned over her, opening her blouse, fingering each button with his long fingers, stroking the bare flesh down to the low line of her slip. She turned a little to lie on her back, and put her arms about him under his T-shirt. She caressed his bare back, felt the strong muscles there, his tension. He shifted, to lie down with her.

He studied her face tenderly, then kissed her forehead. His hand stroked her throat and shoulders. "Isolde?"

"Ummm."

"Last winter, when we first met. You were a virgin. It shocked me very much, you know?"

She chuckled, hiding her embarrassment. "I thought you would faint!"

"I did faint. I fell over on you in unconsciousness. It was so—unexpected. I thought all American women lost their virginity at about fourteen or fifteen."

She opened her eyes wide. "What? You are joking. That is not true."

"How surprised I was to find that. I had not intended to take a girl's virginity. I was not such a—what do you say—a

76

thoughtless brute.'' He said the word *brute* in a delicious accent. She loved his Russian speech, the way he said things; she loved everything about him, his thick straight blond hair, his dark Tartar face with the high cheekbones, his faun's mouth, his broad shoulders, his lean hips, his long legs, his muscular form . . .

''Oh, I wanted you tō do that, Demi,'' she confessed, in a low tone. ''The first one—''

''And who was the second one?'' There was a faint sting in his words. He drew back to look down into her face.

She shook her head.

''Nobody? May I believe that? No one else yet?''

''No one.''

''Ah.'' He bent down and pressed his lips to her cheek, slid them to her ear and nibbled at the lobe. ''I am stupid. I want you to myself. Jealous brute. Impossible brute.''

She laughed softly against his mouth, turned her head so she could press more warmly against his face.

''You are taking some pill?'' he asked bluntly.

She knew she blushed. ''Yes.''

''Good. Because I cannot keep from taking you today.'' They were silent for a time, holding, kissing. Then he drew her up and to the bedroom.

She undressed as he did, frankly, unashamed of their fine bodies. She lay down on the bed, as he finished taking off his shoes. He gazed down at her.

''I noticed first your long legs,'' he said. ''I came into the practice room to begin class, a little late for me. I like to warm up by myself first. I saw you at the *barre* in the back, you were moving your long beautiful legs, so sensuously, so beautifully, taller than anybody, finer than anybody in the room. I looked up from your feet to your hips, I liked what I saw. I was reluctant to look further.''

He lay down beside her, his naked body beside her, and she was breathless with anticipation. His long arm wound around her waist, he put his other arm under her head. He picked at the braids, she reached up and began to unwind them.

"Reluctant?"

"Um. I thought the rest could not possibly be so good as those limbs."

"And you were so disappointed when you finally looked," she teased.

He smiled slowly, down into her wide eyes. He had such a sensuous smile, starting in his eyes, moving down his cheeks to soften them, then opening his faun's mouth so square and large. "Um. I looked at your hips. Good, I thought." He caressed one with his hand. "Round and ripe. And then the waist, small and taut. The breasts, round and firm, I would like them in my hand, I thought." He suited the gesture to the word, cupping a breast in his palm. "And then the face, cool, yet the exciting color of rosy cheeks, and coral mouth, the haughty nose in the air—" Softly he pushed up the tip of her nose.

She laughed. "You like my haughty nose?"

"Um. So haughty nose." He kissed the tip. "Then I looked in the blue eyes, so large, to say they look like lakes is so cheap. What like? Oh, like pools in the forest, dark blue, shadowed. I thought, she is worried about something. What? How can such a glorious girl be worried? And I looked last at your hair, so tightly braided, and so flaming red gold in the morning light. The window behind you—gray and somber, and you there in the blue leotard, and the leg warmers which could not disguise how beautiful you are. And I wanted to see that hair unbound and on my pillow, and those blue eyes soft and happy. Like now." And he bent and kissed her eyes shut, and ran his fingers through her loosened hair.

He rolled over lazily, to half lie on her. Her long legs matched his, his thighs matched hers, both muscular and hard, from exercise, long years of dancing. He wound a leg about hers, and she responded as though they danced together, by instinct, her legs curling to his.

Their lips met, clung, experimented with open-mouthed kisses. Tongue caressed tongue. She pressed her tongue into his warm mouth, tasted his teeth, the sides of his cheeks. He settled more on her, his breathing quickened. But he lingered over her, not hastening.

They courted for a long time, drawing it out luxuriously. They knew the movements of this dance, they had done it before. Yet each time was different, a revelation, a closer being. He would come close, press into her, then draw out, and wait, kissing her breasts, her nipples, teasing her with nips at her waist and thighs. His hand went over her, smoothing the silk of her skin, feeling the taut muscular frame it covered.

Excitement and heat had built up in her. She moved restlessly, shifting under him. Her thighs had opened wide. He lay between them, holding himself on his elbows while he kissed her, and rubbed his long body on hers. When he touched her soft intimate parts with his, she began to shiver.

"Um, you are so soft, like silk, like warm water on the beach," he murmured.

Her hands moved down over his back, slowly, her fingers digging into the spine. She went lower, to his hips, trailing over them, teasing him. He crouched on her, and touched her with his hard maleness, pressing his thighs to hers.

His face grew intent, hard, glowing with passion. She glanced down their bodies, as he held above her for a moment, and the sight terrified her a little. Could she hold him? Was it possible? Then he came down on her, and she forgot everything as he brought them slowly together.

Higher and higher he came, until he settled on her with a sigh of pleasure, and held. He held her close, still, not letting her move as she longed to do.

"Demi—oh, darling—"

"Ummm?"

His head was on her breast, he crushed her into the mattress, hard like hers, the soft pillows under her.

"Oh, Demi, darling—"

"Tell me what you wish, Isolde," he said, with mischief in his tone. "Can you tell me?"

"Oh, darling—how can I say—"

"You tell me now."

"Oh, Demi—oh, please—do it—now—do it now."

"Say the words," he teased. "I am just learning the English. What is this?" And he moved on her.

She cried out softly. Something was exploding in her, high and light and like fireworks. She crumpled up, loving the sensation, wishing it would go on and on— He moved on her, powerfully, and the feelings did go on, and whirled her higher and higher into ecstasy—

She felt him finishing in her, jetting inside her, filling her gloriously, causing her to spin high again. She exploded softly again, and again, and again—clutching his back, scratching him with her fingernails, pushing her hips up to his to get more and more.

She sank down, and he followed her, kissing her passionately, while he still remained in her; their bodies rolled over on the bed, over and over, frantically seeking satisfaction. She half-fainted under him, and he rolled over, and held her with his arms, limply, wet bodies together. His legs straightened slowly, with a jerk then, finishing the movements.

Presently, as he lay with her, and drew the sheet over their weary bodies, he murmured, "How am I going to learn the English for that? Everytime I ask, you distract me!"

"We don't need words," Isolde murmured, her hair falling across her face. He brushed it back tenderly, so he could see her face. "It is like dancing, you do not need the words."

"Um. You are right, my darling. You are right. No words. Just the movements, the *pas de deux* of love."

He said the word *love*, so tenderly. Would he ever truly mean it? Isolde wondered. But for now it was enough to lie there with him, his arm across her, under the same sheet, sleeping on the pillow with her.

She watched his face tenderly, her eyes half-closed in the dimly lit room of that afternoon. It was so good. Every time it was better, for each learned what the other wanted to do. It was like a dance, of two people, tender and intimate, with ever increasing possibilities of new movements. It was a dance of love, for her. Would it ever be truly that for him?

Chapter 6

The winter season ended, but the work went on briskly. Rosita worked with several of the choreographers, and Madame Olga had special sessions with her. That spring she appeared in several small ballets, sometimes as the second lead. She was one of the cygnets in *Swan Lake*, and a Spanish doll in another ballet where Lupe had the lead.

Dimitre Kerenski had come to watch her dance flamenco on two occasions, at the apartment. Delphine had worked the record player. Isolde and Dimitre sat together on one of the long sofas facing the small platform under the winding stairs, and watched keenly, intently, as Rosita danced.

It had been difficult to dance freely, to forget the audience. It was not like a nightclub with dim lights, her family behind her, Oliverio playing his guitar and speeding up as she did. But she managed to forget Isolde and Dimitre for minutes at a time, dancing more and more quickly and passionately, her heels clicking, her fingers and the castanets keeping up an exciting rhythm.

Dimitre had been sitting up, arms on his legs, watching intently. At the end he nodded. "Ah, yes, yes, the Gypsy dancing! How exciting—if I could but capture that in ballet—"

He mused, paced up and down, stared again at Rosita in the scarlet flamenco dress that Maria had made for her.

He was creating a ballet especially for her, he said.

"But I am not good enough!" she had gasped. "The steps, Madame Olga said—"

"I know. You have danced ballet only a little more than a year. But you advance quickly. I shall build the ballet around you. Your steps will not be difficult, not the advanced steps. As you mature, we will change the ballet, add more advanced movements and difficult steps, make it even more exciting. For now, I wish to capture the mood, the feeling, of a Gypsy moving about in her world, aloof, unattainable, touched by the people about her, yet not affected so much—always she moves on."

Rosita worked with him then, all through the spring, after their season, until they left New York and went to San Juan. Isolde was very restless. Dimitre had gone to Europe as a guest artist in the Royal Danish Ballet, then to the Riviera in a small exclusive company there.

She worked them hard that summer, continuing to press Rosita to learn new movements, new steps, to advance quickly. She had passed Delphine long ago, Delphine was now in the class behind her.

Rosita found time to dance with her family in nightclubs and spent Sundays with them. Delphine came along sometimes, to sit on the sidelines at the club, or backstage, helping with costumes. On the beach, she loved playing with the babies, and always took one or two of them into the water with her. Zach was always so busy, so was Kevin, that Delphine seemed glad to get away from the gloomy Hamilton house where her mother still mourned behind drawn shades.

The summer went by so quickly. Rosita had a birthday party ahead of time at the last of August, then returned with Delphine and Isolde to New York City. Her September birthday on the twelfth was always lost in the confusion of beginning school and beginning ballet, and the exciting fall season of New York.

She was now sixteen, taller, now at five feet three. Madame Olga measured her, murmured, "I hope, dear child, you will not grow any more. You are perfect now."

Rosita gave her a shy smile. "Shall I put weights on my head, madame?"

Madame Olga gave her a sharp tap of her pointer, pleased at this sign of spirit from her most promising young pupil. "Now, my dear! We accept what God gives, eh?"

"*Sí*, madame." The Russian temperament, with its melancholy and fateful acceptance of what would come, suited the Spanish Gypsy temperament, which was similar. Fate would deliver, God would decide, one bowed one's head and accepted. But not without crying out, shaking one's fists to the skies. The wild spirit was not tamed by the world.

Isolde was dancing less this year, directing the careers of Rosita and Delphine. She accompanied them to class, talked to Madame Olga about them, consulted with the director, Miss Eleanor Stanton, about their futures.

Delphine was a cygnet this year, and in the line of *Les Sylphides*. She had become more serious about her work as she was given more important roles. Her red blond head was noticeable, her delicate precise movements were applauded by more than one critic. Isolde was pleased with her.

Rosita understudied a visiting artist in *Les Sylphides*, and when the girl became ill on two nights, she had the lead, and did well, to Isolde's great pleasure. Rosita had not been terrified, she was too accustomed to working before an audience. It was a job, which one performed as well as one could, and she could not understand girls who had tremors and fits. Her cool was praised by the director, and she told girls to imitate it, not quite realizing it came from years of experience, in a girl of sixteen. "Look at Rosita, she is sewing ribbons on her shoes, not chattering and terrifying others," she had said sharply before one performance.

In the third week of the winter season, Dimitre Kerenski's first large ballet was presented. He was understandably nervous behind the scenes as they were preparing the stage for it.

It would be the middle number, sandwiched between two shorter more familiar ballets. If it went well, his name as a choreographer would be taken more seriously. It was terribly important, and Isolde seemed even more excited than he was. Rosita alone was calm. She had the long difficult lead.

"The Gypsy Wanderer" was the title of the work. Dimitre had talked to Rosita at great length, casually it seemed, but with intent. He asked her about her life, her family, the winter months in Spain, their people in other countries. Then he had looked in books at the library, studied, thought, talked to other Gypsies he found in New York.

With his own Russian melancholy and sensitivity, he had put together a long ballet of three parts. A Gypsy girl—Rosita—roams alone from one country to another. Momentarily she stays in Russia. The five persons there are all in Russian peasant dress, except for the lead, a dark Tartar prince who falls in love with the Gypsy girl. She dances with him, a fiery Russian dance, then leaves him, with but a look over her shoulder. Dimitre had stressed to Rosita that she must show she is sorry to leave him, but something calls, some restless tendency, an eagerness to see other places, to move, to wander. No man can keep her for long.

The next scene was in Hungary. She is in a camp of Hungarian Gypsies, and there is playing of violins, laughter, and much dancing about a campfire. Her lover is a Gypsy, with scarf about his head, fiery manner, jealous. Another girl is envious, and jealous of her, there was a dance of the three of them, the lover, the Gypsy and the rival, in which the lover finally turns from the rival, and bends the Gypsy over his arm, ardently. But the Gypsy tires of him, and turns, with a final leap over the campfire, to their applause. She then walked slowly away, out into the world again—into the wings, swinging her shoulders, proud, independent, needing nobody. A lonely figure, yet indifferent to the needs of the group.

The third and final scene was of a Spanish gypsy life. The scene opened with several Gypsies singing and laughing when the hero dances wildly. He is accepting their applause and admiration when the Gypsy girl comes in. He stares, he strides to her, she dances with him. She seems one of them, she dances with them, stands to watch them, with hand on hip. They are like her, she seems to say; she likes them, she could live with them.

But her theme music calls, a single haunting violin in the orchestra. Her head turns as she listens, distracted. The hero draws her into a love duet, a beautiful *pas de deux*, gentle, then more and more fiery, until he kisses her passionately. She slips from his arms, listens to the violin in the distance, and then begins to move away. He clasps her, but she slips away again, moving further—he holds out his hand to her, pleads, she has her head turned to the distance. She moves away, dances about the stage, momentarily one with them, then in a last wild leap she is gone, and the Spaniard sinks to his knee, his head bowed.

Dimitre had rehearsed her in the spring as he evolved the ballet. In the autumn, he had spent long hours with her, going over and over the steps. As he had promised, he kept the steps within her range, so she would not strain beyond her experience. He wanted it to look completely polished, smooth, as though she did it with ease. She found she stretched with the practice, and by the time opening night came, he had added more difficult *cabriole* (leaps combined with a quick movement of the legs striking each other in midair). He had also put in many *pas de bourrée,* and some difficult turns, which she had practiced with Isolde until she could execute them with ease.

Madame Olga had been uncertain about the wisdom of this. "Why not keep it simple, dear Dimitre?" she had asked.

"She can do it," said Dimitre, and Rosita did. It took many more hours of practice; sometimes she felt she would drop with exhaustion. But Isolde encouraged, Alan Landis nodded his head with satisfaction as Rosita leaped across the stage, more and more gracefully.

Now she stood in the wings on opening night, waiting for her music. Her hands were warm, she felt calm as usual. It was

85

just another performance, yet everyone around her was so
excited! Dimitre looked pale, Isolde leaned against a wall, her
dressing gown about her, and her fingers playing with the silk
belt.

Delphine stood ready to go on in the first scene—the
Russian dancers—charming in a peasant dress of cream with
red embroidery on the hem and full sleeves. She hugged Rosita,
stood there with her until the music started.

"The family arrived," she whispered. "Zach is here, and
Kevin, mama and grandmama. They will be in the fifth row
center."

Rosita nodded. "I don't know if I can see them for the
lights," she said calmly, but a little nervous flutter started up
in her stomach for the first time.

"Don't look, forget everybody," advised Delphine, knowing her friend. "You will become the Gypsy girl. I know you
will do it as you always do. Pretend you are in the nightclub,"
she murmured, as the music began. Madame Olga shooed them
on stage, the little group of Russians. Rosita waited beside the
ballet mistress.

Madame Olga said nothing, she just held Rosita's arm in
her firm grip until time for her to go on. Then she let go.

Rosita flew out on stage, in her first grand leap into the
center of the stage. Run softly *en pointe*, then the leap, right
into the center of the group surprised to see her. She flung up
her arms, spun around in greeting to them, and began to dance
with them. From then on she forgot everything but the dance.

Madame Olga had said to smile as she danced. Dimitre
had brusquely overruled her. "No, I want her usual expression, that somber melancholy, that proud alone look. *La Soledad*,
it is."

They accepted it. Rosita did not have to think about grinning, as she called it. Others had such pretty smiles, but to her
dance was an ecstasy, a sober excitement, clear to her bones.
The music caught her up, she whirled and spun and waltzed,
and went up *en pointe*, poised for an endless moment, before
releasing it into a little run.

The audience seemed to hold its collective breath. No sound came. No applause, she did not miss it. She was accustomed to the nightclub when the flamenco went well.

Her *pas de deux* with the Russian, a short stocky man of somber temperament, went well. She danced with him, they met, parted, came together again. She spun up onto his shoulder, rode about on his arm, slid down again *en pointe* on one foot, held by his arm. Her hand slid down his arm to his fingers, he released her—she held up her arms triumphantly, standing alone *en pointe*. Her feet were good, Isolde had said, with a sigh, straight across, the first three toes almost even. It was not difficult for her *en pointe* as it was for many girls. She held it for a breathless moment, then her lover caught her and held her in a swoop—her arms outspread.

She spun off the stage, ending in the wings. Isolde handed her a towel, and she wiped her arms and patted her face as Isolde whipped off the Russian apron of red embroidery. She slipped off the Russian jacket, and donned the Hungarian one, listening to the applause. They had liked it, she thought, pleased. Dimitre was smiling, in a strained manner.

The Russians ran off stage, and out of the way of the Hungarians who came on swiftly to the darkened stage. She listened for the music. It had gone on, not waiting for the applause to die. Dimitre wanted a sustained mood, nothing cut, no bows before the end.

Rosita waited, then Madame Olga nodded. Again she ran on stage, into a daring leap across the Hungarians' fire, an artificial glow set into the stage. Her long legs spread into a perfect one-hundred-eighty-degree split as she leaped across the fire, and she heard a sustained gasp from the audience. Then she forgot them again.

The dance with the group, then the love *pas de deux*, more fiery and joyous with this lover, different from the somber Russians, Gypsy violins from the orchestra, aped by an actor on stage. The wild *pas de deux*, the lover bending over her, she shrugs him off, and with a last wild leap across the campfire, is off into the wings.

The Spanish section was the most fun for Rosita. She loved this part especially, for the atmosphere was hers. She could almost imagine her family standing there, dancing with her, clapping with her. She herself had taught the dancers how to clap sharply with their palms, to use the castanets. Lupe had helped her.

They clapped now, faster, and she danced more wildly, her hair coming down to below her shoulders, dark and wavy on the red frilled jacket over the white tutu that came below her knees. Maria had made her jacket, lovingly, of the stiff Spanish fabric, and the overskirt that opened down the front, of wide frills like her own Spanish dress.

The Spanish lover is tall and slim, like Marcos. They dance a fiery tarantella, her feet moving rapidly, tapping softly on the floor in the quick movements she was so used to making. She likes this dancer, this lover, her gestures say. Her hand over her heart—her glances to him—uncertain—"I could love this man," she seems to mime. But the single violin theme sounds, she pauses, head turned, *en pointe*, arms curved— The lover tries to plead with her to remain. The single violin is louder, more insistent. He swoops with her in a curve, she clings to him, her head turns again.

He lets her go for a moment, strides proudly about the stage. He gestures to the other Spanish dancers, look, how beautiful is the girl, and she is mine. But as he turns away, the violin sounds, loudly, and the Gypsy girl spins about the stage, her distress showing. She loves them—but her destiny is to wander. The violin sings, and she must go— A single spin, then a series of spins and a final leap into the wings, her legs out into the one-hundred-eighty-degree split.

Behind her on the stage, the Spanish lover discovers she is gone. He sinks to one knee, his head bowed, as the stage is darkened. The curtain descends, the music ends in a single long throbbing note from the violin. The Gypsy has wandered on.

Wild applause came from the audience. Madame Olga hugged her. "You did well, Rosita!"

Lupe was there, in a dressing robe, ready for her next

role, her eye makeup dark. She held out her arms, hugged Rosita, kissed her on both cheeks. *"Brava, gitana!"*

Isolde was crying, tears streaming down her cheeks, Delphine was smiling and crying. Dimitre took her hand and pushed her on stage as the curtain came up for the bows. He was pale with emotion.

Rosita came out, and shyly took the hands of her cavaliers. They kissed her hand in turn, and indicated she should stand alone before them. She skipped off stage, to more wild applause, and wiped her face gingerly with the towel before Madame Olga pushed her out again.

The cavaliers bowed, she bowed, the Russians and Hungarians and Spaniards bowed. Then the chorus went off stage, leaving the cavaliers and Rosita. They bowed, she curtsyed. A page came on stage carrying a great sheaf of red roses, and put them into her arms.

It had never happened before. Red roses, and so beautiful — But she had seen how it was done. She removed a red rose for each cavalier, and handed it to each in turn. More wild applause.

Then the unexpected. The audience was beginning to stand up. Some came down to the front of the stage and flung single flowers up to her, a small rain of flowers. Then a yellow bouquet. Another yellow bouquet. The cavaliers picked them up, she could not hold them all.

She retreated with the flowers, handed the roses to Delphine, the others to Isolde. Went back on stage with the cavaliers. Then alone, standing, a small slim figure alone on the wide stage, flushed, serious, her arms out to the audience, acknowledging their applause, her gaze searching for them, unable to believe it.

She saw Zach then, his bright red head standing out in the dimness. He was applauding vigorously, grinning up at her. She saw Kevin, his solid kind face beaming and happy, clapping. Mrs. Hamilton, nodding and smiling as she clapped, and standing for her. Tiny Mrs. Sonia Lothaire, still seated, but smiling and clapping and wiping her eyes in turn.

And others. She heard the cries from the balcony, "Rosita!

Rosita! *La Soledad! La Soledad!"* The Spanish voices, *"Gitana! Ay, gitana, gitana!"* And more cries of *"La Soledad,"* as the other Spanish Puerto Ricans from New York yelled their approval of one of their own. They had been reading avidly about her in the few notices in the New York English-language newspapers, the more florid and voluminous writings in their own publications. They knew who she was. Some went to San Juan for weeks at a time, visiting their relatives and friends. They went to nightclubs, and they knew the Dominguez family, they knew Rosita, *La Soledad.*

Rosita bowed to them, bowed again, retreated shyly backstage. Surely the curtain must come down. It went down, then up again. They would not quit, that audience. It was an emotional event. The orchestra director came out with her, and Dimitre on her other side; they kissed her hand, retreated, leaving her alone on the stage. She kept bowing. There were no more flowers, they had run out of flowers. They ran up to the stage, yelling to her, "Rosita, *gitana! Ay, gitana!* Rosita Dominguez! *Brava, brava, brava!"*

A critic reported crossly the next day, "It was an unwarranted demonstration. This is a sixteen-year-old ballerina, talented, yes, but not great yet. She shows potential, no more. The steps were not so difficult, she did nothing in the dancing that another ballerina could not have done. It was the emotion shown that did it, the music, the sensitive choreography—"

But tonight that mattered little to the audience. They held up the performance for almost fifteen minutes while they demanded bow after bow. Rosita went out again and again, and finally as she stood alone, moved and almost crying, she looked at Zach, and put her hands to her face. She kissed her fingertips and flung the kisses out to him—and it looked as though she kissed her tips to the audience. They screamed, they yelled, they clapped, they yelled some more. Zach was grinning and kissing the air to her, his lips pursed, teasing, but pleased with her. The warmth of it filled her.

The curtain came down for the last time, and Rosita was back in her dressing room. Isolde came in, and Delphine, setting her flowers on the dressing table. Dimitre came in, hastily, he was in the next ballet. He kissed her cheek, both cheeks, dramatically.

"You did all I asked, more and more," he said, and added something in Russian, in a sort of growl. He hugged her, beamed at her, and left. He was satisfied, she knew.

Isolde flung off her dressing gown, Delphine helped her pull on the tutu and zip it up. "Oh, my God, what a night, what a marvelous night! The first of many. You did so well, Rosita, I was so proud—my God, I cannot be calm! How can I dance?" But she examined her makeup, smoothed her hair, and ran out.

Rosita was fumbling among the roses. Delphine took a white envelope from her pocket and handed it to her. She had changed already hastily to her short dressing gown. "People were curious, fooling around with the flowers," she said. "I put the card away."

"Thank you, darling," said Rosita, and opened the envelope. She gazed down at the firm black handwriting. "To my Flamenco Rose. Zach." She kept staring at the words, unbelieving. Then forcing herself to believe he was kind and bigbrotherly. She looked up to meet Delphine's curious gaze. "From Zach—I guess from the family," she added weakly.

"Oh, yes, all those red roses," said Delphine without expression. "Want to dress now? The ballet won't be long. Only twenty minutes, and you have all that makeup to take off." She went over to where their dresses hung.

They were simple dresses, chosen by Isolde. She would wear a long black silk, with low neck and shoestring straps. Rosita gazed at it wistfully, but cleaned her face, and put on her short rose dress with pleated skirt, like a schoolgirl's. Delphine's matched hers, in blue.

The ballet ended, to applause. Isolde soon came backstage, into their dressing room.

"How did it go?" asked Rosita eagerly. Isolde had a big part in this one.

Isolde grimaced. "Anticlimax," she said briefly, and began to clean her face. "Next time, 'Gypsy' will go last."

She cleaned up hurriedly, then slipped on the black dress.

It clung to her slim rounded form gorgeously. She put about her the mink jacket, the girls had their woolen coats on.

By this time Zach was backstage with the family, and the area was crowded with cries of welcome, merging fans and ballet dancers, the director and Alan Landis, Madame Olga, Madame Sonia greeting old friends, and Madame Isabeau Hamilton hugging people she knew.

Zach and Kevin finally got some of the party away in the Cadillacs driven by Pedro and Lorenzo. Rosita whispered to Pedro at their car, "Did Maria and Madelena like it?"

"They screamed," he said briefly, grinning broadly, unusual for him. "Maria split my ears. Guess I yelled also."

She sank back into the plush upholstery, satisfied. She had obtained two rows of seats for them and their family and friends in the middle of the balcony. Delphine had paid for them all, out of her allowance. Maria and Madelena would hurry back to the apartment to prepare for the guests to come following the dinner. But they had seen their Rosita dance!

Delphine sat beside Rosita, squeezing her hand silently in her deep excitement. Zach had put himself beside them, firmly, his mother in the front. Kevin was looking after Madame Sonia in the other car. Isolde and Dimitre were also in that one. They all met at the restaurant, and by that time the others arrived. Miss Stanton, Mr. Landis, Madame Olga, the three cavaliers and their current girls. Amy and Denise, and Bernadine, who had graduated to *La Sylphide*. Lupe and her handsome Spanish husband, from another company.

They filled the expensive restaurant. Rosita was given the seat of honor at the head of the main table, with Zach to her right and Delphine on her left. Isolde and Dimitre found themselves down the main table, but as they were together Isolde made no complaint. The chatter and hum and laughter filled the restaurant, until the strolling violins began.

Zach leaned to Rosita. "What shall I tell them to play, little Rose?"

"Oh, whatever you wish," she replied, startled. He was looking directly into her eyes, his vivid blue eyes so bright.

He whispered to the violinist, beside Rosita, who nodded and began to play Liszt, the Hungarian Rhapsody, and the Hungarian dances of Brahms. The wild Gypsy-theme music filled the air, stilling the talking, as people hummed and nodded their heads, all of them so sensitive to the sound.

She remembered her manners, and said, "Thank you for the beautiful roses, Zach."

Madame Sonia, beside Madame Olga, looked vivacious and lively. Their hands moved as they talked, remembering the old days, probably. Madame Isabeau Hamilton was smiling, melancholy forgotten for a time, talking animatedly to Miss Stanton, looking toward Rosita and Delphine and Isolde in turn.

"Roses for a rose," he said. "Will you dance with me?" He held out his hand, she nodded, and rose to move with him. Isolde glanced up, frowning, following them with her eyes.

It was heaven to dance with Zach. He had inherited all the rhythm of his family, he danced as beautifully as he walked. As naturally. He held her closely to him, glanced down to her dark hair, and said, "I was not surprised tonight, Rosita. You danced with all the fire and emotion you show in flamenco. I was so proud of you. I went backstage during the last ballet, and telephoned your family, at the nightclub. Your father was thrilled, your mother said to tell you they love you."

"Oh, Zach!" Dazzled, she gazed up at him. "You telephoned them?" She could not imagine doing such a thing, and so casually.

"Yes, and you shall phone them at home. I told them you would call at noon."

"Oh—thank you—so very, very much—" She pressed his hand impulsively with her right hand as they danced. He squeezed her fingers in return.

"And there is a little toy for you in my pocket," he added.

"A toy! I am not a child!" she flashed, then was aghast at herself.

He chuckled, pleased that he had a rise out of her. "A toy to make you happier, Rosita. I'll give it to you at the table. It is

93

from all of us, all the Hamiltons. Granny helped me choose it today at Tiffany's.''

Then she realized. He was giving her a jewel. She caught her breath. Today had been incredible, the most marvelous day of her life, and it had not ended.

They returned to the table and he gave her the box. Everyone watched curiously as she opened the velvet box and disclosed a golden chain, with a gold heart pendant, a large diamond in the center. Simple, yet rich. Zach opened the clasp and set the chain about her neck, then fastened it again.

"Thank you all, so very much," she said, near tears, her dark brown eyes shining and glistening. Delphine leaned close and kissed her.

"That looks like a nice idea," said Zach solemnly, and leaned to her and kissed her mouth. She felt the warm pressure, the hard muscular feel of his lips, and could have fainted with the joy.

She ate, but she did not know what. People kept coming up to her, and kissing her cheek, and congratulating her. Miss Stanton left early, but said, kindly, "We must discuss your career, Rosita. It is very promising!"

"I am taking care of that," Isolde said, a thread of steel in her tone. Miss Stanton raised her delicate eyebrows.

She danced again later, with Kevin, with each of the three cavaliers, who complimented her, and said they wanted to dance again with her. Once again with Zach, dreamily. And again with Mr. Landis, smooth and polished, who terrified her because he was so strict and difficult a man under the polish. But tonight he was kind, and said she had done well.

She danced the last dance with Zach, and then they all went home. She went to bed with the golden chain and pendant about her neck, and thought she would never sleep. But she was so tired, and it was two in the morning, that she did sleep.

She and Delphine woke to the muted continued ringing of the telephone. It was in Isolde's room. It was about nine, early for them to rise, considering the late night, and Delphine yawned.

"I suppose we had better get some practice in first," said Rosita, sighing, and got up. They washed, dressed in gray leotards and leg warmers and jerseys, and went down to the first floor; all was silent. Delphine turned on the stereo to a low tone, and they began to warm up—the feet, the legs, the hips, then the waist, and shoulders and arms.

"I wonder how late they were here last night," said Rosita, as they began to move more freely. She held her hand lightly on the *barre* beside Delphine.

"I woke up at four, they were still laughing and drinking, I heard the glasses clinking."

"Um. Someday we will be grown-up, and able to stay up and drink champagne," said Rosita wistfully.

"Huh. I am seventeen, and they didn't let me stay up, and you were the star," said Delphine, still indignant. "I think it would suit Isolde if we never grew up! She may lose control of us then!"

Rosita was silent. It had stung, being sent to bed, even though she had been yawning and tired. And only a sip of champagne from Zach's glass. She had not liked it much, it tickled her nose and stung her tongue, but it had been exciting, her first taste of pink champagne.

Maria and Madelena came downstairs soon. They were smiling and beaming, they hugged both girls. "How well you did! How beautiful you were! Did you hear us shout!"

"All the way to the stage," said Rosita solemnly, and they all giggled. "Did you hear them shout *La Soledad?* They knew me!"

"Of course they know you, they all talk about you from one street to another, in our section," said Maria. They went out to the kitchen to prepare coffee, and then fix breakfast.

Zach came down next, down the winding stairs, all handsome and freshly shaved, in a neat gray silk suit. He grinned at the girls. "I like to see such devotion to work, but this is too much. Come have breakfast with me," and he spanked Delphine lightly on the hips as she ran before him to the breakfast bar.

It was a merry meal, with Maria and Madelena talking as fast as they did, feeding them eggs and sausage for a treat, with whole wheat toast and orange juice and hot black coffee.

Isolde clattered down the stairs, all dressed up in a green silk dress with gold chains and gold bracelets chiming. "The press is coming," she announced dramatically. "Rosita, they have come to interview you—I arranged it—just wear what you have on, and leave the talking to me."

Zach turned about to stare at his sister. "What did you say? They are coming to interview Rosita and will talk to you?"

"Of course, I am managing her," said Isolde, tossing her head in the thick rich red gold braids bound about her forehead and ears. She eyed Zach warily. "And, brother, I don't need you around to dictate what we will do! You know nothing about publicity for dancers!"

"I may not know that. But I do know that Rosita does not look like a glamorous, confident ballerina in leg warmers and a gray sweat shirt," he said brusquely.

Rosita looked down at her plate, unable to go on eating. Delphine caught her breath, ready to give battle, but it was unnecessary.

Isolde was saying, "She is not a glamorous, confident ballerina, she is a child, and I say she will look businesslike and—"

"Rosita, go upstairs and change," ordered Zach, fire in his blue eyes. "Delphine, help her choose something pretty. And you change also. There is plenty of time. Go!"

"Come on," muttered Delphine, grabbing Rosita's hands. They left the bar, and ran upstairs, hearing Isolde's angry complaints with every step.

"You are not to interfere, Zach! This is my concern! You tend to your rum business, and let me—"

In their room, Delphine said angrily, "Oh, Isolde is impossible! She wishes to grab all the attention! She will sit there looking so—so magnificent, and do all the talking! And we will look like orphans in the storm!"

Rosita had to smile. "Delphine, you never look like an orphan in a storm—"

Delphine was going over the clothes in the wardrobe. She finally tossed out Rosita's new red wool suit with fur collar and cuffs, and her own blue matching suit. "There, and some white blouses, and our gold chains—your new one, Rosita."

They washed up, changed, made up carefully, then put on their jackets. The doorbell had chimed several times, and when they finally put on their black high-heeled shoes and went demurely down the winding stairs, they looked lovely, modest, and a little scared.

The apartment seemed full. Zach was greeting someone in Spanish, Kevin was opening the door to a woman reporter, Isolde was trying to talk to a drama critic, an amusement editor of a magazine, someone from *Dance* magazine, and a woman in a black shapeless dress who looked like a crone and was a terribly important former ballerina who took on only the best ballerinas.

It had been a mistake to invite them all at once. Isolde had been sleepy, overwhelmed and excited. Rosita shook hands, greeted them, accepted their congratulations, and sank down into a plush armchair held by Zach.

"Yes, it was very exciting—no, not long, only a year—no, I danced before with my parents' troupe in San Juan—flamenco —sixteen years old—going to high school—thank you very much, you are most kind—"

The cross-interviewing was confusing. They shot questions at her, talked to Isolde, repeated the question she had just answered, asked how she felt, how she felt, how she felt. She felt dazed, frankly.

Kevin came downstairs from the bedroom area. "Telephone for you, Rosita—"

"She cannot come," said Isolde loudly. "Tell them she will phone later—"

"It is her parents," said Zach, glancing at his gold watch. "Come along, Rosita, I'll plug it into your bedroom—" He shepherded her up the stairs, away from the noise and confusion.

He plugged the phone into her phone jack and she sat down on the bed to pick up the telephone. "Talk as long as you like, my dear, I'll hold off the vultures," he whispered dramatically, and made to close the door after him.

She smiled back at him, radiantly. How kind he was, how he understood.

"Hello—papa? Is that you, papa?"

Her father's voice came so clearly he might as well be in the next block. "My beautiful baby! How proud we are! We could scarcely sleep! How do you feel?"

"Oh—so excited—so happy. There are reporters here, to ask questions—"

"Oh, my, we better hang up—"

"No, no—Zach, Mr. Hamilton said to talk as long as we wish." She was crying, wiping the tears from her cheeks. "How good to hear your voice!"

She talked to her mother, to Tadeo, to quiet Oliverio, to Marcos, to Elena, to Luisa, to the older babies, to Cristina, and again to her father. It went on and on, but Zach had said to talk as long as she liked.

She was indeed appalled when she hung up at last, and found she had talked half an hour. She powdered her nose quickly, put on lipstick again, and went down the stairs.

Several of the reporters, including one from a Spanish newspaper, were still there. Madame Sonia and Madame Isabeau had come down, beautiful in beige silk and pearls, looking the prima ballerinas they had been, answering questions about themselves and about Rosita.

"Of course, natural talent, her parents and family such good dancers, of course she has much talent, brilliant—a fine musical sense—" That was Madame Sonia, in her beautiful accent.

Zach was leaning against a wall. Maria was bringing a coffee tray, which she set before Isolde, who had to break off talking to serve the coffee to everyone.

The Spanish reporter turned to Rosita as she sat down opposite him. He said quickly in Spanish, "You are Puerto Rican? You have danced long?"

"All my life, yes. I was born in San Juan, we have lived there always. My grandmother is Alejandra Dominguez, she danced before the King of Spain at his request," she added proudly, because he would know that name.

"Ah, the Dominguez of Seville! Ah, yes, you are related to that line," and he became excited, and they talked faster than ever. She saw Zach leaning forward to listen to them carefully.

"And you know them," she smiled.

"*Sí, sí, sí!* I have lived in Spain myself, I know them, from Seville. I may have seen you dance when you were a small child—yes, yes, a nightclub in Granada! I think it was the Golden Cockerell!"

"We danced there when I was seven, I remember."

"I noticed you! A small, solemn black-haired girl, with bangs, then," and he smiled and touched his forehead. "So you have danced all your days?"

"My mother said that I danced in her womb," said Rosita, naturally, repeating what she would have been shy to say in English. "In San Juan—"

"Yes, yes, they call you *La Soledad*. Tell me about that—" And he encouraged her to speak, writing his notes rapidly in dashing handwriting.

Isolde was cross because she did not know what they were saying, her Spanish was not so good as Rosita's, naturally. But Maria and Madelena listened, and beamed at their protégée, and Zach smiled and nodded, he knew what they said.

And the next day Zach send Pedro around the Spanish neighborhood to gather up all the newspapers, and he brought them back with the English ones. The reporter had a scoop, and it was later repeated again and again, all the words he said about Rosita, the words she had said, the stories she had told to him alone, because he knew the Dominguez, because he was kind and interested.

The headline ran in Spanish, "Rosita's mother said she danced in her womb." And he told the story about *La Soledad*, and how she danced flamenco in Spain, in Granada.

Rosita clipped all the stories, and she and Delphine bought scrapbooks and began to collect all the reviews and stories about themselves. It was exciting to read later, and see the pictures, Rosita in the big chair in the red suit, and an older photo of a big-eyed solemn child with bangs from an old playbill from Granada, and a publicity photo from San Juan, and a pose in her tutu with the Spanish shawl over it, her fan opened.

Some of the critics were kind, after all it was a first big ballet for a sixteen-year-old girl. Others were not so kind, pointing out the flaws in later performances, how she was overpraised and applauded for what was after all an early demonstration of a nice talent. "She will mature," said one. "We look forward to seeing her in two or three years."

"She tries beyond her ability," said one, and Dimitre was angry, because he had deliberately not done that. He had kept her within her limits, though he had helped her stretch them.

But overall they were not bad for her age and experience. She clipped them and saved them, and tried to learn from the constructive criticism and forgive the destructive kind.

The ballet, "The Gypsy Wanderer," became a sort of cult object for the Spanish Puerto Ricans and Cubans in New York. Whenever it was announced, they bought out the place and screamed and yelled, and threw flowers all over the stage. When the season ended, Dimitre was tempted to retire it, in favor of others. "I cannot allow you to continue as only a Gypsy ballerina," he told Rosita ruefully.

He was creating a new ballet for her, this one of a modern type, without story, in white tutu and long flowing lines. It would help her develop in a new style. She smiled at him. "I think I want to become a good ballerina, Dimitre," she said. "Not just a Gypsy girl."

"Good girl, you will learn much this winter and next year," he said, and began to sketch out another ballet for her. She was so pliant, so quick to learn, and she was developing rapidly.

Alan Landis, the chief choreographer, watched her progress, and also began a new ballet for her. He looked at her small perfect body, her long legs, her deft movements, and the grace of her hands and arms. He nodded, and said to Eleanor Stanton, "Next year, a star, because we may not have her long. Isolde is ambitious for her, and talking of Europe."

"Um. I hope she does not push the child too fast. And not

neglect the pretty Delphine. If that one is not watched, she will slip back, because she has not the drive.''

"Right. We will put them together into a ballet, the two pretty girls of the same height, and a tall partner for each— effective, eh? They work well together, each encourages the other.''

And so they made their plans. Dimitre made his, and Isolde made hers. And Rosita and Delphine worked and went to school, studied, went to museums, and dreamed, whenever they had the time.

Chapter 7

The spring season of 1976 went rapidly. Rosita and Delphine appeared in a new ballet by Alan Landis, and worked directly under that strict and talented choreographer. It was a *divertissement* with music by Brahms; a cavalier for each ballerina, and a line of six dancers. That allowed for point and counterpoint, and some lovely, balanced scenes. The piece went over well, and gave the girls experience in non-story ballet. Rosita was blossoming into the dancer Isolde thought she could become.

The girls had looked forward to the summer in San Juan, but Isolde had other plans. They went home for three weeks only, during which Zach was very busy with Hamilton Rums. Rosita was silently disappointed that she scarcely saw him. He seemed older now, more self-confident, and he had a new girl named Elissa. Delphine teased him about Josita, but Zach said casually that she had been last year, and Helena the year before!

"Rake," Delphine pronounced and they all laughed.

Rosita hung her head, she didn't know why she did not find it amusing. He went off then to a directors' meeting, handsome in a white linen suit, absentmindedly patting her head. And she was almost seventeen!

After the success of "The Gypsy Wanderer," Dimitre and Isolde were planning excitedly for them all. One Sunday afternoon, it finally all came together. Isolde had gone up to Dimitre's apartment, helped him prepare lamb chops and salad, and a bowl of fresh fruit salad. Over their cups of hot tea and honey, they had talked eagerly.

"Europe is the logical next step," Dimitre stated firmly. "There we can experiment. Rosita and I can dance in *pas de deux* numbers, and there will be places for you and for Delphine."

Isolde stifled her pangs of jealousy, because Rosita would be the one dancing with Dimitre. She nodded, and sipped at the tea to hide her expression. "Yes, Demi," she agreed. "We should be able to earn our way, and save money for the company later. Where shall we start?"

"Letters to the various companies," he said slowly. "We could draw up a schedule gradually. I have an invitation to dance in Amsterdam in midsummer, you could join me there—but we must have the rest of the seasons planned well, at least the first six months."

Isolde caught her breath, her eyes shining. To work exclusively with Dimitre, to be with him constantly, with the firm excuse of their mutual work—it would be heaven! Let Rosita dance with him, Isolde would watch, would be there to help, to go out with him afterward—Rosita, fortunately, was young, and not interested in boys—or men!

Dimitre talked to Isolde about money problems, practically. "We may be able to earn just our own money, enough to pay expenses. However, the huge offer from Amsterdam shocked me—they offered what is about one thousand five hundred per performance for any star appearances I do. I wonder what they will offer for Rosita?"

"If we state our price, send them her clippings, and refuse to accept a smaller offer," said Isolde thoughtfully, "they must realize she is star quality, though very young. And we shall save all the reviews of her, and just keep on demanding more and more. I think we can do it, Demi."

"Good. And we will have you and Delphine also. Between us, we might make—let me see—'' He took out pad and pencil to try to figure out what they might earn.

It was all vague, they would have to wait for definite offers. It grew tremendously exciting to have the letters coming back, to plan, to work out a schedule for the next six months. Demi thought if all went well, they could save at least half of the money and bank it against the future.

''I think when we have about one hundred thousand dollars saved, we can begin our own company,'' he said soberly, his vivid blue eyes sparkling.

May came, and Isolde did not even want to return to San Juan. However, Dimitre would be going off to Amsterdam to rehearse at the end of May, she would not see him anyway.

They met for one final Sunday afternoon in late May, at the park near his apartment, and walked slowly among the first roses. Isolde thought she would always remember those white and yellow roses, and the small petunias of crimson and white and purple. It was half-pain and half-pleasure to walk, matching her long strides with Dimitre's, and have her hand tucked in his arm.

''Now, you have your airplane reservations,'' he was saying. ''I will arrange your hotel reservations after I get there, and find which hotels are best. You want a double room for the girls—''

She was silent, holding her breath. Would he suggest casually that they room together, or would he request a single for her—to visit her sometimes? Or—would this be strictly business?

''Isolde?''

''Um.'' He had half-turned to her.

''It may take two years or more, you realize this?''

''However long it takes, I want it,'' she said.

''Two years. I will be close to forty,'' he said soberly.

''Oh, no, Dimitre, do not exaggerate!''

''It is a comfort to know,'' he said soberly, but his eyes twinkled with his sudden humor, ''to know that though I may grow old too soon for dancing, I shall not be too old for other—pleasurable—activities . . .''

She opened her eyes wide, innocently, matching his look. "What activities?"

He laughed, and put his arm about her, and his lips were close to her ear. "It is better to show than to speak, eh? Let us go back to my apartment, the afternoon hours are disappearing too rapidly!"

They went back to his apartment, and were soon lying on his bed, naked, limbs wound together in the same rapturous closeness as in the dance, closer, more intimate.

Isolde could not believe it, would some witch cast a spell and make all this go away? Two years together with Dimitre! Yes, they would save money, plan for their company, work together, but it would mean more than this. They were planning for their future together, she would be with him constantly, there would be long hours of discussion of plans, nights together. Dances to work on, intimate talks—and travel from one enchanting city to another—all with him, the man she adored!

Dimitre lay beside her, lazily, slowly caressing her. There was not much urgency in him this afternoon, as though it was not the last afternoon they would spend together. She felt more urgent than he did, almost a despair, thinking of the weeks before she would see him again.

She rolled over to lean against him, her breasts against his tanned chest. "Oh, Dimitre, I wish I was not leaving you this week—" She bent her head against his shoulder, hiding her face.

His lean strong hand caressing her spine, he drew her closer to his body. "The days will be long, the nights longer, until I see you again, my dear love," he murmured.

Did he mean it, or was he only poetically Russian? She wished she knew. She knew she felt that way. But she must not demand that he love her. One could not obtain love that way. She lay there, motionless, her face buried in his hard muscular shoulder.

His hand moved up and down her spine, the emotion welled in her. The love, the desire, the passion mounted in her.

She stifled a noise in her throat. He heard it, and whispered, "I hear the tigress in you, adored!"

She could not play, and laugh, and pretend to growl. She felt too deeply, tears thick in her throat, about this parting, even it was only a short time.

She moved her head in protest, not able to speak. His arms gathered her closer, he shifted her onto his hard lean body. He wanted her, she knew by his thighs, hard under hers.

Deftly he put her on his thighs, and she moved her long legs with his. She half-sat up, Amazon riding his body, her long red gold hair hiding her face, until he brushed it tenderly back from her cheeks and forehead.

"How you match me," he murmured, then said no more, his eyes shutting in ecstasy as she rode him feverishly and ardently. His big hands held her slim hips, he held her tighter, and pulled her down sharply at the end.

Ecstasy came to them both, and waters flooded their sweating bodies, lost in the mad, swirling dizziness of need. She fell over on him, still part of him, and he held her closely, hands caressing and caressing.

They came to each other again before the afternoon was over, in silence, she wanting him furiously, to remember when he had left.

When she was dressed and ready to leave, he took her again into his arms, and kissed her forehead. "What freedom to love," he said, and added something drearily in Russian.

She left, dread in her heart, and was feverish and nervy all during the weeks in San Juan. She could scarcely wait for the time to come when they would leave.

Rosita knew it, and Delphine, but said nothing, not even to each other. The days and hours sped past.

Then Isolde took them off to Europe, where Dimitre Kerenski met them in Amsterdam. They were to appear in several summer companies. The headliners were Rosita and her partner Dimitre. She would have the advantage of his name and reputation, he had the advantage of her youth and beauty and the excitement of her New York reviews.

They did well. Isolde danced a few times, Delphine more often, once in a fine ballet of her own. Men hung about the two girls, Isolde shooed them away, watchful as a hawk about handsome men. No dates were permitted.

Delphine tried to rebel and was sharply reprimanded by her sister. "I have your career in mind! It will not help you to become involved with some romantic young nobody!"

Later on, as they went to a museum by themselves, Delphine confided, "I am glad I am not so good a dancer! I will never be famous. So one day I will be free to marry and have all the babies I want! I am not going to let Isolde stop me from that!"

Rosita was silent, gazing absently at a painting of a beautiful girl with her husband, three-centuries-old painting in the Rijksmuseum in Amsterdam. The man looked a little like Zach, with bright blue eyes, a crinkled laugh line about his eyes, and a generous mouth.

All her life she had been disciplined. She had done what her father told her, and her mother, and her sisters. Now she obeyed Isolde and Dimitre, and the people in the dance company. Whatever they said she obediently followed. She was good, and worked hard, and slept alone—

But warm Spanish blood flowed in her veins. She loved babies, and her happiest hours were spent with her little nieces and nephews. She longed to love and be loved. Was that going to be denied her?

Some ballerinas married, but often that ended their careers. A few made it, struggling with a baby, a husband, a hectic schedule of dancing. But it was difficult for them. Still— were they not happier than those who lived a solitary life dedicated to the Goddess of Dance? Fame had its heavy price. Perhaps if one worked a long time, the work became so all-important that a warm family life was not missed. Perhaps.

It seemed a solitary and dismal way of life to Rosita. She was accustomed to having her big family about her, crowded and warm and happy. Gypsies liked to live closely together. If they had more space, they simply added more people, warmly inviting another family to move in. The more the better, was the motto of her people.

"I am so glad we are together, Delphine. I would be very lonely if you were not here," Rosita said impulsively to Delphine as they ate lunch in a restaurant on the Damrak.

"Of course, I know," nodded Delphine, her mouth full of forbidden ice cream and whipped cream. "That is why I let Isolde dictate to me! We are good friends, I could not leave you alone to her, she would eat you alive!" Though her voice was full of laughter, her pretty blue eyes were more serious.

"But she has always been good to me," Rosita said, feeling disloyal.

"Oh, yes, it suits her purpose. She cannot be a great ballerina, and it makes her bitter. Now she makes plans with Dimitre—I wish I knew what they were up to," added Delphine. "I know she is having an affair with him. They disappear nights and Sundays, and she is always tired and dreamy afterwards. And she won't even let us date!" She made an indignant *moue*.

An affair. Rosita had guessed it, but said nothing. It had seemed rather shocking. Her parents were very strict, and she thought the Hamiltons were also. "She probably hopes to marry him," she said, eating the last of her fruit plate.

"Hmm. I heard he is still married," Delphine said, in a lowered tone.

Their European summer tour was exciting. Isolde gave them enough time to museum-hop, and of course they all went to see the English Royal Ballet at Covent Garden, a visiting troupe in Amsterdam, and the Stuttgart Ballet in Germany. They did some traveling about in the countryside, but Dimitre was not interested in touring much, and Isolde wanted to do whatever he wanted. The girls ended up taking brief one-day tours whenever they could.

Dimitre was working on a new ballet with a solo for Rosita. It was called "Spanish Reverie" and was set to the music of a guitar. She wore a very simple medium-length white dress and her hair hanging loose down below her shoulders. Rosita enjoyed the new blending of the Gypsy style with ballet. It began *allegro*, gentle and dreamy, then built up like a flamenco dance, the tempo quickening to all out fire. Then suddenly the music becomes softly quiet. And she leaves the stage slowly, deliberately, head bent. The audience always loved it, even though it lasted less than ten minutes.

Rosita performed "Spanish Reverie" a number of times that summer, and they put it on the program that winter for the New York Festival Ballet. New York liked it, the critics were kind.

The winter of 1976–1977 was extremely busy. Isolde wanted the girls to complete their high school education that spring, and graduate early. Delphine would be eighteen, but Rosita just seventeen. The nuns protested, it would be too much, she would have to skip over some material. Isolde was inflexible.

"We must go abroad next winter, I want her to finish now," she said determinedly. "Otherwise, she will not get her degree."

The nuns sighed, and acquiesced. Rosita worked like a whirlwind all that year. It was classes all week, six of them, some with Delphine. Then she went to the ballet company, and sometimes had star roles. Isolde had found a retired ballerina, Madame Jeanne Verdi, to give Rosita and Delphine special lessons.

She was a lively little Frenchwoman, who made her living now by coaching. She taught the girls more about mime, hand movements, the gestures for leads in *Swan Lake, Sleeping Beauty, Giselle,* all the big classic parts. It helped them in the lesser parts they were doing, and would prepare them for the future. Isolde wanted Rosita also to learn those ballet parts, for Europe, just in case.

In May of 1977, Delphine and Rosita graduated from high school. They did not remain for graduation, however. The day they were out of school, Isolde and Dimitre whisked them off to London. There was no time even for a visit to San Juan.

They moved so fast that sometimes the letters from Rosita's parents became lost, and she did not hear from them for three weeks. They went to London, then to Amsterdam, then to Copenhagen. From there to Paris, then down to Madrid, by air.

It was quite evident now that Isolde and Dimitre were having an affair. In the hotels, Dimitre always requested two double rooms, and he and Isolde roomed together. "If mama knew—" nodded Delphine. "She knows this is a modern world, but not for us! Whew, if Zach finds out—"

"He must know," said Rosita somberly. "Besides, he is always with—I mean, he has affairs, doesn't he?"

She wanted Delphine to say no, he only dated girls, but Delphine nodded wisely. "Of course. But he is a man, and men have hungers," she said, her little innocent face screwed up in an attempt at sophistication. "It is different for women. If they have a baby and not married—well, girls do it now, but not Hamilton girls! I expect Isolde is on the pill. I know she has quite a stock of medicines."

"Well, it is a modern time," said Rosita, thinking of the way girls talked in the company. But she and Delphine had been sheltered all their young lives. "What with women's liberation and all that—if men do it, why not girls?"

"Because girls have babies, that's why," Delphine said wisely. "Sleeping together, living together, girls get hurt more than men do when it is over. Think of Evelyn—"

Evelyn had been in their class in high school. It had been exciting to learn she lived with a man. But when the man left, she had tried to commit suicide. It had been the scandal of the convent school that year. But the newspapers were full of other stories just like that.

"When I get married," said Delphine, "my husband is going to love me more than anybody in the world! He will love me so much, he would not think of looking at another girl. If he does, I'll scratch his eyes out." She looked unusually fierce. Rosita laughed naturally, though she thought of Zach. If a girl managed to marry him, she would have a time on her hands. He was so interested in women, so many girls, one after another, maybe several at a time. It hurt to think about it. She supposed he was something of a hero to her, he was so kind and handsome and thoughtful toward her.

But he was not for her to dream about. He was a Hamilton.

She was a Dominguez. He was English, she was a Spanish Gypsy. Both were Puerto Ricans, but worlds apart, neverthe-less. The Spanish had come centuries before the English to Puerto Rico, they had settled there and been part of the Carib-bean culture long before the English. Yet the English had taken over, they ruled. They were usually the wealthy ones, though some Spaniards had managed to keep their wealth. Most were poor, however, or lower middle class. Somehow it didn't seem right, not to Rosita. She firmly turned her thoughts back to the dance.

From Madrid they went to Rome, then to Milan, and back up to Edinburgh for the August Festival. Finally they returned to London. Rosita woke up one morning, dazed, and could not remember where she was. She lay looking at the room.

Delphine wakened, yawned. Rosita said softly, "What city are we in?"

"Um, Edinburgh?"

"No, that was last week."

Delphine turned her head, gazed about. "The decor, I think we are in London," she said solemnly.

"Um, I believe you are right."

They returned to New York in September, and plunged right into the last season they would have with the New York Festival Ballet. Then without a pause, they returned to Europe.

This time it was damp, chilly, snowy and rainy. They tramped miserably around in boots, got wet through, steamed over radiators to dry out, and danced when they were cold to the bone. Rosita woke up one morning, and looked about. This time she genuinely could not remember where they were. Was it Stockholm? Or Helsinki?

Then she saw the blue and white delftware bowl, and the hothouse tulips of cream and red and yellow. "Amsterdam," she murmured. "Delftware and tulips, we must be in Amster-dam."

"What are you talking about?" demanded Delphine, her mussed red gold head rising from her pillow. "Oooh, how cold!" and she snuggled back into the covers.

Rosita explained, and it became a little game for them, to

wake in the morning, and figure out where they were from the flowers, the furniture, or some clue in their room. It helped to think about something other than work.

They spent Christmas in Rome, which was thrilling. They were able to visit the Pope in a large audience, and were permitted to kiss his ring. The girls liked Rome, and went from one museum to another, one concert to another, and to many ballets. The sense of history there was awesome, standing in the Roman Forum, and the Coliseum.

In February, Rosita was scheduled to dance her first *Giselle*. Isolde was worried for her, and even Dimitre seemed upset. But Rosita found out his emotional distress was not over her. On several occasions, when she collected the mail, hoping a letter from her parents would catch up with her, she found one for him from Moscow. He would rip it open, glance over the strange lettering inside, and frown, and be like a bear for another day.

Something was wrong, and Isolde seemed infected with it. Rosita and Delphine whispered, but dared not ask Isolde. Her nerves seemed on edge as it was.

"Do you suppose the Russian secret police are after Dimitre?" Delphine asked.

"I don't know. How do they act? Do they write threatening letters?" Rosita's ignorance on the subject was as immense as Delphine's.

Giselle soon absorbed all of them. There were rehearsals, alone and with the company, and with the handsome Italian lead, Piero. He was medium height, with soulful dark eyes and long black fringes about them. He had graceful gestures, and he pretended to fall in love with Rosita, to Isolde's dismay. But he laughed, and gave away the joke to the younger girls.

"I am marry!" he said dramatically, eyes flashing, hand on his heart.

"You are going to be married?" asked Delphine.

"No, no, no, I am much marry already! I have the beautiful wife, and two bambinos!"

One afternoon he took them home to his apartment and introduced them to his beautiful wife, a lovely dark Milanese girl, and two adorable children, a boy and a baby girl. He also introduced them to his sister, an apprentice to a dressmaker, and his parents, and the five brothers and their families! They were all fun, noisy, singing, and playing violins and pianos, reminding Rosita of her family. After that, Rosita and Delphine went with him almost every Sunday.

There was fire in Piero, he threw himself enthusiastically into his part. Rosita met it, and caught fire from him. The director of the Milan company said, "There is chemistry between them, good, good," and encouraged them to work together more. Besides *Giselle*, they did another ballet, a storyless one, in white. The more they worked together, the more attuned they were.

Piero's sister encouraged Delphine and Rosita to commission new dresses, without Isolde's knowledge. Delphine had forced Isolde to increase her allowance when she discovered Rosita was still not receiving anything but the money sent to her parents, and her clothes, room and food. "She can just pay for us both," muttered Delphine. "I know they are making plenty!"

Neither of them knew much about finance, but from listening and keeping quiet they had learned that some of their appearances netted as much as two thousand to five thousand dollars. Of course, that usually meant appearing with Dimitre, and they knew he earned much. "But some of that is ours, what is Isolde doing with it?" Delphine demanded of Rosita. "When we get home, I'm going to ask Zach."

Piero's sister Giovanna took them to her boss, a beautiful dramatic-looking woman who turned out to be practical and kind. She looked over the girls, and turned to her assistant. "Much more older for them, eh?" She found pieces of silk brocade, in deep garnet red for Rosita and silver blue for Delphine.

So the girls had their first long dresses, with tiny satin straps over their shoulders, gathered fabric over their breasts, narrow waists, and full skirts to their ankles. They were thrilled with them. They would wear them after the first night of *Giselle*.

Giselle was a momentous occasion. It had been advertised

heavily, and Piero was popular. On his encouragement, they had given interviews to three of Italy's good critics, and the papers had been generous with space for Rosita.

The night came. Rosita waited behind scenes for her appearance, to come out of the little house at the side of the stage with her "mother." Again she was not nervous, she liked working with Piero, he was like another brother by now.

She came out, began to dance. The audience was appreciative, though she did not hear them. Piero was gallant, handsome, a perfect cavalier, and did not upstage her. The first act ended with the mad scene, and Rosita pulled out all stops, swirling the sword around, her unbound hair falling in her eyes, her steps so fast that they jumped away from her as she leaped and whirled, the sword swinging ever wider. The Italian audience yelled its approval, loving the dramatics even more than the ballet steps.

Rosita and Piero took their bows, Rosita thinking ahead to the second act. That was the true test of a ballerina, for it involved difficult dancing and also acting to make it convincing. The "dead" Giselle appears to her duke, for whom she has died, and must help rescue him from the Wilis, who in revenge will try to make him dance himself to death for his faithlessness. Giselle in love and pity tries to save him by holding him up, encouraging him, protecting him, until the Wilis disappear again.

The second act began, the house was silent, watching. They sensed they were going to see a memorable performance. The scene became tense, the dancing grew spectacular. Behind the scenes, Delphine waited with Isolde, watching, waiting, holding their breaths, as Rosita bends over the helpless lover. She draws him up again, forced by Queen Myrta to make him dance and dance, ever more madly. She and Piero whirl about, more wildly, passionately fiery, until he collapses. Giselle leans over him, begs him to rise again, not to die, to keep on going. She tries to protect him, yet must do the command of Myrta.

Finally the church clock chimes the hour, and he is saved. The Wilis must return to their rest, and they fade from view.

But Giselle also must return to her grave. Albrecht, the duke, gasps for breath, stretches out his arms to her longingly, and begs her to remain, Giselle fades away into her grave. And the young duke stretches out beside the flowers he has brought to her, his heart broken.

The last gesture, the longing arm held out to her, the pitying look over her shoulder as she disappears—and it was over. The curtain fell.

It had scarcely touched the floor when the applause roared through the audience. Rosita and Piero went out and took bow after bow, with the Wilis, with Myrta, with the conductor, by themselves. Flowers were thrown at them, besides the bouquets filling Rosita's arms. She handed a rose to Piero, he kissed her hand, the crowd cheered, they wanted to see the young lovers again, again, again.

It took ten minutes for the audience to calm down. Someone counted the curtain calls, twenty-two. It was in the newspapers in New York the next day, and quoted in the San Juan papers, "Our Rosita Dominguez takes twenty-two calls in Milan, a magnificent Giselle." And the picture of her with Piero.

Afterward, the management wanted Rosita to stay on an additional week. They would put on a fifth week of the ballet if she would stay and do *Giselle* and the other ballet with Piero. Isolde accepted for them, glowing and happy. But Dimitre was quiet, abstracted.

Piero and his family took them out to dinner after the first *Giselle*, and the girls wore their new dresses. Isolde wanted to know where the dresses had come from, and seemed rather upset, especially as some extra young Italians had come and hung about her girls. But matters calmed down afterward, Rosita and Delphine were working hard, and had no time for dates. Isolde saw to that.

Zach wrote, "Who is Piero? Why is he hanging about Rosita?" Delphine wrote back mischievously, "He is a terribly handsome Italian, and we are both in love with him."

Zach wrote back furiously, and Rosita sent a soothing letter to him, explaining that Piero was married. She heard no more from him, and almost wished she had not written, but had let him worry!

Dimitre received another two letters from Moscow, and brooded and became difficult. He quarreled with Isolde, and said he would not appear with them that summer. Isolde was terribly upset, and they all went on to Geneva, thinking they were out of luck. But Dimitre quieted, and danced well with Rosita in a *Swan Lake* act, and two *divertissements*.

By May, they were back in London. Isolde was making plans for the summer, but Dimitre would not let her confirm them. She fretted, went for long walks alone, and returned tired, her face pinched.

Rosita appeared for a final time with Dimitre in a London *Giselle*, which went well. She did not feel the same rapport as with young, handsome, laughing Piero, but her emotional force and energy sustained her, and she received much applause. Dimitre was sometimes good, sometimes excellent. This week he was merely good, and Isolde was visibly worried about him.

The morning after their final appearance with the British ballet company, she and Delphine were still in bed, just yawning and waking up, when Isolde tapped. Delphine unlocked the door and let her in.

She was pale, she had not made up. Her hair was up in a tangle of braids. She wore her gray suit, and looked drained. She sat down on Delphine's bed, and said, "Dimitre has left me."

Rosita sat up, slowly, her arms locked around her knees. Delphine said, "Oh, Isolde," and took her older sister in her arms. Isolde wept, bitterly. Delphine kept patting her shoulders, and holding her head. Rosita got up, and got some handkerchiefs, and rinsed out a washcloth to wipe her face. They could say nothing to comfort her.

She finally calmed down. Dimitre had left in the middle of the night after a bitter quarrel, "Over nothing, nothing!" cried Isolde. "I do not understand him!"

"But where did he go?" asked Delphine, practically.

Isolde shook her head. "I don't know. He would not tell me. He said, cancel all his engagements, he would not come with us this summer. My God, I don't know what to do."

Rosita got dressed and went to the other bedroom, returning with the fat red engagement book. They must cancel everything in which Dimitre was scheduled to appear. She thumbed over the fat five-year engagement calendar, with a page for each week, noting absently their many dates. And beside some were the letters in Dimitre's neat black handwriting, *confirmed, $2,000,* or *confirmed, $4,000,* and on the five weeks' Milan engagement, the $10,000 had been neatly crossed off so it could still be read, and the figure $14,000 had been written in. Rosita was shocked. Were they making so much money? Isolde had never told them.

Of course, they paid for all her expenses. But weren't ballerinas paid more for making more? Or did they consider she owed them more, because they had carried her in the years of her studies?

She put it away in her mind to think about later. She turned over the pages of the next engagements. Isolde wiped her face and blew her nose, and reached for the book.

"I must phone Amsterdam, they might take just us," she said, turning over the pages, slowly. "And then, Copenhagen, the following week, oh, dear, they want *Giselle.*"

Rosita was looking also; the word "confirmed" was not written beside any of them. She pointed it out. "Were they not confirmed? Dimitre did not write it down."

Isolde brightened. "Oh, no, he did not." She studied the entries more carefully. The following week was empty, the next one also, then heavy engagements through the summer, but none confirmed.

She got on the telephone while Delphine set out their breakfast which the maid had brought up. Between sips of hot milky tea, Isolde began calling around.

After the first call, she said, "They want Dimitre. They are angry." She hung up, looking like a lost child.

"Let's go home," Rosita said suddenly.

"What? To New York?" Isolde frowned, "Perhaps Dimitre is there, I don't know . . ."

Delphine exchanged a look with Rosita, and shook her head.

"No," said Rosita patiently. "Let's go home to San Juan. I want to see my parents. Mama has been ill, and I have not seen the babies—let us go *home*."

"Yes, I want to go home," said Delphine. "I am tired and cold. I want to go home and lie in the sunshine!"

"All right," agreed Isolde, suddenly weary. "Do let us go home. Dimitre has left us. We cannot carry on, it is too much. How can I cope with all the travel arrangements, the engagements, the demands for more money—I cannot do all that bargaining that Dimitre did. He was saving money for our company—now that all is gone—all gone—"

She looked like she would weep again. Delphine urged her to eat, she could not. Delphine finally took her to her own room.

Rosita finished eating. Then her mouth set. She wanted to go home. Why not?

She could manage. She called the airlines and made reservations for the next day, from London to Kennedy, and home again. They would stay in New York long enough to get their clothes washed, the maids hugged, rested, then they could go home to San Juan.

When Delphine returned, Rosita said, "I made three reservations to go home tomorrow," and grinned at her friend.

"Hooray!" cried Delphine softly, and they began to pack.

Isolde finished canceling all their engagements when she learned what Rosita had done. "That is right, we cannot go on without Dimitre, not now. I must stop and think."

The next day they went out to the airport, and took the plane to New York, anxious to be home at last!

Chapter 8

Zach Hamilton sat at the head of the table in the boardroom. The quarreling was going on as usual, but it always disturbed him. He had the private opinion that all the fussing and quarreling among the owners of Hamilton Rums had helped bring on his father's heart attack. It certainly could not have helped.

"Enough," he said abruptly, sitting up, and tapping his pen lightly on the table for order. "It does no good to blame each other for the mistake. Uncle William, will you report on the United States sales. We have your figures, they look better than last year, though not so high as we had hoped."

Uncle William looked sullen, his mouth set hard. "I was not the one who said the figures would be much higher! I told you no good would come of trying to sell rum to women! They consider it a drink for men."

"Nevertheless, our campaign using the three lovely models did help," said Zach drily. He pointed to the figures in the chart before him. "Up a steady seven percent; then in the summer months after the campaign had been on for four months, and the heat of the summer encouraged cooling drinks, we went up twelve percent."

Jeronimo Oviedo stirred restlessly. "I thought you said,

Zach, that you had some new ideas for the company. Where are your new ideas? We need something to spur sales abroad."

Zach's gaze rested on his old friend thoughtfully. Jeronimo was even more plump, he was fairly bursting from his white suit. And his face was reddish tan from outdoor sports. Zach had left a call for him yesterday at two, it had not been returned until this morning. He was neglecting his work badly. Yet— they had been friends from boyhood. Jeronimo had left his own home frequently, and the atmosphere of indifference and sometimes hate, to haunt Zach's house. He had been treated as a son and brother.

When Jeronimo had finished college, he had been taken into the Hamilton Rum Company to learn the trade. He and Zach had been close in those years. Now—it was different. He was secretive, jealous at times, giving little jabs of spite.

"We do need new ideas, what have you to contribute?" he asked ironically.

Jeronimo laughed uncomfortably, his black eyes blazed before he lowered his heavy lids. "I'm just in the chemistry lab, my boy! I do what I am told!"

"We could use some more fresh ideas in the chem lab, besides those of Aunt Hortense," said Zach, bowing with a smile to his aunt. She was worth her weight in gold.

"Thank you, Zach. I wish I could come up with something else like the Hamilton's silver rum," she said wistfully. "I wrack my brains for ideas, but nothing has come recently."

"The silver rum is going very well. We need more of the American market, and that helps. Uncle William—what about the new publicity campaign, using the girl in a bikini?"

Uncle William reported on that, and they discussed it for a time. Uncle Morgan reported on several experiments in the lab, one showed some promise.

Then the subject of new machinery was brought up by Uncle Morgan. Stephen thought it was a good idea, they could experiment with that machine to make a new kind of rum, a much heavier body, for a masculine *macho* market, as Aunt Hortense said without expression.

Zach listened in almost complete silence, just putting in a

question from time to time. He had studied the matter, sitting up nights in the study at home, thinking. He did not think another heavier drink was warranted. There was Scotch, vodka, gin on the market. And the rums were heavy enough. No, they needed something different.

As Uncle Morgan rambled on about the machine, which he could get at a bargain price through a friend of his, and as he digressed to what the friend and he had been up to in the old days, Zach's mind wandered.

He had been going out lately with a beautiful dark-haired part-Spanish girl, Melinda Valdes. The Valdes family was wealthy, not as much as in previous decades, but still they held their own. She was discontented about that; she had complained that they did not get to New York anymore, not even often to Miami, where they had relatives.

He had the impression that Melinda wanted to marry him for his money and his prestige. She kept on and on about how important his family was, what a credit he was to them and how she adored his mother.

Last Saturday they had gone out, and she had wanted to go down to the beach, and lie on the sand in the moonlight. Somehow he had not wanted to go. He had taken her home early, and remained half an hour to talk to her parents. He liked her mother, quiet, black-haired, mousy, a little terrified of her stocky husband and his bellowing manner. Melinda had fluttered about, handing him drinks and offering cigars, hovering over Zach with her scarlet mouth pursed close to his chin, long nails on his hand tapping a secret message.

Zach was tired of flirtations and demanding, selfish women. He had not given Melinda any jewels, and last Saturday she had stopped him pointedly as they walked from the nightclub, to stare in the window of an expensive jewelers. She had pointed out a set of rubies and diamonds, and demanded, "Would I not look glorious in that?"

Something in him had gone cold. He had given jewels and even money to the women who pleased him in bed. Melinda Valdes was different, he had thought. She was from a good family, a respectable woman, he had believed. Now she was acting like a prostitute. He was glad he had not gone to bed with her, he would have despised himself.

"I am sure you would, Melinda," he had finally answered. As she had smiled hopefully up at him, he had added, "You must ask your father for them." He had dragged her on.

It was then she had wanted to go to the beach, and he had taken her home instead.

He doodled on the pad before him, seemingly intent on the report. But he was thinking. He was twenty-six, he would be twenty-seven in August. His father, Thomas, had married Isabeau Lothaire at this age, and been very happy with her; they had had four children, and much joy in the years of their marriage. Thomas had told Zach that after meeting and loving Isabeau he had never again wanted to stray. No other woman meant anything to him as she did.

He wanted to marry and have a son. His heart leapt up at the thought. A charming son, of his coloring, and his eyes, perhaps the eyes of his mother. But whom? Who would give him the joy that Isabeau had given to her husband, that Sonia had given to Philip Lothaire? And they both mourned their husbands, and did not look to any other man. The marriage had been complete for each of them, nothing could replace it.

He had been seriously considering Melinda Valdes. In recent weeks he had called her more often, taken her out, brought her home to family events. But now—that scarlet mouth, that arrogant air, her possessiveness—they displeased him. He had certainly courted her—but now he was not even sure he liked her anymore. She could be so—so bitchy—

"Well, Zach?" Uncle Morgan was demanding. "I don't think you are listening to me!"

Jeronimo was smiling, teasingly. "I think he is dreaming of a woman, a beautiful scarlet-mouthed woman with whom he is much seen of late!"

Zach looked at him in a level manner. How did Jeronimo know he was dating Melinda? He had not noticed Jeronimo around the places—of course he might not have seen him. But Jeronimo was always very obvious, coming up, slapping his shoulder, teasing him about his current girl.

As Zach did not answer, Jeronimo added with a laugh, "It is not that I disapprove of this, you understand, Zach, my friend! You should slow down and enjoy life. You are getting old too fast! You need more fun and pleasure, and there is nothing like a woman to provide—"

Aunt Hortense was frowning and shifting in the chair beside Zach's. She disliked such talk, and as a spinster she seemed to hold resentment against men who played around. He wondered if she had been hurt by some such man in her past.

Zach cut off Jeronimo. "We are considering the new machine. It would help in making the heavier rums. But we must think—do we want heavier rums? I think not. The trend, as I see it, is to lighter, more pleasant rums. Lighter drinks. More enjoyable drinks rather than having as our purpose getting drunk as quickly as possible. Drinking rum should be considered as a social activity, not as a pirate downing enough to make himself unconscious."

"Oh, very funny," grumbled Uncle Samuel, flushing darkly. He drank very heavily, Zach remembered with a pang. "One does not deliberately drink strong drinks to become unconscious!"

"Why not? It seems so to me," said Zach, then went on quickly. "About the machine. I think not. It is not our purpose to make more heavy rums. We have enough. Let us vote on that now."

The vote went against the machine, by a bare majority. He adjourned the meeting abruptly, and left the room. He went down the hall to his office.

Mrs. Sarita Myers looked up as he entered the outer room. She was flushed, her dark pretty face reddened, her eyes flashing.

He paused at her desk. "Any messages?" he asked, studying her face.

She handed him the little pile. "And Miss Valdes is waiting for you in your office, Zach."

"In my office?"

"She insisted," she added in a lower tone. "And she

125

asked me for a drink—I could not leave the office to obtain it. I am afraid she is angry with me.''

His mouth compressed. "I'll settle that," he said shortly. He strode on into his office. Melinda Valdes was sitting beside his desk, her legs crossed, revealing their long tanned length under the short scarlet and white linen dress. She was smoking, her big black eyes challenging him.

"Darling, where have you been? I have been waiting for an hour!" she reproached.

"I cannot recall an appointment," he said bluntly. He laid the letters down on his desk, and leaned against it to survey her.

"Don't be so literal, love," she murmured. She rose to lean against him. He was stiff. "I want you to come with me, you look so tired, darling. Let's go off and have some fun."

"Sorry, I have hours of work to do yet."

Her eyes blazed, she seemed about to spit words at him, then she changed her mind. He watched her with cool attention. "Your secretary was so rude to me! I don't see how you can endure her! She refused to get me a drink!"

"Come with me," he said, and held out his hand. She went with him willingly to the outer office, moving quickly in spite of her high-heeled red sandals. "Sarita, you are a damn good secretary," he said to the woman in the outer office. "And you are not a waitress. Remember that, please. Miss Valdes is just leaving."

Melinda's mouth was open as he drew her with him through the door. He forced her to walk with him out and along the hallway, to the elevator. They got on, and went down to the lower floor, where they proceeded to the front door. Melinda controlled her temper with an effort.

"Darling, you are teasing me! You are coming with me, aren't you?" she pouted her luscious mouth at him.

"No. I told you, I have work to do, and I must tell you. You are not to come to my office again. That is for Hamilton personnel alone. All this area is a closed area."

She blazed at him, losing her cool, "You are being perfectly hateful! I have often come here—"

126

His eyes narrowed as she abruptly stopped. "Not again," he said drily. "This is for Hamilton people only. The guards will be warned to be extremely careful about this. So don't try again, will you, Melinda? I'd hate to have you thrown out."

She looked to see if he was smiling, he was not. "I hate you, you meanie!" she flung out childishly, and ran down the steps to her scarlet car sitting in the shade of a tree.

He went back inside the cool building. He paused to speak to the guard, and glancing back out the glass door he saw Jeronimo Oviedo approach the car where Melinda sat, and lean over the door to speak to her. She shook her head. He opened the car door on the side opposite the driver, and she watched him. He sat down, and turned half to her. They spoke earnestly for a few minutes, as Zach and the guard watched.

Then they drove away.

"Hmm," said Zach, and the guard looked at him.

"I'm sorry, Mr. Zach," said the black guard, his tone very respectful. "She said she had an appointment with you, and went on upstairs."

The receptionist was sitting at her desk, looking cool and competent in her white uniform with the distinctive Hamilton emblem on the pocket. Zach went over to her, motioning the guard with him.

"How many people come in like that through the week?" he asked. "A couple, a dozen, how many?"

They looked at each other, the receptionist drew the book toward her, and glanced down several pages. "About a dozen a day, Mr. Zach," she said, finally. "They come in, say they are going to see you or Mr. Morgan or Mr. William, or someone, and go on up to the offices."

"The offices are supposed to be closed to everyone but the family." He drew the book toward him, glanced at the names. "Mrs. Morgan, Mrs. William, okay. But not this man—who is he?"

"A field representative of a bottling firm."

"We make our own bottles, no need for him to come. And this one?"

"A friend of Mr. Stephen, on vacation."

"Well, we are going to clamp down," he said, straightening. "I'll issue a memo today. Nobody is to be allowed above this floor at all. Anyone wishing to see a visitor must come down to talk to him, or meet him or her. I'll get it right out, and make it very clear. I don't want unauthorized persons floating all around the office areas. And the labs also, there is no reason for anyone to be in the laboratories who doesn't belong there." He was frowning heavily.

The guard exchanged a satisfied look with the receptionist. Zach caught it.

"Have people given you a hard time about this?" he asked sharply.

The guard nodded, so did the girl. "All the time, Mr. Zach. And when we try to follow the orders of Mr. Thomas, folks say, don't pay no mind to Mr. Thomas' order, he is dead. We get all confused."

"Well, it won't be confusing any longer. I'll send out the memo at once. Nobody, nobody, not even my mother, is allowed above stairs. That will apply to everybody not actively working in the offices. If anybody gives you a rough time, refer them to me—by phone, not in person."

"What about Miss Valdes, sir? She say she come up, she your girl especial."

He scowled heavily. "Well, she is not," he said shortly. "And she was very rude to Sarita. I don't want her in my office, nor in the working areas. The rule applies to her, very definitely."

"Yes, sir, Mr. Zach!" The guard was quite satisfied now.

Zach went back to his office, and dictated the memo at once. Sarita photocopied it, then had a messenger take it all around to all the buildings. He soon got some flak, as his uncles phoned, and even his brother, to ask what he meant.

"Just reinforcing my father's ruling, which people seem to have forgotten or ignored," he said to each one. "I don't want people in our offices, examining papers on our desks, even looking at the lab work and results. There won't be any secrets left at Hamilton's if this goes on."

About five o'clock, Sarita was ready to leave. She was a

lovely woman, who had worked for his father for years, and had recently married one of the control men in the rum works, Bill Myers. She was Spanish, he was English.

"Zach, I want to apologize for being rude to Miss Valdes," she said, hesitantly. "I refused to go out and get a drink for her. I had nobody just then to take my place in the office."

"No need to apologize for doing your duty, Sarita," he said quietly. "You did just right. Miss Valdes will not be coming up again. This is an office, not a bar."

Sarita looked relieved and happy again. "Thank you, Zach. Well—if you need anything else—shall I stay?"

"Nothing more. Go ahead, or Bill will have my head. I'll take some work home, I think. Good night."

"Good night, Zach," she smiled and left the room.

Zach had meant to stay and work here, but the room was still filled with the smell of Melinda's perfumed cigarettes, and her own strong perfume. He gathered up the papers he wanted to study, stuffed them in his portfolio and departed, locking the doors after himself.

He got into the silver Lincoln and drove himself home. He was tired, edgy. Matters were not going well in the company, he thought there should be some solution, but could not think what to do. Their sales ought to be going up more. How to achieve this? They would go under if they didn't get some smart answers. Many companies put out a good rum, and rums did not have as good a reputation as they should in the States. How to convince people that a good rum was a fine drink?

Absently he drove through the traffic, waited at lights, went on, until he reached Old San Juan. At the very sight of the beautiful light-painted buildings, the flowers overhanging the wrought iron balconies, half-opened wooden shutters sometimes revealing a beautiful living room and porcelain vases and lace curtains—he began to unwind. He loved San Juan, it was home, lovely, gracious, redolent of centuries of Spanish living.

He drove up the street, turned left and then into the driveway beside the Hamilton house. The guard Jaime came out, saluted him with a smile.

"How are you, Jaime? How's that wife of yours? No sign of the baby?"

"Not yet, Mr. Zach. Any day now. Maybe tonight!" he replied cheerfully. "Wife pretty unhappy and cross, I take her ice cream maybe."

"That's a good idea. It's pretty hot weather for a woman waiting for her little one."

"Sure is, Mr. Zach. Want to leave the car out, or should I put it inside?"

"Put it inside, thank you. I won't be going out tonight." He slid out of the hot car, and flinched when his fingers closed it. The silvery metal was burning hot from the sun.

He strode inside the back door, to the cool hallway. The patio was ablaze with flowers, geraniums of red and pink, bougainvillea in long strands of purple and dark crimson red, beds of carnations and of roses, tall spikes of exotic bird of paradise in yellow and purple, gorgeous bushes of rose and scarlet hibiscus, with smaller yellow daisies beside them. He drew a deep breath, and relaxed. How beautiful flowers were, so soothing in their unquestioning beauty. No demands from them, only to look, to enjoy, to find pleasure.

He went up by the outside patio iron stairs to his second-floor room, stepping inside with a sigh of pleasure for the modern advantages of air conditioning. On moderate days, they left doors and windows open to the breeze from the ocean, which cooled the house as it had done in centuries past. Now they had air conditioning for the very hot days, and what a relief when the air was still and humid.

He ripped off his clothes as he crossed the room, taking off jacket, tie, shirt in a few movements. He showered, and put on fresh light clothes for the evening, a light pair of gray trousers, thin blue shirt open at the throat. He stretched. He would not go out tonight. He had thought this morning to call Melinda. Now he did not care if he ever saw her again.

He scowled as he thought of her. He had not liked the way she acted toward Sarita. She was possessive, demanding, flirtatious, and thought of nothing but clothes, jewels, dancing and pleasure. There was more to life than that. He wondered if her head was completely empty.

He went downstairs again, and through the patio, now cool with evening breezes made fragrant by the flowers. He paused to smoke a pipe there, sitting on one of the white-painted iron chairs. How good, how relaxing. He could feel the tight tension at the back of his neck easing.

He went into the drawing room. His grandmother was there, some crochet work in her hands. He went over to kiss her wrinkled cheek.

"Mother not down?"

She shook her head, their glances met. "She must come out of herself," she said sadly. "It does not any good to continue grieving so wildly. It will not bring him back. She is sick with it."

"She needs other interests," he mused, and poured himself a drink of light rum over ice, with a piece of lime. Madame Sonia had her little glass of plain rum, the way she liked it.

He drank, and they went in to dinner together. Kevin arrived as they were on the soup course, and sat down, looking tired. They were all silent as they ate. He tried to make conversation, but they had not much to say.

He and Kevin went to the study following dinner, to work again. Kevin had some experiments from the lab to go over with him. They had tried to make another mixture of lime and rum, to sell as one together, it had not worked, though they had tried a number of combinations. The lime would spoil after a time.

"We are doing something wrong, but I cannot figure out what it is," said Kevin, frowning.

Vaguely Zach heard the telephone ringing. He had disconnected it in the study, not wishing to be disturbed. A few minutes later, Madame Sonia came in, not pausing to knock. Her cheeks were flushed, her eyes bright.

"Zach, please connect the telephone," she exclaimed. "Isolde is on the line from New York, and she cries and cries. I cannot understand her!"

Kevin connected the line quickly, plugging it into the wall socket. Zach picked up the telephone. "Isolde? What is it, my dear?"

Rosita's grave voice came over the line distinctly. "Zach, it is me, Rosita Dominguez. Isolde is crying, I have the telephone now."

She sounded older, mature. "What is it, an accident?"

"No, nothing so bad, no one is ill or injured," she said quickly. "We returned from Europe, canceled all our engagements. Dimitre left us in Amsterdam."

He sensed something was terribly wrong, but she was reserved about it. "My dear, what can I do? Do you want me to come—where are you?"

"We are in the New York apartment, Zach. We arrived this morning. Isolde is very tired, that is partly why she cries. Delphine is crying also, but we will be all right."

"Good grief, it sounds like a regular waterfall," he said lightly. "Rosita, what happened? Can you tell me?"

She hesitated. "It is only that we are all homesick," she said at last. "We wish to come home."

"Then come, my dear girl! No problem. Mother will be delighted, I think she needs you girls here."

"That is good. We will be here for a few days, and finish some canceling of engagements. Then we will fly to San Juan. Oh—just a minute—"

He heard a murmured consultation. Then Rosita spoke again.

"Isolde says next Wednesday. We will come on the plane on Wednesday morning, and arrive in San Juan airport in the afternoon as usual. You will have us met, please?"

"I'll meet you myself. Can Delphine talk now?"

"One moment." Another pause. Her voice returned. "She is crying," she said ruefully. "She says she is happy to be home, but is very tired. Oh—here she is—"

Delphine came on the phone. "Oh, Zach, I want to come home, I'm so tired—everything is a mess—if Rosita had not gotten us on the plane—we've had a terrible time—people shouted at us—nasty—Rosita got us home."

He could not make any sense of what she said. He listened patiently, then said, "Put Rosita on the line again, my dear. I love you, Delphine, be calm, and get home safely. Let me talk to Rosita again." She seemed the only sane person around, he thought.

Rosita took the phone again. "It is all right, Zach. We are all just very tired."

"Why were people cross at you?" he asked.

"We had to cancel so many engagements, and some of the booking agents screamed at us," she said calmly. "I told them nothing was confirmed, and they could get someone else. I said, we are tired, we are going home. However, Isolde got very upset, and she is crying all the time. I will see that she goes to bed soon."

"Yes, take care of them, Rosita. And take care of yourself! Don't get too tired. I'll meet you on Wednesday."

"Thank you, Zach."

"And if you need anything, call me! Do you need money?"

"No, thank you. We will get there," she said firmly. She sounded older, more mature. She was about eighteen, he thought. He had not seen her for much too long.

They said good-bye, he hung up. "They are all coming home, granny," he smiled at the eager woman beside him. "I'll go up and tell mother. That should perk her up!"

Sonia crossed herself and thanked God fervently in Russian. "Crossing the ocean all that time, it is nonsense," she said firmly. "They should come home and stay home. This is their place!"

"I agree," said Zach, and kissed her withered pink cheek.

He was surprised to find himself humming happily as he jumped up the stairs to his mother's room on the second floor. He was feeling lighter, happier and more pleased with life.

The girls were coming home. And Rosita with them. Rosita, with her big dark eyes and gentle face, with the soft black hair and the slight wave in it, with her slim form and dancing feet. The eagerness that lit a light behind her eyes when she was excited. The sober ecstasy when she danced.

He could scarcely wait to see her again. Had she changed much in these long months?

Chapter 9

The plane from Miami to San Juan was completely full. The air stewardesses sighed and shook their heads over the huge bundles and packages and shopping bags that people were carrying on board. But they were accustomed to it.

Half the passengers were tourists, one could tell by the guidebooks, the eager chatter about seeing El Morro and the rain forests, the curious peering from the windows as they approached San Juan airport.

The other half were either returning Puerto Ricans or visitors and relatives, and all had huge bundles of presents and goods from the States, including a small sewing machine hand-carried, thick dress bags and electric blankets.

Rosita was amused and touched as she watched the scene, small children sturdily carrying their share and more, babies peering over their mothers' shoulders in baby totes, fathers trying again and again to gather their families together and not lose anybody. The laughter and chatter in Spanish was so familiar and dear.

The plane landed smoothly, to Rosita's relief. She had experienced all kinds of landings in the past two years—skimming over the ground with a soft little jerk, the bump and hump and bump again that made one's inside joggle, the screech and bump that made them fly up into the air again, and clutch the arms of the chair. And one horrible experience of landing in a rain and lightning storm.

But they were home again, she crossed herself quickly, furtively, and breathed a prayer of relief and thankfulness. She was alive, and well, and home once more.

The plane rolled to a stop. People were already standing, reaching for bundles and children, in spite of the stewardess and her warning, ''Please do not get up—please wait until we reach the gate—the captain asks—''

They laughed and called to each other, and started walking to the front. It would be trying to stop an ocean wave. The plane rolled in front of the gate, and there was a little pause as the steps were rolled up to the door, and then the door opened from the inside.

Rosita got off first, and turned around to see if Delphine needed any help. Delphine followed her down, smiling, blinking eagerly in the sunshine. ''There's Zach!'' she said at once, and waved frantically with her free hand.

Isolde followed more slowly, the girls waited for her patiently. Her face was pale, and her makeup stood out, the rouge like some fever and the mascara dark and smudged. She nodded curtly, and went with them to the inside of the air lounge.

Zach was standing there, right at the door, his hands lightly on his hips. How fine he looked, thought Rosita as he greeted Isolde. He took his sister in his arms, kissed each cheek tenderly. He looked older, there were deep grooves on either side of his face, very tanned from the sun. Isolde rested against him for a minute, he pressed his cheek against hers quietly, and let her calm down.

Then he let her go and turned to Delphine. ''My beautiful baby, all grown-up,'' he teased, and kissed her on each cheek. She clung to him, her hands on his wide shoulders, and blinked tears from her blue eyes. Rosita was gravely waiting, appraising him, in the well-fitting gray linen suit, the white shirt and handsome blue and silver tie. How handsome he was, with his dark red hair and vivid blue eyes in the darkly tanned face. And older, she thought, more mature, confident and even arrogant.

Rosita waited as he turned to her. He reached out a hand, her hand went to meet his, she thought they would shake hands. Instead he drew her to him, and she received his kisses of welcome on each cheek. His hard arm had gone about her, the other hand held hers.

She blinked at him as he drew back and smiled down at her. "Lovelier than ever, Rosita, my Spanish Rose!" he murmured. His quick glance went over her thoroughly, from head to shoulders, to breast, to waist, and down over her long slim legs to her small feet. He smiled, as though pleased. "You are grown-up now," he added.

"Yes, I am eighteen," she said, dazed.

"But you are all too thin and worn," he said, turning to speak to the others. "We will have to fatten you up, and make you sleep twelve hours a night! Then some fun—swimming and picnics on the beach, parties and dancing, nightclubs, and some testing of our new rums!" He laughed.

"Oh, Zach," muttered Isolde pettishly. "We just need a little rest, then we must start work again. I may go back to New York in a couple of weeks—"

His glance sharpened on her, his mouth compressed. He said nothing then, but reached for her jewel-cosmetic case, and carried it for her, and Delphine's. He also reached for Rosita's, she shook her head. "I can carry this," she said. "Thank you anyway."

"I brought two cars and two men for all your luggage," said Zach, with a wry grin. "Come along, girls, give me your luggage stubs—"

Rosita handed them to him, she was taking care of all the tickets and luggage stubs. Isolde was so absentminded these days, she had to take care of everything herself. Delphine was inclined to lay things down somewhere and forget them.

Zach escorted them out to the cars, saw them settled, and returned with the two men for their luggage. Isolde was leaning back in the bronze Cadillac, her head tilted, eyes closed. Rosita, in the silver Lincoln with Delphine, watched her with

Janet Louise Roberts

concern. Isolde seemed to have wound down and stopped like a neglected watch.

The men returned and loaded the luggage in the trunks, then they were on their way, in the blue sunshiny atmosphere of Puerto Rico.

"Oh, how glad I am to be home," sighed Delphine. She leaned forward and began to ask the chauffeur eager questions. Rosita listened in silence, gazing out the window, hungry to see the familiar landmarks.

Presently they were winding into the streets of the older part of the city, past the elegant hotels, then the older hotels, and into the very old part. Old San Juan, and Rosita leaned to look happily at the cream buildings, the rose ones, the shops with the Spanish signs, the children playing on the sidewalks, the tourists hovering over windows of shells and pearls and colorful cloth. Up the cobblestoned street behind the Cathedral, they turned left, and home.

Home, to the Hamiltons. And it felt like home to her, this quiet elegant mansion. The doors were opened, Madame Sonia and Madame Isabeau were just inside, arms out. The hallway was darkened against the heat, but the drawing room was golden with its curtains and draperies, and the sunlight streamed in over the plush sofas and chairs, the lovely gold rugs and the Persian many-colored rugs.

Isolde's mother exclaimed over her daughter. "You are sick, my dearest Isolde!"

"No, mother, just so very tired."

"But you must rest—your rooms are ready—" Her other hand reached out lovingly to Delphine.

Zach said to Rosita, "And you have your same room, my dear. Welcome, and be comfortable."

She turned to him shyly. "Thank you. And—and may I use the telephone, and call my parents?"

"Of course. Come with me." He put his arm casually about her and led her back to his study. It was a brotherly gesture, she thought, he had become accustomed to thinking of her as one with his sisters.

Isolde called after her, her voice sharp, "Don't run off tomorrow, Rosita! Practice in the morning, as usual!"

"Yes, Isolde," said Rosita obediently.

Delphine made an angry sound. "I intend to sleep in," she added. "Really, Isolde, one day off—"

"Not any days off," said Isolde, sounding a little like her old self. "We may take some engagements this summer in New York or around the country. It does not pay to get out of practice."

"The girls need a rest, and so do you," said her mother, a little sternly for such a soft-voiced woman. Her French accent was more clear today. "Girls, sleep in, and rest. We will talk later. Dinner at six, dear Rosita," she called as Rosita went on down the hall with Zach.

In the study, Zach picked up the telephone, listened. "It is connected," he said, and handed it to her. She dialed, smiled at him shyly.

"I'll leave you," he said quietly. "Tell your people you will be over tomorrow. One of the men will drive you."

"Thank you. Marcos will come for me, I think," she whispered, then heard a man's voice. "Oh, papa, is it you? It is me, Rosita! I am home!"

Zach grinned at her, and went out, closing the door after himself. She sank down into his large swivel chair and heard her father's voice speaking, a tremor in the tone.

"Rosita, my baby! Where are you? At the Hamiltons? You had a good trip, you were not sick? Here is your mother, when will we see you?"

"Tomorrow, papa," she said happily. "I will come at noon after you are all up. The engagements," she went on in Spanish. "They are good, *sí?*"

"Oh—*sí,*" he said slowly, and she knew they were not. "We will talk tomorrow. You are well?" Then he handed over the phone to her mother.

Her mother's voice seemed frail and tired. Rosita frowned in worry. She wanted to dash over tonight, but they would have to go to the nightclub at seven-thirty, and she herself was

Janet Louise Roberts

feeling the tiredness of traveling. Her very bones ached from long hours in the plane and the Miami airport.

She talked to all the adults, then hung up and went to her familiar room on the third floor. Her suitcases and cosmetic case were in the room, already. She unpacked one case, then put on a light robe, and lay down. She was asleep in minutes, the whirling in her mind finally slowing down and permitting her to relax.

She had dinner with the family, sitting in silence as they exchanged news and gossip. Zach tried to draw her out, she smiled at him and shook her head slightly, as though to say it is the family's night. Madame Sonia was gracious about her successes.

"You must come to my room and talk to me about your *Giselle*," said the older lady wistfully. "I remember so well, when I danced *Giselle*, I still have the dress, I will show you."

"I will be happy to do so, Madame Sonia," said Rosita.

The next morning, she rose at ten, feeling much better. She had missed beakfast, it did not matter, she rarely ate much. She went to the practice room, and warmed up alone for an hour and a half. Delphine did not come, she must have given in to her longing to sleep until noon.

Rosita returned to her room, showered and dressed in a light blue cotton. She crept down the patio stairs then, and met Marcos, who had come for her at twelve.

They paused to talk to Jaime, whose usually somber face was beaming. He told them all about his new baby boy, how marvelous he was, how healthy, how he opened his eyes and knew his papa already. They congratulated him, and sent best wishes to his wife. Rosita made a mental note to buy a present for the baby, perhaps a little blue blanket. They could always use blankets, for the tropical nights could turn very cool, from the trade winds.

Then they went home. It was a joyous greeting, she hugged and kissed everybody, marveled at the new babies, talked about her ballet successes, the strange cities she had visited. And in turn everyone tried to tell her what had been going on, how her cousins and friends were, who had died, who had been born,

140

who had married, who was engaged, news from an uncle in Spain, a cousin in Cuba.

They had exchanged letters regularly, but some had been lost in the mails, as Rosita and the others had traveled so fast. Now they must catch up.

She talked to her father quietly. "The nightclub, it does not go well?"

He grimaced, patted her hand. "We miss you, my baby," he said. "And mama has not been well, there is talk of an operation for her. She worries much about that, she does not want to be cut open."

She questioned him, he did not want to tell her, but it was what she had guessed. A hysterectomy, and the possibility the ovary was cancerous. The doctor wanted to operate soon, before the cancer spread, if indeed it was there.

It would cost much money, and they did not have medical insurance. She talked to Elena about it, and decided she could help. "I will come to dance every night," she said. "I think I have not forgotten the flamenco! It is in my bones!"

If they did well, they could save enough money to pay at least part of the operation.

Elena got out Rosita's two dresses, the red and the rose, and she tried them on. Both were a little tight, her bust had increased, and she was now five feet three inches tall. Fortunately, the seams were always made wide, and Elena busily picked at the seams of the rose dress.

Rosita found her dance shoes, and tried them on, they still fit. She wore them, worked them with her hands a little, to get the leather to feeling soft again. By evening one dress was sewed up, she had fresh lace on the neck and sleeves, and her shoes in order. She telephoned the Hamilton house, got a maid, and told her she was staying overnight with her family.

That night she danced with the Dominguez. Somehow word went around the Spanish community, and the nightclub became very crowded by the time of the second performance.

Rosita had danced ballet for so long, she had almost forgotten the flamenco moves, in the heel-stamping dances. But it came back. The audience yelled their approval, as she combined ballet splits and *pirouettes* with flamenco flourishes of her frilled skirts.

By the time the third performance was ended at two in the morning, she ached from head to foot. A hot bath the next morning helped, and the workout. Then she went off again, to practice a new dance with Marcos. Oliverio made up a new background guitar song for her, and they worked it out in a few hours.

The nightclub was packed again the next night, and the next. The word had gone out, Rosita Dominguez, our Flamenco Rose, *La Soledad,* was back. Sí, Rosita, *La Soledad,* who is dancing in the ballet all over the world, the one in the newspapers, is back in San Juan, dancing with the Dominguez troupe. It was the chance of a lifetime to see her once more! One must go, it was most splendid, she was more fiery than ever, our *Soledad,* our solemn-eyed girl, with her wistful beauty. And prettier than ever, *sí, sí, sí!*

The Puerto Ricans came and cheered, and yelled "*La Soledad!* Flamenco Rosita! *La Soledad!* Our Rosita!" night after night. The nightclub was packed to the sidewalks, the tables were filled by the best patrons who must promise to have a full dinner and wine and rum before they could have that table. They paid gladly, and sat in evening dress and Spanish costume, to watch and eat, to see the floorshow and applaud.

Papa Pascual did not have to beg for a raise for his family. He hated bargaining, it was beneath his dignity as a Spaniard and a Gypsy. People must realize his worth, he often said, it was not necessary to bargain like a merchant!

The owner of the nightclub paid them more, much more, and the money went into the bank for the operation. By the end of the summer, if Rosita did not have to return to New York, they would have enough for mama.

Her mother came out nightly to sing with them, but she did not dance. Her beautiful voice was more plaintive than ever, so haunting that it made tears come to Rosita's eyes. Gray streaked her shining black hair in the thick chignon, and she stood with dignity, her hands held out to them, as she sang the old Gypsy songs, the Spanish love songs, the homesick songs. And they were quiet and listening, for she sang with more emotion and they loved it.

If only Isolde did not make her leave—Rosita prayed about it night and day, slipping over to the nearby Cathedral, to kneel before the Madonna and pray. "Do not send me away, Madonna, oh, let me remain here in San Juan, to help mama," she would whisper each day and evening, before she went to the nightclub.

Her prayers were answered that June month. Isolde packed, and departed for New York, abruptly, without taking Delphine and Rosita with her. Her mother questioned in vain, Zach could not reason with her. She must go, she said.

Isolde had had a letter from Madame Olga. Dimitre was back in New York, but he would not be there long, she said. Isolde got the next flight the day after receiving the letter.

In his apartment, she lay in the bed, after their fierce and violent love-making. She had slept after, satisfied, so relieved and happy. Dimitre had made love so wildly to her, he must love her, and want her again.

She had feared there was another woman—

But he was the same, only more adoring—

She wakened, and lay there, watching him sleep. She dared to touch his face with her finger, tracing the dark lines of his jaw where he needed to shave. She moved her finger over his chin, loving the scratchy feel. He was so very much a man, she loved him so much.

She leaned to kiss him softly. She could not bear it, to waste the time when he might be awake and loving her again.

He murmured, eyes closed, "Do that again. I feel like the Sleeping Beauty!"

She kissed his square faun's mouth again, her lips moving on his. He kissed her back, gently, not like the fierce, furious kisses of their meeting earlier that afternoon.

Then he sighed, and moved. "Isolde, we must talk seriously," he said, and sat up. She watched in amazement as he slid from the bed and put a robe about himself. It was as though he shut himself off from her.

"I should not have done that," he said somberly. Oh,

143

dear, thought Isolde angrily. He has gone all Russian and melancholy just like Madame Sonia in her moods.

"Why not?" she asked flatly. "Didn't you enjoy it? Was I alone in my pleasure?"

She sat up, the sheet around her waist, defiantly showing him her rounded pink and white breasts, her firm body. He looked, then turned his head away. He sat down in a chair half-turned from the bed. He crossed his bare legs, and reached for his cigarette case. He forgot to offer her one, he lit his own. He was always so courteous, except when he was in a terrible Tartar temper, or in a dark Russian mood.

It was Dark Russian today.

"You know I enjoyed it," he said at last. "But it must not occur again. When I told you to come, it was to talk to you."

She had telephoned him that morning, she had arrived in New York last night. She was tired, cross, apprehensive. She had walked in his door this noon, looked at him, prepared to berate him, to go haughty and Hamilton, nose in the air, aristocratic, ballerina-proud, in her cream suit and red sandals.

She had seen him, taut, hollow-eyed, unshaven, in his jeans and T-shirt, and melted right against him. They had scarcely said hello, when they had started kissing, and moved on to the bedroom.

She waited for him to talk, to tell her what he had to say. He smoked one cigarette, another, broodingly.

"Well? Why did you leave us in Europe?" she finally asked. "Were you—tired of me?"

Jealously, she was quick to note he did not answer that. "I had to stop," he said. "I had to come back, to think. I had to plan."

"And what about our plans? The future, our company—"

"I left the money in the bank. I will take out only what I need these months, and the rest is yours," he said wearily.

"Damn the money! What about our company?"

"I cannot do it. It is impossible. I cannot tell you why."

She was silent, depressed, frightened. She could not reach him, not through those fine hands, that thrilled her so much.

Not through that magnificent tanned body, those muscles that moved so beautifully with hers in the dance and in bed. Not through those enigmatic vivid blue eyes, that Tartar face with the high cheekbones she loved to caress, that cool head with the blond straight hair. He had always kept much of himself to himself, he told her only so much, no more. Now he was removed from her. She could not get through to him. He was alone in the tanned skin, the leopard movements, the taut muscular body.

"Are you going back to the company?" she asked dully. She didn't want to go back, but if he did, she would. She would take Rosita and Delphine with her, they would go back under the management of Miss Stanton and Alan Landis—

He was moving his head slowly, no. "I am not sure where I shall go. Maybe Texas," he said.

"My God! What is in Texas?" She thought quickly, the Dallas ballet, or Fort Worth, or Houston, just wherever he went—

"It is far away from New York. It is different. It is alive and mad at times," he said cheerlessly. "I think I could lose myself there."

She was sitting up, her arms about her knees, hugging herself. He glanced at her naked body, then away, swiftly, as though she did not please him. Another woman, by God, it is another woman, she decided, savagely. And hated whoever it was.

It had to be another woman. He was tired of Isolde, that was clear. They could meet and have sex, but he was too tired of her to want more. She felt humiliated to her heels.

"You cannot tell me what is wrong," she said slowly, her face turned so he could not see the hurt.

"No, nothing is wrong. I am weary, I am tired of New York, I am—so you say—fed up. Nothing goes right. I must make the change—"

Three years, she thought, staring at her knee absently. Three years with Dimitre, but he was now tired of her. The future up in smoke, their future together, the company they would have formed—or had it all been a foolish dream of hers?

Had he wanted only to work with her and with Rosita for a time, gain some money, some fame, then quit?

Lead her on, have someone warm in his bed, earn some money— No, he didn't want the money, he tossed it back to her casually. It is in the bank, he said, take it.

His dark face was absent, moody. He finally said, "Want some tea?" He stood up, ready to leave her, to fix tea.

She did not want tea, but she wanted to be alone, to dress by herself, not with him, not letting his gaze rest on her naked body that he no longer wanted. It would be obscene somehow, for him to watch her dress. She nodded. "Tea," she said.

When he had left the room, she got up and dressed with quick mechanical movement. Pantyhose, brief brassiere, slip, blouse, skirt. She was slipping on the red sandals when he returned, and saw her dressed.

She looked at him, he returned her gaze with a blank look, but there was a dark hurt in his eyes. "In the living room," she said brightly, taking her cup. She picked up her cream jacket and her matching pocketbook with her other hand, and walked before him into the other room. She sat down in a straight chair, her ankles crossed, the neat trim ankles of a ballerina. She drank the tea she did not want. Milky tea. Perhaps after Dimitre went out of her life, she would return to black coffee, she thought.

She finished the tea, set down the cup in the saucer on the table beside her. She glanced about the room. She somehow knew she would not see this room again. He had begun packing, she saw, and it was a shock. A carton half-full of his books, another carton full of records—he was indeed leaving.

"Well," she said slowly, in a calm social manner. She had cried enough for him, she would cry no more. "Good-bye, Dimitre. It was—good—working with you. I learned quite a lot."

She held out her hand. He looked at it, then took it slowly in his big hand. They shook hands, like strangers, like people who had never met before, who would never meet again. She walked to the door.

"Isolde," he said, his voice strangled.

She could not endure it if he said he was sorry for her. She grimaced in an attempt at a smile. "Let us know how you are doing, Dimitre! Don't forget us," she said in a higher tone than usual.

He ducked his head, she thought he would kiss her lips and she could not bear it. She turned her head away. She felt his wide mouth touch her neck softly, at the side of her throat.

Then he stood away from her. He held the door open, she walked out. He had not said a word. He stood and watched her walk away from him, steadily, to the elevator. He was watching her when she entered, and pressed the button for the ground floor.

He was leaning against the door, in the robe, his long legs showing, barefoot, his dark face closed and aloof. His vivid blue eyes watching her, watching . . .

The elevator door closed, and Isolde shut her eyes tightly for a minute. When she opened them, she was on the ground floor, the door was sliding open. She went out to the street, and walked out into the hot sunlight of New York, with horns honking, and dogs on leashes pulling to reach the lampposts, and people crowding at the crossings—

She went home, and to her room, and lay down across the bed. She could not cry any more. She had shed her last tears for Dimitre. It was over. Somehow she must plan for a future without him. Somehow she must fill the days and months, and years. Without Dimitre. Without him, her love.

Chapter 10

"Ready?" Kevin asked. Zach gazed at his brother absently, at the red brown hair, brown eyes, stocky body. He was so solid, in person and in disposition.

From where they stood in the patio, he could just hear the music coming faintly from the practice room, opposite to the practically unused ballroom on the fourth floor. He said, "No, you go ahead. I thought of something I must do first. Tell Sarita I will be late, take all my calls."

"Right. May I take the Lincoln today?" Kevin added, with a grin.

"Go ahead. I'll use the brown Caddy."

Kevin went on out, Zach went to the patio stairs, and began to mount the iron rungs to the fourth floor. He stepped off at that floor, and went around to the practice door.

It was slightly open for air, and inside the music from the stereo was stronger. It was a piano, the music with a solid slow beat.

He pushed open the door, and went inside. Rosita was at the center *barre*, poised. Her eyes went wide.

"Go on," he said, "I'll wait."

She bowed, part of the movement, and he went to a chair

in the corner. He sat down in the wickerwork chair, pushed the cushion behind him, and relaxed, legs crossed, as he watched.

Rosita was lovelier than ever, he decided. She had matured, her bosom was softly rounded, her waist trim, her hips more full. How graceful she was in the dark blue practice leotard, how lovely even in the leg mufflers, ankle socks above the worn pink ballerina slippers. She had removed the gray sweater, and it lay on the arm of the chair where he sat. He fondled it absently, it held a little of her perfume.

Today her hair was not bound up. She wore it in a loose ponytail. The hair that looked so black in the spotlights of a nightclub now showed itself in true colors in the ordinary lights of the practice studio, under the roof that was partly glass. The hair showed brown, deep warm brown, with a slight wave in it, and little tendrils had come loose about her ears. Beads of sweat were on her forehead, she wiped it absently with her towel, then laid the towel aside. The music was slow, steady. She must have just started about fifteen minutes ago, he knew the routine.

The first warm-ups were for the feet, then for the legs, the waist, the upper torso, then the arms, the head. Slowly. Slowly. Pause. Then the next fifteen minutes for the more rapid movements. Later, free from the *barre*, and in the open.

She turned, her foot out, and moved it slowly. Her head moved, she looked at him, continuing the slow count to the music. "You wanted to speak with me?" she asked.

"Yes, but go ahead. I'll wait until the next pause."

"Thank you," she said seriously. She went on. It amused him a little, how dedicated she was.

As he sat there watching, he realized it was not funny. She had worked hard all her life, from babyhood. "I danced in my mother's womb," the newspapers in Spanish had reported. And from then on, he thought.

Dancing was her life, of necessity. She did not sleep late in the morning, though she had crept in at two in the morning. His room was just beneath hers, he had worked late some nights, and had just gone to bed when he had heard her coming up the patio stairs, and into her room. He had heard the soft movements above him, and had lain with his hands under his head, imagining her gestures, removing her jacket, her blouse, her clothes, unbinding her hair.

He gazed at her, the hair came almost to her waist, full and trying to spring from the ribbon that tied it back, full of glossy life. Framing her sober little oval face, that pure chin line, the proud nose, the wide expressive mouth. How ripe her mouth looked, young but sensuous, red-lipped.

There was fire in her, but until now it had showed only in her dancing. He had watched her dance, entranced, when she was only twelve. As she matured, the fire grew, the movements were disciplined, yet there was a passion behind them that held the viewer in thrall.

She posed, held it, then her right leg moved around to circle her back, she arched, held it, came down slowly. He gazed at her, thinking of all the hours of practice, the days and weeks and years, that went into the beauty of a ten-minute dance. Was it worth it? It was to her, and he had to admit when he watched her perform, it was magnificent.

He would never forget the dance in New York, "The Gypsy Wanderer." He had even forgotten for a time that this was young shy Rosita, this magnificent sensuous Gypsy, able to win the wild love of so many men, then strolling away—

Afterward, she had seemed so very young, exhausted, dazed, happy, yet with big sober eyes wondering if this could be her—the one receiving all the praise and admiration—so unspoiled, so timid, so grateful for any gesture of kindness— The roses in her arms, trying to thank him for them. The gasp at the beauty of the pendant— She had scarcely been able to speak. She wore it often, he had been pleased to see.

She was a woman now, he thought, and felt his heart beating faster at the pure beauty of her body, her movements in the simple exercises. Her skin so golden, her eyes so large and beautiful, the brush of her long dark hair against her lean young back . . .

The music finished. She stopped, and went over to turn it off, then returned to him. He got up, she shook her head with a faint shy smile, and sank down onto the floor before him. He put the gray sweater about her, tying it loosely by the arms about her neck.

"Thank you, Zach," she said. He sat down again in the chair, and watched her stretch out her long youthful legs, into a split, bending in supple gestures to keep it stretched, bending, rising, bending, rising.

"I could not speak to Isolde before she left. I think she has not confided in mother, either," he began abruptly. Directness was his way when possible, he hated the deviousness of business language.

The big eyes searched his gaze, then the eyelashes came down, the lids covered her eyes. Her head bent, in watching her legs as she stretched them.

"*Sí,*" she said. "She does not speak much, of what troubles her."

"What does trouble her?"

She finally sat up straight, and stopped working at her body. "Could you not ask her? Or Delphine?" she finally asked, a faint pink flush in her cheeks.

"You are keen and observant, you have a loving heart," he said quietly. "I am asking you. You love my sisters, I think, and you are protective of them." He smiled a little. "They think they are looking after you, maybe it was true once. Now I think you are taking care of them."

"I am grateful to them—"

"Understood. You have more than repaid them," he added, and saw the flush deepen, the grateful look in her face up-turned to his. "You have been a true friend to Delphine, and I think you see Isolde clearly. Now tell me—who is Dimitre? What is he? What kind of man? I did not get to know him well."

The rapid-fire questions seemed to confuse her, or make her wary. Her body was still, held quiet. "Well—he is a Russian dancer, who defected some years ago," she began. "He is a very good dancer, he partnered me, and did it so smoothly. He teaches well, is very patient in the teaching. He is kind, but sometimes—he has a dark mood," she gestured, with both hands before her face, in instinctive mime.

"I remember when he defected to the United States. The newspapers mentioned a wife. Is he still married?"

She started, her trained body gave a little betraying jerk.

"We do not know," she admitted.

"We?"

"Delphine and I. We were worried, because he seemed— very fond—of Isolde. So—" Her head tossed a little, the ponytail swayed, and the brown hair moved on her back. "We went to the New York Public Library, the big one down at Forty-second Street, you know? They have newspapers and many magazines, some on microfilm. We looked him up. We searched for everything we could find on him one day, we looked for hours." Her red mouth made a little *moue* of ruefulness, at their daring to do so.

"And what did you find?" The girls must have been very worried to do this, he thought.

"At first, they mentioned his wife left in Russia, her name was Natasha. She refused to come to him, she berated him. He has no other family, one newspaper said. She had family, no children, though. They were married very young, she is also a ballerina, but not so talented. He kept begging her to come, and sometimes the magazines said in sentimental articles that he missed her very much. But one said they had separated and lived apart before he left Russia."

"Ah! Separated. Did he get a divorce? Is he Catholic?"

"He is Russian Orthodox," she said. "I do not know how they feel about divorce. The magazine articles spoke of this, then they did not speak of it any longer. We looked at every article we could find, and in later years there was nothing about his wife. Nothing at all."

He thought about that, frowning. "And Isolde? Did she love him?"

The head bent, the face was mobile, sensitive, he watched her shrewdly. "Rosita, did they live together?"

Her head jerked.

"Tell me, I shall not speak to mother about this," he added gently. "I must know—"

"Well—in Europe—they shared rooms," she admitted

153

reluctantly. "And when he left us—she was shattered. I have never seen her cry so."

"Tell me about it," he said.

She did, reluctantly, but frankly, when he showed his concern. "And I think she went back to New York to try to see him again."

He nodded, and sighed. "I had a telephone call last night, from Isolde. She sounded cold, detached. She said she meant to remain in New York for the summer, and dance. The New York Festival Ballet is doing some summer work, and they wanted her. She said nothing of Dimitre."

She pondered that seriously, face absorbed. He watched her, she was so young and touching in her unself-conscious beauty, the gentle sweetness of her face, the open quality of her expressions, the wonder in her eyes.

"Perhaps he is there, perhaps they are together again, perhaps it will all be well," she said hopefully.

"I don't know. I'll watch the papers. If you see anything in the papers about Dimitre or Isolde, will you tell me?"

She nodded, yes. "I will watch the Spanish papers also. Papa and Marcos read all the time, mostly the sports!" and her face lit up, she smiled. "I wish I had more time to read. Delphine and I used to go into bookstores and try to find books in English, which we would buy and read in Europe, in bed at night. It was so cold!" She shivered expressively. "And so we went to bed early and read and read. Sometimes we found an English newspaper, and could read what was happening at home."

Her arms had crossed her chest, she hugged herself in the warm room as she spoke of the cold. He thought about something.

"Rosita, do you know what body language is?"

She frowned.

"You know, when you dance, in mime, that is a kind of body language, you speak of love, hate, motherly affection, grief, by the way you use your hands and arms."

"Oh, yes, I understand that. That is body language?" She looked up, expectantly, eager to learn.

"Yes. And in business, it can be important. For instance, I have begun to learn when someone is lying to me. Inability to meet my look, a slurring of words, and so on."

"Oh, that is most interesting!"

He loved the sparkle in her face when she absorbed something new to her. "Now, think about this, Rosita. You have seen this Dimitre with Isolde. He seems an honest man, a good dancer—"

"Oh, yes, he is very good. Very absorbed in work, very precise, very caring in how the work goes. When he does not so well, he hits his head afterward, like this—" And she lifted her small fist and hit her forehead again and again. "And we know he is dissatisfied."

"Good. Now think. How does he act with Isolde? Does he care about her?"

Her face crinkled up, she closed her eyes, and thought. He observed her tenderly. Then she opened her eyes, and nodded. "Yes. I think so!" She sounded excited, her eyes glowed darkly. "I am remembering a time in Helsinki when we were so cold, and an engagement was canceled, and Isolde just stood there in the lobby—we were just going out—and she swayed—and Dimitre went over to her. He took her in his arms, so gently, and his one hand went to her head, and he held it—so—like a mother with her small baby, like Elena with one of her littlest." She gestured, as though holding a baby, with one arm about it, and the other hand behind its small head. "No passion, no anger, no shouting. He said not a word. He just held her."

"And Isolde?"

"She—sort of shivered. It was so cold in the lobby, I remember, someone had opened the door and the cold wind swept inside, and the snow blew in, and Delphine and I held our coats about ourselves, and Isolde put her head down on his shoulder for a moment. She never was demonstrative in public, we were so surprised. Then Dimitre said he would telephone around, and we went back to our rooms."

"And were there other occasions?"

She nodded, eager now. "I can remember, now that you

have said this. Times when we were tired, and the ballet was an hour late—the further south you go in Europe, the later events are scheduled, and sometimes they did not seem to care if something started on time or not. And Isolde would be angry, because we were all getting stiff. Dimitre would make a joke, and hold her hand, or put his arm on her shoulders, and whisper to her. And she would relax and smile, even laugh. They were good with each other.''

Her small face sobered, she sighed. "Yes, they were good with each other," she said again. "That is why it was such a shock when one morning Isolde came and said Dimitre had left us. We did not see him again. He just walked out!"

"And you all came home," he said. She nodded.

"Umm." She rubbed her cheek with a tired gesture, remembering. "I phoned for reservations before Isolde could change her mind," she said with a little grimace. "Delphine and I were so tired of running all over Europe. We wanted to go home. So I made reservations and we started to pack."

"And you came home to me," he said, with a smile, his eyes keen on her face.

She flushed, a tint of rose coming up in her golden cheeks. She had quickly acquired a new tan, from hours on the beach, he thought. "We came home," she said, her dark eyes evasive.

He stood up. She stood also, gracefully, accepting his hand up. She came up with a spring, he clasped her hand firmly, as she would have drawn it away.

He drew her closer to him. He thought to kiss her silky cheek, it looked enticing. He bent, brushed his lips against her face, down the cheek to her chin. Her mouth was very close, sensuously full, rosy, parted slightly. His mouth went to it, and pressed on it.

He felt her stiffen in shock. It roused something in him, the masculine quality of excitement in pursuit. His arm slid about her to hold her firmly. She tried to press away from him, her fists clenched on his chest. His hand went up to her neck, he held her head in place for his caresses. His mouth pressed more deeply into her soft one, taking charge of the silky warm lips.

He felt the resistance shuddering through her slim body. Rosita was not accustomed to this, he knew her innocence with his mind, and now with his body. The little body was virgin, she had known only dance partners, not lovers. She tried to turn her head away, his hand on her neck tightened.

Zach felt a strange burning inside, a flame starting up inside him. This time his mind did not stand aside, and watch with cool amusement as a practiced woman welcomed him. His mind and body were one, burning, wanting, eager, the desire taking charge. His arm slid lower, he held her close to his thighs, as she tried to bend back. She was so much shorter, he could feel her small breasts pressing against his lower chest. He half-lifted her off her feet, she dangled, helplessly as he kissed her again.

The stiffness seemed to melt against him, her fists relaxed and became small palms tentatively against his chest. As she resisted less, he gentled. His lips went to her neck, her shoulder revealed by the rounded leotard.

He lifted his head to look down into her face. Her dark eyes had closed, her rosy mouth was opened as though she had been drinking nectar, and was half-delirious with the pleasure. Her cheeks were flushed deeply under the golden tan. She lay against him, accepting his closeness to her, helpless to fight the attraction. Her yielding wakened tenderness in him, and he handled her more softly.

He held her against him, and his lips met hers again. How sweet she was, how baby-soft and silky against his mouth, how light and supple her body on his. He wanted her completely.

But Rosita was innocent. He forced himself to hard control, and kissed her once more lightly. Then he let her slide down his long body, until her feet once more touched the floor, *en pointe*, he realized as one hand released her neck, the other still lightly supported her. On toes, then on her feet, flat, so she was facing his chest.

His finger caressed her warm cheek. Her head was down,

she could not look at him, embarrassed. She put up her hands, and pushed him away. A light touch, a fairy touch, he didn't have to accept it, but he did.

"You are—very sweet to kiss, Rosita," he said, softly. "I shall want to do that again."

There was no answer. He finally left the room, turned back once to see her drooping form, the head bent, the ponytail over her shoulder.

Zach went down the winding iron stairs lightly, his hand on the white railing, until he reached the patio. Only then did the music begin again in the studio. And he smiled.

He went out to the amber brown Cadillac, and set out for work. It was ten o'clock, the traffic was lighter, and he made good time around the bay, to the brilliant buildings shining in the sunlight, beside the blue waters. He parked in the shade, and strode into the building, welcoming its coolness. It was only a couple of days until July, the full hot summer was on them.

He had been unable to turn his mind to work on the way. His lean body still burned from the contact with Rosita's softness, her slim limbs brushing against his legs, her hips pressed to his, the soft breasts just rounding to womanhood against his chest, he had felt the little nipples peaking in desire. God, how sweet she was, how marvelous to touch—if only he could be the one to teach her the wonders of fulfilled desire!

In the hallway, he finally turned his mind fiercely to work. He had had an idea, a new rum, not lime, but a coffee liqueur. Coffee mixed well with many drinks, another rum maker had tried it, but Zach had a new idea for that. A mild flavor, a good French drip coffee, not enough to overwhelm the rum, but blending with it, it would take many experiments to get it just right— He had thought of it last night when Sonia had poured brandy into her hot coffee.

Madame Sonia was a continental to her fingertips, she had exquisite taste, she had dined with the finest gourmets and the most regal of families and beaux. She had been everywhere in Europe and America, she had been wined and dined and feasted, men had drunk champagne from her size five slippers.

She rarely ate or drank much, but what she did must be of the best quality. Her small nose would turn up at a poorly prepared meal, a poor type of wine or brandy or rum. Zach often had her taste one of his experiments; he could tell by her reaction whether it would be good. Some perfume men had a "nose," she had a "mouth," as Zach teased her. He did also, but he liked to have her confirmation.

And she liked brandy or rum in her coffee.

He grew more and more excited about his idea during the evening, and had gone to bed late writing down his ideas for it. He strode down the hall to his office, thinking about it now. He would talk to Kevin and to Aunt Hortense—

His door was open. Sarita, looking troubled and intense, stood at her desk. Kevin was there also, alert—his solid calm face was unusually flushed.

"What is it?" asked Zach at once. Kevin shook his head, put his finger to his lip. Sarita handed Zach a note.

The note read:

Say nothing. Your Lincoln is bugged and so is your office. I'll show you, then we can talk briefly in the hall. Kevin.

He looked at them both; it was like a punch in the ribs. He nodded toward his office, Sarita closed the door and followed them into the inner office.

Kevin pointed to a small gray wire leading down from a picture on the wall, a portrait of red-haired Morgan Hamilton, who had founded the family so long ago, on the island of Elysia. His keen stare met Zach's every day as Zach worked at the desk which had been his father's, and his grandfather's before them.

Kevin gently moved the gold frame out from the wall, pointed. Zach came around him, looked up. A small white device was stuck on the back of the portrait. He reached up angrily for it, Kevin shook his head vigorously.

They went out to the hall, all three of them. Kevin spoke softly, "I noticed it on your car this morning, the Lincoln you usually drive." His brown eyes glittered. "I turned on the radio, there was a slight interference. That bothered me, I stopped at a garage of a fellow I know, and pulled in, and worked on the radio. I found a recording device inside. I left it there. I came to the office, decided to look around. Found that inside. Pretty obvious, and hurriedly applied.''

Zach rubbed his head. Kevin was so sure of his facts, always, he never rushed into anything. This alarming news stunned him.

"How did you notice that?" he asked. "In the car, I mean? I have driven it since we got it—when—"

"I used it four weeks ago, I didn't notice anything then," Kevin said. Sarita had said nothing, only listening with big dark eyes that made Zach think of Rosita. "At the university, I used to hang out with a fellow who wanted to work for the government as a spy. He was always going around trying to fit bugs on things. When he bugged my bedroom I drew the line, but he told me he had put it in six months before I noticed it. He did terrific work, I asked him how, and we used to talk about it. Cocktails with toothpicks that recorded conversations, in imitation olives, little radios, tape recorders no bigger than a match box or a lighter, things to put in a telephone which would carry a conversation for more than a mile with nothing but a receiver at the other end.''

"Is my phone bugged?" Zach asked sharply.

Kevin nodded his head. "I checked."

"And people were free to wander in and out of the offices for months, until you stopped it, Zach,'' said Sarita. "Anybody could have come in and done it. Anybody you know, that is. Only the family and close friends came into your inner office.''

Both men stared at her. She nodded emphatically.

"Then—you are saying—that someone in the family, or working here, or a close friend—was the one who put the bugs in the office," said Zach slowly.

His mind was racing, so was Kevin's, obviously.

"Yes. And why?"

"The new ideas for rum, probably," said Zach. "And to think I was going to have a meeting about them in my office this afternoon!"

"You've got an idea?" Kevin asked alertly.

"Yes, but now I don't want to talk," said Zach bitterly. He rubbed his head. "God. What a mess. Damn them to hell! Bugging us—and it must be someone working here, involved with the company—or a family member— What the hell do they want from me, blood? Is someone trying to wreck the company? They will bring us all down! This money is the income for all of us, aside from some stocks in a few other places. It is our life, our fortune! We have enough trouble, without our secrets being sold!"

They were both silent, listening. Someone's office door down the hall opened, Uncle William peered out curiously to stare at them.

"I best go to the lab," said Kevin, in a low tone. "We can talk at home—at least, after I check the study!"

Zach did not smile. "Yes, you had best do that. Kevin, go home early and check the house, check it thoroughly. Get help from someone on it, if you need, someone you can trust. I want all the bugs taken out of the house! They can stay in the office for a time, we just won't talk freely here. But, God, I have to talk somewhere!"

"Right. I'll get to it this afternoon. I take it we won't be meeting about the new ideas you have," added Kevin wryly.

"Damn right! I'll say nothing here."

They went back to their offices. All the pleasure in the day had died in Zach. He stared at the portrait of his ancestor, Morgan Hamilton, and the straight blue gaze seemed to stare right back.

How much was revealed? Who had planted the bugs? How much had been recorded? Had they listened in on his private conversations—of course they had! Business and his talks with Melinda, and his mother, with whoever had telephoned, with whatever concerns he dealt with. They would know how many bottles had been made, how many kegs of wood ordered from Kentucky whisky distilleries, the estimate of sales. He had discussed everything, the advertising campaigns in the United States and how well they had done, the ideas for the next campaigns, the lime liqueur which had not worked—everything! If someone in the company was doing this, it must be someone who feared Zach had ideas he would not share. That was a puzzle.

He had almost revealed his new idea for the coffee liqueur! Damn, how close that had been! He scowled at the portrait, and Morgan Hamilton stared back blandly.

"Who the hell," muttered Zach, and then remembered that he should not even talk out loud to himself!

He decided he could not live with the bugging. When Kevin came around again at noon, he had his brother remove the bugs from the portrait and from the telephone. They searched the office, Zach inexpertly, and found another bug in Sarita's telephone. Kevin removed that also. At least they were clean now, but someone who listened would know they had discovered the devices and removed them. What would they do next?

Chapter 11

Delphine lay back on the hot sand, under the shelter of the huge yellow umbrella, and relaxed. She felt so good. When she thought of the cold days and nights in Europe, the long hours of practice and dancing when she was so cold she could scarcely feel her feet, they were so numb, she shivered. Never again! Somehow she must get out from Isolde's control.

Zach and Kevin were busy with the factory. Her mother had retired into a numb gray world, and not even having the girls home seemed to bring her out. She had had a mild stroke a year after their father died, and had been slow to recover. The doctor had not been surprised, he had said, "It often happens this way. She is young enough, she may come out of this. But when a loved husband and partner dies, the will to live frequently dies with it. She must have a new reason for living."

"Aren't we enough?" asked Delphine spiritedly, and Zach had put his arm about her.

"Patience, little one," he had said quietly. "We will bring maman out of her grief one day."

But they were all so busy, and nobody seemed to care enough. Even Grandmother Sonia would sit with idle hands, gazing into space, before sighing heavily and picking up her current embroidery project.

It was a house of quiet soul-numbing grief, and Delphine could not endure it. She lay abed late, and practiced with Rosita only every two or three mornings. She was sick of practice, sick of ballet, sick of dancing with fervor when she felt like playing. Her school friends had gone on to college, or married, or had interesting jobs—one was in newspaper work, another in television.

What was in the future for her? Delphine stared into space and saw nothing. She had never been allowed to date, she had stormed that Isolde was more strict than her mother!

Well, things were going to change, she promised herself that sunny Sunday afternoon.

Instead of remaining home, she had gone to Rosita's house with her. She had risen early, they had gone to Mass together in the Cathedral, and then Marcos had come for them. Zach had said all right, absently, and her mother was in her room with the shades darkened.

The house of Rosita's family was in an old section of town, the paint was freshly whitened, everything nailed neatly in repair. It was a big house, not grand like the Hamilton's, but pleasant, the rooms tiny and old, and Rosita's former room in the attic entranced Delphine. Everyone was so close! The unmarried men and boys had a dormitory-type room. Two of the married couples lived there, and Cristina and her husband came often. And the house burst with small children!

She sat up as one of the children crawled near to her. The little girl held up her arms, and Delphine smiled at her and drew her into her arms tenderly. What a soft plump body, what big dark eyes and curly dark hair! She was an adorably pretty child, one of Tadeo's and Inez's. And several of Elena's were playing nearby, absorbedly digging in the sand with pails, buckets, little shovels, giggling and shoving and singing and talking.

The little girl she held was sleepy with the sun and the picnic food they had eaten. She curled up on Delphine's knees, and leaned against her, her thumb went to her rosy baby mouth, she sucked lustily, then fell asleep against Delphine's breast. Elena glanced at her, smiled.

"If she is heavy, put her down, it will not disturb her," she said softly.

"She is not heavy, she is so sweet," Delphine said. One hand brushed back a long curl from the eyes. Silky and dusky hair, beautiful face, firm chin, she would be a little beauty when she grew up.

They all looked after each other's babies. It had taken her a while to remember all their names, and who belonged to whom, for all went promptly to an aunt as readily as to a mother, to an uncle or older cousin as to a father. And they vied to go to Grandpapa Pascual, tall, handsome and distinguished.

Her gaze went curiously now to a small group standing nearby. Oliverio was seated on the sand, softly strumming his guitar with his skilled long fingers, his head bent over the instrument. Pascual was directing four of the others, Tadeo and Inez, Rosita and Marcos.

They were composing a new dance for the four. They called it "Shadowplay." It would add interest to their night-club act, Pascual had decided. Delphine had discovered that Rosita went out every night of the week to join them and dance. She had said nothing, but she longed to join them, and one night she would! She could just watch, and help backstage, as she had done that summer a couple of years ago.

Pascual motioned to Inez. "Now, you will first do this movement, turning three times, then to Tadeo. Then Rosita, you will begin just as Inez is finishing, turn three times and go to Marcos."

They walked it through slowly, then went on to another move, and another. Within half an hour they were dancing it through, slowly, as Oliverio played slowly.

"Good, good, rest now, and then we will do it again, faster," said Pascual, with satisfaction. He went to sit beside his wife, Margarita, and bent to kiss her cheek. "You feel well, yes?" he murmured tenderly.

Rosita came to sit down beside Delphine. "You are not bored?" she whispered anxiously.

Delphine gave her a quick loving smile. "Bored? In your big beautiful family? Never!"

One felt the warmth of them just being there. Marcos did not sit down, but went to pitch a beach ball slowly to one of the little boys, and two others ran to join in. Felipe with his big mischievous eyes was darting about, teasing his mother Inez to come in the water with him. He was six, his little sister was three. When she refused lazily to go into the water, Tadeo rose and took his hand.

"Come, my son," he said in Spanish, "we will wash off some of your sand and your lively spirits in the water!"

Those nearby laughed, and Felipe shrieked with pleasure and ran into the water with Tadeo. He bounded into a wave, flung handfuls of water at his father, until he was picked up and hugged by Tadeo, and let go, to swim farther out.

Delphine watched them with a smile. Rosita lay back, and rested, her slim body relaxed on the sand. She was still tired, Delphine thought she did too much, but the exhaustion was gone, her face calmed. She was acquiring a golden tan once more, her limbs and uncovered shoulders and face were glowing with health and sunshine. So much better than last winter, when they had all been pale and drawn, with black shadows under their eyes.

Oliverio was still playing, idly, dreamily, making up a tune. The sun was warm, the blue sea rippled like shot silk. Families nearby were finishing their luncheon, stretching out, drinking or swimming. It was a crowded beach, but so bright and happy. She heard someone's laugh ring out, a shout of teasing, another burst of laughter. How much better than the dark glum house, though she felt guilty at thinking so.

Rosita was half-asleep, her head on her curled arm, under the yellow umbrella. Under the red umbrella, Inez lay sleeping. Elena was murmuring to her mother, and Jacinto had gotten his guitar and was playing with Oliverio, softly, murmuring about the melody, arranging as they played so that Oliverio took the tune at times, and Jacinto at others. Delphine loved it. It was such a beautiful sensuous experience to lie with her toes in the sand, the baby on her breast, the melody rippling about her, the sun warming her.

Drowsiness of midafternoon fell on them. Marcos and one of the boys stopped playing, and dropped where they stood, to curl up and sleep a while. Rosita was deeply asleep. Tadeo waded in with Felipe, and lay down beside Inez, his hand on her waist, his face turned toward her sleeping face. Felipe seemed to have such restless energy, he jumped and bounded about, trying to find someone to toss a baseball with him. Luisa scolded him softly, "You will wake up your mama, Felipe, be good!" He grinned at her mischievously.

The baby Martina stirred on Delphine's breast, and struggled a little with a nightmare, scowling with her dark eyebrows. Delphine turned, and laid her down gently between herself and the sleeping Rosita. She sat up, stretched and finally stood. She was getting stiff, she would swim a little while.

She ran down to the water, lovely and trim in the one-piece blue suit which was smart this year. Bikinis were not favored on the Spanish-style beaches, and she had worn this new suit. It was flattering on her figure, anyway. Rosita was so pretty in her yellow one, which matched Delphine's in style.

She waded out into the warm surf, and struck out with her arms briskly. She loved to swim, she was good at it, her father and Zach had seen to that. She swam out a ways, then turned to lie on her back, dreamily. Her blond hair was tied up, she hated swim caps, and anyway, she would always wash her hair when she got home after a swim.

She turned in the water, sensing someone near her. "Felipe," she said reproachfully. "Does your papa know you are here?"

He gave her a gap-toothed smile, and shook his head. "Everybody's asleep. I can sleep at night," he said. He swam away from her, then around in circles. "I had some lemonade," he giggled, "and it was icy and cold! Mama said no, but she went to sleep," and he laughed.

"Oh, Felipe, you are a caution," she sighed, but had to laugh. He was so full of pep and trouble.

He swam away from her, confident in the water, striking

out. She decided to follow, he was swimming away from the beach, and very few people were in the water in this hot midafternoon. She swam with easy strokes, enjoying the sun on her tanned skin, the coolness of the water as they went out further.

Then suddenly she heard a choking cry, saw a little hand up in the water, and Felipe went under. Delphine did not even have time to think, she swam after him, dived, and grabbed at the arm. She missed, went under again, grabbed again, and caught him by the leg. He was tumbling over and over in the water.

She pulled him up, held his head above the water. He was choking, sputtering, his face turning a funny shade. His eyes bulged with terror and the choking of the water he had swallowed. He began to struggle, fighting her. She could scarcely hold him.

She caught him behind the head, held him with his back against her, so his flailing arms could not hit her and knock her out. She began to tug him to shore, glancing there to make sure of her direction. Someone on shore was standing, she raised one arm and shouted. "Help! Help!" Then she concentrated on keeping Felipe above water, and trying to get in the right direction. His little legs were kicking wildly, then more feebly as he weakened.

Delphine began to weaken. She was strong enough for herself, but holding a fighting terrified child was almost too much. She concentrated on keeping them both above water. Someone was coming. She could see the strong arms flailing the water, the strong tanned legs kicking. She relaxed and tried to soothe Felipe. "Calm, dear, calm! Someone is coming for us. Calm yourself, Felipe!"

He was sobbing, choking, fighting. She could not hold him much longer. Then Marcos was there, his anxious face appearing in the water beside hers. She gave Felipe to him thankfully, and took a deep heaving breath.

"Felipe! You be quiet or I will hit you!" Marcos's stern voice had more effect than Delphine's soothing one.

The boy calmed a little, sobbing, and clung to Marcos

with his arms about the older man's neck. Marcos gave Delphine an admiring look from his warm brown eyes. "How are you? Hold on to my shoulder, and I will tow you in."

"I'm—all—right," she panted. "I can—make it—"

"Do as I tell you!" he said sharply. "Catch hold of my shoulder!"

She responded to the masculine authority with limp relief. She put one hand on his hard muscular shoulder, felt the strength of it, and relaxed in the water. He began to swim, with the limp Felipe hanging on his neck, Delphine on his shoulder, moving them to shore.

Several of the Dominguez were standing up, peering out at them. A man shouted, then ran to the water, and began to swim toward them. Another followed. Soon they were surrounded by four of the men, and Tadeo took Felipe from Marcos. Marcos turned to Delphine in the water and said, "Turn on your back, I'll take you in."

Gratefully, she turned over, and lay back while he put his hand under her chin firmly, and began to tow her. He swam easily, more slowly now, no desperate movements.

They came to the shallow water, he stood up, so did she, and he reached out his brown hand to take hers. She felt it clasp her slim brown hand, firmly, warmly, comfortingly. They walked in behind the others, and came up on the sand, where Tadeo had Felipe on his stomach, pumping water out of him.

Felipe gagged, cried out, vomited, got rid of seawater and lemonade and some food. Then he cried in his mother's arms.

He was not spanked. His father spoke to him firmly, sternly, but with warmth and understanding in his tone. Then he picked up Felipe, wrapped him in a blanket, and strode to the car, with Inez and the other children following.

"We had best go home also," said Marcos, turning to Delphine. He still held her hand. He stared down at her. "And I thought you were just a little pretty girl, a decorative flower for some man's lapel," he began to smile, mischief in his dark eyes, so like Felipe's.

Delphine smiled, her mouth trembled, she shivered with

cold and reaction. Rosita came up with Delphine's blue terrycloth dress and wrapped it about her, then held her close.

"Oh, Delphine!" she cried. "Oh, Delphine—if anything had happened to you . . ."

Marcos put an arm about each of them. "To the car," he said. "Jacinto, their blankets and gear—eh? We'll meet you at the house!"

Jacinto nodded, his brown face warm and relieved. He and Oliverio organized the children into picking up all the balls and blankets, the picnic baskets, the thermoses and umbrellas, and followed the others to the cars.

Delphine's shoulders felt warmer with Marcos's arm about them, and she felt his warm tanned wet body against hers.

Marcos drove, with Delphine between him and Rosita, four of the children in the back. He drove well, casually, easily, and Delphine watched the brown hands on the wheel, the dark hair on the back of his hands, the strong wrists. He was all muscle and hard strength, and so reassuring.

At the Dominguez house, Delphine went up to the attic bedroom with Rosita, where they had left their summer dresses. They showered, dried their hair, dressed. Delphine still shivered, as she thought of what might have happened. She might have drowned, so might have Felipe.

She slipped into her blue print dress with the yellow hibiscus flowers dramatically spilling over the print. She brushed her hair back, into a long blond ponytail, and tied it with a matching blue ribbon. Rosita was in her rose cotton, her feet bare but for thin sandals, her hair tied back with a rose ribbon.

Their eyes met. "Thank you, Delphine," said Rosita soberly. "Dear God, we must go to Mass tomorrow morning, and thank the Virgin for your safety, and Felipe's. It was too close."

"Yes, I will, I know it was close. Mama must not know."

Rosita looked troubled. She said slowly, "She might not want you to come with us again. But your family should know—"

Delphine looked away. "Then I'll tell Zach," she said, and crossed her fingers behind her back. She didn't want to tell anybody, even Zach, for he might prevent her from coming again with Rosita, and she could not bear that. "Besides, it won't happen again," she said more cheerfully. "I'll be on guard with that little imp!"

They went down to the large front room, a combined living and dining area. The long table was being set buffet style, there was no room for them all to sit about the table, so on Sundays when all gathered, they used the buffet. Plates and napkins and forks at one end, then all along the two sides were huge steaming bowls of food. Delphine sniffed hungrily.

First a huge pot of black bean soup to be spooned into bowls, and covered with a generous sprinkling of raw onions. Then a platter of meat loaf, rich with spices, onions, tomatoes, green peppers. Some of the children sliced it and put it between slices of brown bread, for sandwiches, which they munched as they sat on the front steps of the house.

Pots of steamed corn on the cob, green beans and bacon, cooked apples with cinnamon and nutmeg. Platters of cheese of several kinds, crackers and bread, slices of yellow cake; a large bowl of mixed fresh fruit: pineapple, apple, oranges, bananas, mangoes, passion fruit.

Delphine ate hungrily, Marcos had filled her plate. She sat on the porch steps beside one of the little girls, and he sat down on her other side.

She glanced up at him, she felt more calm now. "I want to thank you," she said.

His dark eyes met hers, and she felt a shock at the blaze in them. "Later," he said. "I will take you home with Rosita. We will talk then."

She blinked. He was gazing deeply into her eyes, his handsome strong face was unsmiling. She had to look away, shyly. A thrill was going through her, a strange, unfamiliar thrill. This was Marcos, whom she had known casually for years. Yet all of a sudden this afternoon he seemed a stranger.

The children were a little subdued, the adults talked more quietly than usual. Elena scarcely ate, hugging her smallest baby, her Madonna face brooding. Death had come so close that sunlit afternoon.

Presently Oliverio brought out his guitar, and began to

play. Margarita listened for a time, then she began to sing, and Elena to sing with her. Their beautiful plaintive voices rang into the evening air, some of the neighbors sitting on their steps, smoking or eating, grew quiet to listen.

Marcos took Delphine's plate away, returned to lounge beside her on the grass of the front yard. Rosita was leaning back against her father's knee, he was stroking her head slowly, her eyes were closed.

Delphine felt a little thrill as Marcos sought her hand in her full blue cotton skirts, and held it. Unexpectedly his voice joined in the singing, it was something about home and loneliness and the winter that follows summer.

Oliverio finished with a long stroke of his hand. "Too sad," said Pascual briskly, "Play the one about the donkey."

The children chimed in, laughing. "Yes, the donkey, the donkey!"

So he played the gay donkey serenade, and the children imitated the sounds, and they all laughed and sang lustily. Some of the neighbors children wandered over, and sang also.

They sang and talked a little, and sang again. And they were quiet while Jacinto and Oliverio played their guitars, making the silken dark blue night throb. Delphine had never felt so happy. This afternoon, possible death in the bright blue waters. Tonight, warmth and closeness of a loving family, song, and Marcos's hand holding hers as the stars came out.

About nine, Pascual said, "Enough, to bed for the children."

Rosita decided she must go home and sleep, she was almost asleep against her father's knee. She kissed them all, one after the other, and they hugged her and said, *"Hasta mañana,* Rosita!" Alejandra held her long, the aged arms quivering.

And they kissed Delphine also; she started by kissing Felipe, and Martina, and the other children, and pretty soon she was kissing Mama Margarita, and Elena and Cristina and Inez and Luisa, and then a kiss on the cheek for each man in turn. She came to Marcos, his lips were warm and lingering on her cheek. Then they went to the car, and he put their gear in the back, and tucked both girls in the front.

He took them home, not saying much. He drove into the side driveway, and Jaime came out, pistol in his belt. Marcos got out, greeted him and came around to help the girls out. This time, he escorted them around the back hallway, and into the darkened patio.

Rosita kissed Marcos, and said, "Thank you, my most dear Marcos, for my Delphine."

He squeezed her, and let her go. She started up the stairs, turned to look for Delphine. "Go ahead," said Marcos, in a quiet tone. "I will speak to Delphine."

Rosita hesitated, then nodded, and went on up to the third floor. Her skirts fluttered in the slight breeze as she disappeared in the glass doorway.

Delphine was waiting, her face upturned. Marcos was so—so exciting, so handsome, so all male. Yet so kind, so good, so gentle—so wonderful with the children, so dependable—

She gazed up at him. His face was dark in the moonlight, little light spilled into the patio, only that of the two electric-lit lanterns. Flowers gave out subtle fragrance, and a bird chirped sleepily in the hibiscus bush in the corner.

"How do I say thank you for Felipe?" said Marcos, and put his big hands on her shoulders. "Such a small girl, such a lot of braveness in that beautiful body." His voice shook a little. "If I had not seen you both—"

"How do I say thank you for Felipe, and for me?" she murmured, a little roguishly. She felt so melting with emotion, so glad to be alive, so excited at his presence—

He smiled, she saw the slash of his white teeth, as he bent. "Thank me," he said.

She put her slim arms slowly about his shoulders. She had done this in the dance, sometimes she had been momentarily thrilled when the man was handsome and she felt some emotion toward him. But this was real, not a dance—

Their lips met. And she felt a deep shock. She thought, of a sudden, "My life is going to change—right now—it will never be the same again!"

Their mouths clung, he held her more tightly against him, she felt his lean strength all down her slim supple body. He held her more closely, and his mouth seemed to drink from hers. Long, long moment, and they clung. Her hands tightened on the hard muscular upper arms, his hands were locked at the slim back.

"Dios!" she heard him mutter, then his mouth came down on hers once more. He drew her back further into the shadows of the patio, and she clung more desperately, wild with the emotion welling up in her, the unfamiliar sweet strange emotion he brought out in her, she had never felt it before, it was so different, so overwhelming, so shocking and honey-sweet—

He drew a deep shuddering breath, and drew back.

"I must go. *Dios,* but you are beautiful!" In the moonlight, he took her face in his hands, studied it with the piercing gaze of a lover, and kissed her forehead.

She felt the unbearably soft touch, and her hands touched his hard wrists. They stood there, silently, in the darkness, and they knew. They belonged together.

They could not cope with the knowledge, the two young lovers who had never loved before. Love had flamed up so quickly between them, after years of casual friendship.

She stepped back. "I—I will see—you—next Sunday?" Next Sunday, so far from now—so many many hours stretching out before they would meet again—

"Next Sunday," he said. "You will come with Rosita—"

"Yes—yes, Marcos."

He touched her face with his fingers softly. Then he took her hand, and led her to the stairs. She mounted them, still clinging to his hand, until at the fourth step she had to let his fingers go—what pain to let him go—

He watched her go up the stairs. At the second floor, she turned, she could just make out his face, his white shirt, below her in the patio. She put one hand to her lips, and blew a kiss to him. He caught it, she saw his hand go to his mouth, and he blew the kiss back to her. She caught it, hugged it with both hands to her yearning breasts.

174

The next Sunday finally arrived. Delphine dithered, and finally put on a ruffled blue cotton, because Rosita said it was the color of her eyes. She tied back her red gold hair, that had been sunburned to almost blond, and was ready.

Marcos met them, and his quick smile and deep look told her he too had counted the hours. They went to the beach, and sat on the sand, and talked.

Everyone paired off, and talked, or they sat in a circle and talked, or sang. And they danced, barefoot on the sand, practicing routines.

Delphine learned that Marcos was unhappy in the dancing, much as he loved it. She watched the strong brown hand pile up a little hill, and smooth it out again, as he talked.

"I went to the university for a time, but we could not afford to have me continue," he said simply. "And I wanted so much to be a chemist, not like Cristina's husband, you understand, to work in a pharmacy and make up prescriptions. I want to be a real chemist, to work at creating new things." His handsome tanned face was flushed, his dark eyes studied her to see if she realized what his ambitions meant to him.

"How far did you go?" she asked anxiously. "One year, two?"

He shook his head. "I have only the equivalent of about one and a half years," he said sadly. "And I took mostly mathematics and chemistry, to prepare. I am so far from graduating—it will be years, trying to take one class each morning, and dancing until two the night before— It is impossible. Oh, well," he shrugged and smiled. "It is not so bad a life, to dance. It is my heritage, I am a Gypsy."

Both felt instinctively that they must not be seen much together. Both families would try to stop them. Already Father Pascual was peering at them with worry. Delphine jumped up and ran into the water, splashed around. Inez came out, swam with her, talked about Felipe and how subdued he was for a while, and how grateful she was. And Rosita swam with her.

Moments together had to be stolen, and it made their romance all the more exciting. In the darkness, Marcos would

175

hold her hand. Or he would bring her a bit of *tortilla* with cheese on it, and tip it into her lips, laughing, as though joking with her, his fingers brushing her mouth in a secret message. In the water, sometimes, those radiant summer Sunday afternoons, they swam farther out, and held hands in the water, and looked at each other.

When he brought Rosita home from the dancing in nightclubs, sometimes Delphine waited in the shadows of the patio. Rosita would say good night, and after she had gone inside, Delphine would slip out and whisper, "Marcos?"

And he would come to her, in silence, and hold her, and their lips would meet with excitement and desperation, because it had been such a long time, so many hours, since they had last kissed.

Delphine and Marcos did not talk about the difficulties that surrounded their love. It was an enchanted summer, and they did not want to talk about problems.

He did say he was unhappy about the dancing in flamenco, that he wanted to return to the university. She did tell him on the sunny afternoons on the beach that she dreaded the return of Isolde, the probable return to ballet. "For mother does not know what is happening, Zach is too busy, and the others are helpless against Isolde."

"But you love dancing, do you not?"

"Oh, yes, I love it, but it is not my whole life," she said, glancing away shyly from his keen dark eyes. "I want to marry, to have babies—like Elena. That would make me very happy. Of course," and her mouth pursed primly, "I would have to love the man very, very much."

"That is taken for granted," he said soberly, and his strong mouth quirked. "One must love much to endure the bonds of matrimony! A wife can be a shrew!"

She laughed, and flung sand over his lean tanned body, and he wrestled with her, until Pascual said ominously, "Now, Marcos, Delphine is our guest—she is not one of the little boys!"

"I know it well," he muttered to Delphine, and she blushed to the tips of her small ears.

Several of them would practice dancing, and she would watch, and know what Marcos said was true. They did need him in the troupe, and they were a close-knit, loyal family. She would sit with her arms about her tanned knees, and observe how they created a dance, how they worked together, by instinct, from years of living and working together, so that one scarcely needed to speak, they would move as one, or follow the other.

She was so proud of Marcos, his lean grace, his pantherish dancing moves, his proudly held head, his handsome face, his brilliant mind—his loyalty—his goodness. He made no move to try to take her, though some nights when he kissed her she could have melted right into his bones. She was so weak with him, he could have picked her up and lain with her on the hard tiles of the patio, and she would have welcomed the pain and the glory. But he did not, he kissed her deeply, held her gently, and let her go.

And if Pascual looked at them with trouble in his face, and Mama Margarita shook her head and crossed herself, and Rosita watched and wondered—the two young lovers did not see or care. There was a glory around them, in their movements toward each other, their laughter, their speech. Their secret love bloomed in their faces, though they knew it not.

Chapter 12

Zach turned the large amber Cadillac into the driveway and drove slowly back to the garage area with a deep sigh of relief. The August sun had burned mercilessly in his eyes, in spite of the thick sunglasses and sunshade on the car. The drive from Ponce was a murderous one at times, with the traffic heavy, and the twisting, winding roads and switchbacks making some people feel actually sick. He had felt it himself today, the constantly twisting turns and the necessity of changing speeds again and again.

He had been gone three days, he would be glad to be home. The trip had been necessary; he had to talk in person to some men whose sons worked at the rum factory. Was someone stirring up trouble in the factory, or was it just part of a general unrest? The men had been reluctant to talk. He had finally gone to a priest, and discussed the matter. The priest had promised to try to get some answers for him.

He pulled in, got out of the burning hot car. Jaime was not there, he would come on duty later. He greeted the other man, a new one, he noted.

He walked slowly into the patio, was about to turn to go up the staircase with his suitcase, when he saw a lovely sight.

Rosita had turned from contemplation of a hibiscus bush of scarlet flowers, and stood against the bush, in a lovely cotton dress with gathered bodice, narrow straps, full skirt to her knees, brown bare legs, and brief brown sandals.

"Well, you're a pretty sight for tired eyes," he smiled, his spirits lifting up.

She smiled and her whole face lit up. "Zach, you are home early!" She came shyly over to him, and he put his arm casually about her waist. He bent and kissed each cheek, reveling in the warm silky feel. She gazed at him with her large dark eyes, and moved back.

"How are you?" he said, wanting to know. He searched her face, noted with satisfaction that the dark shadows were gone. She bloomed golden with sunshine and health. Her round shoulders were tanned also, and her arms brown. Pink ran up in her cheeks as he stared down at her.

"I'm fine. Did you have a good trip?" He turned her and moved with her clasped in one arm, the suitcase in his other hand, and walked through the patio to the dim cool hallway beyond at the front of the house.

"It was so-so," he said, frowning slightly. She fit just under his shoulder, he liked to feel her soft, slim, rounded body moving with his, though he had to make his steps shorter to accommodate hers. "Troubles—I'll be glad to forget them for a time. What have you been doing?"

"Oh—dancing, practicing—and we had company for luncheon."

Her body was so close to his, he felt the tension in it. "Who was that? Has Isolde returned?"

"Oh, no, she phoned from New York last night and wanted to talk with you, though."

"Must not have been urgent, she did not call me in Ponce. What did she say?"

"Not much, she sounded tired and hot, she said New York is at its very worst in July. I think it is very much worse in August, though!"

"Glad to be here?" He smiled down at her. She nodded

vigorously, and her long dark hair swung in the thick ponytail behind her back. They had come into the dim hallway, he set down his suitcase with a little sigh of relief.

A maid came at once to take the case, and beam at him.

It was midafternoon. He was surprised when his mother's voice called from the formal drawing room. "Zach, is that you, my dearest?"

Her voice sounded more lively. He moved with Rosita to the beautiful golden room, and found the draperies moved back, sunlight spilling in and illuminating the mirrors, paintings, and faded Persian rugs. His mother was seated at the silver tray of coffee and tea. From the cups set about he surmised their guests must have recently departed.

He let Rosita go reluctantly, and bent to kiss his mother's cheeks. "So. You look beautiful, mama!" he approved. She did look well today, in a soft black dress with jet earrings. He moved over to his grandmother, kissed her cheeks. "And Madame Sonia, imperious as ever! I don't know how you escaped the revolutionists, they surely thought you one of the czar's family!"

It was not a joke she appreciated, and she frowned at him. "Truly a dreadful time, Zachariah! I did escape with my ballet costumes, as you know, and my jewels. Speaking of jewels, you should have been here for luncheon!"

"Don't tell me, you were all so hungry you ate the family diamonds!" he joked again. He flung himself down in the large armchair opposite the sofa, and grinned at them all. Rosita hesitated, then sat down gracefully in a straight chair, her ankles crossed like a good child. But her body was no longer that of a child, slim as she was, it was rounded in all the right places, he noted with approval.

"Miss Valdes was here with her fiancé," and Madame Sonia's keen dark brown eyes studied him intently. "Jeronimo was all over her, hugging her and kissing her, even during the meal. A disgusting exhibition before us. We should have set them across the table from each other, Isabeau."

"Modern times, mother," said Isabeau, mildly for her.

She disapproved of demonstrations in public. Her French up-bringing had made her most conscious of etiquette and niceties of society. "They came, Zach, to thank us for the wedding gifts. Also to show off her own, I think. She wore an outrageous display of diamonds and rubies! We could not help remarking it, mother and I, that in our day one never wore diamonds in the daytime. Never. They were reserved for after the sun went down."

"Hear that, Rosita? When I give you diamonds, you must only wear them after sundown," he said, mock-gravely, for the fun of seeing the color rise in her brown cheeks once more.

She shook her head at him. "How you tease," she sighed.

He laughed, and turned back to his mother. "So, did they both seem very happy?" he asked idly. He did not care much. The engagement had come as a shock, he did not realize that Jeronimo and Melinda had even been going out together, let alone contemplating marriage. It must have happened very suddenly that summer. He wished them joy of each other, but did not expect it. Melinda was a selfish girl, intent on pleasure. Of course, Jeronimo liked his pleasure very much—perhaps that was the bond.

"Yes, yes, laughing all the time, teasing each other. Melinda showed us the diamonds and rubies carefully, and told us about the long strands of pearls that Jeronimo had given to her to wear at the wedding. In the Cathedral, Zach, in just two weeks."

"What a haste," said Madame Sonia, thoughtfully. "It makes one wonder if they have anticipated the marriage."

"Mother!" said Isabeau, reprovingly. "Not before the child!" She glanced at Rosita.

"I think this child has grown up. Eighteen, going on nineteen, right, Rosita?" said Zach. "But it does no good to gossip, and I am tired. I'll check my study—did Sarita bring my letters to sign, and the mail?"

"Yes, dear, she came at ten o'clock, I believe," said his mother. "I gave the material to the maid, and she set it in your study, she said."

"Good. I'll go back there, and do an hour of work or so, then I'll take a good Spanish siesta. The light on the road was blinding today. Rosita, would you be so kind, ask a maid to bring me a sandwich and a pot of black coffee?''

"Of course," and she rose quickly, to go to the kitchen.

"A nice child," said Madame Sonia, smiling to herself. She picked up her needlework. "So good and kind, so willing to be of use. We have been talking of my old days, the ballet years, and she is so patient in her listening!"

"She loves your stories, mother, so do we all," said Isabeau, sounding reproving somehow. Zach gave them both a long, thoughtful look. The two women were both so perceptive, so sensitive to relationships. They had made him somewhat perceptive also, and he liked to talk things over with Madame Sonia, she was so shrewd. She had had to be, to remain alive and out of reach of the many lovers who would have taken her over. The lot of a ballerina in a czarist society had not been an easy one, not if she cherished her virginity. Madame Sonia's proudest boast was that she had been a virgin when she met and married Philip Lothaire in Paris.

Rosita returned, "The tray will be in your study in five minutes, Zach," she said. 'May I help in any other way? Your suitcase to unpack?" she added anxiously.

"No, thanks. I can do that, thank you, *pequeña*." He went out, touching her cheek with a long caressing finger in passing. It was good to be home.

He went back the hallway to the combination library-study where he and Kevin now worked. His father had been in command of that room for so many years, and his father before him. Every time Zach entered it, he felt his father's presence there, as though he watched, guided, guarded.

He walked into the study, stopped still. He glanced from one place to another, the desk, the filing cabinet, the typewriter table, the smaller desk—in shock and incredulous anger.

The room was a chaos. It seemed as though a thunderstorm had swept in, a cyclone! Papers were strewn over the floor, the drawers pulled out, messed about, the usually immaculately neat desk covered with file folders, envelopes, scraps of paper, notes, all in wild disorder.

He yelled, "Rosita, Mother, Madame Sonia, Angelica!"

They all came running, except Madame Sonia, who nevertheless made good time on her ebony and ivory cane. They stood aghast and horrified inside the door, eyes wide, hands out in dismay.

"What in the world—oh, good God in heaven," cried Rosita. "What has happened here?"

Angelica the maid chimed in, berating, exclaiming, bursting with anger at who had dared to make such a terrible mess! Isabeau started to pick up some papers, Zach stopped her.

"No, no, I must call the police," he said more calmly.

"The police! My son!" gasped Isabeau Hamilton. "What can you mean?"

"I mean, this is no windstorm from an open window, this is no idle mischief," he said grimly. "Come out, everyone, I'll lock the door. The police must take fingerprints."

He telephoned the police on another phone, then as they waited he questioned everyone crisply about their whereabouts, who had come that day. He found that Sarita had come about ten, Jeronimo and Melinda about eleven, a florist about eleven-thirty, a friend of Madame Sonia's at twelve for luncheon. Jeronimo and Melinda had departed about two. Rosita had practiced all the morning, until the maid had told her guests were here and Madame Sonia wanted her to come. She had bathed, changed and come downstairs at quarter to twelve, she said.

Kevin had gone to the office at eight-thirty, and was not yet home. The maids had come and gone as usual, to the bakery, one to visit a sick mother, two to early Mass.

The guards were on duty as usual; he went out to question them, just as the police were arriving. He returned, and talked to them.

"Have you had any trouble at the factory?" the older one wanted to know, as they stood in the mussed study.

"Yes, quite a bit," he said. "We are threatened with a strike, not the usual kind. The issue is not money, some want shares of stock as bonuses, and eventually a seat on the board. We have refused, it is now a completely family-run organization."

"Ah—and these letters—" One policeman had discovered the pile of mail that Sarita had brought, and among the letters were three more threatening ones.

They were the usual he had begun receiving about a month before. Crudely pasted on yellow pages were scraps from newspapers, spelling out threats. "If you do not meet demands from us, you will be killed. Your family is not safe. Do not think you fascist capitalists can control us."

The others were in the same vein, pasted on with newspaper words.

Zach took out a file of letters from one drawer and handed it to one man. "More of the same. I have had about two dozen now. And we get telephone calls. Several have come at home now."

They questioned him about that, then about their personal lives. Did he have a personal enemy. "I have not had time to make enemies," he said wearily. "I'm too busy working."

The men smiled in sympathy, and gently questioned the ladies, with Spanish deference. They wrote down notes, while a fingerprint expert arrived and began to work all over the room. Zach asked the ladies to return to the drawing room, and he waited with the men. Kevin returned home, grimaced at the mess.

"Did you tell them about the bugging?" asked Kevin practically.

"No, not yet," he said, and told them. Kevin had invited his expert friend from Washington, D.C., and the man had come down for a holiday and a week of checking their home and offices. "I think he got them all. This was about a month ago."

"Well, since then, you had company," said one man, and gently turned out a landscape painting from the wall.

"God, no," groaned Zach, running a tired hand over his face. They fingerprinted the white bug attached to the painting, and then examined the rest of the office. The telephone had another little bug inside the works; they removed it at Zach's request.

"I guess we'll have to check daily," said Kevin.

"I can come over once a week," offered one policeman, looking thoughtful. "If you will keep a list of all your guests, and I check once a week, we might come up with some idea of when it happens, and who is present."

After they had left, Kevin and Zach and a maid sorted out the pages, and straightened the desks. Zach signed the letters, two would have to be retyped, for dirty marks were all over it, from someone's shoes. The maid shook her head sadly, clucking over the disorder.

When she had gone back to her usual work, Kevin asked Zach, "Did they get anything important?"

"Thank God, no. I had everything still in my head, and it's going to remain there until we get some idea of who is doing this."

"Any ideas?" asked Kevin in a low tone.

Zach shook his head. Yet—something lingered in the back of his mind. Jeronimo, and his high living. How had he been able to afford all those jewels for Melinda Valdes? He knew to a penny the salary he received. His father had some money, but was stingy with it.

He went up, washed, changed to a casual suit, and prayed there would be no guests for dinner. He did not feel scintillating. As he came out, Rosita was just descending the stairs, and he caught up with her, and put a casual hand in her arm. She smiled shyly up at him, her eyes big and anxious.

"You must be very tired now, Zach," she said. "All that mess, just when you come home weary!"

He grimaced. "I've felt better. I could look at you all evening, and not grow tired, though," he teased, giving an admiring look to her.

She was slim and vital in a yellow polished cotton dress of slim princess lines, his pendant on her throat. Yellow high-heeled sandals made her feet even more narrow and dainty. So simple, yet so lovely, her small face glowing and pleased with his compliment.

They finished descending the patio stairs and came down to the tiled floor, near a huge hibiscus bush. He snapped off a yellow flower just spreading its petals, and held her still while he pushed the stem carefully into the braid at the side of her small ear. "There," he said. "A flower for a flower. But it should be a yellow rose. I must tell mother—yellow roses must be planted at once."

"Oh, Zach, how you tease me!" she laughed, a little bubbling gay laugh that surprised and pleased him.

They went on into the hallway, and to the drawing room. Zach said at once, still holding Rosita's arm, "Mother, we must have yellow roses planted at once, to have some for Rosita's hair. Don't you agree?"

His mother glanced up, her face showing her surprise. Madame Sonia was more prompt, "We have a beautiful yellow rose already, Zachariah," she said, with a twinkle in her dark eyes.

"Oh, well done, Madame Sonia!" he laughed, and bowed to her. To his delight, Rosita spread out her skirts in a deep curtsy, her head bent, her hands flirting gracefully. He could not keep from it, he took her nearest hand and kissed it, then showed her grandly to a chair. Her face was flushed with laughter and pleasure.

Delphine ran down the inside stairs, and into the room. "What is the joke, I heard you laughing," she said hopefully. At her bright face, Zach felt a pang. There had not been much laughter lately in this house. No wonder the young girls slipped away so often.

Angelica served the dinner, they talked as they ate, about the possibly strange robbery, for nothing seemed to be missing. Zach said bluntly,

"I think we are going to have more trouble at the plant. Evidently they have some method of obtaining entrance to the house also. I have ordered more guards for the house and plant. And also I want to assign some of the men to be bodyguards for all of you."

There was an outcry, especially from Delphine, her eyes flashing. "I do not need anyone, I am not involved in the company, I do not work there!"

"No, darling, but you own stock," said her mother practically. None of them spoke what was obvious to the men and older women, that the girls would be fine candidates for kidnapping, and holding hostage. They knew Zach would turn heaven and earth to get them back. He set his mouth grimly. He had to protect them, gentle little Delphine, and sweet Rosita.

Rosita spoke up after Delphine had cried out, "I will not need any men to guard me, thank you, Zach. My brothers always guard me well. And I am not at all a member of the family, though everybody is so kind to me."

Delphine saved Zach from putting his foot down. She said stormily, "If I have to, Rosita has to, or I won't!"

Madame Sonia said drily, "I hope that Rosita never has to have all her hair cut off, for Delphine would insist on doing the same!"

They all began to laugh, even Madame Isabeau, and the tone of the conversation lightened. Madame Sonia changed the subject deftly, and began speaking of some dangers in Paris after the Russian Revolution.

After the family dinner, they all went back to the large drawing room. Zach leaned back heavily in a chair, he was dead tired from the journey, and then the shocks that followed. He listened in silence to the conversation, his mind turning over and over what had happened. Rosita slipped away, Delphine with her, and it was only after they did not return that he realized they must have gone to Rosita's family at the nightclub. Little devils, how swiftly they had gotten away! He missed them. A little of the brightness had drifted away from the drawing room, as though the golden lights had been turned down.

With the guards alerted and their numbers increased, there was no more bugging of the phones and office for the next couple of weeks. Zach worked harder than ever, but he kept his new plans to himself, he could trust no one, and no wall or window. There was time, he could wait until after the autumn harvest of sugarcane before setting his plans in motion. Yet he felt impatient at the wait. He had fresh ideas for the new line he wanted.

The marriage of Melinda Valdes and Jeronimo Oviedo in the Cathedral went off without a hitch. Zach sat in their family pew with his family, minus Rosita. She had slipped away that day, and was with her family. He missed her, he frowned slightly as he began to realize how much he missed her when she was not there. She did not usually say much, but she smiled, was alert and interested, and her soft questions could start Madame Sonia on some of her fascinating reminiscences, or Madame Isabeau on hers, to forget the recent sad past. And Delphine laughed more with Rosita, and even Kevin forgot his solid absorption in work, and spoke up. She was a catalyst, he thought, from his chemistry courses, someone who made things happen. A sweet and lovely catalyst, with good results, he thought, with a smile.

Thinking of Rosita, her beauty, her grace, the way she had looked last evening with a red hibiscus in her dark hair, wearing a simple red linen dress at dinner last night, he forgot he was at the wedding of a former girl friend.

Delphine nudged him. "Look at all those jewels, I bet they set Jeronimo back a pretty piece!"

He did look, saw the elaborate white satin dress—in August—in Puerto Rico! And the long strand of glistening pearls, more pearls in her headdress, in the form of a small tiara that could be removed from the veil and used separately another time. Four bridesmaids, in yellow, pink, blue and green. Four ushers, and flowers all over the church.

A very pretty and elaborate wedding. How had the Valdes's afforded it, he thought irrelevantly. Not his business, of course. Yet—yet—Jeronimo was wearing a smart white silk suit, with jewels on his hands.

At the wedding reception in the Valdes home, Zach noted more items, his attention sharpened by Delphine. The engagement ring was a mammoth diamond surrounded by more diamonds, until Melinda's slim hand looked overloaded. She wore a diamond bracelet, and the long strand of pearls, the pearl and diamond tiara. "Vulgar," sniffed Madame Sonia, later. "Half would have done quite well."

Zach commented casually to Madame Valdes about the

charming display of jewels. Her face lit up. "Gifts from the bridegroom," she said proudly, with relief. "He is so very good and generous, our Jeronimo!" She was evidently pleased and relieved also, to have their only daughter married, and so well.

They had champagne and cake, sandwiches and more wine, then departed thankfully as soon as they decently could. Delphine kept darting little looks at Zach, and on the way home, she asked, "Are you grieved at all, darling Zach?"

"Grieved?" he asked absently.

"At the wedding of your girl friend to your best friend!" she said explicitly. "I think you've had a great escape!"

Madame Isabeau and Madame Sonia said at once, "Delphine! You are indiscreet and rude!"

"One does not say such things!" added Madame Sonia, shaking her head. "What have I taught you?"

"To speak the truth," Delphine giggled. Zach laughed with her.

"You're a caution, Delphine," he said indulgently. But he was quiet the rest of the day, and the ladies exchanged significant glances.

However, he was not regretting the loss of Melinda Valdes; he agreed with Delphine that he had had a great escape. But something else did trouble him. Those dresses paid for by the darling bridegroom, kind generous Jeronimo. And all those jewels, on his bride and on himself. Zach thought he had never seen before the immense ruby Jeronimo had worn today.

Where the hell had he gotten the money for all that? He wasn't into drug-trafficking, was he? That was a horrible thought, it made him frown and wonder, turning even more quiet. His good friend Jeronimo was a wild one, but surely not—not so illegal and reckless as that? Drugs were a dreadful business, causing untold horror and human misery. Jeronimo knew that—he could not have gotten into that stuff!

But if not drugs—how had he gotten so much money, so very fast? Or had he bought the jewels on time—and if so, on what surety? It was a puzzle, and Zach could not figure it out, nor did he feel like confiding in anybody else to try to work on it. It would have to remain a puzzle, he supposed. If Jeronimo had gotten deeply into debt, someone like Zach might be called upon to pull him out again, as Zach had done in the past. But not such large amounts—Zach was not about to sink all that into such a venture. He had other worries and responsibilities now.

Chapter 13

Isolde returned in mid-August, and shattered the fragile peace of the Hamilton household. She had not seen Dimitre, she told Delphine shortly, when the girl innocently asked.

"That Russian!" she snapped. "He is impossible! He is such a contradiction, so dynamic, then so—so all Russian melancholy! There is no talking to him!"

She looked fragile enough to break, black smudges under her eyes. Rosita had thought she had on too much mascara, until one morning when she saw Isolde just risen from bed, in her dressing gown. Isolde had paper white skin, and her eyes looked bruised. They told of many sleepless nights, and feverish activity the rest of the time.

She returned to San Juan in time to celebrate Zach's twenty-seventh birthday, on August 12. It was a happy family occasion, with only Rosita present as an outsider. She was not allowed to feel an outsider, she was welcomed, Zach kissed her on her cheeks as he did the rest of the women, when he thanked her for her gift of a silver blue cravat. He pulled off the tie he wore and donned the cravat at once, posing, his red hair standing up in waves, his blue eyes devilish with laughter and mischief.

Then the work began, the following Monday. Isolde scolded

Delphine for having gained five pounds, up to one hundred eleven pounds. She put her on a diet at once, to Delphine's fury. "But I don't want to go back to dancing!" Delphine protested in vain.

"What will you do with your life, be idle, and a parasite? Oh, no, you have too many years of dancing lessons and money put into your career," Isolde said firmly.

"But I don't want—I don't want to continue," Delphine wailed.

"Nonsense, you are just idle and spoiled by the summer."

Delphine tried to protest to Zach, he smiled indulgently and pulled a red gold curl. "It won't hurt you to go back to school to Isolde," he said. "Only don't let her push you too hard."

"He does not understand how strict she is," she wailed to Rosita, rebelliously. "There are no half-measures with Isolde! And she talks of returning to New York in September! Oh, I don't want to start that again, Rosita!"

"Talk to your mother," advised Rosita, troubled for herself. She owed Isolde so much, she could not protest. Isolde had given their family a generous amount as soon as she returned, her mother would have the operation in early October, when there was a bed for her at the hospital, and her doctor returned from vacation. With the money earned this summer, and Isolde's gift, they could pay for it.

"She just pats my shoulder and says a ballerina must have discipline! I tell her I don't want to be a ballerina, and I don't think she believes me!"

Delphine set her mouth. She seemed unusually angry, and Rosita wondered if Marcos had anything to do with this spurt of rebellion. But they had little choice, Madame Sonia approved of their hard work, Madame Isabeau thought it was only natural, because of Delphine's heritage, Zach was too busy with his work, and Kevin knew little about it.

So they set to work, and practiced long hours. Class for two hours in the morning, a small break, then rehearsals, in any ballets they could contrive with just three dancers. Isolde was scouring Puerto Rico for any partners, and made use of two young men who had come on holiday. Then one tried to kiss Delphine when Isolde was out of the room. Both were promptly banished, to Delphine's glee.

"I didn't like them anyway, swarming all over us! They just wanted the money to run out at night and have fun with their women!" she said.

"Oh, Delphine, they were not bad. And they had worked hard all year."

Delphine turned up her nose. "The very sight of this house, and Mama in her diamonds gave them ideas! Money is evil, Rosita!"

"The lack of it can cause much more evil, and much harm," said Rosita practically, swinging her leg carefully, studying the angle of her foot.

"But the Bible says money is evil."

"No, the love of money is the root of all evil. Not the money itself. Father explained to us that it was the unreasonable greed for it that was evil."

"Oh, well. I didn't like those boys anyway," and Delphine's pretty mouth pouted in discontent.

Isolde was driving Rosita even harder than Delphine. She was feverish, demanding perfection.

"No, no, no, that is not good enough! Try again, listen to the music, and then do five *bourrées* in turn, again, again!"

Rosita wiped the sweat from her face and arms, then obediently did it again and again, until her legs ached, and her small feet hurt. She had good feet, and usually did not mind being *en pointe* for an entire ballet, but now she ached all over, including her feet. And since she was continuing to go out and dance in the nightclub until two in the morning, she was not getting enough sleep and rest. She began to lose weight.

To her credit, Isolde did not know about the night dancing. Rosita thought she would forbid it if she found out. But her family needed her. She was part of several acts, a duet with Marcos, a quartet with Marcos, Tadeo and Inez, a dreamy solo to the music of Oliverio and Jacinto, and her usual solo in the line of dancers.

Also, she and Delphine had formed the habit of having a warm-up in the morning, eating luncheon with Delphine's mother and grandmother, then going out. Marcos would pick them up at one or one-thirty, frequently, and they would go out to the beach for a couple of hours, to swim, rest on the sand, sleep, talk. They could not do this any longer, for Isolde kept them practicing after a meager luncheon.

Rosita's golden tan faded, and she felt tired all the time, after only two weeks of this harsh routine. She had been accustomed to it in New York and Europe, but now she was out of practice. She must get accustomed to it, she told herself, and of course in New York she had not gone out six nights a week to dance vigorously. When they all returned to New York, or went off to Europe, it would be different. But it would be all work and no play for them both. Delphine also looked white and tired, and complained to Zach.

Zach returned early from the office one early September day. Rosita was performing one *pirouette* after another, in a chain across the floor, diagonally. Delphine watched, angrily, her mouth tight, as Zach walked in the door. Her one hand rested lightly on the side *barre*. Isolde was clapping her hands sharply in the beat.

"One—and two—and three—and four—no—no, go back and start again."

Rosita snatched the towel, wiped her soaking head with it, then went back to the corner. Zach hesitated, then leaned against the mirrored wall and watched, without saying a word. She scarcely noticed him just then.

She went back and began again, as Isolde started the music. "One, and two, and three and four and five and six— that is better! You must concentrate more, you must make every turn perfect! Now go back and try again—"

Rosita's legs were trembling with weariness. She had scarcely had a break today. She drew a deep breath, so she would not yell a protest, like Delphine, and went back to the corner.

"Stop," said Zach, and his voice was cold and loud. Isolde whirled on him.

"You are not in command here, Zach!" Her blue eyes flashed with fury, her red gold hair flamed about her face, coming loose in little tendrils from the tight coronet. "If you cannot be quiet, go!"

Rosita stood in the corner, arms out, ready to go, as soon as the music started. Her dark eyes were wide, Delphine wore a little pleased cat grin.

Isolde reached out for the music switch on the stereo, Zach reached out after her, and snapped off the switch again.

"Damn you, Zach, let us alone!" Isolde yelled, her nerves shot. "You attend to your business, and let me attend to mine!"

"The girls are my business," he said calmly. "Look at them, Isolde, they are thin and tired. This is wrong!"

She did not bother to look. "They must be back in condition as fast as possible! We are returning to New York in two weeks, and I want Rosita ready for *Sleeping Beauty* and *Spanish Reverie* as soon as we return. She must, must be ready!"

It was the first Rosita had heard about this. She had never done *Sleeping Beauty*, it would be a whole new ballet to learn. No wonder, the many *pirouettes* and turns. But the thought of leaving San Juan and her family just at this worrisome time of her mother's grave illness disturbed her very much.

Delphine cried out, "New York! No, I won't leave San Juan, and maman. She needs me, she said so. And I don't want to go back to that horrid routine! Getting cold and tired and miserable, just to be on stage!"

"Now, don't start that again!" Isolde's furious voice was dangerously grim. She stared at her young sister. "You have goofed off all summer, and now you rebel at getting into condition! You would waste years of training for your career—"

"I don't want this career! You want it! But I won't be your substitute, and let you make a whipping girl out of me!" Delphine stuck out her soft chin and tried to look completely in control. Rosita looked from one to the other, troubled, not knowing what to say.

"This matter of a career must be discussed, Isolde," said Zach, with more calm now. "Stop for today, I'll take the girls out to the beach for a swim and some sun. Look at them, pale

197

as ghosts, and twice as thin. We must talk this over more calmly later on—I'll stay home tomorrow and we will talk about it.''

"There is nothing to talk about!" Isolde was raving mad, her long hands clenched into fists. "I am going to train these girls, especially Rosita! She has a magnificent talent, and she is going to be a great ballerina! I am her agent—"

"Really, has she signed a contract with you?" Zach asked crisply. "I had not heard about it! Rosita, have you signed a contract with Isolde?"

"Nonsense, we don't need a signed contract," said Isolde, angrily. "Rosita is being paid by me, and she has been trained by me for years—"

"You mean, she has submitted to your demands, for some reason, probably the family she adores," said Zach, and now he sounded very hard and tough. "Well, this is going to change. We'll talk about it!"

"No reason to talk," Isolde faced up to him, hands on her slim hips, almost as tall as her brother. "We are going to train hard, the three of us. We are going back to New York, and I am going to have control of this! I have my future to look out for, I am going to teach, and form my own company—"

"What about me?" cried Delphine, suddenly in tears. "What about my life? What about my desires? I never wanted all this, I thought it was fun for a time, but now—now—I want to live, I want to be a real woman—"

"You are just a child," said Isolde contemptuously. "At your age, I was a woman!"

"I'm going to talk to mama!" yelled Delphine, and in a flash she had run out of the studio, and was racing along the hallway.

"You idiot, don't disturb mama!" cried Isolde, and ran after her, distracted.

Rosita had been feeling a flood of emotions. Surprise at Zach's entrance, dismay at Isolde's plans to return to New York, wonder, grief, amazement—Zach was looking at her as though he could read all the flitting expressions on her face.

She stood frozen in the corner, the sweat drying on her body, chilling her in the warm room.

"Fate," Zach said cryptically. "Come along, Rosita, little rose. We have some talking to do."

He held out a strong compelling hand to her. She walked to him, dazed, obedient, willing to let him command. He took her slim hand in his big one, looked down at it.

She looked up at him, puzzled. "Talking?"

"Yes." He drew her out of the sweat-smelling room, into the breezy hallway, and she shivered. He frowned. "Run down to your room, my dear. Put on your swimsuit, and a robe over it, get your gear, and meet me downstairs in five minutes."

"Five minutes?" She seemed unable to say anything but an echo of his words.

He led her to the inside stairs, and walked down to the third floor with her, and around the corner to her room. "Make it fifteen minutes. I'll tell Angelica to put up something for us to eat, and I'll gather up the beach gear. Come on, let's get away before some thunderstorm stops us."

His grin made her feel light and giddy. He pushed open her door, she went inside, he clattered on, down the patio stairs to his room. She stepped into the shower, allowed herself two minutes of his fifteen to wash away the perspiration and tension, then dried herself, and put on her one-piece yellow *maillot*. Over it she slipped a flowered caftan that came down to her ankles. She picked up two towels, a head scarf for her wet head, a slim purse with compact and lipstick, and was ready.

She felt as on the days when school let out early and she and Delphine had an extra two or three hours to do what they wished. She skimmed down the patio stairs, lightly, as though her bones did not ache and her feet burn in the light beach sandals. Zach met her at the bottom of the stairs, and handed her down the last steps, catching her fingers in his lightly.

"All set," he said, with satisfaction. "I like a woman to be on time!" Arrogant, masculine, hard lean body in his jeans and open shirt over the swim shorts.

The car was ready, Jaime was putting in a huge beach umbrella and transistor radio, a basket covered with a napkin, with a thermos sticking out. "All set, Señor Zach," he said, with a kindly smile at Rosita. "You go for a swim, eh? Today is good, very hot and dry."

"Yes, it sounds like heaven," she said, with a happy sigh. "How is the baby today?"

"He goes well, very well. Very loud and noisy all the time," said Jaime. "Very healthy."

They all laughed, and Rosita slipped into the car seat. Zach came around, slammed the door, and turned on the key. They slid out smoothly, the silver Lincoln so airy, so sleek and even-riding, it made her family's old cranky car seem like something out of an amusement park.

"Oh, where is Delphine?" Rosita asked suddenly. "She was coming along—" She peered back anxiously.

"No, she is crying on maman's shoulder," grimaced Zach. "I did not disturb them. We'll talk later. This afternoon, we two have things to say."

He sounded firm, frowning slightly at the windshield and the traffic before them. It was about four o'clock, the cars streamed out of San Juan toward the hotel district and beyond to the countryside, and were joined by more from the factory areas. He concentrated on driving, watching his chance to dart into the one stream that led to the highway.

Rosita sat back, not disturbing him. He might mean to scold her, or question her, or straighten things out, or—she did not know what. It was enough to know she would have his undivided attention, sheer heaven! She longed to touch his arm, bare to the elbow in the rolled-up blue sleeve. Dark with hair, on the hard brown skin, the wrist strong as he turned the wheel, his long fingers lightly on the wheel. She loved to look at his hand and arm, it was so—so Zach. Strong, tough, yet gentle also, holding one up in the dance, someone to lean on and depend upon.

She glanced out the window, adjusting her yellow-framed sunglasses on her small nose. How lovely it was today, her Puerto Rico, with the palms waving in the slight breeze, a splash of yellow hibiscus bush, a hedge of rose hibiscus and another splash of yellow Allamanda.

The Lincoln whizzed past the entrance to the public beach where she and her family usually went. She glanced questioningly at Zach, he did not turn his head, but he must have sensed her movement.

"There's a private beach a little further on, it will be less crowded today," he said briefly.

They reached a fence, locked, with a guard at the gate. Zach honked lightly, a sleepy guard came out, opened the gate, waved them on. The silver car slid down the graveled path, past more gates, open now, and out near a beautiful private beach. Only half a dozen people were there, and Rosita marveled at the huge long creamy sand beach, clear and clean, with the ocean rolling slowly in long blue waves and white spume beyond it.

Zach stopped the car, and helped her out. "Find a nice spot, Rosita, I'll bring the gear," he said, sounding suddenly cheerful and happy. She hesitated, everything looked so nice, so unspoiled.

He walked along beside her then, carrying the beach umbrella. He stopped, staring about critically. When they were dozens of yards from anybody else, he pushed the stem of the umbrella in the sand, anchored it firmly, then went back for the basket and towels.

He returned, dumped it all down. "Let's go in first," he said, and helped her take off the caftan. She felt his hands on her shoulders, lightly removing the gown, and his critical approving look down her slim body in the yellow suit.

He began to unzip his jeans. It was suddenly so intimate a movement, that she could not bear it. She began to walk toward the water. "Wait for me!" he said. It was an order.

She waited in silence. He came up, caught her hand, he had removed his shirt and his sandals. They ran together to the water. He held her hand until the waves separated them.

She struck out into the surf, a little yellow fish, at home in the big salty blue waves. She splashed about happily, diving under, coming up to laugh into Zach's bronze face so close to hers. He did not swim out, as she had expected he would. He remained close to her, swimming with her, following her about, like a guardian fish, she thought, with an inward giggle.

She was tired, she did not swim long. When she turned to shore, he followed her again, catching her hand once more as they came to the surf, stood up and walked in to the beach. She dropped on the sand under the big gaudy orange and yellow umbrella, and picked up a towel to dry her arms briskly.

He loomed above her, behind her. He began to unfasten her hair. "Oh, what are you doing?" she asked, startled.

"Your hair is wet, it will never dry like this," he said, all briskness and commanding of voice. He unfastened the coronet, unwound the braids, and began to spread out the length of soft dark brown satin. She felt the wetness on her shoulders, then he took another towel and began to gather big strands in it to dry them.

She slipped on the caftan against the chilling wind. The evening would come before long, they did not have long to stay, she thought with regret. She cherished each moment, willed it to lengthen. She lay back on the sand, closed her eyes.

He lay down beside her, stretching out like a great satisfied cat. "Don't go to sleep," he said, amusement stirring in his tone. "I want to talk to you."

"I'm listening," she murmured, able to hear him forever, wanting to go to sleep with his voice in her ears.

He put his big hand on her shoulder. The shock of it made her eyes go open and wide, looking up into his bronzed face. He had turned serious.

"Rosita, have you thought much about your future?"

"Well—no," she said slowly. "It is up to Isolde. I suppose I will learn more parts, more difficult ones, and maybe more star roles—and then—"

"No, no," he said impatiently. "Do you really want to do as she says? Do you want to be a great ballerina?"

She sat up slowly, he sat also, and sat cross-legged opposite her, as though an antagonist. He reached out absently for the thermos and two glasses, poured some cool rum mixed with fresh lime juice. She sipped a little, cautiously, he drank down a glass, then poured out another one, which he set on the top of a covered dish of sandwiches.

"A great ballerina," she said slowly. "I don't know if I have the talent for that. But Isolde thinks—"

"Forget Isolde. Think about yourself. For the next few years, you would work very hard, you would have to continue to be very disciplined. You would get up each morning, practice for two hours, rest, practice more, eat lunch, practice all afternoon, rest a couple of hours. Then in the evening, production, an all-out effort, dripping with sweat, for the sound of people's hands clapping together. Question, is that what you want? Is it worth it?"

She said in a low voice, "Is that what you think of it, ballet? Is that all it is?"

"God, no," he said impatiently. "My mother and grand-mother were fine ballerinas, granny was a great one, in fact. Everyone says so, though I never saw her dance seriously. She was past it. Rosita, when you are twenty, you will be going up the ladder of fame. I have seen you dance, I have been moved and exalted by your dancing."

She could not speak, troubled by some dark meaning in his voice. She sifted sand in her hand, made a little pile, smoothed it out beside her knee. He seemed to watch her hand intently.

"When you are twenty-five," he continued, "you will be receiving fine notices, some criticism, but good direction. Isolde may not be able to keep you in her control," he added drily. "You will be becoming great, offers will flow in, agents will offer high fees, bigger companies, guest appearances."

"If I don't break my ankles," she added, with a flash of humor. "It does happen! The best of plans go oft awry, as that Scots poet wrote."

"Heaven forbid, but as you say, it could happen. If not, if you are lucky, God smiles on you, and the critics and the people, you go on up and up. You reach thirty, you are at your height. People flock to see you, your fees are very high. Then— then you start to slide down. You think of the future, you take in some pupils, you teach, you advise, you dance less, unless you are one of those few who can continue maybe to forty. Maybe you are the Queen Mother, who does not dance, but moves on stage gracefully. Maybe you are the widow, the beautifully moving tragic figure seen briefly."

The lovely, stirring, deep voice paused, he seemed to hit at her without touching her, those hurtful deliberate words. Her head was bent, hidden by the shining dark drying hair.

"Is that what you want, Rosita? Tell me!"

She thought of Elena, her Madonna face bent lovingly over her baby. She thought of Cristina, transformed by her own child, weaned away from selfishness because of the needs of her husband, his children, their children. She thought of her mother, face serene and splendid, in spite of pain and aging, because her children were gathered about her, and loved her deeply, and her husband loved her as no one in his life.

"What would you do, if you could do anything in the world, Rosita?" He lifted her face with a finger under her chin, and gazed down into her soul.

"Oh, to marry and have babies," she whispered, with desolation. "But it is not possible. Marriage is not for a serious ballerina, Isolde says so."

He laughed shortly, as though in relief. "Thank God you are not an image of Isolde's making, much as it might appear on the surface. Oh, Rosita, I shall ask you now. Do you have any feeling for me?"

Feeling for him? Oh, God, she had love spilling over for him, she had devotion that would wipe his feet with her long hair, she had hands that burned to do something to help him, an anxious heart that longed—but what was she thinking?

She brushed back her hair, her hand touched his. He tilted her chin until she had to gaze into his blue eyes, or shut hers. She gazed, was lost, in the deep ocean blue, in waves of hot emotion.

"Why?" she cried out in torment. "Why, why, do you ask me such a question? I am Rosita Dominguez. I am a ballerina, I am—I am—what am I?"

She finished in desolation. He smiled, so tenderly it caught

at her like a strong vine, so possessively, it terrified and dominated her. He drew her slowly toward him, his hands on her
small shoulders.

"Oh, Rosita, my little rose, my adored. I know what you
are, a lovely little girl, a more lovely woman, all grown-up,
now, ready for love, and marriage. Aren't you, aren't you?"

He drew her close, wet body to wet body, and held her,
his gaze flashing over her from head to heels before he drew
her so close he could not see her. His warm mouth closed over
her lips, possessed them, hurt them with his hard passion before he gentled. She lay on his arm, and felt the hardness of it
beneath her neck, as he pushed back her head so he could kiss
her chin, her throat, down to her rounded breasts just revealed
by the top of her *maillot*. She felt stinging heat there, as though
he branded her with his lips, made her his, marked her as the
belonging of Zach, the possession of Zach, his woman, his to
flame up, burn up, turn to ashes at his will.

In the shelter of the beach umbrella he kissed her senseless, his hands molding her to his body, holding her to him
until she felt his sinewy arms and chest and thighs burning on
her round limbs. Rosita moaned, and put one tentative arm
about his neck. This slight encouragement made him all the
more ardent. He kissed her lips, until her mouth answered, and
opened to him, so that they were one breath. Her fingers explored the hard-rock strength of his neck, shoulders and back.
As she timidly explored, he was more bold, learning her curved
form with his fingers, with the palm of his hand, stroking,
caressing, wanting more.

He finally put her down, breathing hard. "Rosita," he
said huskily. "Any more, and I won't wait for the wedding!"

She blinked up at him, so shocked by all these new sensa-
tions that she could not think at all. Zach was running so far
ahead of her that it was hopeless to catch up. He was laughing,
and kissing her, and pulling her along, but she could not see
why, all this was mysterious and sun-bright, dazzling.

He pulled her down, and lay with his hand on her waist,
his head on his other curled arm, gazing intently at her. "Rosita,
I'm talking about marriage," he said gently. "I want to marry

you. Soon. Very soon, I don't think I can wait much longer. I waited for you. I saw you as a child, growing into a girl, growing up, into a lovely, marvelous woman. I want you, I love you. Say it, for God's sake! Am I alone in this wanting?''

"Oh no . . . you're not alone," she managed to say. "Oh, Zach, do you know what you are saying?" she burst out. "It is not possible . . . you and . . . and me . . . so far apart always, so different . . .''

"Different, as a man and a woman are different," he smiled, stroking boldly down over her thigh to her knee, and back up again. "Have we not always known what was in each other's minds and hearts? Could we not always talk without saying a word? Remember that first time we met, in the nightclub where you performed with your family? Remember when Isolde wanted you to come with us, and insisted on wrenching you from your family? You know what I thought, what I felt.''

"You . . . " she said slowly, understanding, "You wanted me to come. But you wanted me to stay with my family. You knew how I felt, torn both ways.''

"Yes. And the night you danced the Gypsy wanderer. How I felt then, wanting to gather up your small exhausted self, and say, Gypsy, stay with me! Your wanderings are over!''

It could not be, his beautiful voice murmuring these wonderful words to her. His striking blue eyes, so imperious, softened by love for her! It could not be, but it was. His hand, possessively on her hip. His face so close, flushed with passion, burning with desire kept with difficulty in check.

"I am crazy to make love with you," he whispered, though there was no one about to hear. "I want to love you, make you mine, take you to my bed, wake with you in the morning, see your lovely sleeping face next to mine on the pillow. God, darling, I cannot wait! How soon?''

Daringly, she placed her finger on his cheek, in the dent graven by his worries and long hours of work. She caressed the strong chin, let her finger wander up to trace the other cheek to his nose, to one eye, to his forehead, then down again, to rest on his mouth. He kissed the finger, his blue eyes gazing at her as though daring her, willing her, forcing her to say she would belong to him.

"Zach, if you mean it—"

"If? Shall I take you now?" he teased, and came up, bending over her, his face very close. His lips teased hers, he bent up, propped on an elbow, very near to her, body pressing against her body. "Soon, Rosita? A couple of weeks at most? We could plan, I can get away two weeks from now—have to go to Elysia anyway. We could make that our honeymoon! Yes, we'll do that," he went on eagerly. "Take the sloop, get to Elysia, stay at the plantation for a couple weeks, all on our own! You to myself, with nobody around—what heaven! What do you say? Just say yes, don't say anything else, don't stop me, don't deny me, or I'll go stark raving mad!" He began to laugh with joy, brushing his mouth against her shoulder, tasting the salt, licking it with his impudent tongue.

She could not speak, waiting, breathless, for the moment to end, for her to wake up from some fantastic, incredible dream. But she did not wake, the sun burned lower in the west, and Zach was saying,

"Darling, say yes. You will, won't you? I've been so wanting you—I know that now. You will fit into my life so beautifully, you will fit against me so marvelously—" He pulled her close to him, she felt their bodies fitting as though they danced a *pas de deux* and moved in unison as perfect dancers together—but Zach was not—was never—a stranger. "Say yes?"

She could not resist, though she wakened and found it bitter daylight. "Yes," she whispered. "Oh, Zach, I do love you. I love you so very much—"

They kissed, and could not let go. He finally pulled her up. The wind was cooler, the evening was coming.

"We'll go home, spring the news," he said merrily. "I can't wait to tell mother she can now plan our wedding!" And he laughed.

Wedding. His mother plan the wedding! What about her family? But Zach was up, brushing them down, gathering up the uneaten basket of goodies, the umbrella, the towels. She took some of the gear, and she walked with him across to the car, dazed, happy, yet—yet—wondering about the future. Could they—from their separate worlds, really unite as one?

Chapter 14

They arrived back at the house about eight o'clock. Zach escorted Rosita up to her room, kissed her hard on the mouth. "Change, come down, we'll eat together in my study, and make plans. I'm starving!" His look told her he was hungry for more than just dinner.

In the peace of her room, Rosita looked about, dazed. Could it have been less than four hours ago that she had been here, changing to go out with Zach, worrying about her future? And he had swept her away, changed her whole life—with his love!

He loved her, he loved her. She paused in soaping her small body, clasped her hands over the soap, gazed at the bright yellow tiled wall of the shower. He loved her! It was incredible! She had fallen asleep and dreamed it!

Tall, handsome, wonderful Zach, so strong, so dear, so wonderful—wonderful—marvelous—and he loved her! And he was waiting for her! She hurried then, dried herself, slipped on a slim rose-printed cotton, white sandals, and went downstairs. Zach was in the drawing room, she heard their voices.

Shyly, she stood in the doorway, he felt her there, he turned and came over to her. She looked at him anxiously, he was smiling, but she felt tension in him.

He put his arm about her, tucked her under his broad shoulder, as though he would protect her. "I couldn't wait, Rosita, I have started to tell them our news. We are going to be married," he told the group.

He must have said it before, for the shock was already on their faces. Madame Isabeau in her sheer black was sitting with her slim beautiful hands clasped before her, as though in prayer. Madame Sonia was half-smiling, brown eyes alert and shrewd. Kevin just looked stunned. Delphine—Rosita looked anxiously at her friend. Her mouth was open, her eyes wide—then the girl jumped up and ran over to them.

"Rosita, to be truly my sister!" she cried in delight. She kissed her, hugged, moving to push Zach back for a moment. "Oh, I'm so happy—when is the wedding?"

"In two weeks," said Zach smoothly. His mother cried out.

"Impossible! You are insane! Pause, and think! Zach, I know you quarreled with Isolde about this, but truly, this is not the solution! We must talk calmly—"

Isolde was not in the room. Rosita shivered a little, dreading it when she heard.

Madame Sonia put up her hand, beckoned to Rosita. "Come here, my dear." Zach let her go, she went over to the older woman, knelt down before her. The elderly ballerina touched her tenderly on the head, then leaned to kiss her on each cheek. "Bless you, my dear," she murmured. "May you ever be happy!"

Tears rushed to Rosita's eyes, she whispered, "Oh, thank you, Madame Sonia! You are not angry—my career—and everything?" Anxiously she searched the aged wise eyes.

"I saw it coming," said Madame Sonia, with a smile. "You are right for each other. Be good to him, my dear, he needs your gentleness and goodness."

Rosita impulsively kissed the aged graceful hands, and Madame Sonia leaned over her and kissed her forehead.

Kevin was standing, exclaiming, insisted on kissing her. Madame Isabeau was much more reserved, she had her doubts, but she managed a few stiff words of welcome to the family.

Then Zach took them away, to his study. The maid brought a tray of food, they ate, and drank coffee, and talked.

"I think we can manage a wedding in two weeks," said Zach, smiling at her over his coffee cup. "There is no need to draw it out. I want you in a white dress, with a white veil, and the pearls—"

"But not diamonds," said Rosita, finding she could joke a little. "Not diamonds in the daytime!" They both laughed, joyously, and Zach reached out and took her hand in his.

"Your ring. Will you mind a family diamond, or shall I get something just for you?"

She was blissful, just at the thought of his wanting her. "It doesn't matter—"

Zach opened the safe then, and took out jewelry boxes with reckless abandon. He laid out the pearls, chose one strand the right length for her throat, for the wedding. He set a pearl tiara on her head, said it was just right. And there were the diamonds, some emeralds, and an old sapphire ring in a setting so ancient—Zach told her it had belonged to an ancestor, one Tess Hamilton, long ago. "I must tell you about her, on our honeymoon. We are going to Elysia, where she lived with my other great-great-great-something grandfather."

He found a ring that almost fit her slim hand, and said he would have it made smaller at once, and solemnly measured her finger with a piece of string. "But you will come with me tomorrow to the jeweler's. I want your ring on that hand right away, the mark of possession!"

He was so dear, so joking, so loving, that she could not take it all in. They talked a bit about the wedding, she would have Delphine as her attendant. Her father would give her away.

"Oh—my father!" she gasped, her hand going to her mouth. "I have not told my family!"

"We'll go there tomorrow also," he said at once. "What time—about noon? Will they all be there at noon?"

What would her family think? It would be such a shock— they had no idea—And she was supposed to dance with them tonight, it was too late now—

She sat there, her face troubled, and he seemed to read her mind. "Darling Rosita, I know it will be a surprise to them. It will seem very sudden. But I have known my own mind some time now, it seems very natural to me," he said gently. His hand folded around hers, squeezing them reassuringly. "We can convince them that we know what we are doing, can't we? We have known each other for many years, we are not strangers. We have grown in love—I know I liked that little girl in braids and pigtails long ago," he smiled. "I liked her courage, her gallantry, her talent, her serious little face, her loyalty to her family." And he picked up her hands and kissed them.

"Oh, Zach, and I have thought of you with such love—such longing—and I knew it was hopeless—" She admitted it with a deep blush. "You seemed so far beyond me. But when you came to my debut in New York—and you paid such attentions to me—I felt—I felt—so happy—so. . . ." She could not say the words.

"I think Isolde was terrified then!" he laughed. "She tried to shoo me away from her lamb! I think she felt the threat that I could be to her plans. I did not intend to let her sacrifice you on the altar of her ambitions! So long as you enjoyed the dancing, fine, and you were growing up, and a friend to Delphine. You seemed happy, radiant, and so lovely on stage! I wanted it for you. But it gradually came to me, how lovely a wife and partner you would be for me! And I am selfish, what I have I keep!"

She felt then a light pang of anxiety.

Her family still needed her. And Isolde had had such plans for her—

Zach kissed her good night, and led her up to her room, his arm about her. "Tomorrow—about nine, darling girl. We'll start out then, the jeweler's, and the church, we must talk to the Padre. And your family at noon, and more plans. About your dress—I want you in white, but mother will help you with that—"

She went to bed, to dream that she was in a white wedding dress like seafoam, and drowning in the veils, so that she yelled, and fought free, to find herself tangled in the sheets.

Silly, she thought, and lay awake with heavily beating heart, until she calmed again.

The next day skimmed past. The jeweler altered the ring at once, while they waited, so that they went to her family with his ring on her finger, an immense diamond set in a cluster of smaller point diamonds, on a gold ring. They had bought the two wide-banded gold wedding rings, one for him. "For I shall wear your band of possession also," he laughed, looking pleased with the beautiful bands they had chosen together.

At her house, the family sat on the porch, staring at them. Her father was literally so stunned he could not speak. Her mother gasped, "Rosita—married—to Mr. Hamilton?"

Only Marcos took it in at once. "He seemed to like you very much, Rosita!" he smiled. "I wondered about that—" And he kissed her cheeks, and shook Zach's hand happily. Rosita thought maybe he was thinking of Delphine. But Delphine was an heiress! And Marcos a student, and a Gypsy dancer! Her family would never agree!

But that was what she was—a Gypsy dancer! Oh, how could it be true! Zach sat beside her on the wooden porch swing, her hand clasped tightly in his, and beamed on them all. He looked so young today, almost boyish, but for the dark lines on his tanned face, and the weariness under his eyes. He worked too hard, and she thought tenderly, even as she worried about the marriage, that if he did marry her she must take such care of him, as Madame Sonia had said.

"I know you wonder," said Zach, finally, coming down to earth. "Her future, her career—all up in smoke. But she wants to marry and have children, she said so. And I don't want that hard life for her, the life of a ballerina. It is so lonely, so disciplined, so difficult. She is too tender a girl for that." He smiled down at Rosita, and put his arm about her possessively. "Her career shall be as my wife, and the mother of my children! All in good time, of course!" he added, as Rosita blushed hotly.

Her father finally roused himself from his daze, kissed her, blessed them both. But Tadeo and Inez sat with dark brows frowning, worrying, Rosita knew, about the nightclub act. She found a moment to speak to Inez, hastily in the kitchen, as they prepared cold drinks.

"I would have left anyway, Inez," she said quickly. Elena was there also, with a baby on her broad hip. "Isolde was speaking of leaving for New York in two weeks, for ballet engagements. She would have carried me away. So I could not have danced anyway, in the act."

"Is that why you are marrying him?" asked Inez bitterly. "For the money, the softness, the ease? Oh, you will have a sweet *dolce* life, that is for sure!"

"No, Inez, I would marry him if he did not have a penny," said Rosita quietly, holding fast to her temper. "I love him."

"It is easy to love where there is money!" said Inez nastily, and Elena rebuked her.

"Since when has Rosita been greedy and selfish? No, she has had all the money sent to papa, never has she kept anything for herself! You should not begrudge her such a life of ease, she has worked hard since she was able to walk and dance!"

However, when she and Zach departed in midafternoon, she had the sense that they felt she had failed them, and was deserting them. Even Oliverio had been more silent than ever, his dark eyes brooding. Surely they did not think she was marrying only for money, a life of ease!

She rested, on Zach's orders, then came downstairs. It was such a strange day. She had not danced one step, she had not had a moment even to work out in the practice room. She must not get out of condition, she thought—yet why not? Zach did not seem to expect her to dance again! How odd that would seem!

She came down to the drawing room early, in a smoke blue chiffon dress and blue sandals, her long hair tied back loosely as Zach liked it, with a blue ribbon about the ponytail, not in the tight coronet of braids. Zach was before her, and so was Isolde, the first they had seen her. She had been out with some friends, had slept late, and was now in a very belligerent mood. Her mother had informed her of the wedding.

She turned on Rosita. "You are a little fool!" she spat.

"You cannot give up such a promising career! I told you, you will be a great ballerina! You will be applauded on the stages of New York, London, Paris, Milan—"

"I would rather marry Zach," Rosita said simply, when Zach held out his large hand to her. She came to stand beside him, feeling the warmth of his protection. "I wish to thank you, however, for your great care of me, and the interest you have shown—"

Her polite speech was cut short. Nobody else was in the room, it was early. Isolde cried out, "Oh, yes, you are grateful for those few years, the years of my great expense and care for your career! Then just when you are ready to really make a return on my money, you give up! You will get married and have babies, you say! That is my reward!"

Zach began angrily, "You knew it was a risk, Isolde! Any ballerina can opt out, and she might have turned her ankle, hurt herself—left anyway—"

"She has not hurt herself! She is in perfect condition! And I demand that you stop this nonsense, and break this foolish engagement! You have some stupid chivalric impulse, Zach, you are protecting a girl who has been working hard! But that is part of her life—"

"Not at her choice," he said shortly. "She was driven by you, and by her need to help her family. Well, that is over, if they need help, I shall be proud and happy to help them."

"And have an entire huge family on your hands forever!" she sneered. "And all because Melinda Valdes threw you over for your best friend! You are on the rebound, and longing to show her she means nothing!"

Rosita caught her breath, shrinking from Zach, and from Isolde's fury. Zach merely shrugged. "Nonsense," he said mildly. "Now, Isolde, stop all this sound and fury, it bores me. Come on, congratulate us, and help us plan the wedding—"

"Plan the wedding! Never! Now, Rosita," and Isolde turned to Rosita, not noticing her white face and shaking hands. On the rebound from Melinda Valdes! Rosita had not realized that! Oh, could it, would it be that? Could Zach do that, to use her because he could not have Melinda Valdes of the warm beauty, the scarlet mouth and too-knowing eyes? "Now, Rosita! You must listen, you must do as I say! I have trained you for years, you must not give in to an impulse, just because you are tired! Think of New York, the excitement of the season, and Madame Olga assured me you are being considered for great parts! Alan Landis himself said he would be glad to have us back, he has missed you! They plan to do *Gypsy Wanderer* this season, it is a great hit—he will give you Tonio Montez as your partner, think of that! There are such plans, you cannot throw them over—"

Rosita was staring blindly at Isolde, not hearing the coaxing imperious tones, not at all. On the rebound from Melinda Valdes, Oh, Zach, she thought, you would not hurt me so!

The others came down, Delphine slipped her arm about Rosita's waist. "Have you planned your wedding dress, darling? I want the same style! May I wear pale blue? And carry roses, Zach, are we to have roses?"

"Of course," he said, smiling at them. "A church full of roses for my Spanish Rose! I'll call the florist this afternoon, he is ordering hundreds from the States."

"Tell him he is crazy, mother! Tell him he is out of his mind!" cried Isolde, frantically, seeing Rosita slip out of her grasp, her plans for the future company, her efforts at commanding both Rosita and Delphine. "This is such a wild idea—and in two weeks! They must have time to think about it—delay it—why the rush?"

Madame Isabeau looked speculatively, coolly at Rosita, down her slim thin form, and Rosita flushed, and shrank from the look. Did she think it was—necessary? That Zach had made love to her, that she was pregnant? Oh God, Rosita could have fled from them all.

Madame Sonia said quietly, "Isolde, you are being hysterical. These two young people belong together, I have seen it. You will understand one day. There is an aura about them, I know it, I saw it when I saw them dancing together. It was meant to be."

Rosita felt bewildered. Did Madame Sonia mean this, or was she just being kind? They went in to dinner, she could not eat, her stomach felt like it was turning over and over, as though she were on a ship bucking in the waves. She sat at Zach's right, the place of honor, with Madame Sonia on her right, and felt buttressed between them, but Madame Isabeau darted little bewildered looks at her, and Isolde was angry.

In the study later, she tried to speak to Zach about it. He wanted to talk further plans, he said, but when they came inside, he shut the door firmly and took her in his arms. "Not a kiss all day," he moaned, with a smile, and began kissing her softly all over her face, her chin, her cheeks, her eyelids, her forehead, sliding down her nose, to land on her mouth. Then his kiss deepened, until she was breathless, her hands clutching his sleeves.

His mouth was so deeply on hers, so hungry and over-powering. Her lips opened to protest, he was hurting her, and he nibbled at her lower lip in a sensuous way that drove every thought right out of her head. He drew her over to his chair, and sat down, pulling her onto his hard thighs. She lay against his chest, and tried to get her breath. His head pressed against hers.

"Oh, darling, such a long time, two whole weeks," he said.

She felt rather frantic. She sat up, pushing him away firmly with her palms against his chest. She felt his heat through the thin shirt, the thick hair on his chest, and her fingers curled up against him. "Zach—I must speak to you," she said seriously.

"Yes, darling. Tell me how much you love me," he said.

"Oh, I do, I do," she breathed. "But Zach—" She could not ask him about Melinda Valdes— "Isolde said—she said, she was making plans for the winter—the ballet—perhaps we should put off the wedding for a time. I mean—she did put a great deal of—money—into my career—I feel guilty—"

Zach frowned. He said curtly, "Isolde is not now in charge of your life! I am!" He was arrogant, certain of himself.

Melinda Valdes, sultry, scarlet-mouthed, dynamic, the image of her floated before Rosita like a nightmare.

"It has been very sudden," she managed to say calmly.

"I think your family—they are—shocked. It would be better to postpone our—our engagement—let us think about it for a time. If I go to New York—"

"No!" he said flatly, and his blue eyes glittered dangerously. "You said you wanted this, I won't let you back out! Are you getting cold feet?"

"Yes," she said, looking away, for fear he would read her mind. She wanted to belong to him, she wanted to be his wife, to lie at his side in the great bed, and one day bear his son. Oh, God, how she wanted this—but— "It is too quick—our families are not accustomed to the idea. It would be better to wait—" And she tried to pull the diamond ring from her finger.

He caught her hand, held it cruelly tight. "No! No, you don't back out now! Rosita, you said you loved me! You agreed to marry me! I'm not letting you slip away! Our families? Who is getting married, us or our families?" He became even angrier when she tried to persist in breaking the engagement.

So they went ahead with the wedding plans, though Rosita had to shut her mind and her ears to doubts. She had her own worries. She heard whispers, and Isolde did not bother to hide her fury. The relatives came to an engagement party the following Sunday, and she heard more whispers. Her own family was uneasy in the big Hamilton house and left early.

When they departed, and Elena turned to smile at Rosita, she heard one of the uncles say, perhaps Uncle Samuel, "And they are Spanish Gypsies! God, what are we coming to?"

It hurt her badly, and she went pale. Delphine heard also, and flung her uncle a furious look. Melinda Valdes Oviedo had come with her new husband, and they were laughing with other guests, casting curious looks at Rosita. Zach did not seem to hear them.

Elena made Rosita's wedding dress, they had planned it together. It was like one of her flamenco dresses, only in white eyelet, in seven layers of the skirt. The bodice was rounded and demure with sleeves below the elbow. The skirt was narrow at the waist, then one small ruffle of eyelet below that, another larger one, then another, until it ended at her ankles in the widest most beautiful ruffle of white eyelet, so she looked like a dainty dancer with high-heeled white satin shoes. She carried white roses, made up to Zach's wishes, with a single red rose buried deep in the bouquet.

Rosita had gone home to her family the last three days. She dressed for her wedding in the small attic room she had shared with Luisa. She looked at herself for the last time in the narrow long mirror on the door.

Marcos escorted her out to the chauffered silver Lincoln, and got in the back with her and her father. He was one of the ushers, the others were not in the wedding party, but would sit in front rows.

She arrived at the Cathedral, trembling, waiting in the back for the music to start. The elegant church was filled with baskets of roses, white around the altar, yellow and red and pink in other baskets. White ribbons at the pews, a white satin runner laid over the carpet to the altar.

Zach waited at the altar for her. Finally that was all that mattered, he was waiting, for her. And it was the Saturday after her nineteenth birthday, she had celebrated quietly at home with her family, opening Zach's elaborate gifts to her before she had left the house, the Hamilton house that would be her home. Her birthday had been the twelfth of September, just one month after Zach's, and their wedding day September 16.

She walked slowly to the altar behind Delphine, on her father's shaking arm, as he walked tall and proud and distinguished beside her. So fine in his shiny black formal outfit, with the white ruffled shirt, the outfit he wore for dancing. And Marcos stood there, so fine, so like their father. And Kevin, as best man, and then Zach right before her.

Delphine's pale blue eyelet dress matched hers, Luisa had made it, and she carried a bouquet of pink roses. The two girls stood there, listened to the words of the priest, knelt, rose, and Rosita was comforted by the closeness of her dearest friend.

Their hands were joined, they said their final vows, the golden rings were exchanged. Then they knelt for the wedding

Mass, and received Communion together for the first time as a married couple.

It was so very final—

Until death do you part. Death. Death. A long time away, God willing—

Zach turned, and put back her veil, tenderly, and kissed her lips, lightly, a formal kiss before their audience. His eyes promised more later, a warm blue gaze with joy and a pledge.

They went to the vestry and signed the register, and Delphine and Kevin signed as witnesses, then Marcos added his name. Her father kissed her, on the forehead, and blessed her in Spanish, deeply moved.

The reception was in a large hotel, El Convento, just across the street from the Cathedral. The huge dining room was filled to capacity, the food served on a long buffet table to the side, and the bar taken over for the event. The El Convento waiters ran about, smoothly seeing to everything, faces beaming. The Hamiltons were well known, and of course Rosita Dominguez was known also, their own *La Soledad*, their own flamenco girl, known before they had heard of her fame as a ballerina.

Some distant relatives from Ponce, and some guests from the United States and from England had flown in, and had rooms at El Convento. The reception went on and on, until almost two in the afternoon.

Rosita had noticed unhappily that her family and friends lingered in one corner of the room, away from those of the Hamiltons. There were cold looks between them, Uncle Morgan was horrified at the connection. Uncle Samuel had made several snide remarks in her hearing. Even her own relatives seemed just as suspicious about their motives for marrying. Her own Granny Alejandra had rebuked her.

"I knew no good would come of this ballet! Why could you not have remained with your own? You are a Gypsy, a flamenco dancer! Have you forgotten your proud heritage? What will our relatives in Spain think?"

It hurt Rosita to hear her, to think she was disappointing her grandmother. It was ironic to think that her grandmother and her father were both disappointed in the marriage! They were proud and high-strung people, close-knit, suspicious of outsiders. And her mother was hurt, thinking they were losing Rosita. The last night she had wept over her.

She thought, even as Zach helped her cut the elaborate five-tiered wedding cake, that they were both shocking their families. It had all been so sudden, nobody had been able to stop them. Was that why Zach had done it so quickly, had swept her off her feet, had pushed the wedding plans on? And why? Why did he not wait, and let himself get over his love for Melinda? Or did he want to hurt the girl as he had been hurt? Did she still love him, that Zach thought Melinda would be hurt by his marriage?

Zach left her side, to take a piece of wedding cake to Madame Sonia. She heard the whisper again, as some guests stared with open curiosity at her and her white tiered dress. "Gypsy!" she heard one say. "A Gypsy dancer! Imagine! Men have always been carried away by dancers!"

It was wryly amusing to think she could carry Zach away! She was so small and slim, he was tall and muscular and tough. Yet she knew what they meant. He had been swept away by passion for her, lust, probably, they meant. They could not believe he loved her. She found it difficult to believe herself.

Rosita gazed about the huge dining room at El Convento, saw the small stage at one end, and remembered suddenly that she had once danced here! Yes, when she was a child, she and her family had had a two weeks' engagement here, and she had danced on that very stage!

The music that had been played softly by a chamber music group suddenly grew louder. Zach came to her with a smile, his hand out to her, and she could see nobody but him. She forgot her worries, her radiant smile met his happy look.

They began to dance together, her white full skirts whirling about his white linen legs, as he turned her quickly in the waltz. Others began to dance also, joining in, the laughter and music lightening her spirits.

Zach did not release her to anybody else. Jeronimo Oviedo

came up, his fat face red and beaming, and tried to get her to dance with him. "Dance with your own wife!" laughed Zach, and whirled her away again, leaving Jeronimo scowling in rebuff.

Marcos grinned at Rosita, and winked at her, he had Delphine in his arms. How handsome a couple were they, thought Rosita absently, and then was turned from them by Zach's strong arm, as he moved her around the crowd, deftly. Delphine's blue eyelet skirts were swirling about Marcos's long legs, clad in his black formal suit. How closely she had been held in his arms—how very close—oh, dear, thought Rosita as Zach turned her again and she saw her brother with Delphine bent across his arm.

How very closely they were dancing, eyes sparkling at each other, matching smiles and dreamy faces. Oh, dear, would people see, would they notice? Marcos must release her to someone—but no, he shook his head, Delphine clung to his arm and laughed.

The room grew warmer as more people danced. Rosita stopped at the side of the room near the buffet table, and Zach put a glass of cool lemonade in her hand. He knew she did not care much for champagne and wines and rums, except a bit on special occasions. Of course this was special, she had had pink champagne with him over a piece of white wedding cake, and followed it with a bit of his silver rum.

The drink cooled her, she smiled vaguely at someone across the room. Her father was dancing with her mother, how well they moved together after so many years of marriage and dancing together. How graceful, they made everyone else look clumsy—except—the couple moving together, swaying together—

Rosita blinked, horrified and turning cold. Oh, God, was Marcos still dancing with Delphine? People were whispering, staring at them. Zach was frowning, his mouth a straight hard line. "What the devil," she heard him mutter. He turned from Rosita, motioned to Kevin. Kevin nodded reluctantly, and went to Delphine.

Rosita watched, in sheer horror, as Kevin tapped Marcos

on the shoulder and motioned to Delphine, his kind brown face smiling. Marcos had paused, he looked down at Delphine. Delphine laughed! Oh, that wicked mischievous girl! She was shaking her red gold curls decidedly, and pulling Marcos away with her! Kevin gazed after them thoughtfully, then shrugged, and moved to another guest, asking her to dance.

The music quickened. Zach turned to her, his mouth still hard. Rosita looked up at him helplessly. She felt pained and hurt. Somehow she was good enough to marry Zach, he had insisted. But he did not like the idea of pairing Marcos and Delphine! Oh, those young ones, how reckless they were—and how hopeless—if they loved—Delphine would never be permitted to date him, much less marry—

Zach's look softened as he saw her troubled face. He drew her again into a dance. Whirling around with him, she almost forgot her worries. She passed her parents, gave them a radiant smile, they answered with a fond smile to her. Mother looked ill yet, her eyes shadowed, but Pascual, how very handsome, how straight, how beautiful he was! His head was arrogantly high, as in the dancing in the nightclubs.

Then she heard the whispers, saw the direction of the stares. She and Zach were moving into the turn of the room near the orchestra, it was playing more rapidly, it went into the flamenco theme! Oh, what in the world—Rosita's heart seemed to pause, then beat again much more rapidly.

Zach hesitated, the other dancers did also, and turned to watch. A stunning couple in the center of the floor! Dancing the rapid wild passionate flamenco! And it was—it was Marcos and Delphine!

In the midst of her worry and anguish, Rosita could still appreciate the stunning beauty of that young pair. Marcos, so handsome, so like his father, but with the added glory of his youth and his love, that shone out of him. And Delphine, so softly lovely, so yielding in his arm, her red gold curls tumbled about her lively face, the blue eyes blazing—

Their steps matched perfectly, they slid and glided and he spun her about, recklessly, yet carefully, showing his adoration of her in the stern hold of his arm. He would not hurt her, the gesture mimed. Her heels clicked impertinently, his answered, they moved about each other, in close abandon, her face laughed up at his: They clapped briefly, the music increased in speed, and their lithe young bodies moved in a perfect love duet, the classic *pas de deux* of the Gypsies.

Across the room, she saw her father watching, his arm still about his wife, their faces matched in trouble, yet pride. How beautiful his son, the seed of his body! How like him, how glorious! Yet it could not but lead to disaster, his face clearly said it.

All the family and their guests watched the magnificent young couple, the laughing, glorious, glowing pair that danced in beautiful rhythm, their steps matching as if they had danced it before on some heavenly stage.

Zach's breath caught, he clicked his tongue against his teeth in impatient worry. Rosita heard him, could not look at her brand-new husband, for very shame. That her brother should dance this way with his sister, in public! Making a show for all to see—

Yet how fine they were. She swelled with pride, even as she gazed in tense concentration. Would the music never end? The guests of the wedding were gathered about the sides of the room, having moved back to give them room. All stared, as in frozen concentration, like the guests at the party of Sleeping Beauty, falling into their hundred-year-sleep. The waiters had paused, trays in their hands, to stare and wonder. No one ate, no one drank, no one spoke, all gazed, unable to take attention from the couple.

And Marcos swirled Delphine about on his arm, smiled down at her, his face sternly set in the flamenco style of look, his body proudly arched in a perfect curve of back, down to his tapping heels. Delphine arched in response, her slim rounded body curved as though to match his. Her blue skirts whirled— whirled about him, as though closer and closer to a flame.

The music came to a final loud conclusion. The heels clicked together, precisely, and the two dancers flung themselves to a proud final pose. Someone began to applaud, Marcos bowed, Delphine curtsyed, with the sweetly dazed look on her face telling Rosita clearly, that Delphine had completely forgotten where she was.

The music began again, more conventional, a fox-trot. Marcos and Delphine began to dance once more, swaying together, but now other couples were on the floor, music and laughter swelled in the room, talking was beginning again.

The scene was over, but not forgotten, Rosita knew by the anger in Isolde's face, the bewildered coolness of Isabeau Hamilton. And Zach was angry also, Rosita knew by the tension in his arm as he drew her into the fox-trot. A few dancers in the corner were dancing singly, in the gay abandon of disco, the others were more sedate. And everybody was talking, talking, glancing toward Marcos and Delphine.

Zach left her briefly, near Madame Sonia, and they spoke of anything but Marcos. She saw Marcos leave Delphine, and go over to his family. Zach spoke to them, smiling, but his back was stiff. Pascual had his head up, he spoke quickly, nodding to his family. Rosita clasped her hands together anxiously. Oh, not a scene, she prayed. Not a scene, not her beloved husband and her adored family—

Zach returned to her, and put his arm about her waist. He whispered to her, "Your family is leaving, want to go over and kiss them good-bye?"

She nodded, her heart plunging. Kiss them good-bye! Was that how he thought of it? No, she must be sensible, he meant only that they were going away on their honeymoon, and would not see them for a few weeks.

They proceeded across the room with difficulty, for the crowd seemed reluctant to let them pass. Zach had to push and smile, and shake his head in mock anger, before they parted to let them go. They came to her parents, and smiled. Rosita's mouth trembled. Her mother looked exhausted, she was ill.

Rosita kissed her mother, her father, and each one of them, quickly, for they seemed anxious to leave. They departed then, and she gazed after them as they went out into the lobby.

"It is not forever!" teased Zach, turning her back into the room. "I shall not give you time to miss anybody!" She blushed, and wrinkled her nose at him to cover her confusion, and he bent and kissed her nose quickly. The little moment gave her comfort to tide over the hour before they could leave.

Then they returned to the Hamilton house, a few blocks away, to change for the trip on the sailing yacht, to Elysia.

Chapter 15

The Hamilton yacht seemed huge to Rosita, yet all too small when they had set off and were on the Atlantic Ocean to the north of San Juan. They soon turned to the northwest, headed to the Turks and Caicos Islands. Two sailors were managing the large sailing vessel; they turned on the motor once they were clear of the harbor, and made good time in the afternoon.

"How far is it?" Rosita asked, leaning on the railing. Zach leaned beside her, so handsome and dear in his dark blue jeans and shirt, his red head shining in the sunlight.

He gave her a quick comprehensive look, taking in the simple yellow cotton dress with ruffled bodice, the straw sunhat. He had said not to take elaborate clothes, they would live simply on their honeymoon, and she had not bothered to buy new clothes. She could not afford it, and she had not wanted to take his money for that.

"Almost a thousand miles straight northwest," he said. "My ancestors settled on an island in what is now the Bahamas chain, or near enough. They bought some of the island, a large plantation. Some years later, a cyclone wiped out much of the towns there, and other people left. St. Michael is now a sleepy little town of about fifty people. The Hamiltons bought the rest of the island, and have owned it ever since.''

''Oh.'' Imagine owning a whole island. ''How large is it?'' She visualized a little sandspit, yet he had said towns had been wiped out.

''About fifty miles by thirty miles, very roughly. There is a long hill down the center of it that is not cultivated, but allowed to grow wild in pines, coconut trees, flamboyants, bougainvilleas, also some orange and lemon trees which are cultivated. Some of the Hamiltons loved flowers so much they improved the hibiscus bushes, and encouraged more of the jasmine, both yellow and white. You'll see them—and dozens, hundreds more varieties of flowers, all tropical.''

''It sounds like paradise,'' she breathed.

He smiled down at her, and slid his arm about her waist. ''That is what it is, Elysia, which is paradise,'' he said.

They sailed on and on that night; he had said they would proceed slowly, touching on several islands on the way, to take on fresh fruit and vegetables, fresh water, and go ashore to wander about.

They ate their supper sitting on the deck, in small white-painted deck chairs, with their food spread on a cane table. She scarcely knew what she ate, Zach kept gazing at her instead of the moon and the sea.

She had seen their cabin when they came aboard. It was a small neat room, with shiny redwood panels, and tiny round windows. Cupboards were built in, cunningly, the beds were set in also, two of them, she had been relieved to see. A small bathroom with a shower was to the side of their bedroom. The sailors slept on deck most of the time, and one kept near the wheel, or at the wheel in stormy times. Zach did not expect a storm, but one might come up, he said cheerfully, as though that prospect did not daunt him.

Nothing much daunted Zach, she thought. He just swept it all before him, as he had swept her into the marriage. He laughed away objections, or just set his chin and said that was the way it was. He knew what he wanted and went after it—so how had he lost Melinda Valdes? That was a puzzle, and one that hurt to think about. She put it from her mind, firmly. She had made vows before the altar, some aloud, and some in her mind, that she would be faithful to him, love him, obey him, honor him, all her life. And she would do her best to make life happy for him. His life was not easy, he had many responsibilities, and endured much for his family and the company, and the thousands of employees. She would help him all she could.

One of the black sailors cleared away the table and plates and glasses, and went down to the galley to wash them, singing a crooning cheerful melody with a Barbados lilt. "Went down to Jamaica town, got me a honey don't give me a frown—"

Rosita hummed along with him, tapping her sandaled foot to the jaunty tune. Zach laughed down at her, and took her hand in his. "I got me a honey don't give me a frown," he said softly.

Rosita laughed with him, hoping the darkness hid her flushes. She dreaded yet longed for the night to come. Her mother had talked to her, and Elena, and she knew with her mind what was to come. But she didn't know it yet with her body.

And she wanted to belong to Zach. She wanted to lie with him and learn him, and have him touch her with his caressing hands. In the past two weeks, he had kissed her so much, he had roused deep longings in her that she had suppressed all her growing days. She had been so innocent, she had stayed away from men, Isolde had seen to that. She had wanted no complications for her budding ballerinas—and then Zach had swept along with his demands! How angry Isolde was—what would happen when they returned to San Juan? Would Isolde have left for New York by herself or with Delphine? Delphine was still storming, refusing to leave, refusing to practice at all.

The moon shone on the darkening waters. The sailors now talked idly at the wheel, their mellow laughter rang out at times. The white sails billowed over their heads, the wind sometimes gave them a whack, and the sails straightened with a crack, and the masts creaked. But it all was normal, Zach assured her.

"You'll get used to sailing, Rosita. I enjoy it very much,

we'll go out Sundays and holidays when we don't want to swim. I want you to enjoy life now, not work so hard all your days.''

"What work will I do, Zach? Your mother has charge of the house—''

He hesitated, he had evidently not thought of it. "Your main job is me," he said, with a laugh. "Keep me happy! Mother will look after the house, yes, but she will encourage you to gradually take charge. She said she was moving out of the master suite, and will have it fixed up for us by the time we return.''

"Oh, Zach!" she gasped. "I would not ask that of her! She came there as a bride—''

"But father is dead," he said quietly, folding her hands in his. "She told me it has been a subtle torture to remain in that suite without him. She wants to move to another room, perhaps mine, and become reconciled to his loss. She has brooded long enough.''

"It is—good of her—but—''

"Believe me, darling, it is for the best. I have noticed a good change in her these past two weeks. The marriage has stirred her out of her languor and grief. If she does not sink back, she will begin to make progress. It has been too long, this deep grief and refusal to face life again with courage and hope.''

"She may think she has nothing left to hope for," said Rosita, softly. "I know how I would feel, if anything happened to you.''

"Darling, I adore you!" he whispered, his voice shaking. He stood up, held out his hand to her. "Come, I don't want to wait any longer!''

It was a sudden, eager, imperious demand. She came with him, shaking a little, ardent, yet timid.

They went down to the cabin, and he lit one of the lamps. They had electricity, but he preferred to use the oil lamps, the candles on the small inside table in stormy weather. He undressed rapidly, he did not seem to stare at her, yet she felt him looking at her.

She took off the yellow sundress, the slip and brassiere, the sandals and panties. All such small things, yet they had protected her from his gaze, from the world. Such a symbolic gesture, discarding her shield from his eyes. As though she let him see her as she was, through to her bones.

He took her hand, then drew her into his arms against his naked body. In the yellow lamplight, he glowed golden and bronze. She felt the springing wiry hair on the chest, the dark red hair that shone copper now. She wondered how she looked, as he pressed her hair back, her hair that streamed loosely down over her back, and gazed into her face.

His head lowered, he kissed her forehead, her cheeks, her mouth. His one arm held her to him, bending her back, he bent over her like a dancer. She knew that move, she did know the physical mime of love, she had not known love itself.

Now she began to know. His mouth, so eager on her own, so hot and ardent. Her lips opened, his tongue slipped into her mouth and played about, to teach her a deeper caress. His hand on her back moved up and down, slowly, coming to her hips, fondling them, then up again to her waist. Finally he lifted her and carried her over to the bed.

"You are so light, like flower petals," he murmured. "Do you live on whipped cream?"

"No, no cream at all," she joked unsteadily. "Isolde would forbid that!"

"Lettuce leaf and skim milk," he grimaced. "Forget Isolde. She has no say over you now." He laid her down gently on the bed. He lay down beside her, so much longer than her, so much broader, she was a little afraid. Her hand went to his chest, as though to hold him off.

He murmured to her, love words, gentling words, as he kissed and touched her. "Little darling, adorable one, my lovely Flamenco Rose. So pretty, so sweet, a little girl, my own—"

She wanted to match his words, she was too shy to speak. She would have to learn that also, she thought. Her arms went about him, touching his chest, his back timidly. It seemed strange that she had the right to touch him. Her fingertips

231

seemed unusually sensitive, feeling him delicately, learning the hardness of his skin, the toughness of his body, the muscular structure under the skin. In dancing, she had sometimes felt the hardness of a male dancer's body; Zach felt like that, in condition, strong.

She had thought Zach would take her quickly, her mother had said men sometimes did. She had sounded dubious about Zach. Spanish men, she had said, were more sensitive to a woman's needs. She did not know about English men! Rosita had discounted her mother's unspoken prejudice.

Rosita was relieved and surprised to find that Zach lay with her a long time, caressing her, talking to her, making love with his deep melodic voice. His hand wandered over her, as though idly, her body melted against his, and she lay curled to his body. His fingers went to her breast, moved over it gently, touched the taut nipples.

She gasped a bit when he touched her there. Her nipples were so alive to his touch, they rose up, and he leaned to her and took a nipple between his lips and pulled at it. Then he licked around the breast, all around, deliberately, as though he enjoyed the touch of the softness. As he kissed, his hand went lower, to her waist, down her spine, over her hips, over and over.

He began to kiss her all over, also, bending over her, kissing from her chin to her heels, and up again. She quivered with longing, and caressed his shoulders with her fingers when he came near to her again. This time when he lay down, he lay half on her, one leg over her, pushing her thighs apart with his leg, casually, yet with purpose.

His fingers went again to her hips, then around the smooth thigh to her inner thigh. She shivered at his touch, he paused, then went on slowly. Presently he came to her intimate parts, and caressed them gently with his fingers and thumb. Going over and over her, until she felt the heat of response building inside her.

Finally he moved over her, and slowly brought them together. He had left the lamp on, she could see him in the dimness, through half-parted eyelids, and he was so large—

above her like a dark shadow—yet her lover, not a stranger—She felt him inside her, pressing firmly, and something gave her a sharp pain.

"Oh—Zach—" she cried out, and clutched at him, tried to push him off.

Tears ran down her cheeks, involuntary tears, she had not meant to cry. But it did hurt, that quick sharp pain. He soothed her gently, lying back beside her. But he was determined, and again mounted her, and this time he pushed home, inside her.

It hurt again, not so sharply, and he moved slowly back and forth. He cradled her in his arms, and kissed her wet cheeks, and insisted on pushing further inside. When he finally came, and the pain eased, she was glad, and relieved. He drew back, and lay down beside her, breathing hard.

He took her in his arms, then, soothed her, but he was sleepy and relaxed, pleased with her. He went off to sleep. She did not sleep soon, lying rigidly for a time, until she calmed down, and finally could relax. The lamp burned low, she finally got up, and washed herself, in the little basin in the bathroom, donned a nightdress, and lay down on the other bunk.

Zach was sleeping deeply in the other bed by the porthole. Was he happy? He seemed so. Her mouth twisted wryly. Her mother had warned her, and Zach had tried to be careful with her. The next times would be better, Elena had said.

She finally was able to sleep, and slept deeply into the morning hours. She wakened as Zach bent over and kissed her mouth. She wakened, opened her eyes, blinked up at him, intensely startled to see a man there.

He was dressed like a deckhand, in a light blue pants outfit, sandals, sleeves rolled up. He had brought her coffee, and set the mug beside the bed. She sat up to drink it with him, and eyed him cautiously over the edge of the mug.

His face was thoughtful, gentle; he had not shaved that morning, and a film of red hair lined his chin. She liked him like that, unshaven, off guard, softened from the hard business image.

He touched her cheek with one finger. "How are you, Rosita?"

She nodded. ''All—right,'' she managed to choke out. ''Sore?''

She nodded, her cheeks beginning to burn.

''It will be better next time. Not tonight, another time,'' he said quietly. ''You are so small, and I'm a big man. We'll take it easy, I don't want you to dread that I will be pouncing on you at all hours.''

''Thank—you,'' she whispered.

''Love me anyway?'' he said, with a grin, but his blue eyes, vivid as the sea, were anxious.

''Yes, Zach, I love you—very much,'' she managed to say.

''And I love you more every day,'' he said. He kissed her shoulder where the nightdress had slipped aside. ''Finish your coffee, and get dressed. The sea is glorious today!'' He smiled, and left her to wash and dress alone. She was grateful for his consideration. She had the feeling not all men were so sensitive to a girl's shyness.

She loved the days in the sun. They walked around the deck in sandals or tennis shoes, when the deck got slippery. They gazed into the distance, and Zach told her about the early days, of pirates on the Spanish Main, of the Spanish treasure ships which had come this way, of his ancestors and how they had come. One of his ancestors had inherited Elysia from an American Loyalist who had been threatened with tarring and feathering during the American Revolution. He had come to Elysia, bought the plantation land, brought his wife there, and eventually had three children.

''But the wife and children died of a fever, so the story goes. The plantation went to Morgan Hamilton, who had just left the English Navy following the end of the Napoleonic Wars. He married a girl out of a tavern on the shore, just before he set sail. And they were my ancestors,'' said Zach, with a grin.

''A tavern girl!'' gasped Rosita. She was a Gypsy dancer, was that above or below a tavern girl?

Zach smiled again, teasing her long strands of hair, winding them around his hand. ''An ex-sailor and a tavern girl, but a lovely one. Their portraits are at the Hamilton house in San Juan, but copies of them are in the main room at Elysia plantation. I'll show you them. And tell you their story, it is quite a romantic one! She smuggled her only living relative aboard the ship, and her brother and she planned to make their living somewhere in the Caribbean in case Morgan discarded her.''

"She thought he would discard her?" Rosita cried out in dismay, anguished all over again.

"Well, he had no such intentions! He fell in love with her right away. He won her in a card game, so the story goes."

Stranger and stranger! And Zach told the story so cheerfully. Isolde had never told her any such story. Could Zach be making it up? Isolde was so proud and so aristocratic, talking about her elegant family, her grandmother who had been a Russian ballerina, her French mother of a fine family.

Zach was laughing. "You think I'm making it all up! Wait till you get to Elysia. Some of the servants there are descended from those who waited on Morgan and Tess and their children. One of the girls, Dolores Abaco, is descended from a pirate!"

"Now I know you are teasing me," she said firmly. He only laughed again, and shook his head.

Several times they went ashore on an island, visited the town, wandered from shop to shop, stopped to eat at a primitive restaurant, on the waterfront, dining on fresh fish, fried breadfruit, or bowls of black bean soup with onions. They always had fresh fruit, which Zach washed and opened with a knife at the table, passion fruit, pineapple, papaya or limes. The coconut had to be chopped open with a machete, and it was offered with a broad grin by a black boy. The mango was past the season, it came in a jar put up by a native woman.

Zach did a curious thing each time. He would ask for the local rum, and taste it carefully, sipping at it, sometimes rinsing out the glass with juice of a lime, and trying another. The waiter would watch him, and bring another kind, seeming to understand he was comparing brands. He would show him the bottle, talk to him about whose rum it was, and where it was produced.

Rosita was content to taste it, usually with a half a glass of lime or papaya juice combined. The pure rum was too strong for her.

They would wander back to the ship, to find the sailors had taken on fresh food and water, and were ready to depart.

One afternoon, the sky clouded over rapidly with a black cloud, and soon it began to pour down rain, a sudden squall that drenched the sails, the deck and themselves. The sailors and Zach fought to get the sails down, and they drifted for a time with the immense waves until the squall was over.

Rosita had gone below stairs, into the cabin, to lie down and fight the seasickness which seized her as the ship threatened to overturn, the mast swaying recklessly from side to side. When it was over, she was immensely relieved. She came up on deck, to find the sailors sleeping in the wheelhouse, and Zach minding the wheel.

Zach turned and smiled at her, beckoned her. One sail was up and the brisk wind was blowing them sharply on their way. She came to him, he tucked her into his shoulder, and said, "I'll show you how to steer," and he did show her, though she would never dare do it alone.

It was fun, though, to feel the ship responding to the slightest turn of the wheel, to feel them being whipped along by the sharp wind. To hear the sail slapping, the waves running under the ship, to see the blue shining sea, the clouds fading away behind them.

The lines of worry and sleepless nights were fading from Zach's face. He was becoming even more bronzed, he hated wearing any kind of hat, and his red hair was burned golden. Rosita usually wore a sunhat, but even she was turning golden brown over most of her slight body. "Your legs are more gorgeous than ever," Zach told her, and grinned at her blush.

On the fifth day, they reached Elysia. They could have come faster with the motor used more often, but he had wanted a lazy trip. They docked in a sleepy harbor, and everybody in town came down to watch. There was so little doing, that the return of the Hamilton yacht was an event.

Rosita was surprised to find a car had come to meet them,

driven by a black smiling native. Zach explained, "We get a new car every couple of years, ship it by freighter from the States, run it good, then give it away to some family as a prize for something. That way we keep having cars here, freighters bring us oil and gasoline for them. They are never scrapped. When one breaks down completely, it is used for spare parts for the other ones."

The car was a Ford Fairmont, in a lovely shade of blue, and they put their luggage inside and were off. The sailors would live on board the yacht, taking care of it, and visiting their friends on the island until time to depart.

It was a dusty ride over an unpaved road along the windward side of the island of Elysia, up the coast, to the last plantation. Remains of two other plantation houses were on the way, Rosita looked at them curiously. The white and pink coral frames still showed among the weeds. "Other families who sold out eventually," Zach explained briefly.

The fields were full of low stands of sugarcane. It had been planted not long ago, following the June harvest, and July clearings. It would mature in about sixteen months. The harvests followed each other, and there was continuous work throughout the year. Zach pointed out old mills where sugar still was processed, a huge wooden frame building where the sugar in crude form was boiled into molasses. He explained the process briefly. She tried to take it in, but realized she was too sleepy and dazed by everything to understand.

Zach was driving with about one-fourth attention, hanging out the window, driving slowly, studying the cane fields, waving to workers vigorously. This was a business trip as well as a honeymoon, as he had said, she realized with surprise.

They finally reached a lane of crushed coral, and he drove up between rows of ancient coconut palms. Before them was a large old house, many times painted and refurbished. The shutters were green, freshly painted. The base was of pink and white coral, a two-story house with a wide wooden veranda all the way around. The doors were flung open, they were beautifully carved, very old, she thought. Perhaps the original ones.

Large French windows of glass were set all around the

front veranda, to the sides. Zach parked, and said, "The servants will bring in the luggage, come on!" He seemed anxious for her to see the old plantation house.

A girl stood shyly at the front door, a beautiful dark girl with bushy black hair, golden earrings in her small ears, a beautiful smile on her face. "Dolores Abaco," introduced Zach. "This is my wife, Rosita Hamilton, Dolores."

"How do you do, Missus Hamilton?" The soft velvety voice was friendly, sweet.

As they climbed the wooden stairs, Rosita could not help answering the girl's friendly curious look with her own. Was this child really the descendant of pirates?

She showed them inside, with a proud delighted gesture of her graceful hand. Rosita gasped as she entered. The entire first floor was open, a cooling breeze swept from front door to back. Pillars upheld the second floor and divided the first floor into rooms. On the left front was a study with an old desk, chairs, glassed cabinets, and bookcases. On the right front was a beautiful drawing room with shining redwood sofas covered in rose and blue watered silk. Small costly tables inlaid with marble and semiprecious stones displayed statuettes of jade and ivory and porcelain. China vases were filled with tropical flowers: hibiscus, jasmine, anthuriums.

The older furniture was of mahogany and cedarwood, and equally beautiful, though more simply made. There were cabinets filled with beautiful shells and porcelains, a huge dining table and chairs to match of cedarwood, an open cupboard held a complete dining set of Limoges porcelain. Everywhere Rosita looked were evidences of loving care, precious antiques beside more modern items. Copper kettles filled with more flowers were perhaps once rum buckets, she thought. Ancient rifles and pistols hung in racks on the walls, along with several swords. The floors were shining parquet, grooved from the footsteps of many generations.

Several portraits decorated the walls of the room. Zach pointed out one of a man with gray red hair. "Supposed to be Uncle Thomas Hamilton, from the Revolution in America," he said. A matching portrait showed his wife and three children, who had died of a fever.

Rosita was even more interested in a portrait of a tall red-haired man, who looked so much like Zach, with bright red hair, dominating blue eyes in a bronzed face, wearing a handsome blue silk suit with ruffled sleeves. The girl who sat in the chair set before him was blond with thick curls about a small pretty face, and her blue eyes shone. She had a firm chin, though, and the face while lovely was not that of a society woman. A child was held in her arms, a boy of about two, with bright red hair and an imperious expression. The man stood with his hand on her shoulder, as though to say, "This is my property!"

"Morgan and Tess Hamilton," said Zach. "And their first son, Morgan. They had four others, and five girls, two died young. The others survived, and live all around the Caribbean. That is, their descendants live here!" He laughed softly. "They are all so real to me, that I think of them as still alive." He gazed up at the portrait with affection.

Zach took her upstairs then, where Dolores had put fresh sheets on the huge beds in the master bedroom and the lovely one in front of it. "Where master and missus stay," explained the pretty girl shyly. "When you want to bathe, I will bring hot water," and she indicated the tin tubs.

Zach grinned at Rosita's surprise. "I didn't warn you, this house doesn't have water piped in. I usually swim in the sea. But don't you go without me! There is sharp coral out there and the tides can drag you under. I know where it's safe. Never go without me!"

"All right, Zach," she agreed, gazing about with more fascination at the furnishings. "Does Isolde come here?"

"Isolde? Never, not after a couple of experiences in our youth." he grimaced. "No, she doesn't care for the primitive life, she told us all emphatically. And mother didn't care for it either, though she couldn't refuse father anything. She would go wherever he led."

Rosita nodded, she understood that. She would go wherever Zach led. Besides, she loved this place already. She touched the carved bedpost, imagined pretty blond Tess in that bed, gazed from the windows, and imagined what they had seen in the old days. Zach came to the window, put his arm about her, in a gesture that was already natural for him.

"I'll tell you their whole story while we are here," he said. "They fought off a slave rebellion, greedy neighbors, an attempt at murder by a nobleman who wanted Tess. They had some wild times, but they survived. We are survivors, we Hamiltons."

Later he told her, as they ate dinner in the cool dining room, that many of the servants were descended from slaves set free by Morgan and Tess. Some had wandered away to other islands, but many had remained, to intermarry, or marry those who had come here to settle.

They had their old customs. They cut the cane and harvested it, set the cane in the rollers, boiled the molasses, and prepared it for the wooden barrels. Those barrels were taken to the factory in San Juan, where the rest of the work of making sugar and rum went on. This was one of several island plantations now owned by the Hamiltons, and supplied the San Juan distillery amply, so they had no need to buy from other suppliers, and could keep careful control on their quality.

After the cane was cut, and the harvest completed, the children of the former slaves had a cane party, at which a cane king and queen were chosen, presents given as though it were Christmas. Cane time was even more important to some of them than the Christian holidays. They had their work songs, their evening songs, their party songs, their dances.

"Do they still believe in voodoo?" Rosita asked thoughtfully, thinking of the cane workers in Haiti and other Caribbean islands.

Zach nodded. "Yes, it is mixed up sometimes with Christian beliefs. But it is there, a heritage from black Africa and the other islands of the Caribbean. I have gone to voodoo ceremonies, especially when I was young and they indulged me. They don't often want whites there, not at the real voodoo."

She was silent for a time. It was so strange, here in this

plantation house so full of history. She could almost feel the strong vital presence of Morgan Hamilton, so like her red-haired Zach. The gentle firm face of Tess haunted her, so strong and yet so small. And she had lived, and borne so many children, and wielded a rifle when she had to, and endured. They were those who endured. They were survivors, the strong ones.

Zach was like that. Rosita hoped she was also. She thought she was. For the Gypsies were survivors also, those persecuted throughout Europe, the ones who laughed and defied and even died for their freedom to roam. She remembered the stories her father had told them, of the Gypsies under the Nazis who had been given identity cards and told they had to use them. The Nazis would come to their campfires, and order them to show their cards—only to find that they had used them in card games, and there was no telling again who was who!

And they had fought for their freedom. Alejandra's husband, Alfonso, had died in 1939 during the Spanish Civil War. Others had died also, her uncles and granduncles, fighting guerrilla warfare, for Gypsies knew every mountain pass, every rock and crevass and dangerous road through the snowy mountains to the north in Basque regions. They could slip from country to country, using their Gypsy identity to find relatives and countrymen to hide them and slip them further, so that Gypsies always managed to get from Russia to Portugal, from Spain to Belgium, from England to Greece, with little trouble.

Zach reached for her glass and filled it with Hamilton rum, the new silver rum he had brought with him. "What are you thinking, Rosita?" he asked.

"I was thinking about my Gypsy people," she replied, watching his face, for his reaction. "We are survivors also."

He did not show disapproval when she spoke of her Gypsy heritage. How did he truly feel? He smiled, raised his glass, and waited for her to raise hers. "To us, Rosita, and our people. May the ghosts of our ancestors watch over us, and be proud of us, the survivors!"

Relieved, she drank to that with him.

Chapter 16

Zach stirred on the hot dry sand, and wakened. He blinked at the sun, squinting his eyes behind the dark glasses. From its position it was about eleven in the morning, and getting hotter. The sun was blazing hot by noon and until four in the afternoon.

He turned over and looked at Rosita, sleeping beside him. These days and nights had been good for them both. She had relaxed also, sleeping more, eating better, her color deeper and more rosy and golden. She had needed the rest as much if not more than he did.

She was lying on her stomach, her slim limbs sprawled in luxurious abandon. Her hair was in a single long dark braid down her back, over the yellow *maillot*. He leaned over her, studied the beautiful body of his bride, the lean, trim waist, the widened hips, the long neat legs, the beautiful feet. Then back up to her shoulders, her small head, the dark hair. He bent over, brushed the braid aside, feeling the heavy weight of her thick hair on his wrist, and kissed her neck.

Rosita stirred, murmured, "Ummmm," and he smiled. She was just getting accustomed to him. At first, when she wakened she would stare up at him with dark bewildered eyes.

243

She rolled over, stretched and yawned, "Time to get up?" she murmured in a sleep-husky voice.

"Yes, it's getting hot. We'll have one more quick swim to wash off the lotion and sand." He helped her up, steadied her as she stumbled in her sleepiness. They walked down the sandy beach, their private one in front of the plantation house, and waded into the sun-warmed waters.

They had to be careful. Out just a little further was pretty deadly white coral, where they could cut their feet open with a single careless step. They avoided those places, swam for a few minutes lazily, then came out again, to run up to the house with their gear, bottles of lotion, towels, sunglasses.

In the house, it was almost dark after the bright sun. Dim and cool. Dolores appeared, to smile and suggest tea.

They toweled themselves dry, put on casual clothes, and came down again, to drink hot tea with milk, the way the English did, said Zach. Rosita nodded. "I remember from London, how delicious it was on a cold rainy day. I never thought I would drink strong hot tea with plenty of hot milk—but I did, and soon enjoyed it very much."

"And it tastes good on a very hot day also," said Zach, smiling across at her. How very lovely she was, in a pale yellow sundress with gathered bodice, sleeveless, showing her golden arms. Lovely, and warm of heart, abandoning herself to him in bed with a delicious trust that she would follow wherever he led. How had he gotten so lucky, he sometimes asked himself. To find a pretty wife, intelligent, gentle, with such a sweet nature. A man's dream! He sometimes shuddered to think what he might have gotten—a shrew, a virago, as some of his men friends had done. It was difficult to know what was under the smooth surface of some girls, all smiles and willingness on dating—but whew, after the marriage— what a change! as one man had told him angrily.

"You know what I would like to do today?" said Rosita, setting down the fragile porcelain cup gently, gazing with pleasure at the white surface and the gold rims, with the violets scattered on the white. "I'd like to look through that old trunk you found the other day. They looked like journals, some of those books, not just reading books.''

"Why not? I'll bring it dówn from the storeroom, and we can have a time with it. I was curious about that at times, but never bothered to look through it.'' He went upstairs, found the small flowered trunk in the back storage room, and carried it down to the dining area. Dolores promptly scolded him.

"Mr. Zach, that is so dirty! Whyfor you bring it down here, huh?'' She was setting the dining table carefully, taking pleasure in the creamy linen mats, the bright yellow plates and cups, the wooden-handled silver. She looked with great displeasure at the dusty object he set down on her clean floor.

"Give me a rag, Dolores, I'll clean it úp.''

She gave him a rag, but said disapprovingly, "You take that right outdoors, Mr. Zach, and clean it up on the porch. We don't want that dirt in our food, do we?''

He grinned at her, and took it outside obediently. He scrubbed it up gently, with a damp cloth, then a dry one, and soon it was pretty clean, though dirt had been ingrained on the cloth-covered trunk, and the flower pattern had faded.

He opened it out on the veranda also, and took out the first few books. Rosita wandered out there, and sat down in a rocking chair beside an iron table painted white. He began to set the books before her, she took the cloth and dusted them as he took them out. She glanced inside one after another.

"Oh, Zach, look, a poetry book!'' She glanced over the poems, reading eagerly. "Milton—and some Bible verses, and Robert Herrick!'' She had opened it to one page, and began to smile.

"Read that one,'' he commanded curiously, taking out some other books.

She chuckled, richly, delighting him. She so seldom laughed aloud, at least she had not with him. She had with Delphine, he thought. He dusted briskly as she read.

> Gather ye rosebuds while ye may,
> Old Time is still a-flying

And this same flower that smiles today,
    Tomorrow will be dying.

"Um—appropriate," he grinned down at her, glancing significantly over her slim body. She wrinkled her nose at him, and he bent and kissed her nose.

"I was just thinking about convent school. Our English teacher disapproved of this one," she laughed. "She was an old nun, a bit dried-up," and her eyes shadowed. "I should not laugh at her, she was a good soul."

She was kind, even in her thoughts, he realized. She leafed absently through the volume, set it aside to read later. "This must have been Tess's trunk," he said. "Her books, she has her name written in some, look," and he showed her the flyleaf.

He carried a small pile of books through to the living room area, and set them carefully on a cloth that protected the parquet floors. Dolores would have his skin if he ruined her beautiful floors that she waxed so carefully every week. He went back for another pile, Rosita helped him carry the rest of them.

"Lunch is ready, folks," said Dolores, smiling from the dining area, so they went back. It was delicious as always.

She had prepared fresh corn on the cob, and they ate it with melted butter dripping from the cobs. There were pork chops, cooked with hot tomato sauce, green beans and onions cooked with bacon. For dessert a bowl of mixed tropical fruits, papaya and pineapple, oranges and limes, and chunks of fresh coconut. They drank silver Hamilton rum mixed with lime juice, and finished with hot black coffee in old fragile porcelain *demi-tasse* cups.

As they left the table, Rosita sighed, "Oh, I'm full! I am not used to so much—and I am so out of practice! Zach, I really must do my exercises tomorrow morning."

He had kept her in bed with him mornings, rising only to go down to swim in the blue ocean. "Oh, I think I give you enough exercise," he teased, to see her cheeks turn pink.

"You know what I mean! Ballet exercises. The bed railing at the end is a proper height,'' she added thoughtfully. ''I can use that as my *barre*.''

She swung one leg absently, holding her hand on her hip.

''Forget work for now, I am,'' he said, and held out his hand to her, as they walked to the dining area. She slipped her hand readily into his, he squeezed the fingers.

They sat down on one of the sofas, he picked up some of the books to glance over them. Rosita started on another pile, and soon found treasure.

''Zach, I think this is Tess's diary!'' she exclaimed. ''Listen to this, 'Morgan went over to Señor Quintero's today to consult with Vincent. He returned with the following recipe for making coconut liqueur. Begin with three-year rums, and prepare the following coconut mixture. Take the milk of a dozen coconuts—' ''

''Hey, let me see that!'' exclaimed Zach. She handed the worn red journal to him, and he read it intently. ''My word, Rosita! Just what I wanted.'' He felt dizzy with excitement. ''This is the old way of making coconut liqueurs!''

''Is it still a good way?'' she asked with interest.

''It may be. That's what I have to find out. Morgan Hamilton made a good grade of rum in his day, and some old folks talk about the liqueurs that Hamilton's used to make. We dropped them about the time of Prohibition, and never went back to them. The formulas were discarded, somehow, in a clean sweep when we built the new plants. Grandfather said we would not go back to them, but he used to talk about the liqueurs—not perfect, but excellent when they worked out right.''

He turned over the pages, found another reference, and read it eagerly.

''Listen to this, Rosita! She says, 'Morgan has been trying Señor Quintero's suggestions for making a coffee liqueur. I boiled strong Brazilian coffee for half an hour until it was the consistency of thick ropy molasses. Then Morgan added more sugar in the amount of—' My God, Rosita, just what I wanted!'' he said, with great excitement. He turned over pages hastily, but did not immediately find more.

"Is this important, Zach?" she asked, puzzled. She picked up another red journal, and began to leaf through it.

"Terribly important, honey, or it might be," he said, with his voice lowered. "I want to try to come up with a new line of rums to improve our business. We have been experimenting with various mixes, but some don't turn out well, our lime one was a dreadful failure. But Kevin and Aunt Hortense are continuing to experiment—" He stopped, having found another reference. He muttered, " 'Take the juices of a barrel of oranges—' "

"If this is important, let us mark the places," she said practically. She went over to the desk in the other area, and brought back some white paper. She tore it into long strips, and began to set them into the places in the journal, carefully, so the fragile pages would not tear. While Zach read in growing excitement, she began to turn over the pages in a second journal gently.

He read, thinking, "If this works, Rosita, oh, if this works—it might not, I mean, this is primitive chemistry—but if it works—"

"Why should it not work, Zach? The people who used to work with herbs in the old days came up with good medicines, before they ever knew much about chemistry. Our botany teacher told us that. And people drank the liqueurs and enjoyed them."

They gazed at each other, her cheeks were pink with excitement, he felt shocked and tremendously thrilled. If this was the answer to their puzzle—what a boost to their work at the factory! He tried to calm himself, it might not be. But what if—what if the answers to all his searching could be contained in these little journals of his ancestor, written so long ago, and sitting so innocently upstairs in the storage room of the old plantation on Elysia!

While Zach read and wrote down notes, Rosita searched the other books, and sorted them. She set aside the poetry books, the volumes of Milton, Shakespeare, Chaucer, Edmund Spenser, John Donne—she kept thinking that Tess had had a fine taste for the classics. And she found some books with a heavier black underlining—could it be Morgan's?

She set aside also the heavier volumes of philosophy, some history, and then discovered some few tomes of science, on the sugarcane industry in the Caribbean, the making of rums, the flora and fauna of the Caribbean area, and so on. She would show them to Zach when he finished with the journals.

Tess's journals finally lay in a neat pile on the small table beside the sofa, some eighteen little red journals, in her neat handwriting. Readable after all these years, she wrote with such a clear fine hand. Some of the pages were of accounts, she listed the prices they obtained for their muscovado sugar, their fine white sugar, their one-year rums, their two-year, and so on to their best six-year rums. She wrote of everyday events, some pigs were born, some trees were uprooted by a storm. They had planted more hibiscus starts from trees and bushes in the hills. Louis Abaco had brought them some white jasmine starts, and she had planted them about the house. Rosita marked the pages with white slips of paper to show Zach when he was through perusing the liqueur recipes.

Zach kept shaking his head in wonder, and ever-growing excitement. "Listen to this, Rosita!" he would say, and read another recipe. "They kept experimenting with liqueurs, and this one was a success, Tess notes. The one with lime! Lime liqueur, and we have it all wrong—Kevin told me the other day he was unable to get it right, the fresh limes did not work, and here is the answer! Boiling the lime juice—adding the rum and sugar gradually while continuing to boil—"

They went through two journals that day, he continued that evening, as Rosita began to write out some of the directions from the journals for him, sitting at the big desk. He looked over at her bent dark head as she wrote, thinking, "This is where my ancestor Tess sat and wrote, probably at the very desk, and Rosita looks so natural there!" He felt closer to his new little wife. They were continuing the tradition of working together started by Morgan Hamilton and his Tess.

The next day, he went out to the cane fields early to

observe them, and asked Rosita to go along. She agreed eagerly, put on heavy jeans and a jacket to protect her tender skin from the sharp cane, and in boots walked through the fields with him. She was quiet, her face alert and eyes alive with wonder at all the sights. Some of the younger ones were weeding the cane fields, others worked with the planting of more fields.

In the heat of the afternoon, they scanned through more of the journals. Zach finally went back, put the journals in order by year, and said, "We'll have to read them more carefully, Rosita, and discover which recipes worked, which experiments were discarded, and so on."

"Then we should bring the journals back to San Juan with us," she said thoughtfully. "I have longed to do that, Zach, I should like to read what Tess wrote about her life here in the old days."

"We'll do it. When we are ready to leave, we'll take the books with us. I'd like to have them in the library back home anyway." Then he paused, frowning slightly. "I think we'll keep them in our suite, Rosita. Not in the study, at least not for now. I want these kept private, all this information. Okay?"

She nodded, unquestioning.

"You see," he went on, "this information could be valuable. We have secret formulas for our rums, most companies do, and if we come up with some good liqueurs, I'll want to keep those formulas secret also. If anybody finds out where we got this information—could ruin our efforts."

"Who would do that, Zach? Other companies?"

He hesitated, then told her, "Rosita, it may be within our own company." He told her about the bugging operations. Her eyes were very wide, as he told the extent of it. "You know what happened in the study at home," he went on. "The office has been bugged again and again, it really has me angry. I cannot figure out who is getting in to do this, because guards are stationed there all the time."

"That means that someone within the company is doing it," she suggested, without surprise.

He nodded. "I'm afraid so," he said, quietly. "Rosita, I

will be telling you things from time to time about the company,
I have to talk to someone, and I don't know anybody more
likely than a wife to confide in," and he hugged her close to
him. "Especially a wife like you! I don't want mother or
granny to know, Isolde and Delphine are not to be confided in,
okay? Only me and Kevin."

She nodded, her face solemn, and he kissed her mouth.
"I will be very careful, Zach. Thank you—for trusting me."

He was a little startled. Yes, he had trusted her, unquestioningly, he felt he could trust her with his life. She was such
an honest child, she always had been. Quiet, and dependable,
never discussing any of Isolde's business, until he had asked
her direct questions.

Finally, reluctantly, after almost a month on Elysia, he
decided they must go home again. "Much as I hate to leave
this paradise," he said, regretfully.

"I feel the same way. But we must go back to work," she
sighed.

"We?" He teased her chin with his finger. "I must work,
I don't want you to slave for Isolde. Okay? She may think she
is getting you back again, but I don't want you driving yourself
or letting her drive you."

"But, Zach, I do want to stay in practice," she said,
distressed. "I did work hard all my life in dancing, it is part of
my life."

"Well, maybe two hours of practice a day, to stay in
shape," he said, and let his gaze wander down her slim rounded
form. "Not that I have any complaints about your shape!"

She was a little more rounded, filled out about her hips
and breasts, a glow to her of more sleep, good food, rest,
happiness, the sunshine and swimming, the love-making.

They sailed home in four days, making faster time, because Zach figured he had better get home on Saturday, and be
ready to work again on Monday. He had ideas he was eager to
work on—yet, how could he do the experiments if he had to
keep everything secret?

He would work with the experiments on paper, he thought,

and continue to read through Tess's journals. Rosita could help him there, and he explained what he wanted to her. She agreed eagerly to help him.

They arrived home in late October, on Saturday, October 21, tied up at the dock, and Zach phoned for one of the limousines to meet them. He had the litle flowered trunk of books with them, their luggage, straw hats, fishing poles bought on one of the islands, two cases of rums of other companies to sample, boxes of sugarcane samples. The chauffeur laughed and shook his head when he pulled up.

"You been on holiday, Mr. Zach?" he grinned. "You look mightily like one of them tourists!"

"I feel like one too," he said, helping load the gear. "We had a good time on Elysia, and the cane is coming fine."

"That's good, that's good," and his gaze approved them both. "Sunshine and fresh air, and lots of time to swim and such. You look mighty good!"

At home, his mother said the same, kissing him. "Oh, Zach, it has done you a world of good," she said spontaneously. "You look so refreshed. Thank you, Rosita," and she kissed Rosita with the first genuine smile she had given his wife. Zach was pleased, he knew his mother had not fully approved this marriage.

Rosita smiled back, kissed her, and Madame Sonia even more warmly, and Delphine with a big hug.

"Delphine, show them the rooms," said his mother. "I've been trying to fix them up, Zach. But you might want new paint on the walls, Rosita might want another color."

"Oh, I'm sure they will be just fine," Rosita murmured.

Zach did not commit himself until he saw the rooms. His mother had made up fresh curtains of filmy white organza, fresh draperies of rose in the bedroom and blue in the parlor. The Persian rugs had been taken up, cleaned and put down again. The ornaments had been carefully sorted, his mother had taken her favorites, and set out what Rosita might choose or discard.

Delphine said, "Mother thought you might have things of your own you would want, Rosita. Or you may gradually acquire things. I thought you might want your big picture of Pavlova on the wall, that painting we gave you in New York.''

"Oh, yes—if Zach does not mind!''

"I don't mind. Come look at the other portraits," said Zach, spotting them in the parlor. "Here are the originals of Thomas Hamilton and of his family, and the one of Morgan and Tess and little Morgan. Here are some smaller ones of other ancestors.'' He showed Rosita all around the suite.

The walls were of cream, the long French windows opened to the balcony when they chose to let in more air. The smaller bedroom had another bed, which Zach could use when Rosita was having a child, or ill, or when he came home so late that he didn't want to disturb her.

His room was in amber and gold, the master bedroom in rose with multicolored Persian rug and rose and gold furniture. The sandalwood dresser had a fresh rose and gold skirt. The lovely upstairs parlor was cool and attractive in blue and white with touches of rose and gold. Everything was spotless and inviting.

His mother might not fully approve the marriage, but her manners and conventions were impeccable. The new bride must be welcomed as she herself had been welcomed when she married Thomas.

Rosita showered first, then left the bathroom to Zach. He shaved off his growing beard and mustache, with a grimace for their toughness after five weeks, and promised himself a haircut on Monday. When he returned to the bedroom, Rosita was dressed in a pale champagne-colored silk short dress that showed her long golden legs.

"There were new dresses in the wardrobe, Zach," she said shyly, her cheeks pink with excitement. "Did you buy those for me before we left?''

"I ordered some made here, some sent for from New York, with the help of Isolde and Delphine," he said. "Delphine supplied the dress that fit you best, I gave that to one of our *modistes* here—I think that is what she is called. She promised to use the greatest care in having them made. But if they don't fit, you are to return them to her, and go back for fittings.''

"Oh, Zach, you are so very kind to me!"

"Believe me, darling, it is very easy," he smiled, and kissed her fresh glowing cheek. "Let's see what has come," and he opened the wardrobe door to survey the row of gowns. At one end were her own cottons, and some linens, with a couple of evening frocks. Then the new gowns; he approved a champagne taffeta in full length with a slit skirt, a layered blue silk, a rose linen suit with matching blouses, an aqua suit, a turquoise day dress, a silky dress in amber, one in pale gold. "Good, I hope you will like these. And others will be coming from New York, I think these are all San Juan makes—" He examined the labels quickly. "Yes, these are all from San Juan. So the designer dresses are yet to come."

"Designer dresses? Zach, I don't need that!" she gasped.

"Darling girl, I'm afraid you will. As my wife, you will be appearing at receptions, dinners, entertainments for visiting dignitaries, public appearances with me at San Juan functions—"

She visibly gulped, her eyes wide and rather frightened. "Zach, are you—so important, really?"

"Yes, my dear," he grimaced, and laughed. "And so are you. Not just as my wife, but your reputation as a dancer is well known throughout Puerto Rico, as well as New York, London, Paris, etcetera! As a former prima ballerina, and my wife you will be carefully observed, and I mean to make it worth their time!" He pinched her cheek lightly.

She said something quickly in Spanish, shaking her head.

"And," said Zach, "you will need suitable dresses for showing off the family jewels. Kevin took them to be cleaned for you. Diamonds, the Hamilton rubies from pre-World War I, and other things—"

"Oh, Zach!"

"And the sapphire pendant and earrings and ring of little Tess, Rosita! You will be glad to wear those, won't you?"

She relaxed and smiled. "Oh, yes, something of hers. That would make me very happy!"

He put on her an amber necklace, and gave her the matching earrings to wear, and had the satisfaction of seeing her glow at dinner. She looked so lovely, with her new golden tan, her beautifully simple silk gown, he was very proud of her. His mother was animated and smiling, in her pale gray and lilac dress. She looked so much more lively.

Madame Sonia was quietly pleased, glancing from one to the other, and nodding in satisfaction. The honeymoon had been a success, her Zach was happy, and Rosita more lovely than before.

Delphine was eager to have her friend back, and chattered animatedly about what they would do this winter.

Isolde said sternly, "And practice is what we will do!"

"No way," said Zach, as Delphine began to pout. "The girls may practice to keep in shape, but I don't want them working so hard. If you want to go on in ballet, Isolde, that is up to you. My wife is not going to. And Delphine—well, we shall discuss that later."

Isolde was furious. And the next weeks she was even more furious, as she found that Zach meant exactly what he said. She had to scrap her plans for them for the spring season in New York, for he would not allow her to work Rosita hard. Delphine would not do it, if Rosita did not.

Instead Zach was taking pride in showing off his beautiful wife to San Juan society. He had never cared much for running around in a crowd, but he did want them to go to musical events, dinners, dances. And always Rosita would have a beautiful designer gown to wear, and family jewels, diamonds, sapphires, rubies, amber, pearls. He had family dinners, of course; they often gathered on Sundays, and for holidays, and Rosita must be gowned particularly well, for they were critical of her.

He wanted Rosita to be at ease with them, able to dress so beautifully she could forget it, and smile and relax. And his confidence extended to her, so she seemed to enjoy the events, though she was still so shy she did not speak much in company, but only smiled and clung close to his side. One day she would grow in confidence that would then match her beauty, he thought.

Chapter 17

At breakfast, Zach finished his coffee; he seemed absent-minded. Rosita sat beside him quietly, trying to plan her day.

She was worried about her mother. The operation had been a success, she had returned from the honeymoon and no news of her family, to find with relief that all had gone well. She had not confided in Zach for he might feel he must pay for the operation. Generosity was automatic with him, but she did not want her family dependent on him, and her father would not stand for it either. His pride was strong.

And she must talk to Isolde one day about the money she had paid them in August. Must that be returned? Rosita thought of the sums she had seen on the calendar engagement book, and mentally shook her head. She thought she had earned what Isolde had given to the family. She had received no wages at all, just board and room and travel expenses. And she had earned much for them in those two weary years. Surely that made up for her expenses in the early years. But she must discuss it with Isolde.

Then again, why should she? Those sums haunted her, two thousand dollars, five thousand dollars and even that sum of fourteen thousand dollars after she had made such a success of *Giselle*.

Isolde had taken care of her for four years and a little more. Clothes, food and shelter, ballet shoes, training, trips, travel home.

Yet Rosita had brought in large sums of money, far more than had been given to her parents. Of course, Dimitre had often danced with her, but that *Giselle* had not been with Dimitre. The success of the ballet with that wonderful Italian young man had been due to them alone, the chemistry between them, their harmony of body and spirit, the laughter and friendship they had shared.

The more Rosita thought about it, the more she thought she had really paid back Isolde for the years of payments to the Dominguez family. She had done what Isolde demanded unquestioningly, she had practiced, performed, followed directions. That she was not going on in ballet was a big disappointment, but Isolde could not expect to dominate her entire life!

Rosita would never demand to be paid for those years of performing, but neither would she ask her parents to pay back any money. She had defected to Zach and marriage, yet she felt she owed Isolde no more. They were even.

Zach finally said, "I won't be home for dinner, Rosita. I have a business meeting, don't know how I can get out of it," and he sighed.

"Those advertising men from the States?" she asked, her thoughts veering to him anxiously. He looked so tired again, and it was only a month since they had returned home radiant and glowing with health.

He nodded. "Yes, we must discuss the campaigns. Uncle William is determined to put in scantily-clad women, and I am dead against it!"

"Right on," said Delphine automatically. "Women's lib shall reach even San Juan!"

"Delphine, don't use vulgar slang," said her mother. "But I must confess I agree with Delphine, for other reasons. I do not see that women with no clothes on should cause men to drink!"

Zach burst out laughing, so did Kevin.

"You know what I mean!" said his mother severely, her delicate porcelain face pink. "Don't tease your mother!"

"Sorry, mother," said Zach. "However—to return to the question at hand— I shall not be home for dinner, in fact, don't expect me until two in the morning. Kevin and I must give the men dinner and somehow persuade Uncle William to go along with us. We should wind up things tomorrow. I want them to open another type of campaign."

"Families," said Madame Sonia unexpectedly. "You should show families in your ads. At least, man and wife, perhaps entertaining graciously, with rum drinks made so beautiful with pineapple sticks, and the ladies in gorgeous dresses, so feminine."

"An intermission at the ballet," said Isolde, rousing from her brooding to enter spiritedly into the conversation. "Beautifully clad people drinking beautiful drinks, discussing the ballet—with a poster beside them of a ballerina in a classical tutu—"

"And a scene on the beach," Delphine suggested, beaming. "People in smart swim togs, and a little table of drinks, beautiful cool drinks with different colors, silver rum, gold rum, on the rocks, and in mixes, like Tom Collins."

Zach put his hand to his head. "My family!" he laughed. "You dazzle me. Okay, I'll put it to the ad men. It sounds great to me. Rum as a drink for beautiful people." He stood up, smiling around the table. "Thanks, everyone, I appreciate your ideas. Darling, don't expect me back until two or so—I'll use the other bedroom," he added in Rosita's ear, regretfully, and kissed her cheek.

She said quickly, "I think I'll go over to the family today, Zach. I haven't seen them since last week."

"Fine. Give them my love. Everybody okay?"

She hesitated, his keen eyes noted it. "Well, mother has been ill, she is much better," she said, with caution.

"Why didn't you say so? Anything I can do?" He was immediately concerned, and she was grateful. She shook her head, smiling.

"Father has managed everything, thank you. I just want to make sure she isn't trying to do too much."

After Zach had left, Delphine said, "Let me come with you today, Rosita? I haven't seen your family for a time."

Rosita nodded. "Of course, if that is all right with your mother."

"I do hope you might practice first," said Isolde gloomily. "Or I'll be up there by myself," she added accusingly.

"Yes, I would like to practice, I try to every morning that I can," said Rosita quietly. Isolde usually arose later, and was just coming as Rosita left. Delphine had been there only once in a while.

"Then I'll come too," said Delphine.

"Slowly, darlings, you just had breakfast," said Madame Sonia. "Shall I come and count for you?"

Rosita felt relieved. Madame Sonia was a more gentle dictator than Isolde. "Please do, madame. It would be kind of you to help us."

"I'll come also, a little later, and we'll work on hands today," said Madame Isabeau unexpectedly. "I was talking to Delphine the other day, and I think she is having trouble with some gestures."

That pleased Isolde immensely. Her mother was taking an interest in life once more. They had a good session that morning that lasted a little more than two hours, with Madame Sonia counting and suggesting the exercises, gradually building up from the gentle first movements to the more trying difficult ones.

The last half-hour Madame Isabeau took over the class. As Madame Sonia sat in an armchair at the side and watched, the three girls followed the direction of Madame Isabeau. It was odd to see the dainty Mrs. Hamilton in a gray leotard and short skirt, ballet slippers on her feet, and leg warmers smothering the lines of her legs, earnestly going over the hand movements like a ballet mistress which she had been once, for a time after her marriage.

Her grace reminded Rosita that she too had once been a prima ballerina, in the Paris Ballet. How lovely she must have been in *Giselle*, and *Sleeping Beauty*. She had such grace, she was small and porcelain-exquisite, like a Royal Doulton doll figure.

The class over, and Isolde glowing with satisfaction, they all left the studio. Rosita went to her room, showered, and put on a warmer dress. It was November, and the days could be chilly, the nights cold. The rains were overdue.

Delphine met her at the stairs, and they went together. Marcos was waiting for them, Rosita had telephoned him to come at twelve. He beamed at seeing them both, especially at Delphine in her demure blue suit and tiny hat. His gaze lingered on her.

"How is mother?" asked Rosita, giving her brother a little punch to remind him that Delphine did not know about the operation.

"Pretty good, she gets tired readily, but the doctor said it was to be expected."

"What is wrong with her?" Delphine asked alertly.

Rosita evaded, and hoped her family would also. But she soon learned that Delphine was as persistent as ever. Within an hour, she had learned of Margarita's operation, and her look reproached Rosita. "Why didn't you tell Zach?" she asked quietly, when they were momentarily alone. "He would have wanted to know!"

"Yes, he would have wanted to pay also, and my family is proud," said Rosita. "I don't want him to feel he has to pay for my whole family! And father would not permit it."

"Rosita, I think you do not know Zach," said Delphine, thoughtfully. "He will not thank you for shutting him out."

Rosita felt puzzled. She did not mean to shut him out, she just wanted to keep the family's affairs private, and her family felt she had taken enough money from Isolde for them. She had earned that money. Otherwise the Hamiltons owed them nothing. They could manage, they had always managed, even in war times.

She talked to Marcos about the act. "It does not go well," he said flatly. "Cristina wants to come back in, but you know her husband does not wish it, and there are the children. If she starts a baby, and has a miscarriage, he would be very hurt and angry."

"I'll bet she never figured on having four children," laughed Luisa. She was happy now, she had a boyfriend who seemed serious. A truck driver, but such a nice man! Not a dancer, he had three left feet, he said, but he loved to see her dancing. And maybe she too would marry one day before long.

"What about if I danced with you when I could?" asked Rosita. "I cannot often leave the house, nights, but when Zach is busy like tonight—"

Marcos seized her hands. "Would you, could you? It would make such a difference!" he said fervently. "Even if the audience never knew when you were going to dance, it would encourage them to come! And papa would be encouraged also—he is sometimes in despair, and thinks we should hire more girls."

"What about me?" asked Delphine pertly. "I could dance too!"

"Flamenco?" he smiled.

"Why not? You know I can fake the foot movements, and do the hands," she said with cheerful heresy.

Rosita protested; Pascual, when approached, hesitated. "I do not know what your family would think—if you dance in a nightclub," he said, going to the heart of the matter.

"Why not? Rosita is even more important now than I am, she is Mrs. Zachariah Lothaire Hamilton, and she dances!" Delphine laughed up at him, pouted and got her way.

Delightedly, she dressed in one of Cristina's dresses. Elena measured her and took the dress to take out a seam at the waist by about one inch. While Elena changed the gown, Pascual and Marcos went over steps with her, as Oliverio and Jacinto played the music. They practiced a couple of hours, had an early dinner, relaxed, then practiced again until time to leave for the nightclub.

Delphine glowed with excitement, the days had been so dull for her and the nights worse. She knew no men to date, she had been so sheltered, and her family guarded her all too well. As a wealthy girl, and beautiful, she wanted to be loved for herself, and was also wary of who she dated. With Rosita's family, she felt loved and wanted, they treated her so naturally. Delphine knew Rosita suspected she was much drawn to Marcos. They were much alike, these two glowing people, living and with a sense of fun, caring about others, gentle and lovable.

The two girls caused a sensation at the club. They knew Rosita, they shouted their welcomes to her, *"La Soledad! Flamenco Rosita! Our own Rosita Dominguez!"*

Some knew vaguely that she had married, but not to whom, others knew and were curious. But she was there, dancing more beautifully than ever, with her lithe body, her more mature frame, her sober little face shining with pleasure.

She did a lively solo, combining flamenco and a little ballet in the *pirouettes*, and the crowd went crazy, adoring her, enjoying what she did to the music of Oliverio's guitar. She danced one duet with Marcos, a daring rumba-bolero, with swoops and lifts that had them gasping and cheering.

Then Delphine took her turn, she had insisted on being in the line. She could not tap rapidly, but she had a lovely little face and an intriguing smile, a little demure grin that made them watch intently for what she would do next. Her little feet spun her around and the red skirts flicked her heels again, again. She could ape the movements of the other girls, and she took the edge of her skirt in her hand and fanned her feet recklessly, prancing about the stage. She got a big hand the first time, and that encouraged her.

Marcos was thrilled with her, that was evident. During the intermission, he begged Pascual, "Let me dance with her, papa, we can do a rumba easily."

"Please, Papa Pascual," begged Delphine, dimpling at him, and flirting her golden eyelashes.

"Very well, you children will be the death of me," but he smiled happily. "First, Rosita, then Marcos, alone. Then Delphine alone. Then the duet of Marcos and Rosita. Then Tadeo and Inez in duet, then Oliverio solo on guitar. Then Elena sings and Luisa dances to her song. Then Marcos and Delphine. Then the four-part one of Tadeo and Inez, Rosita and Marcos. Then mine, solo. Then all together for the finale.''

He worked it out rapidly, his mind used to such improvisation and changes in the acts. They nodded, and rested before the next part, Luisa and Elena making the coffee for them.

Delphine and Marcos walked through their duet, he explained what he wanted to her, and she nodded and nodded, her shining red gold head lifted trustingly to his dark one.

It went beautifully in the next performance. Rosita was cheered loudly, so were some of the others, then Delphine and Marcos came out to dance together to a dreamy rumba, then changed gradually to fire. They swooped together, paused, hesitated, dashed into the next move, dramatically, seeming to move as one mind and heart. He gazed down at her, into her eyes, and drew her to him, then flung her out into the dance, then back again, and she responded like a lover. They finished in a deep dip, with her over his arm. The audience loved it.

It all went so well that Delphine begged to go back again. Her mother was calmly pleased that Delphine enjoyed going to the Dominguez house, she knew that they were very careful of the girls. The men were always careful of their women, those Spanish men, she said to Madame Sonia. Delphine would be safe with them.

So Delphine joined the family act, and often went over the steps with Papa Pascual, or with Tadeo, or with Marcos. She enjoyed practicing the flamenco, and Rosita relaxed. Zach was often out evenings, he seemed to have to work late many nights, and to wine and dine business associates from the States or from the other islands of the Caribbean.

It helped Rosita fill the time also, and she loved being with her family. She and Delphine often went twice a week to the house, and on to the nightclub. If Zach was to be out late, they remained until the end of the final act, at two in the morning. If Zach would return early, by silent consent they had Marcos take them home at eleven-thirty, after the second act.

It meant that Rosita often slept late. Zach came in her

bedroom at about ten one morning, yawning. "We are both sleepyheads," he said, smiling. He sat down on the edge of the bed and kissed her lightly. Then he bent closer and began to kiss her shoulders and arms hungrily. "I have missed you, *mi querida! Mi alma*, my darling—do you not miss me also? If you do not, I shall be very angry!"

With mock ferocity, he growled at her throat. She laughed softly, and wound her arms about his hard body, and drew him down to her. He pulled back the sheet between them, and they were silent as they kissed and kissed again. He lay down with her, and rolled over to look into her sleepy rosy face.

"I was going right to the office," he sighed.

"I am a good Spanish wife," she said demurely. She released him, letting her arms fling wide. "So, go to your work, señor! I bid you good day!"

"You are too anxious to let me go!" He smothered a chuckle in her throat. "Ummm, you taste delicious."

"You are hungry for your breakfast! I shall ring the bell and order much bacon and eggs and piles of oranges and many cups of very strong black coffee!"

"You are mean to me. I want my wife!"

"Oh, is that what you want?" She could not tease longer, stroking her long fingers over his unshaven cheeks. Her eyes half-closed, she gazed at his strong mouth, parted in a half-smile. Her fingertip traced along his lips, she wanted him also. He was such a lover, so tender and gentle, then so passionate. "Oh—Zach," she sighed, and her slim body arched up to his. "Zach—do you—want me—now?"

"It is the first time you have asked in words," he whispered. "I cannot deny you—oh, my love—"

They came together slowly, sweetly, in silence, only their panting sighs telling of their ecstasy. They moved to be as one, his body on hers, hers soft and welcoming. He moved luxuriously on her, caressing her with his entire body. Her arms were about him, the hands moving over his back, down to his hips, up again along his spine. He felt the frantic touch of her fingers, growing more passionate, more ardent.

Her back arched again, more imperiously. He held back,

letting her take command of the movements. She came up again, pushed up against him, driving him more deeply between her thighs. She could take as much of him as she wished, and as he lay there lazily content, it seemed, she became more daring. She held him tightly with her arms, and arched again, gasping as he came deeply into her. His chest rose and fell against her rounded breasts, it was the most sensuous experience yet. It was as though they danced, he held still, and she wound herself around him, flirtatiously, then more deeply involved, finally desperately seeking ecstasy and the final climax.

It came, she writhed against him, her body seemed to float in air, spinning, spinning, her mind almost blanked out in delirious pleasure. He filled her with his pleasure, then and made her climax again. She was twisting in his arms, trying to get closer and tighter about him, and he let her do as she wished, only holding her gently.

She whirled down to earth again, spinning more and more slowly, until she lay flat on the bed, gasping for breath. He stroked her wet thighs gently, lovingly, until she was more calm. They lay together sleepily, finally drifting off to sleep from the wildness of passion.

They did not wake again until after twelve. Zach finally got up, ruefully. "My little witch! I could lie here all day with you." He bent to kiss her softly, and draw the sheet up to her shoulders. "Rest, sleep some more. How can I work today, thinking of you?"

Sleepily, she pursed her lips for his final kiss. He touched them, groaned, and dragged himself away, to shower and dress. She slept again, not waking for two more hours. Oh, what a lover he was. She blushed, all by herself, to think of her daring with him. But it had pleased them both so much!

The days passed so pleasantly, sometimes in practice with Isolde and Delphine, sometimes with her family when she could get away. The nightclub proprietor was pleased with the Dominguez, and came to talk to Papa Pascual about the act.

"Will the girls come often and dance? It is they my customers come to see now!"

Papa Pascual frowned in thought, turning to look at Rosita. "My daughter is married now," he said with quiet pride. "It is up to her and her husband, who so kindly gives his permission for her to come sometimes. but her husband comes first, you comprehend!"

Rosita blushed, and avoided Delphine's glance. She had not asked her husband's permission, she just came. "Sometimes I can come twice a week, or maybe three times," she said hastily. "However, I cannot promise. I always do what I can, I enjoy so much dancing with my family."

"Well, that is good enough for me, you and your friend will come so when you are able to come," he said, and signed another month's contract with Pascual for a higher amount.

It was a tremendous relief to Pascual, and Rosita stifled her guilty feelings. Her family was proud, and if she could help them earn their living, nobody was the loser. She took nothing from her husband, and she wanted to be with her family. And Delphine was free to do as she chose. Marcos certainly liked it that way! He loved dancing with Delphine, and on rainy afternoons they danced in the front room, the carpet rolled back, and practiced rumbas, sambas, cha-chas, and rumba-boleros. Delphine always wanted to learn more from Marcos! She was becoming adept in the flamenco style, Pascual was careful to teach her the technique.

They came home at eleven-thirty one night, and Rosita was relieved when she heard Zach coming in stealthily about midnight. She rolled over and went back to sleep, she always felt better when she knew he was in.

It seemed scarcely a minute later, when she heard the muffled thud of a shot, then some loud curses. It seemed part of a nightmare, she wakened with heart thudding, listening. Then she heard Zach jump up, and she knew something was wrong. She snapped on the lamp beside her, and slid from the bed.

Zach looked in, said tensely, "Stay in the bedroom! Rosita, don't move—"

She saw the lamp shining on the weapon he held in his hand. Barefoot he went out and ran down the stairs wearing

267

only the pajama bottoms. She heard voices, someone shouting, another shot.

"Oh—God—" she said, and put her hands to her breasts. She finally ran out into the hallway, her negligee about her shoulders, and saw Madame Sonia come from her room at the other corner of the house, gray hair mussed, her robe held about her.

"What is it? What is going on?" she quavered, and said something in Russian fearfully, crossing herself. Rosita went to her and put her arms about her.

"I don't know. Zach went down—with a gun—"

"God have mercy!"

The two women stood tensely, the young one and the old, until Kevin raced up the stairs. "All right, it's all over, the police have come."

He looked tense and excited. "What happened?"

"Someone got into the house. Zach is having a look around. Jaime was shot—"

"Oh, no!" Rosita cried out. but it was not Zach who had been shot, and she was able to relax and be under control once more. "Madame Sonia, you must go back to bed, you are shivering and the hallway is cold. Come." She took her back to her room, tucked her into the four-poster with the silvery blue canopy.

"Oh, come back and tell me what happened, my dear," Madame Sonia begged. "I cannot sleep now—"

"I know. I'll find out and come back with some hot tea for you," Rosita soothed. She went down, to find the guards roaming the house, and Zach looking bleak.

He said, "The safe was rifled. Just beginning to get things out, I think, when Jaime surprised him. I don't know yet what is missing—damn papers all over the place."

"How is Jaime? Is it serious?"

"Shot in the lower shoulder. He is off to the hospital. I asked them not to whine the ambulance siren, it will waken everybody for miles—and I don't want people to know about this." He looked cross and miserable.

Rosita got out trays and cups, made some tea, and took it

up to Madame Sonia and Madame Isabeau, who had wakened to join her mother. The girls slept through it, on the other side of the house. Isolde slept with ear plugs, she was so sensitive to noise, and Delphine slept like a baby.

She persuaded the two older ladies to go back to bed and sleep, once they had their tea and exchanged news. Then she went downstairs once more, to find Zach and Kevin locking up the house. They returned to the study, she went along.

Zach was picking up the papers, the police had gone through very thoroughly and it looked worse than before.

"Nothing seems to be gone," he said wearily. "Thank God, I didn't put the important stuff in here. And the jewelry seems to be intact."

"What were they after this time? And what do you mean, 'important stuff'?" asked Kevin.

"Just some experiments I'm writing out, nothing far along yet." Zach was evasive, and Rosita kept quiet, remembering the hours he spent in his room, reading the journals, writing out formulas, muttering over his pages of ideas.

"I think Jaime must have surprised him as he was starting to look," said Kevin. "But what I want to know—how did anybody get in the front door? It is always locked at night, and often in the daytime."

"With a key," said Zach baldly. "Somebody has a key. That means changing all the locks. I'll get at it tomorrow."

"I'll do that," said Kevin practically. "You have enough to do. What else shall I do?"

"See Jaime at the hospital, and take his evidence, and then get the police in on that. If he wants anything, promise it to him. I can't be grateful enough. The person might have come upstairs, and frightened everybody."

Only Zach did not mean "frighten," Rosita thought. He was really afraid someone else might have been hurt.

They all finally got back to bed, and some sleep. Zach was cross the next morning and told everybody they would have to be very careful.

"I'll hire more bodyguards for us all. Isolde, you must not go out alone. Rosita, be very careful. Fortunately, you have some nice tough brothers! You don't go anywhere else, do you? The dressmakers, or hairdressers?''

"No, I do my own hair, and you have given me enough clothes to last ten years," she said, with an attempt at a smile.

"I wonder if it would be best for us all to go to the country," he said, scowling at his untouched plate of ham and eggs. "There are fences wired electrically and guard dogs. We could all be safe there. Yes, that might be best—"

"I will not be penned up like a—a prize horse!" Isolde cried. "I am a human being. How can I plan my dance, and form a dance troupe, and see my friends if I am guarded like a—a Russian prisoner!"

"I think you are overreacting, Zach," Madame Sonia said. "We do have guards, thank God for those like Jaime. I must send him flowers and a note of gratitude, and see if we can do anything for his family. But not removal to the country—I for one do not intend to be a prisoner of fear. I have seen what that can do. Rather live in danger, than lock one's self into a cell."

Isolde gave her a grateful look, Madame Isabeau nodded, though her little porcelain face was unnaturally white today.

"Mother is right," said Madame Isabeau. "We must go on as before, we have a position in society, and it does not do to let one's self show such panic. And I for one do not care for the country!"

Zach looked disgusted, but Kevin said, "Look, we can scarcely go back and forth to the factory every day, as we need to do, Zach. It is a three-hour drive, each way. I think with additional guards, and new locks we'll be all right. Some of this may be involved in the strikes, you know."

All Puerto Rico was seething with labor unrest, strikes flourished like weeds. Their plant had been threatened, and the management was meeting with the labor leaders to discuss the new contracts. Zach rubbed his forehead.

"Yes, it may be that. Though what anybody hoped to find in the safe for the labor contract, I fail to see," he sighed.

"Has it anything to do with the terrorists, I wonder,"

mused Madame Sonia. "In Russia, I know they would do anything. And the newspapers are full of what they do to the naval installations."

"We are not in the government, thank God," Zach said. "I have troubles enough. But we are considered capitalists, of course. Since we hire thousands of people who might not have jobs without us! I don't know what they think they will do when they succeed in wiping out all factory management. Do they think they could run the plants as well as we do?"

That did not call for an answer. He got up and went to work as usual. Kevin arranged about new locks, and supervised the exchange that very day. Rosita and Madame Isabeau went to the hospital with flowers, to see Jaime. They found him half-conscious, weak, but grateful for their visit. His family was all right; his brother was taking them in while Jaime was away.

They assured him of their gratitude, told him to ask for anything he needed. They came away, sober that he had taken a bullet for their sake. "He is such a good man, I felt so secure with him there," sighed Madame Isabeau, worry in her wrinkled forehead.

"Alfonso is just as devoted, so is Julio," said Rosita, quietly. "And Enrique will walk the house each night, Zach has arranged it. I think we will not be troubled again. The guards have been doubled, and more hired at the plant to be trained, Zach phoned at noon."

"Yes, yes, I know. I wish he did not have our troubles on his shoulders, it makes him old before his time. And I think of my dear Thomas. He died before he should have, Rosita, for his worries," and her voice shook, she pressed her handkerchief to her mouth.

Rosita dared to take her slim hand in both of hers. "Do not distress yourself, maman," she said softly. "Zach would be so upset for you. We have long worried over you, that your grief lasted so. Can we not persuade you to believe that your husband has gone to heaven, and lives in joy among the saints? He was such a good man, so kind, so generous."

Tears spilled down the thin cheeks, she put her head against Rosita's shoulder. "I know—I know—but I miss him so much!" she sobbed.

The chauffeur kept looking over his shoulder, troubled also. "But life goes on, Madame Isabeau," he said, unable to keep from joining in the conversation, with the freedom of an old servant. "The Good God knows why, but we are in life for some purpose, and God knows you have a fine family and devoted sons. Rejoice in them, and hope for their sons!"

Rosita held her breath, worried that Madame Isabeau would rebuke the frank man for his speech. Instead her mother-in-law sat up straight and wiped her eyes.

"You are right, Alberto," she said. "You are so right. I weep, when others have so much less than I. I am ungrateful. I have four strong children, who are devoted. My health is good, thanks be to God. Why am I so weak, so others must take my weight also? I will thank God every night for what I still have, instead of berating God and the Virgin that I have had a severe loss," and her voice shook, but her sniff told that she had controlled her tears.

"That is right, Madame Isabeau. You are wise. Thank God for our blessings," said Alberto, and drew up in front of the house with a little flourish, and turned into the driveway. "You may be sure that we shall watch and guard with more care than ever, Madame Isabeau and Madame Rosita," and he nodded firmly. He jumped out to help her out, holding her frail arm securely. She reached up and patted his bronzed cheek with her thin hand.

"You are a good man, Alberto. God bless you, and thank you," she murmured, and sailed into the house with some of her old assurance.

Rosita followed, wondering at the strength of frail women, who found courage when they might be expected to collapse. Well, all the Hamiltons had that stuff of which heroes are made, she reflected, and they were all survivors.

And so was she, she thought again. She went in the house, to find Madame Sonia had ordered tea and sandwiches for them, as though she had known when they would return.

They talked, calmly, then, not about the attack, but about the coming days. Madame Sonia had invited a friend for luncheon on Friday, they would have some Russian dishes prepared. Madame Isabeau had asked her dressmaker to come, so she might order some new dresses for a grand reception. And Rosita would need new dresses, she said.

"Oh, no, Madame Isabeau! You have not seen my closets!" Rosita cried.

Madame Isabeau brightened, so did Madame Sonia. "May we look?" her mother-in-law asked, with the curiosity of a woman whose interest in clothes has been revived.

"Of course." After tea they all went up to look at Rosita's dresses, and Delphine came also, and advised on what dress to choose for a December ball at one of the Spanish houses in the suburbs. "We ought to plan our colors together," Rosita suggested. "As we used to in New York."

And they talked about that, she and Delphine, for the interest of the two older women, and the day passed pleasantly, the dangers of the night mercifully forgotten.

Chapter 18

Zach could have moaned from sheer weariness. He was not just physically tired, he was mentally exhausted and exasperated. Stress had worn him out more than actual work.

But he thought he had won his points finally. The delegation of United States regional sales managers had protested vigorously at his ideas for a low-key family style campaign for his "fruity rums" as they called them. "Rum is a man's drink, yo-ho-ho and a bottle of rum," one man kept saying, as though very clever.

Zach had had finally to put his foot down, and remind them he was president of the company, and wanted it done this way. The men had muttered. He would have to keep close watch on them, to make sure they handled it properly. Others were always so sure they knew just how to make a fortune.

As his father used to say, "If they are so clever, why aren't they out there making their fortunes? No, they will do it my way!" Zach also felt those sentiments.

They were all tired and hungry by eight o'clock, and he invited them to dinner with him at a nightclub, where they could dine and watch the floor show. Nine of the men accepted his invitation, two others went back to the hotel to sleep against the morning plane time.

His uncles went home, disgusted with him, because they had not wanted it this way, either. They fought him all the way, on general principles, he thought, not because they believed in the old campaigns. Kevin took the two men back to their hotel, and went home.

Zach escorted the others to a nightclub that was not far from the factory. They had a rather good dinner, of steaks and baked potatoes, they refused any native foods, which did not surprise him. Most tourists and infrequent visitors to the island were suspicious of the native foods, not realizing the Spanish had lived on them for four and a half centuries! And the Spanish had flourished.

Oh, well, why am I fighting the tourist battle tonight, thought Zach, and ordered black bean soup for himself. The native food was good, he had marinated steak with tomatoes, corn *tortillas,* and a dish of fresh pineapple to end.

Then the floor show started. He had his back to the stage, indifferently, giving the best seats to his guests. One man opposite him whistled, his red face beamed over his tight white collar. "Wow, look at those dolls! Gimme the redhead!"

"I'll take the dark girl in red," said another man, his eyes moving as he ran his gaze up and down her body. "Man, those curves! And watch how she moves," and he whistled loudly in shrill approval, drawing the disapproving attention of some Spaniards at the next table.

Might as well watch and enjoy, relax by staring at some pretty girls, thought Zach, and quietly moved his chair around. He sat down again, leaned back and prepared to get some pleasure from the evening. He heard the appreciative applause, the shouts, the whistles.

"*La Soledad! La Soledad!*" one man shouted, and several men clapped sharply to the music as the guitar began a quick strumming.

Zach gasped, his gaze went right to the stage, from the man who claimed his attention. "What is *La Soledad?*" the man was asking.

Zach could not reply. He was gazing at his wife, in a red frilled flamenco dress, dancing on the stage before them! They were back in the corner at a large table, the lights were away from them, she could not see him. But he could see her!

Horrified and stunned, he stared as his wife went into her flamenco dance. Her skirts swirled about her slim ankles, her sober face was enraptured by the dancing, as Oliverio bent over his guitar and strummed more rapidly. Her feet went faster and faster, her arms weaved over her head, her hands clicked more rapidly on the castanets. The dance ended with a triumphant rumble on the guitar, and Rosita dipped into a low curtsy. The applause was deafening.

"Wow, wow, wow!" yelled one of Zach's sales managers. "What a honey! Let's get her over to the table after! What a figure, and how she can dance! Do they or don't they, Mr. Hamilton?" he ended with a laugh, his face bright red, his lips wet.

Zach felt sick. They were talking about his wife! Another man was discussing frankly her charms, her figure, her breasts, her legs, as Rosita stood clapping for Marcos to dance. Zach stared at her blindly, unable to see clearly for the furious mist before his eyes. When he got her home he would give her the talking-to of her life! Daring to come here again—his wife—

She was Mrs. Hamilton! She had a position to uphold! And there she was, dancing on the stage, showing her legs to all of them— He shook his head in disbelief. What was he thinking? She had danced before, he had thought little of it, except that she was beautiful and graceful and he was beginning to love her. But now she was his wife—his wife—and he was full of jealous rage.

She was displaying herself on the stage, before all these men. How often had she come? He had been gone so many nights! Damn! All those times she had said she was going to her family—had she come here? All those days and nights!

He had missed Marcos's dance. Now a girl with red gold hair came out, in a blue frilled dress with white dots, and smiled demurely at the audience as she began to dance. Her fingers clicked the castanets, she was not so skilled as Rosita, but she was pretty with a lovely figure, and much grace. Zach blinked.

"Oh, God," he muttered. It was Delphine! His sister was dancing on the stage!

"Look at the redhead! Ain't she purty!" one man drawled, with a laugh, exaggerating his accent. "God, I could take her right back to the States with me, and set her up! I bet she would come, lots of girls are anxious to get away from Puerto Rico! Hey, look at them!" he laughed as she kicked her leg straight out. "God, what gams!"

Zach sat there, burning with fury, swallowing his rage. The girls were dressed in flamenco dresses, heavily made up with mascara and rouge. If they ever did meet these sales managers, he hoped the men would not know them in ordinary garb. But oh, God—he had to get them out of here!

He had to sit through the whole act, hearing the lascivious comments of the men. He had heard such remarks before, but not about his wife and sister! The longer he waited, the more furious he became.

He saw the whole show through a haze of fury. The solos, duets, the four-part dance. He knew it was good, they all danced well, the audience applauded wildly. But that was his wife they applauded, when she lay over Marcos's arm, and that was his sister dancing a suggestive bolero with Marcos! They looked like a real love duo, those two. He watched, with incredulous fury, as his sister leaned back against Marcos, twined herself against him, twisted around, and smiled up at him. Marcos bent over her, bent her backward, and seemed to kiss her.

And how long had this been going on? Dancing like that on stage!

As soon as the show was over, and the lights came up, and the Dominguez were back in the dressing room, Zach stood up. He briskly got taxis for his guests, paid the bill, and told his chauffeur to wait for him.

Then he strode backstage, black fury in him. He heard the chatter and laughter in the dressing room through the partly opened door. He opened the door wider and walked in.

Pascual saw him first, and straightened from leaning against the wall. The dressing room was so small there were few chairs, and Marcos, Oliverio, Tadeo and Pascual all stood. The girls were seated, Luisa was pouring coffee.

"Ah, Mr. Hamilton! You must have coffee with us! You saw the show, yes?" Pascual was beaming.

Zach looked right at his wife. Rosita looked guilty, her childish face was apprehensive and shocked. Delphine—he looked at her. She looked defiant, her fists clenched.

"What the hell has been going on?" roared Zach. "Rosita, you come home with me this minute!"

She gasped, and the room went quiet. "But Mr. Hamilton—señor—" said Pascual, standing straight and tall, his face distressed. "What do you mean? You did not come to see us perform?"

Zach thought of the businessmen with him, their comments and crude jokes about his wife and sister. Such anger burned in him he could scarcely speak.

"To see you perform? No, I brought a group of businessmen here for dinner. And what do I find? My wife and my sister, performing for them—in a nightclub! A sleezy nightclub! Making a show for such men—" He gulped down his rage with an effort. "Rosita, you shall never come here again! My wife, Mrs. Hamilton, dancing for tourists! Like that! And my sister—Delphine, come away at once!"

"But señor Hamilton," said Margarita's dignified voice, and his wife's mother was standing before him, her plump face worried. "Did you not give permission for Rosita and Delphine to come to us?"

"Never," he said flatly. "I had no knowledge that they were doing this. Believe me, it shall not happen again! I have never been so—so horrified—"

"But she danced beautifully! And Delphine learns well! You do not think they dance well?" Pascual Dominguez was unable to comprehend what was wrong.

"They danced well—like nightclub dancers!" cried Zach, so angry he did not measure his words. "I will not have it. She is my wife!"

"But she has danced before with us, all her life!" Marcos had come forward, his face red with anger, his handsome figure taut. "She is a dancer, Mr. Hamilton! You should have thought of that when you married her!"

An appalled silence fell over the room, for just a moment, before Zach spoke again.

"I married Rosita, yes, and she is my wife. She has a position to uphold! I thought she understood my wishes! I have to make them more clear, it seems! Come along, Rosita."

Rosita had stood, her hand holding to the back of the chair, the shawl slipping from her shoulders. "Zach, you must not say such things!" she whispered, her eyes black with anger. "How can you speak so to my father? He is the best dancer in the world! And this is not a sleezy nightclub, it is a very good one! We are honored to dance here!"

There were tears in Margarita's dark brown eyes, but she kept her gray head raised, her stance dignified. "There is evidently some mistake, Señor Hamilton," she said formally. "We did not realize Rosita did not have your permission to dance with us. She must have your permission, of course, for whatever she does. She is a good girl, a good wife. Go, Rosita, go with your husband."

Pascual's jaw was set and Oliverio was muttering darkly to his guitar. "*Sí*, she must go," Rosita's father said. "I protest your words, though, Señor Hamilton. Rosita is not disgraced by dancing with us. We are the Dominguez family, we are professional dancers of the highest caliber, our standards have always been high!"

"And your family have been dancers also," Tadeo said, stirring from his stunned silence. His dark eyes flashed. "Your grandmother, your mother, your sisters, have all danced in the ballet—on the stage, before men! What is the difference? They also have danced in public! It is not a disgrace!"

"*Silencio, todos,*" said Pascual, in a firm tone. "Señor Hamilton has a right to forbid his wife to dance. Señor, we apologize. We did think she had your permission. Rosita, you will go now with your husband."

Delphine burst into tears, holding her handkerchief to her eyes. "Oh, Zach, how could you!"

Rosita stood her ground. "I shall not go until you have

280

apologized to my family for your insulting words!'' she cried, fire in her eyes and in her pose, hands on hips. In her flame red dress, she looked as though she had caught wildfire. She looked like a defiant Gypsy, thought Zach, amazed. "Tell them you are sorry for such words. They are my people!''

"Like hell!'' Zach said. His red hair felt as though it stood on end, he could have spanked her. "Come with me, now, or I'll make you very sorry!''

"Make me sorry! I like that! It is you who are unbearably rude and vulgar and stupid!''

"Rosita!'' her father snapped. "You will not speak so to your husband! You make me ashamed!'' He shook his head in disapproval. "Such words for a wife to her husband! You know better than this!'' He said more in Spanish, forcefully, unable to say all he wished in English. Her mouth pouted, her face turned sullen.

Her brothers stared at Zach, so angry that he felt it in heat waves coming at him. Her sisters were grieved, her mother had slow anguished tears rolling down her brown face. Delphine was twisting her hands together, gazing from one to the other. This was more than a prank, she seemed to say by her uneasy actions.

Zach strode over to Rosita and grabbed her wrist. He hurt her, she flinched, but he did not let up his grasp. He had trusted her, and she had done this to him! He could never trust her completely again.

He felt ripped in two by his feelings about this. That she had gone behind his back, sneaked out—with his sister!— again and again—for Delphine showed much practice—and had been performing in a nightclub. And never telling him one word about it!

"Come with me!'' he said, authoritatively. "Come, Delphine!'' He pulled Rosita with him to the door, though she tried to hang back, her heels digging into the floor. "If you don't come quietly, I'll put you over my shoulder and take you out like the child you are!'' he yelled at her.

Ashamed, her head drooped, and she came more quietly. Delphine followed them meekly, in silence, appalled by the scene. Behind them, the men muttered ominously. He practically flung Rosita into the car, where the chauffeur respectfully held the door, and tried not to stare at them. Zach pushed Delphine into the car after Rosita, and got in himself, to sit in grim silence as they drove home around the bay, and along the cobblestoned streets of Old San Juan.

It was past midnight when they went into the quiet house. Delphine muttered good night, and started up the patio steps with the familiarity of long practice.

"I'll speak to you tomorrow, Delphine!" he warned her.

"All right, Zach," she said, but she did not sound obedient, only sullen and furious.

He and Rosita went into the other part of the house, and up the inside stairs to their room. He held the door for her, the corner door to their suite, and she went in, head held high, still wearing her red dress with the polka dots and frilled skirts, the high black comb in her dark hair.

He shut the door, turned on the lamp. "Now, Rosita! Tell me what you mean by this!"

"My family needed me," she said.

His mouth tightened. "Needed you! You are married to me now! You are my wife! You have a position to uphold! How long have you been dancing with them?"

Her chin went up. "All my life!" she snapped, her dark eyes glowing with rage. "All my whole life! Since I was a small child! They are my people, I am a Gypsy dancer. Didn't you know that? Didn't you know that when you insisted on marrying me? I am a Gypsy dancer!"

Rosita felt like punishing him for his behavior. She was outraged, hurt by his words to her family, dismayed by his harsh behavior to her. He looked down on her family!

"Now, Rosita, what do you mean by going behind my back, sneaking out like that?" he asked, and his blue eyes were so wide and fiery that she felt rather afraid.

"I told you I was going to my family, and besides you were busy!"

"You did not say you were going to dance on the stage!"

282

"I have danced often on the stage! Your sisters dance on stage, so do your friends—and my friends—in New York! Your mother was a ballerina! So was Madame Sonia!"

"Not in nightclubs," he said, and tore off his jacket impatiently. He began taking off his trousers, his shirt, as though unaware of what he did.

She was suddenly weary. She dragged at the zipper of her dress, trying to reach around the back. Zach came to her, turned her around, and unzipped her.

"Thank you," she muttered, and stepped out of the heavy full skirts. Under it she wore only pantyhose and brassiere. She unfastened the bra, and took it off, and reached for her peach-colored nightdress laid out on the bed. She became aware suddenly that he was standing and watching her. She felt naked, as she had not felt since her wedding night. She yanked on the nightdress, and took off the pantyhose from under it. She went to the bathroom, scrubbed off her thick makeup.

When she returned, he went to the bathroom, and she heard the shower running. She lay down, exhausted by the evening and by the scene.

What had they done? She felt the delicate fabric of their relationship had been rent into pieces. And her family! How she felt for her family. They must be so upset, so insulted. She thought of her mother's face, wet with tears. Her mother was still not well, infection lingered, the doctor was worried. This was not good for her.

When Zach came back into the room, she sat up against the pillows glaring at him. "How could you have insulted my family so?" she accused abruptly. "The things you said tonight—they will never forgive you, neither will I! You insulted us, you insulted the Spaniards, the Gypsies! You do not know how we feel!"

"Now, don't make this an international incident!" said Zach tightly. "This is between you and me!"

"Then why did you insult my family! The Spanish were here in Puerto Rico four centuries before you Americans!"

"My God, now you'll throw history in my face! What the

hell does that have to do with the fact that I don't want my wife dancing on a stage in a nightclub, with men looking at her legs and asking if she is available!'' he stormed.

Rosita stared at him, in shock. ''Are you crazy?''

''No, I'm not! But you are, if you think I'll put up with this!'' He sat down on the edge of the bed. ''Rosita, do you know what men say about you on the stage?''

She put her hands over her ears. ''I don't want to hear you! You are mad! Why should the filthy talk of gutter men affect me?''

His mouth twisted, he pulled her hands down so she could not pretend to misunderstand him. He held her wrists strongly in his hands. She glared at him.

He gave her a shake. ''No more arguments! You just listen to me, Rosita! No more nightclubs! No more dancing with your family! If they want to make a living at it, that is their business! If they need money, I'll be glad to give it to them! But you shall not dance with them again!''

''Oh, you don't want them to earn a living at the one job they know!'' she cried, absolutely appalled at his ignorance. ''What are they supposed to do, those Spanish Gypsies? Clean streets, wash gutters, drive vegetable trucks? You would deny them their talent!''

''Don't be stupid! I am talking about *you!* Mrs. Zach Hamilton, a woman with a position in San Juan, in Puerto Rico, in the world! You are a woman with dignity to maintain! What will people say——''

''You should have thought of that when you married me! You should have known I would disgrace you!'' She was close to tears of anger, and of hurt.

''Don't be silly, you don't disgrace me.'' His voice gentled, he was staring at her slim form in the peach nightdress. His hands softened on her wrists, he slid his hands up to her shoulders, sending an unwanted thrill through her. ''Come on, honey, calm down. It's over, you won't do it again——''

His calm assumption of his dominance infuriated her all over again. What arrogance, what—*macho!* He was a male chauvinist pig! She did not dare say so, but she thought it!

He pushed her against the pillows. It was the final outrage, that after insulting her and her family, shaming her before them all, he wanted to make love to her!

"Don't you touch me, don't kiss me!" she yelled, and pushed him away sharply. He was astonished. Then she hit him on the chest when he tried to pull her closer. "You treat me like a naughty child, and now you want me to be a woman! You insult me, then you think I should love you! Let me go!" She beat at his shoulder in a frenzy as he laughed and kissed her neck.

"You are a child, Rosita, and a woman, and a desirable wife," he whispered, turning amorous so quickly that she could have struck him with a knife. "Come on, honey, be quiet. Let me . . . . let me have you . . ."

"What am I? A doll to be hugged, then thrown into the corner when you are finished? Am I to have no brain, no heart, no feelings, no pride? Let me go—stop that—don't kiss me—" She tried to yank herself from his arms.

"Oh, Rosita, stop it. I'm tired, let's go to sleep. Only let me love you first—come on, honey—"

"Don't *honey* me! You insult me, like a pig! Don't think I will forget it for the pleasure of your kisses! Stop that!"

He was laughing at her, and her rage increased. When he pulled her by force into his arms, and laid her across the bed, she kicked and punched at him until she was out of breath. He turned angry, and wild, as she had never seen him. His passion seemed to increase with her fighting, he held her down by his strength, his legs across her thighs, his arms holding her shoulders and arms. He forced her to accept his kisses on her mouth, and when she was out of breath, he managed to get between her legs.

"Zach—don't—I hate you—I hate you!"

He shook his red head blindly, his blue eyes were dazed and passion-blind. He held her down, and forced himself on her, and it hurt, almost like the first night, only now he was not gentle.

She cried out, in pain, and he did not hear her. She made herself lie still for him, so it would not hurt so much. Her struggles had made him only the more passionate. Nothing mattered but possession. He pushed back and forth on her, groaned, and then fell heavily forward on her.

He calmed down then, rolled over, and went to sleep. It was frustrating and infuriating to Rosita. She waited until he was deeply asleep, then got up, retrieved her nightdress, washed herself shakily, and went to bed in the other room.

It was a long time before she slept. She kept rehearsing speeches to fling at him, hurting words, violent words, dignified formal farewell speeches, as she went out the door and left him forever.

He looked down on her as his other relatives did! She remembered every look, every word, every muttered insult of his uncles and their wives and children. She dredged up every smile of a guest of the American and English colony in Puerto Rico. Every sly look, every snide smile, every whisper of the words, "A Gypsy, yes, a Spanish Gypsy, her family are flamenco dancers in nightclubs!" He had said, "A sleezy nightclub—" as though he despised them. Yet he himself went to them, he had first seen her there.

Maybe he had wanted to make her his mistress! Maybe only her innocence had made him marry her—for a time! He looked down on her as well as on her family. He said she disgraced his old name—*his*-distinguished family name!

Well, the Dominguez name was much much older and more famous than his! The Dominguez family went back many centuries in Spain, they had been known as dancers from three centuries ago! Yes, they were famous, they were respected!

The Hamiltons went back only to about 1800, and his ancestor had been a sailor and his ancestress a tavern maid! So the Dominquez family were more distinguished than his! She thought of flinging that to him in the morning!

Yet—yet it was all a part of what the Americans and English thought of the Spanish. They had been the conquerors, and so the Spanish were the dogs, the servants, the outsiders of society. Rosita writhed and thought over every insult in San Juan, every look down the nose in New York when they learned she was Puerto Rican. Her best friends, she thought forlornly, had been their Puerto Rican servants! She ignored Delphine's close friendship, the friends of ballet school, the classmates in the convent.

The cultural and class differences between the Hamiltons and the Dominguez were typical of the ones between the Americans and the Spanish on the island of Puerto Rico. Yet the Spanish had come first, more than two centuries before any English. It was their land, it had been their islands, until the Americans had come in their arrogance, to fling out the Spanish rulers, and take control of the island. Newcomers! And they thought they were better than any of those who had been there for four and a half centuries!

Her fiery temper surprised herself. For all her life she had given in, to her family, then to Isolde, then to Zach. She had been obedient, unquestioning outwardly. Only in her dancing had she showed her fire, her rebellion, her temper and fierce longing to be herself. It was only during the music that she was outside any man's control. She was above and beyond ties. In the dance, she was Rosita, *La Soleded*, the Flamenco Rose: fire and flame, temper and heat, volcano and eruption, all Spanish grace and wildness, Gypsy and solitary bird-spirit, flying where she would in the clouds. She was free.

Until the music ended, when she must reluctantly return to earth and applause, obedience and control.

Now she lay in bed, wide-awake in spite of her weariness, thinking over the years of her life, when she had obeyed all to whom she owed respect. Must she continue like that? She was herself, she was Rosita. For an hour or more she thought of leaving Zach.

But where would she go? Back to her family, to put herself under them again? Much as she loved her father, she recognized his firm authority. No, that was no escape.

And did she want to leave Zach? She loved him, she knew, so deeply that to leave him would be death to her heart. She thought of Madame Isabeau, so grief-stricken over her husband's death. What if Zach died? She shuddered, and knew she could not leave him unless he forced her to go. To leave would be dying.

She finally slept, wakened, slept again, restlessly, turning over and over in the bed, tossing back and forth. Dawn came, she wakened, stared at the lightening sky, turned over and slept again, heavily.

She finally wakened when Zach turned off the shower and came out into the room.

"What are you doing in this bed?" he asked, amazed at her. "Why didn't you remain with me?"

"Because I could have hit you again!" she blurted out.

"Oh, Rosita!" he laughed. "Forget it. I was angry last night. But you won't do that again, will you?" He bent and kissed her nose, and went to dress.

She fumed all over again after he had left and run downstairs to breakfast. Their quarrel had meant so little to him! He had forgotten his insults to her and her family so quickly! It made her feel curiously desolate.

Chapter 19

Zach was deeply worried about the strike that was threatened. It was just a week before Christmas, he had hoped the labor troubles could be cleared up and new two-year contracts signed before Christmas. Instead, a dissident faction within the union was making heavier demands, and the vote had been postponed.

He had talked to the union leaders, they were sullen and upset. They wanted more say in the management of the factory. He could scarcely keep his patience and temper. Why should they have any say in management? They did not have money invested in his company, they owned no stock, if they lost money it would not come out of their pockets!

He finally said it one day, and they were furious. "And if we lose money, you wish to have cuts in pay?" he asked. "You want to have a big share in the profits. What if we lose money?"

They stared at him, amazed. "Why should we cut our pay? That is your fault if you lose money! But you don't lose money, you make much money, and we want big bonuses!"

"If we make much money, you want some of it. When we lose money, you don't want any share of the troubles. Is that fair? Is that just? A factory owner has the responsibility in the good years and the bad ones. What if we go bankrupt? Will you contribute money to get us out of trouble?''

"That is just like you capitalists! If we ask for a share in the profits, you cry and complain you don't make much!'' cried one of the labor leaders.

"A capitalist is a man who has enough capital to put money and faith into a business,'' explained Zach, knowing he was talking to mostly deaf ears. But he was so angry, he went ahead in spite of his cool brother's warning shake of the head. "He hires men, gives them work, pays them, takes all the risks. If he loses money, he must endure it, and if his business fails, he loses his capital entirely. But if he makes money— you say he should give the men all the money!''

"Not all the money, just our fair share,'' said the man.

"Then you should take a fair share of the losses! Let me see, last year on our heavy rums, we lost over one hundred thousand dollars. How much of that will you pay?''

The lawyers finally cut in, afraid of the results if Zach went on, with his red-haired temper. The labor leaders walked out, saying they would take a strike vote soon. Zach remained, to hear the reproaches of his terrified uncles.

"How could you talk like that? That does not help us. You have to give them soothing syrup, and tell them how good they are.''

"Not honesty,'' he said bitterly. "Nobody wants honesty. I am sick of this talk of unfair capitalists. We lost money for three years running, but I didn't cut the labor force! We kept them on, until the good years finally came, and the harvests were good. Now the rums are mature, and ready to sell, and they want a big hunk of the profits! If they want their share, they can have a share of the bad times also!''

"Zach, you are being unreasonable,'' said Uncle William. He sighed deeply. "I guess you are tired. I have never seen you act so in a meeting. You are usually so calm.''

Zach was silent. He knew he was being unreasonable. His personal life had been upset recently, and he was taking it out on others. That would make the factory suffer. Rosita was being difficult, he feared she was tired of marriage. She was a fiery little thing. Her temper had flared again and again at him, and he could not take it meekly. He was the man of the family, and by God she had better realize it!

There was a rally that afternoon, after the labor leaders reported the results of the meeting. They tried to take a vote, two men disrupted the proceedings, and started a fight. The guards were called, then the police.

As a result, Zach fired the two men, on consultation with the labor men. "Yes, they are troublemakers. But the men will be angry if they are fired, and will take their cause," they told him.

"I looked up their work records. They hired on only three months ago, and have made more trouble than work ever since," said Zach firmly. "They are supposed to work in bottling. Instead, they had taken much time off to work in rallies and try to get elected to their section of the union. No, they have to go."

So he fired José Serrito and Antonio Plácido, his brother-in-law. José was a big stupid man, he was under the thumb of his small, shrewd, vicious brother-in-law, Antonio. Zach had the feeling they had hired on just to make trouble. The labor men were uncertain, one thought they wanted work, but were mentally disturbed. Better to placate them, they said. Zach did not agree.

"Whether they are troublemakers out of principle, or mentally disturbed, I don't want them in Hamilton's."

He went to them, and fired them in person. They were furious, and threatened him with a knife. A guard had come with him, the men were disarmed and told to leave the factory grounds at once. Their cards of identification were taken from them, a platoon of guards escorted them to their car and off the land.

A newspaper reporter got hold of part of the story and tried to interview Zach. He told him curtly what had happened, and thought no more of it. Instead in the afternoon paper, there were big headlines. "Hamilton's fires union men. Strike threatened." A distorted story appeared under that. The reporter had not understood.

"Jeronimo Oviedo wants to see you," Sarita Myers said, in the doorway of his office.

"Tell him I am busy just now," Zach began, when Jeronimo came in behind her, pushing her out of the way.

His face was flushed, his manner belligerent. "Look, Zach, just because I got lucky and married Melinda instead of you, is no reason to snub me. I want to talk to you about the labor unions!"

Zach had been working on some detailed plans for trying experiments on the liqueurs. He shoved something over the papers, as Jeronimo's curious gaze seemed to be trying to read the pages upside down. "All right, sit down. What was that stupid remark about your wife?"

Sarita closed the door tactfully after herself.

Jeronimo grinned, his face flushed. "I know how you felt about Melinda. But she preferred me, and then you went right off and got married to that little tart Gypsy!"

"What the hell!" said Zach. "Watch your tongue, Jeronimo! You don't speak of my wife like that!" He was wondering inside, in the midst of his fury, if others thought and spoke of Rosita like that. Was something of this manner behind her anger and questioning about his attitude toward her family? He respected her family, they were good professional dancers. He just didn't want his wife and sister dancing with them again. They had a position to uphold, that ought to be clear.

Jeronimo reached right out and tried to turn over the pages on the desk. "What are you working on?" he asked brazenly.

Zach struck his hand away forcefully. "Get your paws off! It's none of your damn business what I'm doing. Have your say and get back to your own work!"

"All right, all right. God, you are touchy today! I'm here about Serrito and Plácido. You should not have fired them, have you seen the papers?"

"I have seen the papers, and called them with a more complete story. Any other remarks?"

"Look, man, you should be more careful! They are union men."

Zach waited ominously, a frown gathering.

Jeronimo rambled on, about the dangers of antagonizing union organizers, the troubles if a strike should start, how Zach should handle it differently, how he could handle it well.

"You should be more careful, you have a quick temper. Let me handle it, Zach, I can do it. You have to treat them with kid gloves."

"Damn if I'm going to give in to that demand," said Zach. "You don't own shares, Jeronimo, or you might be less willing to hand over control of the company to them!"

"Hell, I'm not talking about control! I just think they should be listened to—"

"Not when they want shares in the company and seats on the board, and part of the profits," said Zach flatly.

"Well, sometimes you have to give in. I like docile workers," said Jeronimo. "You have to keep them happy, throw them little goodies now and then. Let them think they have some control. What about giving them a few seats on the board, non-voting? That would keep them happy—"

"And give away the formulas of the Hamilton rums?" asked Zach sarcastically. "You know better than that, Jeronimo!"

"Well, the men should be more docile, anyway," said Jeronimo. After his puzzling point of view, Jeronimo finally went away, and let Zach work.

The next day, the union met, and voted to strike on January 8 if their conditions had not been met. Zach appointed Uncle William and two lawyers to meet with them, warning the men not to give in on any of the major points. He did give them some leeway about wages, based on the profits of the past year when the figures came out early in January.

"If the rums sell well, and I think they have been doing better in the States, then we can afford up to about ten percent wage increases to the senior workers, and seven to the medium, and five to the newcomers." He would not go further than that, it would stay within the government guidelines in sum totals.

In the next several days he received several crudely printed letters, threatening violence to factory plants and to himself and his family. He filed them, and warned the guards to take every care. He was in no mood for Christmas cheer, but the season had come anyway.

And there was to be a huge reception in his home, for some American businessmen and a congressman here for vacation. It was amazing how many visiting congressmen surveyed conditions in Puerto Rico when snow came up north and the warmth of the Caribbean beckoned. Zach wondered how much they learned of living conditions while lying on the beaches and dining in the homes of the wealthy.

The reception was scheduled for the Friday before Christmas. It would last from four until ten in the evening, with dinner for a dozen guests. Others would be coming and going from four to seven, with cocktails and tables of hors d'oeuvres. So he came home early from the plant, showered and changed, and went downstairs promptly at four.

The ladies of the family were gathered in the hallway and the first guests were coming in the huge front doors, wide to the sunny afternoon. His first look went to Rosita, and he swelled with pride in her.

She wore a new designer gown fashioned with a touch of Spanish. It was rose red, in panels like those of her layers of flamenco skirts, each layer lined in black braid. A stiffened collar stood up about her slim beautiful throat, emphasizing the necklace of bright diamonds. Her earrings were diamonds, and her slippers were red satin. She glowed with dark beauty. The dress was short enough to show her long legs.

Delphine standing next to her wore a matching gown of blue silk, and the sapphires which were her heritage. She was lovely, her red gold hair dressed in curls to her throat.

Isolde wore green, an imperious color that suited her height and dignity. His mother and grandmother were in shades of purple and lavender silk, with pearls.

Rosita turned slightly when he came up to her. Her smile was reserved. He kissed her cheek formally, and wished he could shake the pride out of her. Yet he loved her for it also, he thought ruefully. They would have to have a good talk one of these days, and get things straightened out between them. Perhaps Christmas would be a good time, a time of peace and goodwill. She resented what he had said to her family, misunderstanding him, he thought. And he had been a bit rash in his words, he had been so upset.

Rosita was thinking she wished the day was over. She had dreaded it. The whole Hamilton clan was coming, besides the many guests.

She wished it even more as the day wore on. They finally took turns staying in the hallway and greeting guests, while others circulated in the large drawing rooms, the dining room which had been temporarily turned into a drawing room, the music room behind the drawing room. The house seemed crammed with people, and the shrill voices rang unpleasantly in her ears.

The beautiful flowers were practically obscured from view by the lovely gowns of the ladies and the men's legs as they moved about. She had been so proud of their arrangements, she and Delphine had done them. Tall spikes of gladioli flown in from the States, mingling with tall red and pink anthuriums, sprays of jasmine, several pots of scarlet red poinsettias, and a lovely bowl of Christmas roses.

She moved slightly from one aching foot to another. These high heels were not nearly so comfortable as ballet slippers. She smiled brightly at the curious Uncle William and his wife. She heard them mutter as they moved away from her to the drawing room, "She looks good for her background!"

Another sting. She compressed her lips, forced them to smile again. Jeronimo Oviedo and his wife Melinda came up to her. "Isn't it tiring for you?" Melinda said brightly, her black eyes avid and cold. "You aren't used to all this, are you? Now, I was trained for such occasions. I even studied standing up when I was a teenager. Just to prepare myself for receptions!"

Rosita did not believe her, she could not imagine the hard, selfish girl doing any such thing. She vaguely remembered reading that the present Queen Elizabeth of England had done so—that she could believe, but not Melinda Valdes! Her devoted parents would never have demanded such a sacrifice no matter what their ambitions for her.

"How nice," she managed to murmur. She hated the way Jeronimo studied her so insolently, his gaze traveling over her shoulder, her throat with the diamonds sparkling on it, the low neckline of the gown in front, the tight waist, over her legs. She felt like squirming under it, it was so boldly intimate and insulting.

They finally moved away. "Gypsy girl," she heard Melinda say clearly. It had been meant for her ears. Rosita felt afire with fury. The girl could have married Zach, she had chosen that—that fat slug! Did Zach still miss her—she watched sharply, unable to tear her gaze away, as Zach went up to them and greeted them. Did he smile more warmly at Melinda? Did his look linger on her wistfully? She thought so. She had been his mistress, everybody said so. Someone had said in her presence that he had married Rosita on the rebound. The events had certainly taken place in a short time, Melinda's marriage to Jeronimo, and Zach's marriage to Rosita.

It made her feel faintly sick. She turned around, caught the shrewd gaze of Madame Sonia. The older woman came closer, took her arm in her frail hand, murmured, "And are you enjoying this occasion, my dearest Rosita?"

Rosita's mouth twisted a little, she managed to murmur, "Yes, of course, Madame Sonia."

"Poof," Madame Sonia said. "Neither am I!"

Rosita laughed, it was so unexpected. Several people turned about to see who laughed, in such a clear bell tone. Some smiled at her, some frowned.

All of Zach's relatives were here, she realized later, all his uncles, Aunt Hortense, cousins, relatives by marriage of his uncles' wives, and so on. And not one of her relatives had been invited! Of course, they did not move in Hamilton circles, her people were Spanish Gypsies, not San Juan society.

She thought, my father would have stood as straight and proud as any of them, he looks as distinguished. My brothers are as handsome, more handsome than many! My sisters are as gentle and charming. But none of them had been invited. Zach had not even thought to include them.

She raged inside, events were piling up to make her feel

an unwanted outsider. Isolde had wanted her only because of her ability to dance well. Delphine was her friend, Madame Sonia was kind, but Madame Isabeau was still distant and aloof. Rosita was aware that Zach's mother had not fully accepted her, and Isolde did not accept her as a sister.

The guests finally departed. She heard other things that made her sting. Remarks about her behind her back. Sneers at Zach's "taste for women," and about Gypsies. They said little about "dancers," for many of his family were dancers themselves. Ballet dancers, it seemed, were accepted socially, flamenco dancers were not! How terribly unfair, especially when she had been a ballerina for four years!

The dinner seemed long drawn-out and she felt miserable. She could talk of little things, and smile and listen, she tried to do all this, and was aware that Zach was smiling at her approvingly as she talked to a congressman and his wife across the table. She spoke of Puerto Rican history knowledgeably, and its social problems briefly, and the congressman asked some questions about the poverty. She said what she knew of programs going on, Zach took it up quickly and carried on the talk.

The congressman asked about the coming strike at Zach's factory, Rosita was surprised, for she had not read about it much. There had been some newspaper articles, Zach had discounted them, something about two fired workers. He made little of it now, shrugging and saying they were negotiating, and it would soon be settled, he hoped by New Year's.

"A matter of amount of wages within the government guidelines," said Zach.

"Yes, yes, it is important for the economy for us to be cautious. Inflation is getting worse instead of better." They discussed that at great length.

The guests lingered long after dinner, drinking coffee, rum and brandy. They finally departed after midnight, and Rosita dragged herself to bed, tired out. But Zach had been pleased, he kissed her cheek and said, "You looked glorious tonight, my darling. And you were a very charming hostess."

"Thank you," she murmured. "I am glad you were satisfied."

"I thought everything went well. The flowers were lovely."

She brightened a little. "I enjoy the flowers so."

"It shows." He smiled at her, and went to the other room. He did not return, she slept alone, glad to be alone, yet missing him. There had been constraint between them for days.

On Sunday, the day before Christmas, they all went to Mass in the morning, and in the evening for the midnight Mass. On Monday, the relatives would stop in during the day, bringing gifts, receiving some, drinking from the giant punchbowl, talking of family matters. Other guests would come and go. The family exchanged gifts in the morning after the early Mass, which some attended.

Rosita felt overwhelmed by her gifts. She had given Zach such ordinary things, she felt, shirts and ties, books of history and biography that she knew were his taste. She had given similar presents to the others, from her and Zach together. Zach had told her there was money in a bank account, she must charge things, or get what money she wanted, he had no time to buy presents. Anything would be fine, he had said.

But the family's gifts to her showed so much more thought, money and imagination that she felt very guilty. Isolde gave her a box of ballet slippers, two dozen of them in all colors, white, pink, blue, violet, black. From Kevin was a beautiful charm bracelet of gold, with a charm of ballet shoes that had garnets on the little toes. From Madame Sonia and Madame Isabeau came books and records of ballet and dance music. Delphine gave her a porcelain doll in the form of a ballet dancer who looked rather like Pavlova, Rosita's idol. And Zach—she opened one huge box, and gasped with shock.

A mink jacket, the beautiful dark sheen of ranch mink, in a dark brown, just her size, that set off her pert, lively face. She modeled it for them over her Christmas green light wool dress, and they applauded her.

"Marvelous, beautiful," approved Madame Sonia. "You will wear it in New York when you and Zach go there."

"When are you going?" Isolde wanted to know at once.

Zach groaned. "I am not planning a trip—it is just sometime, when I want to get away *alone* with my wife!"

Isolde grimaced.

Then Zach tossed another small box into Rosita's hands. It was tiny, unwrapped. "I can't wrap presents," he excused himself with a grin.

She opened the leather box, found a magnificent diamond bracelet with the letter *R* picked out in more diamonds. She gulped, said, "Oh, Zach," in a feeble tone.

"Let's try it," he said, and set it around her wrist, and fastened the clasp, and the chain. "Like it, honey?" he asked in a low tone.

She wondered at once, if this was an expensive apology that he could not speak in words. She nodded, her head bent, wishing he had said the words that he was sorry about what he had said about her family.

"Thank you very much, Zach," she managed to say. "It is—too much, really."

"Not if it pleases you," he said quietly.

She admired the gifts of the others, they cleared up the paper wrap, and set some of the presents about for their guests to see through the day. She took the mink wrap and the diamond bracelet upstairs, put the bracelet in her jewel box, and locked it in a drawer.

Guests came and went during the morning, the luncheon was a buffet affair, people eating when they wanted.

Rosita had gifts for her family, although Zach had said nothing about going over there. About one-thirty, she found herself getting more nervous and upset about that. She had telephoned her parents on Saturday, she had not seen them for a week.

Finally she took one large present down to the garage, and spoke to one of the chauffeurs lounging there, ready to drive anybody wherever one wished. "You are free? Could you take me over to my parents' home presently?"

"Of course, Señora Rosita! As you wish, always!" He beamed at her, and put the gaily wrapped package in the back of the car.

"Thank you, I will come down at once, with the other gifts," and she ran back upstairs to get the other packages and her purse, and a light cloth jacket.

Zach was in the large drawing room, she heard his laugh and teasing words to someone. Delphine was there also, she would not trouble her. She crept out again, with the other things, and went out to the car.

At her house, she thanked the chauffeur as he put the packages in the arms of Marcos and Tadeo. "Thank you so much, my brothers will take me home when I am ready. Merry Christmas to you," she added in Spanish.

"A most happy Christmas and a very good year to you, Señora Rosita!"

He departed, her brothers carried the packages to the house amid exclamations about how fine she looked, and how many presents there were, and how was her family at home?

"They are all well, thank you, there is a big festivity in their large family. All come to the house and bring presents, and eat and drink, even as you are doing," she said, and managed to sound merry and uncaring.

Marcos looked at her keenly, but said little. They escorted her into the house, wished her Merry Christmas. She hugged her mother and sisters, and all the little ones, who were running about winding up toys and hugging dolls and talking gaily.

It was so good to be with them, in the small crowded house, with everybody talking at once. Her mother looked much better, Rosita managed to talk to her privately with only Elena there. "You are better? The doctor is pleased with you?"

"Oh, yes, so much better. The new medicine is halting the infection. One more treatment, he said that should be all, probably."

The drawn lines were fading, the eyes were more clear. Rosita smiled in relief. "Oh, I am so glad, it will be truly a happy Christmas now."

They opened the large boxes she had brought, which she said were from her and Zach. There were many exclamations of delight.

Rosita had bought many lengths of fine materials she had found in the best shop for fabrics. Lengths of dress materials in fine colors of rose, blue, yellow, of silk fabrics for flamenco dresses, lengths of fine white lawn for the men's shirts. And she had found white frilling of a good stiff material, and long lengths of beautiful lace. They would make splendid costumes for them all for the next year. Alejandra was very approving, saying, "That must have been made in Spain, these materials!"

"Why, I think they were, granny," said Rosita, pointing out the labels she had left in of those made in Spain. She had tactfully taken out the ones which had been made in France and in the United States.

They had a beautiful gift for her, of a magnificent yellow flamenco dress in full length, with seven frills layering the skirt, each layer finished in fine lace. And there were black shoes for her, in the box.

Pascual looked uncomfortable about the gift. "I do not know when you will wear it, *mía*," he said. "However— perhaps one day—" He shrugged eloquently.

She did not know either, and had a sinking feeling in her stomach that it might be never. But she smiled her pleasure, and tried it on at once, to find it fit perfectly, of course.

Elena and Luisa had made the dress, Cristina and Alejandra had finished the edges with lace, they were best at that fine handiwork. Her mother had painstakingly crocheted the collar of lace.

She played with the babies, making their acquaintance all over again. How Delphine would have enjoyed them, she adored the children, and they loved her, for she was so gentle and so much fun.

Marcos was very quiet, she thought. Oliverio sat in a corner and played his guitar. Luisa's boyfriend had come for the afternoon, and sat and held her hand, beaming helplessly his pleasure at having such a fine *novia*. He was a nice man, jolly and good-hearted, just right for sweet Luisa. They would be married in February, when he had a vacation coming.

About six o'clock they were talking of having supper, and

Rosita said she would stay with them. But a car drove up, the Hamilton chauffeur who had brought her, and Zach beside him. He got out, smiling politely, and came to the steps where she sat with her father.

He wished them all Merry Christmas, they thanked him for his gifts, which he did not know about, but concealed his ignorance. They talked about fifteen minutes, then he and Rosita left.

He turned to her in the back of the car, and said in a low tone, "You did not ask me to come with you, Rosita."

She tossed her head. "You did not suggest coming!"

"You know I would have wished to do so. I did not miss you until two o'clock, then the chauffeur said where you had gone. I realized then you did not want me to come, so I left you to remain for a time with your family."

His blue eyes reproached her. She looked away, feeling guilty, and so angry. She did not want to quarrel with him on Christmas Day, so said no more. They returned home in a strained silence, and had dinner late with the family, exhausted and glad to relax with only themselves.

"And how are your family, Rosita?" Madame Sonia asked mildly. "You enjoyed your visit? They are all well?"

"Well, thank you, Madame Sonia. They wished everyone a happy Christmas."

"You took our good wishes, I hope," said Madame Isabeau, looking faintly disturbed and ashamed. "They should have come today for the celebrations."

"They were not asked, madame," said Rosita, with hostility showing in her tone. She stared down at her plate, her appetite lost.

There was a shocked, strained silence for a minute. Zach finally said, "It is understood in our family, that all our relatives and friends are welcomed on this happy day, and all holidays. We hold open house. I thought you knew this, Rosita, I apologize for not making this clear. Your family would have been most welcome. Next time, they must come."

"Thank you," she said, politely, not believing him. He

had said nothing at all about her family coming. They did not want her family here.

Delphine was silent, also, not eating, staring at her hand. Did she miss Marcos, or had that been a little summer fling? Rosita did not know.

Kevin tactfully said something about one of the cousins who had been ill, and the conversation was changed. Rosita said nothing more, she was conscious that she was spoiling their joy in the day, but she could not help it. She felt an outsider, and she wondered again and again. Why had Zach married her?

Chapter 20

One morning in early January, Isolde was in the practice room on the fourth floor, with Delphine and Rosita, going through warm-up, when the maid came to the door, panting from the long flights of stairs.

"Señorita Isolde, one comes to see you."

Isolde frowned. "Tell them I am busy," she said indifferently.

"It is a gentleman, so tall," and the maid held up her hand very high. "He has the blond hair, the blue eyes, so very tall and handsome, and he says his name, and talks to Madame Sonia in Russian!"

"Oh, my God!" cried Isolde, "and I look like this!"

She dropped her sweater, and raced out of the room, down to her bedroom. She showered in such haste her hair got wet, she was all thumbs trying to pull on her clothes. She could not choose what to wear, she could have wept. She was keeping him waiting, why had he not telephoned, oh God, where was her most attractive blue wool? She finally managed to put on everything, bind up her hair, and descend the final stairs more slowly.

She heard his deep calm voice through the open door of the drawing room. She entered in a dignified manner, her gaze going hungrily to him as he sat talking to her mother and grandmother. He stood up at once, unwinding his long legs.

She came to him, he met her halfway, and held out his hands. She put both of hers in his, he looked down at her gravely, and drew her hands up to his lips. She felt his lips on her fingers, lingering.

"Isolde," he said.

"Dimitre," she said, in a little croak of a voice.

His hands squeezed hers before he released them, he smiled down at her. He looked different, somehow. His face was open, shadows gone. She sensed there was some profound change in him. She had been so close to him she knew every fleeting expression, even though she had not always understood him.

"I have much to discuss with you," he said quietly.

"Ohhh," she drew a deep shuddering sigh. Was she dreaming? Would she wake, to find this was a hopeful dream and she was alone once more? She glanced at her mother. "May I take him to the music room, mother?"

"Of course, you may talk here if you wish," said Madame Isabeau, still studying Dimitre Kerenski speculatively. "Your grandmother and I can retire upstairs—"

"No, no, we will talk and then return," said Isolde, quickly. "Madame Sonia, would you ask the maids for Russian tea, in about an hour? With hot milk?"

"Of course, darling," said Madame Sonia. Her dark brown eyes sparkled with excitement, she sensed something important was happening. That man had come all the way to San Juan, it must be important! "Russian tea, in one hour, darling."

Isolde led Dimitre through to the music room behind the drawing room, and closed the door. Her mother would forgive her, but Isolde did not really care if she did or not. Mother was still formal and old-fashioned. Isolde hungered to be alone with Dimitre.

He did not take her in his arms. He motioned her politely to a comfortable chair near the piano, and sat down beside her

306

on the matching plush armchair. He crossed his legs, gazed into space.

"This is a very lovely home," he said.

"Thank you. You—had a good flight?"

He nodded. "I arrived yesterday evening. I walked around Old San Juan for a time. Most charming and old world."

"We enjoy it here very much. Where are you staying?"

"A hotel called El Convento, near the Cathedral." He cleared his throat, recrossed his legs the other way.

"I hope you are comfortable."

"Yes. Isolde, my wife died in Moscow about a month ago."

He said it so abruptly she could not take it in for a minute. "Your—wife—died?"

He nodded. Still he did not look at her. Instead he stared at the far wall, where portraits of the family were arranged in a close mass.

"When I defected, the ballet company was on tour in Paris," he said slowly. "My wife was not in the touring company, she was left in our flat in Moscow. Often, they did not let husbands and wives tour together, for fear of defection. She did not consider it anyway, she was from a large and rather well-off family in Kiev. She enjoyed visiting them, she often invited them to us. I did not like many of them, and showed it. They were very gossipy, vicious at times in their attacks on others, I grew weary of their words.

"In Paris, I managed to get away, hide, and friends smuggled me to England in time. I wrote to my wife, Natasha, told her I wished her to come out on a visa if she could obtain one. She never answered me directly. Another friend who defected later told me she was hysterical with anger about my leaving, and took it personally."

"You had separated anyway?" asked Isolde boldly. She had long wanted to ask him this.

"Not formally. I was often away, but her home was mine. Her father was in the Communist Party, she had many privileges. She enjoyed it in Moscow, artistic freedom meant nothing to her. She was a rather good dancer, but never got farther than a small part. She resented this also.''

He was silent for a time, then sighed and went on, as though the memories made him somber.

''I remained in England only a short time, and came to the States. You know my history from then. When I realized my wife would never come, I asked for a divorce. Angrily her father replied that he wished her to get one, that I was a disgrace. But nothing from her. The matter did not progress. I was busy, besides I wished to marry no one. It did not matter. I let it go. Then I met you. I wished to be free. I wrote to Natasha, and to her father. It was only then I discovered her father was dead. Her sister wrote bitterly that they were in trouble, that enemies said they were suspicious people, because of me. I had caused them much trouble, Natasha was no longer dancing in the ballet. They were in poverty. I was troubled, tried to find ways to send them money and make sure they received it. She had been moved from Moscow to Kiev, that made it more difficult, as I knew no one but her family there, and could not check up on the truth of what her sister said.''

He sighed heavily, expelling his breath as though they were bad memories.

''An English ballet dancer went to Moscow, I asked him to try to find out what happened to Natasha, if there was some way I could get news and send money to her. I wanted a divorce, it seemed impossible. I could not add this trouble to her. It was then I left you in Europe, I had decided to try to pursue the matter myself, in any way possible short of going to Russia. When the dancer returned, I spoke to him. He said Natasha was ill, he thought it was mentally ill, but she was not in a sanitorium, she was being cared for at home. That meant she was not a political prisoner, thank God for that.''

''You still love her?'' she asked, wildly jealous at the tenderness of his tone.

''Not for many years, since soon after we married,'' he said quietly. ''I soon found her selfish, thoughtless, wildly varying in moods—there is mental illness in the family, I

decided not to have children with her. But I pitied her, and felt
some responsibility for her. In any event, I learned that she
was very ill, her sister finally wrote to me, and told me she had
died. Soon after, the state authorities confirmed this to me.
This was one month ago. I felt so—I cannot express how I felt.
Relieved, sorry, anguished for her. Such a sense of freedom,
yet guilt also that I felt free.''

"Oh, Dimitre." Isolde finally managed to put her own
feelings aside, to comfort him. "It was not your fault. You
tried to get her to come—"

He shook his head. "I did not really want her to come.
This made me feel the more guilty. I was glad to be away from
her, from her torrents of screaming and insults, from her jealousy that I was rising to stardom while she remained in small
parts, artistic jealousy as well as personal. I had but to smile at
my partner, and was treated to such rages that it became un-
bearable. Poor Natasha, she never felt secure. And when her
father, who idolized her and spoiled her, when he died, it
evidently triggered a final breakdown. But her relatives did not
tell me, her sister did not write in answer to my letters, for over
a year, about this. They always disliked me, this was their
petty revenge. Even when her sister did write, it was in such
spite. She said it was my fault, I had driven Natasha to her
death. If I had not defected, the fortunes of the family would
be higher than ever. All, all was my fault. And I could not
deny it.''

"Oh, Dimitre, as though that was your fault!" Isolde
cried, appalled.

He nodded, decidedly. 'Yes, it was. An entire family is
suspect from then on, when a man defects, or a woman. The
suspicion is there, from friends, enemies, authorities, all. They
were watched, spied on, promotions refused, the factory finally removed from my father-in-law's management, his privileges curtailed. All because I defected.''

Isolde was silent. She rarely read the newspapers, ballet
was her passion, politics meant nothing to her. She was impatient at talk of Puerto Rican strikes, of terrorists, all that meant
to her was interruption of vital things such as concerts, ballet

performances, the arts. But here was Dimitre talking in a tired, level voice of matters beyond her belief. How could rational, sane people behave like this? How could a government punish an entire family because of the actions of one man? It was incredible, but it had happened.

"But now—I have finally come to believe that I am free," said Dimitre, and stretched out his long arms in a gesture of intense joy. "I am free at last! Free of the past, of Natasha and worry about her. Her family can fend for themselves, they usually land on their feet, my brother-in-law is now in the Party, and will redeem their honor," he added drily. "They have all rejected and denounced me, as having driven their beloved sister to her death. That should help their status somewhat."

"Oh, Dimitre! How horrible!"

He reflected. "Yes, horrible, but rational, according to their lights. You do not understand the Russian system, Isolde, either of the past or the present. I think your grandmother does, however. I like her immensely, we can talk."

"Yes, you both speak Russian," said Isolde.

He smiled at her with whimsical humor. "Yes, we both speak the same language," he said.

He brooded then, gazed at the pictures on the wall. Then he turned again to her.

"You will realize, Isolde," he said quietly, "that it is very soon after the death of my wife to consider marriage. I have lived long with the thought of her—I cannot believe she has died, that I am free to marry."

Hope bubbled up in her. Marriage? He spoke of marriage? She could not believe it.

"I wish one day, to be able to ask you to marry me," he said, with curious grave formality. "I love you, you know this. I think you have loved me—" His gaze was a question.

"I love you terribly. Oh, Dimitre," she managed to say. Where was her poise now, her assurance? She felt like a green girl!

He did not reach for her; instead, he smiled at her, with

grave tenderness. "I do not deserve you," he said. "I treated you abominably. But I was so hurt, so—so distressed. I could not dance well, I knew I did badly." He tossed back his head, his beautiful Tartar head, like a restless stallion. "I despise myself when I cannot dance well. I betray myself. I hate myself," he said dramatically, but she understood. She had the same feeling. "I could not be kind to you, because I hated myself."

"I understand," she said, and she did at last. She could look beyond her own hurt feelings, and comprehend what had been going on in his life, in his head and heart. Loving her, and bound to another, exasperated beyond endurance at the walls that kept him from learning what was going on in Russia.

"You are good, and kind, I do not deserve you," he said and sighed deeply. "One day, I shall ask you to marry me, when I can forget, and be calm once more, and under control. One day, when the sun shines, and we are happy, I shall say to you, dearest Isolde, will you love me always? Will you marry with me, and make me the happiest man in all the world? You will comprehend why I cannot ask at this time. We must think, and talk, and walk together, and dance, and perhaps make love, together. And one day, will be the right time."

She wanted to cry out, that now was the right time, whenever he wished! But somehow, she did comprehend him, that he had been hurt and confused, that he knew he had hurt her, that they must indeed wait, and become close once more. Then one day, he would take her hand, and kiss her, and they would marry.

She could be content now, to wait, for the right time.

She smiled, and touched his hand rather shyly. "There is often sunshine in Puerto Rico, Dimitre. You must learn to enjoy the warmth here, and it will heal you. The sun is healing."

He picked up her hand and carried it to his lips.

They talked for a long time, now about the future and of ballet. "I have some engagements for the winter, but they can be cancelled," he said. "One company is in Texas, and I can fly up there and fulfill that. Another company is on strike, that is canceled already. The others I will cancel, that is, if you wish to remain here, Isolde!''

He was consulting her, he was looking at her with questions in his eyes. Excitement and pleasure welled up in her, her life took on a much rosier hue. ''I want you to stay for as long as you will, Dimitre,'' she managed to say. ''I want to discuss a ballet troupe with you. I think one day we can form our own, don't you think so?''

He nodded. ''The ballet movement has caught on so strongly in the United States, and indeed in the world. I think there is room for another ballet troupe. But we must engage good dancers, teachers, and plan carefully. Too many are hastily planned, and soon go under for lack of care. But I wish to work with you, whether we both go with a troupe, or whether we form our own.''

''Oh, Dimitre, that is what I want also.'' Somehow they were both standing, and he took her tenderly in his arms.

His lips met hers, they were gentle at first, and she leaned against him, hungry for him, yearning for him. That he had come back to her—the shadows gone, those terrible moods past—at least she hoped so—

His arms went about her more closely, his hand on the middle of her back pulling her to him. His lips turned hot and passionate, full of desire. She wished they could go right upstairs to her bedroom—oh, God, why were they not in New York? If she had been in New York when he discovered about his wife, they could have been in bed by now! She felt a primitive hunger for him, an urgency that was impatient of all restrictions. But they were here in her mother's house, and reluctantly she drew back when a tap came at the door.

His arms had dropped, he turned to the door as Madame Sonia opened it. ''The tea is ready,'' said Madame Sonia, smiling at them happily. ''You will come now?''

Isolde nodded, her face flushed, her mind in a tumult. There was so much to say, so much to talk about, so many plans to make. She was blissfully happy. Dimitre was free, and he had come at once to her! The past doubts and disappointments were explained and forgiven. Dimitre had been so change-able, so difficult, because of his wife and his worries about her. And of course he could not propose when he was still married to that woman.

Madame Sonia said merrily, "You will wipe the lipstick from your mouth, Mr. Kerenski?" She handed him a handker-chief.

He shook his head, smiled, took out his own large white handkerchief and wiped his mouth. "Thank you, madame," he said in Russian, his blue eyes twinkling. "You are most kind."

Rosita and Delphine showered and changed, and came down to luncheon with the family. The men were not there, but they were curious to see Dimitre once more.

Delphine muttered, "We shall be working hard again, you watch! I knew this was too good to last."

"Don't you like Dimitre?" asked Rosita curiously, as they walked over to the stairs.

Delphine shrugged. "Well enough, though I could have killed him when he left us cold. But I'll bet Isolde is already making engagements for us for the spring. We'll be working like demons whether we want to or not."

Delphine seemed strange these days, impatient, dreamy, quick-tempered, then abstracted. Rosita wondered if she were seeing Marcos, or had forgotten him. Delphine never spoke of Rosita's brother, and now that they were not dancing in the nightclub with the Dominguez, Delphine did not go to the fami-ly on Rosita's quick afternoon visits.

Dimitre greeted the girls warmly, with kisses on their cheeks. Rosita thought he looked better, not so drawn and brooding. They moved into the large dining room for luncheon, Madame Sonia pushing Rosita to the head of the table, where Zach usually sat. "Take the head, it is your right, darling!" she whispered.

Rosita hesitated, but Madame Sonia pushed her again. Reluctantly, she took the head, no one said anything. It seemed odd.

The conversation was taken over by Isolde and Dimitre,

with a few chiming remarks by Madame Isabeau. Rosita silently signaled for changes of course, as she had seen Zach do, and whispered to the maid for the proper wine.

Isolde was talking about rehearsals, and Delphine nodded to Rosita gloomily, in an "I told you so" look. "We should prepare several small numbers, to get us into condition"

"What are the prospects here in San Juan?" asked Dimitre, spearing his lettuce salad.

"Not much," shrugged Isolde. "An occasional visiting troupe, the others are all booked up. We will probably have to return to New York."

Delphine opened her mouth to protest, Rosita kicked her leg lightly under the table. "Wait," mouthed Rosita. They would talk to Zach about that!

Delphine nodded, and ate her fish in brooding silence.

Isolde and Dimitre discussed a *pas de deux* of Dimitre and Rosita, from *Swan Lake*. "And I want you to rehearse with her in something from *Sleeping Beauty*," said Isolde briskly. She glowed, she beamed, she burst with ideas. Her cheeks were pink, her blue eyes sparkled, she wore an electric blue woolen dress that set off her red gold hair.

"Rosita can do *Spanish Reverie*," said Isolde. "Rosita should rehearse *Gypsy Wanderer*." Rosita should do this and that and the other; she was full of plans for Rosita.

Madame Sonia spoke up in a short silence. "Dimitre, my darling lad, did you know that our Rosita is now married to our Zach?"

Dimitre Kerenski turned from his absorption with Isolde to gaze at Rosita in amazement. "Rosita, married to Zach? When did this happen?" He glanced at her hands, at the gold and jeweled rings.

"Last September," she said quietly.

"But you—married! You are only a child!"

"Nineteen," she said defensively.

He recovered and gave her best wishes. "You may be sure you have my sincere best wishes upon the happy occasion. I had not heard—but what will this do to our plans? Will your husband permit you to dance?"

Rosita did not know. She had no chance to speak.

Isolde said, "I'll speak to him, but I'm sure he will not mind. Our family is deeply into ballet!"

But not into flamenco, thought Rosita bitterly.

"Have you kept in practice?" asked Dimitre.

"Yes," said Rosita.

"Oh, well, that is all right then," he said, and turned back to Isolde.

Madame Sonia raised her delicate eyebrows, Madame Isabeau looked very thoughtful. Dimitre was as bad as Isolde, thought Rosita. Nothing mattered but ballet.

She retired to her suite of rooms following luncheon, she had much to think about. Dimitre and Isolde had left right after lunch, to talk some more, they said. From Isolde's glowing look, Rosita wondered if they would take up their affair where they had left off. Why had he returned? In fact, why had he left?

Delphine had disappeared in the direction of her room. Rosita took out the box of ballet slippers Isolde had given her for Christmas. Might as well sew on elastic and ribbons, she decided. They would be needed soon.

Madame Sonia tapped on the door, and Rosita jumped up to encourage her to come in. "May I, dear Rosita?" she smiled. "I am so full of talk!"

"Of course, I am delighted that you came."

She saw the box of slippers, the little sewing box of rose velvet that Zach had given her. "Oh, do let me sew some slippers, I have not done so for a time."

She took a pair, and asked where Rosita wanted the ribbons sewn on. Rosita brought her a pair of her old slippers, for matching, and they settled down in comfort to sew and talk.

Rosita's questions were answered. Madame Sonia had had tea with Dimitre, and talked in Russian to him. She knew all about his wife Natasha, and how she had died, and how Dimitre had felt, and that he had come back to work full time with Isolde.

"And how is he to work with? He is a good dancer, a

good partner?'' asked Madame Sonia, sewing with tiny neat stitches.

"Yes, excellent," said Rosita, her head bent over the slippers she was sewing.

"Very demanding, yes?"

"Well—he is very particular. But one feels very secure with him, he is very strong, and makes one feel protected."

"Ah, good, good. You have seen him dance often with Isolde?''

"Sometimes, but not often. She has more solos, you know."

"Ah, her height. I fear that, always. The prima ballerina cannot be so tall, it is too bad. You are the right height and weight.''

"So they say."

"You are not happy, my darling?"

Rosita glanced up quickly, gazed into the shrewd brown eyes. "Well—sometimes. At times I am—puzzled. I don't know what to think."

"About marriage and dancing?"

Rosita nodded. "Should I have married Zach? I still do not know why he married me—I mean, it was so sudden, and he did not let me stop and think about it—" She was flushed.

"Zach dated many girls, but he said nothing about marriage, until one day he says he is going to marry you, right quick," said Madame Sonia, snipping the thread neatly, and spreading out the ribbon to study it. "I think he loves you very deeply, but he is so busy with the factory. The strike worries him, you know."

Rosita nodded, a crease between her eyebrows. "I know that. He has so many responsibilities.''

"I think it is harder for modern girls," said Zach's grandmother. "When I married, my husband directed me from then on. He permitted me to dance in ballet until I was pregnant with my first child. Then, no more, I might damage myself. Later on, I became ballet mistress for two years, but he disliked it, that I was gone from home so much. So I stopped that. I have not regretted that. My happiest years were with my dear Philippe. The war—God, the war. Wiping out my dearest one.

How I hate wars, so senseless, so violent. Wiping out such a good fine man. For what reason?''

"That is what my grandmother Alejandra says," said Rosita. "My grandfather, Alfonso, died in the Civil War, right at the end. He had lived through all that, she said, and then a bullet right at the end of the war, and she mourned him so bitterly. There was such violence in Spain, you know, so many terrible things, and the Gypsies had to hide in caves, she told us of those times.''

"I should like to meet and talk with your grandmother, I think we have much in common," said Madame Sonia, in her delicate porcelain beauty. Rosita thought of tough old Alejandra, her fierce black eyes, the black gray hair pulled back from her tanned lined forehead, the wrinkled hands, and tremendous loyalty to her own. The Gypsy who told fortunes, and brewed herb tea and dosed her own with medicines she created, and muttered Catholic blessings mingled with Gypsy words. She wondered if they would have anything to talk over at all, this old Russian ballerina and her Gypsy grandmother.

At dinner, Isolde promptly asked Zach about Rosita's dancing. "We need to get in condition right away," she said.

Zach seemed preoccupied. "Why? What difference does it make?" he snapped.

"Because we might need to be ready for a visiting company," said Isolde. "And besides we might form our own company, but that is in the future.''

"Don't include Rosita in your plans," said Zach absently, and started to rise from the table.

"Zach! I want Rosita to start practicing tomorrow morning!" cried Isolde. Dimitre watched them with grave curiosity.

"Rosita, do you want to dance ballet?" asked Zach, pausing, to look down at his wife. "Have you missed it?''

She hesitated, Isolde glared. "I have missed it, yes," she began, and wanted to ask him to discuss this with her in private. But he was already moving to leave the room.

"Very well, then, dance a little if you wish. But don't work too hard on it, I don't want you tired out and exhausted as you were last winter," and he disappeared down the hallway.

Kevin got up to follow him.

"Oh, really, what is he so grumpy about?" groaned Isolde. "There is no talking to him!"

Usually placid Kevin glared at her angrily. "There was a strike vote, it failed by a very narrow margin! We are still talking contracts, but it is difficult! Don't you care about where your money comes from?" he snapped, and he strode out.

"Dear me, even Kevin is bad-tempered," sighed his mother.

"What is he talking about?" asked Isolde. "As though it mattered!"

Rosita felt furious. "He is talking about the strike of workers against Hamilton Rums," she said clearly. "They do not have the new contract worked out, they are demanding much higher pay, and the company might fail. If it does, we are in trouble, and thousands of men will be out of work, adding to the troubles of Puerto Rico!"

"*Brava,*" said Madame Sonia, and patted her hand.

"Oh, really," Isolde said disinterestedly. "What about the new ballet we were talking about, Dimitre? Can you choreograph it soon?"

Dimitre looked grave, but began discussing the dance with her. The others were silent. Delphine had slipped in late, during the fish course, and seemed nervous and fidgety.

The practices started the next day. Isolde seemed to have forgotten that Zach said Rosita could dance "a little," and Rosita and Delphine were worked as hard as ever. They had an hour and a half class, then a fifteen-minute pause. Then rehearsals, until a very brief luncheon in the practice room. Then more rehearsals, and systematic practice on very arduous roles for Rosita, and lesser ones for Delphine. Delphine grumbled under her breath, and later to Rosita, but she obeyed. As though she did not really care about anything, Rosita thought.

Madame Sonia volunteered her services as ballet mistress, during class, and Madame Isabeau came later to help with various fine points. Isolde sometimes directed, Dimitre sometimes. And later they would disappear for the rest of the afternoon, going off to talk, they said.

"An affair, if you ask me," said Delphine.

"She is looking for more dancers," said Rosita, stretched out on her bed, as Delphine prowled around the room.

"Huh. Much good it will do. We'll probably have to go back to New York to line up more dancers, if they want their own troupe."

Rosita looked at her toe as she wiggled it in the air, her whole foot ached, both legs ached, she ached all over. Did Zach really care about anything? Did he care for her? She knew he was very busy and tired, coming home late at night, sleeping alone, groaning in his sleep.

She could not bother him with her troubles now, he had enough to worry him. But did he really care about her? Was he tiring of his passion for her? Now that he had had her as a wife for several months, was that all he wanted? She had not started a child, her mother had delicately asked her if she were taking "something against children." She was not. She wanted a child, but she did not have one yet.

But did Zach want one?

They were both Roman Catholics. But divorce was not the serious big forbidden topic it used to be. Even Catholics got divorced. And Dimitre had tried to get a divorce, Delphine had found out. If Zach decided Rosita was not good enough for him, he might want a divorce.

His relatives seemed to think she was not good enough for him, calling her Gypsy, flamenco dancer, the girl from the Spanish area, "that one," and so on. Had Zach decided she was not aristocratic enough for him?

If Zach did discard Rosita, she thought, she must be able to earn a living. She did not want to live on alimony, that would be horrible. And she did not want to live idly all her life. She must be prepared to earn a living. So she might as well obey Isolde, and practice all Isolde wished, and do her *pas de deux* dances with Dimitre.

She had come to love Zach deeply, but she did not trust his love for her. It seemed to be compounded most of passion, and she thought that passion could die and leave only ashes.

She felt stormy and angry about Zach. Why had he done

this to her? Why marry her so suddenly, then neglect her? Why despise her family, but marry her?

And yet, she lived for the nights in his arms, few those were lately. She loved him, she wanted him, she felt secure only when he held her.

However, if he had become indifferent, there was no future for her with him. She might as well prepare herself to leave him. And that meant working very hard in ballet, so she could leave him and still make her living.

Chapter 21

Zach returned in late afternoon from the labor meeting, feeling exhausted, but much encouraged at their progress. They were getting closer matching offers and demands. Another meeting, and they might be able to make an offer that would have a chance of acceptance by the union membership. It took so much patience, and he had so little!

But he was learning, he thought, to control his temper, to persist, to explain their position and problems in words all could understand.

He strode into his office. "Sarita, try Jeronimo at home again. Does anybody answer?"

She shook her head, only the maid had answered. "I'll try again, Zach," and she dialed the number.

He sat down at his desk, unlocked the top drawer and took out pages to work on. Sarita came to the door, her face troubled.

"The maid is very upset," she said. "She asked me to telephone the parents of Señor or Señora Oviedo about them."

Zach looked up. "Oh? What has happened? Illness, an accident?" He reached for the telephone. Sarita waited. "He didn't phone in today," he continued as he dialed. "Unlike him not to show up for two days like this. One day, yes, but not two, and not to be at home at all—hello? Señor Oviedo? Zach Hamilton here. Do you know where—"

He stopped, listened in amazement. Señor Oviedo was pouring out words in an angry torrent. "He is disgracing us all! And that sinful hussy he married—I could strangle her with my two hands! They are off to Mexico with no regrets—I cannot lift my head again!"

"What is it? What do you mean, off to Mexico?"

"I think you best come here, or I shall come to you," said Señor Oviedo after a pause. "My wife weeps, I do not wish to leave her, she is in hysteria over this disgrace!"

"May I come now?" asked Zach, frowning over this puzzle. "Is it convenient?"

"Convenient, when you wish, Señor Hamilton! But you may wish never to set eyes upon us again! You will never forgive us for raising such a dreadful heartless traitor of a son!"

"I'll be there in twenty minutes, Señor." Zach hung up. He thought a minute, then phoned Kevin. "Kevin, meet me in the parking lot right away, we have to see Señor Oviedo, something is wrong about Jeronimo."

"Oh—right, I'll be along—"

They reached Oviedo's residence, in an expensive new section of San Juan, within minutes. A terrified maid let them into the drawing room, and tiptoed away. Señora Oviedo sat in black in a large chair, her handkerchief to her swollen red eyes. Señor Oviedo, plump in a too-tight suit, received them with dignity, but he also had been weeping.

He indicated chairs, called them both "Señor Hamilton," and not the familiar "Zach" and "Kevin." He was formal, visibly upset, not putting on an act, but genuinely grieved and scandalized.

When Zach heard the story, he was also. He could not believe it for a time, knowing that Señor Oviedo had always disapproved of his lighthearted rake of a son.

"Jeronimo and Melinda—how I despise that woman who has led my son astray!—they have left San Juan forever! Nobody will ever receive them again—they will be forgotten and their names never spoken again!''

Señora Oviedo wept again, hopelessly, into her wet handkerchief. Zach waited, with what patience he could command.

Señor Oviedo went on. ''My son and his wife—they came here last Sunday afternoon after Mass—they went to Mass! I hope they went to Confession first, but I think not! They came here for a pleasant afternoon. But they did not linger. Let me tell you, I sent them from the house! I hope you will not blame us when you hear how shocked and angry I am with my son! Oh, such a one! How horrible a thing he has done—''

Kevin and Zach exchanged significant looks—they were beginning to see the light. Oviedo wanted to cover himself completely before telling about his son, Jeronimo. He did not want to lose his place in society. But this obviously must go deep—

''You said Jeronimo and Melinda have gone to Mexico? Where in Mexico, and why?'' asked Zach as calmly as possible. He was tired, he wanted to go home and rest, have a good dinner with his family, play some music perhaps to relax him—

''To set up their own rum distillery,'' said Oviedo bluntly, and wiped his forehead, peering at them behind the cloth with anxious little black eyes. ''He has been setting it up for some two years, he was brazen enough to inform me! He has partners there. It seems that he has learned enough of the Hamilton rum formulas to earn that part of his partnership. They are supplying the money, they have built a plant, they have hired workers, and are ready for production. Now he goes!''

Zach stared at him blankly. Kevin said quietly, ''And he has been planning this for some time, while he worked for us? Señor, tell us about this.''

He nodded unhappily. ''Yes, Señor Hamilton. My son evidently acquired the idea about two years ago. He was approached by some Mexicans who wished to produce and sell rum in northern Mexico, they had bought some fields of sugarcane, they knew how to manage the crushing process. But they needed aid from then on. He flew over there, surveyed the possibilities, he said, and decided to go into business with them. He gave them advice, told them how to build the plant, and from his experience with Hamilton's he was able to assist them in achieving all this.'' He waved his plump hands vaguely, not able to explain about the processes.

Zach was silent, his tired brain racing. Jeronimo setting up a rum distillery in competition with Hamilton's. Using Hamilton experience and knowledge, using his work with them to buy into a partnership with Mexican businessmen. Using Hamilton formulas—but wait. Jeronimo was not on the board, and he was not a Hamilton relative. He would not have access to the secret formulas, only the preliminary ways of treating the sugarcane, the molasses and rum mixtures, the vats—

Kevin was probing, Zach heard the voices dimly. Señor and Señora Oviedo had known nothing about this, only that Jeronimo liked to spend his vacations in Mexico. And then when he married That Woman, that Melinda Valdes, that scheming vulture, that female who craved money so much she cared not how she achieved it—then Melinda had insisted on going ahead more rapidly with the plans.

''And he bragged to us that she had assisted him in spying on the Hamilton firm! She places the bugs—she said *bugs?*—on walls in offices, listened on the radios, I do not know how this works, Señor, believe me! They even went so far as to steal into your home, and open the safe there, to go over papers! When I heard this, I said, 'you are criminals, thieves, lower than the lowest!' ''

It took another hour to get all the information about the operations out of Señor Oviedo, he repeated himself, apologized, swore he knew nothing about it, he was in disgrace, he wept, he waved his hands in agitation. They believed him, he was too angry not to be truthful.

Zach and Kevin went home, and telephoned the relatives. All came over following dinner, they held a four-hour meeting.

''I confess I am relieved,'' said Kevin, calmly, as Uncle

William raved on about traitors and betrayals. "Now that Jeronimo and Melinda have fled the country, at least we know who has been doing the bugging and breaking into the house and the offices. It was not the labor organizers, nor any terrorists. It is a straight case of company thefts, and attempted thefts of formulas."

"That is true, that is true," muttered Uncle Morgan, running his hands through his thinning red hair. "But how much did he learn? That is the question."

"We will probably not know until his rums come out," said Zach thoughtfully. "Aunt Hortense, did he hang about the labs, do you know?"

"He tried to, he even came to sit in my office, but I shooed him out, let me tell you. Never did like that lazy young man, though he was your friend," Aunt Hortense said. "And I saw to it that I locked up with my own padlocks every night."

"Uncle Morgan, how about you?"

"I'm afraid I was not so careful," he admitted reluctantly. "But damn it, I will be from now on!"

Zach did not remind him that it was like locking the barn door after the horse was stolen. He turned to Stephen, his cousin. "How about you, Steve?"

"I am a fanatic about secrecy," grinned Steve. "Thank God! I learned the formulas, and locked them in your safe. Never kept them around, and I worked alone."

"Well, there is a chance he learned our formulas for the older rums, but not the silver one, then. And now we can proceed with my new ideas," said Zach thoughtfully. "I'm relieved, as Kevin said. Now that we know who was prying about, and he has departed for Mexico, now we can proceed with fresh ideas."

"Well, I hope you have some, my boy," said Uncle Morgan heartily. "I don't mind telling you, I am appalled! That young whippersnapper—"

"And he was my friend!" Zach burst out, furiously. "We had him in our home since he was a small boy, we felt sorry that his parents were so strict with him and neglected him at the same time. He seemed so—so friendless! And he took advantage of that friendship to steal company secrets! I cannot ever forgive him for that!''

''And Melinda?'' asked Uncle Samuel shrewdly, his eyes narrowed. ''You dated her, didn't you? Close to marriage?''

All of them stared at Zach. He shrugged, thinking about the rum being produced in Mexico.

''She could have done nothing without him, she knew nothing about chemistry,'' he said absently. ''Now we will have to wait until the Mexican rums come out to see what they have done, how much damage to our regular line. But meantime, we can get started on the new things—''

''What new things?'' asked Uncle Morgan. ''You keep saying you have new ideas, what are they?''

Zach smiled. ''Some great ones. You know, I have been wanting us to do a new line of liqueurs, but the formulas were difficult. Well—I have discovered some formulas on coffee liqueurs, coconut, lime, apricot, banana—''

''My God!'' cried Steve, excited, slapping his knees. ''How did you come up with them?''

Zach only grinned, he was not about to tell them where he had the ideas. The journals of Tess Hamilton were safely locked up in a drawer in his bedroom. ''Never mind! Just know I have some ideas, and have been working them out on paper. Now we can experiment in the labs, and really go to work on them.''

''Tremendous, you can count on me to work hard on these,'' said Aunt Hortense with satisfaction. He opened the safe, and took out some of the scribbled papers he had been fussing with. She took the first one eagerly, and began going over it, murmuring the formulas intently.

After hearing about Jeronimo and Melinda, Zach had felt free to bring the pages down to the study, and lock them in the safe. Now he also felt free to discuss the new liqueurs.

''Let me have something to do, Zach,'' said Uncle William. ''How soon can we come up with something? I'll work nights on a new campaign, if that would help!''

''And let me have something to work on in the lab,'' said Uncle Morgan, reaching out eagerly for a page. ''What do you want me to do?''

"The coffee liqueur, Uncle Morgan, if you will," said Zach, feeling new energy and a surge of pleasure in his family. They could be ornery and difficult, but when problems arose, they could sure rally around. "Let us think first about the coffee liqueur and the orange; according to the formulas, they should be the simplest to produce. Uncle William, you dream up an ad campaign to put them over, we can plan on having them in production within a year at the most, perhaps even in six months. I'd love to get them out by this summer—let's see, it is the end of January— How fast can we work?"

"Once we take out any problems with the formulas, we could be in production by June, anyway, couldn't we?" said Kevin, and took out a pad of paper to scratch away at plans.

"If Uncle Morgan does the coffee, and Aunt Hortense the orange, what do you want me to do? Help one of them, or proceed on one of my own?" asked Steve, an eager flush on his cheeks. He had never worked on one wholly on his own, Zach thought.

He went over the pages, carefully. The pineapple looked fairly simple, and would be a good summer drink. He handed that page to Steve. "Here is the pineapple suggestion. Remember that the formulas are about two centuries old, based on ways of working that long ago—"

They gaped, he grinned, "No, I am not going to tell you where I got them! But an ancestor of ours did work on these. And I got them legally! They are ours, no question about it, and we are free to work on them and improve them for our own."

"Well, you are a surprising young man," said Aunt Hortense, primly, giving him a smile of approval. "What else do you have up your sleeve, Zach?"

He read off the pages briskly, proud of the work they had been able to do between them, he and Rosita. "Coconut, orange, apricot, banana, pineapple, mango, papaya, mint—spice maybe—nougat—"

"My God! Fantastic," cried Steve, his eyes shining. "We can get out a whole line of them. How long will it take?"

"Depends. How accurate can these formulas be, when

translated to large quantities? Can we obtain enough pineapples and oranges to process? Can we get the containers soon from the States? Can we train more workers, or will we need to take workers from the rums to work on them, and train others for this?''

They discussed the problems for a long time that night, and met again the next two days to work on them. They were more closely knit, more cooperative than he had ever seen them. He felt jubilant about that, and that carried over to his next meeting with the union leaders.

The rum factory had been running over with rumors about Jeronimo Oviedo and his wife, and their hasty departure from Puerto Rico. Zach decided to tell the whole story, honestly, and enlist their cooperation in the problems.

They listened intently. He told the labor leaders what had happened. ''We were spied on, the safe at home was broken into, our guard shot. Bugging devices were set about at home and in the offices. We did not know who was doing this. It was my former friend Jeronimo,'' and he heard them muttering and saw them shake their heads.

''You can imagine how I feel,'' he went on slowly. ''This is a blow from the hand of a friend. However, as the saying goes, 'God can make good come from evil,' and so it is. Now we know what has happened. Now we can feel free to go ahead with other friends, other plans, with a free spirit.'' When he talked in Spanish, he found himself using their idioms, their expressions.

He told them about the new line of liqueurs. ''We can now feel free to go ahead with this. It will mean promotions for some men, to supervise the new lines of rums. It will mean training others, we will need to hire more men. Kindly inform the men to apply for these positions, and I wish your recommendations on which men are so careful and so reliable that we can depend on them with this new important work. Also take lists of men who wish overtime.

''It will mean that soon all our men and women can go on full time, there is no more need for part-time work and spacing it out. Progress will be made soon on a new addition to the distillation building, we will require a dozen new large vats. We shall be hiring by June.''

He explained it all carefully, then answered their questions.

''Now, we do not believe we can offer higher wages than our previous offer, which is within the government guidelines. However, the new supervisors who are promoted to those jobs will receive higher pay for their more responsible work. Those who work full time will receive more than when they worked part-time. Those who wish overtime will receive more for that. On this basis, are you willing to sign a new two-year contract? That is the question I wish you to put to the labor members.''

One supervisor had a question. ''What about those Mexican rums, Señor Zach? What if they are better than ours?''

From their anxious faces, it was a real problem.

Zach said, firmly, ''I do not believe they will be. I have asked our sales agent in Mexico to be alert for the rums, and send bottles of samples to me as soon as they are produced. We will examine them carefully. However—they will be made from guessed-at formulas, stolen by a man without honor. They will be produced by Mexican laborers unaccustomed to such work. They will be made in vats not supervised by men such as Hamilton men. And they will not have the knowledge, intelligence and skill of our Puerto Rican people! No, I do not think they can match us! What do you think?''

He ended in such a strong tone that they began to cheer and applaud. He thanked them, and left the meeting, so they could discuss the matters alone.

They took a vote two days later, and the contract was approved by ninety-five percent of the workers. With that settled, he could forget the problem for a time. He had Kevin supervise the reports of the supervisors, decide whom to promote, and he himself began ordering the new vats, the building of an additional section to the distillery, the testing of the new formulas as Aunt Hortense and the others called them to his attention.

He could not sleep well at nights. He worked until after

midnight on plans for construction, on letters from the States, on bids for various sizes of vats, on variations of the formulas for the liqueurs presented by the chem labs. Then when he did go to bed, he was exhausted, too tired to sleep, tossing and turning in the narrow bed in the room next to Rosita's.

He was brusque, finding it hard to control his temper. He left the dinner table abruptly one evening, unable to endure Isolde's chatter about ballet, and some gossip about neighbors. He went to the study and shut the door, and sat with his head in his hands. The burden was going to crush him, he had never felt so tired in his life, his head ached abominably, he felt nobody in the world understood what he was going through. Was this how his father had felt, in those years and months before his fatal heart attack?

Rosita tapped on the door, and entered, before he could bring himself to say, "Come in."

"Zach, I am worried about you," she said quietly, closing the door after her. She came over to his desk, and stood beside him, where she could look into his face. "Whatever is the matter? Do things go badly?"

He took her hand, and drew her down on his knees. He felt her sink against him, and put her head on his shoulder. She felt soft and warm and gentle against him.

"It is just—that I am so tired," he said finally.

"It is more than that, darling Zach," she said, her voice coming from the depths of his jacket. "You are worried, you work too long at nights. You will break down, I fear, if you continue like this."

Her hands came up, and she stroked his neck. Her touch was soothing, he relaxed a little. "No, I am too young yet to break down," he said ruefully. "I am feeling sorry for myself, I guess. I don't know how dad managed!"

"He worked too hard also. Oh, Zach, I don't want you to become so exhausted. Cannot you go more slowly? Must it all be accomplished at once?"

"I guess not," he conceded. "I just feel such urgency. The men want more work, some have been out of work so long, we have been hiring. When I say the work will begin in June, they look so hurt—so—their shoulders go down, they hang their heads. They are hungry, Rosita, and they ache for their families.''

"You cannot do everything at once," she said. "And there are the welfare programs, the food programs. They will not starve before then. Still—if some could be hired now, and the training begun—" She lifted her head and looked at him hopefully. "Even part-time now—"

He thought about that. Their faces had begun to haunt him. "Perhaps we could," he said slowly. "I would have to discuss it with the union leaders. But we might hire now, and put them on double with an experienced man each, to begin training slowly. Instead of giving overtime, we could hire more men to train, it will be more expensive, but worth it in the long run. Yes, I'll talk to the uncles tomorrow—on Monday, rather. Tomorrow is Saturday, isn't it? and they won't be in.''

"Don't go in either, Zach," she coaxed. "Could we go on a picnic instead?"

"In February, darling?" he laughed, and hugged her.

"We could—we could drive somewhere, and sit in the car, and gaze at the ocean and the sky. And talk. We have not talked for so long.''

She was right, they had been strangers to each other for too long. She slipped from his lap, and came around to stand behind him. "I think your head aches," she said, and began to hold his head, and rub her thumbs firmly on the back of his neck.

He groaned with pleasure. "Oh, that feels good—"

She rubbed over his head, his neck, his forehead, her stroking slow and even. She hit the right spot, and he said, "There, that's where it starts, right there. Rub it again." And she rubbed firmly over the area from behind his ear to his forehead and down his cheekbones. He could have purred like a cat.

Then she held his shoulders, and worked them back and

forth until he was able to relax. He slipped off his jacket and she worked on his shoulders through the shirt. It felt so very, very good. The tension began to drain from him.

"There, is that better?"

"Much better, honey. Let's go upstairs, I'll turn in early, I could sleep for a week."

He took a shower, and went to bed. Rosita was lying there in her thin nightdress, and he lay down flat on his stomach, yawning, and put his head on her breasts. She was soft, yet firm, a strong little girl with a beautiful body and long silky legs.

He stroked over her with his hands, then apologized, "I want to make love to you, but I'm too damn tired."

She laughed softly, to his surprise. "I didn't entice you up here!"

"You didn't?" He wished he could bring himself to make love, he adored seeing her all softened with laughter, her face sparkling, her dark eyes shining.

He shut his eyes, his lips against her breasts. "Talk to me, honey."

Her hands softly stroked his head, she rubbed her thumbs firmly on his temples. "What about?"

He remembered something that had been bothering him. "About your family. Your mother was ill, and I keep forgetting to ask—is she better now?"

The hands paused for a moment, then she resumed stroking firmly over his head. "Yes, thank God and the Virgin. Mother had some medicine for the infection, and it worked well. She is well again, and sings in the nightclub again. Luisa still dances, she is going to be married in mid-February, and they will go on a honeymoon to his relatives in Ponce. He wishes to introduce her everywhere, he is such a nice young man, with many people all around Puerto Rico and in New York City."

She talked on calmly, yet he sensed some note of unease in her voice.

"And they have good engagements?" he asked finally, when she had paused.

"Oh—well, no, Zach. It does not go well." Her voice

became troubled. "I wish I could help—but I know you do not wish me to dance with them."

He rolled over and gazed up at her. "No, I don't, honey," he said gently. "You got too tired, and it was not safe, not the way Puerto Rico is right now. Our family is wealthy, I hired the guards for a purpose, you know."

"Yes, I know. And there was Señor Oviedo—but that is finished, and she has left, hasn't she?"

He did not understand her words. "They both left," he said. "Well rid of them, too. And to think Jeronimo or a hired killer shot Jaime! I won't forget that."

"He has recovered and is well again, thank God."

"Yes, thank God. Rosita—if you need money for your family, you will ask me, won't you? No reserve about this? What worries you, worries me."

"It is not money they need, Zach, though I thank you for the offer. It is engagements. They are proud people, my father will not take money now, since I am not dancing in public in the ballet. It would be—charity, that is what he would think."

"Not between a man and his son-in-law."

She was silent, but he sensed her trouble.

"Do they dance now?"

"Yes, in a nightclub, but the pay is not good this month. Only Luisa and Inez are dancing, and Inez is pregnant. Cristina offered to come back, but she has four children now, and her husband is reluctant."

"Well, if they need money—Rosita, for God's sake! We have plenty—"

"Yes, but it is not the money, Zach. They have much pride, and they wish to dance well, and be paid for that. It is their work, their living."

"Perhaps Marcos will marry, he is a very handsome and fine fellow," said Zach lightly. "If he married a girl who danced well, that might solve the problem for a time."

"That is another problem. Marcos," said Rosita.

"He isn't in trouble, is he? Not Marcos!"

"No, no, no. He is not that kind. But he wishes to go back to the university, and get a degree in chemistry. He has always wanted this, since high school, he likes chemistry so much.''

"Hum.'' If Marcos wanted a job, he could have one in Hamilton's. "How far along is he?''

"He has only gone one and a half years. He needs two and a half years to graduate, then he speaks of graduate university. Papa just holds up his hands in horror. It is impossible, for the money, and for the troupe.''

He was silent. It seemed an impasse. He could offer to finance Marcos, but they would probably be too proud to let him. And they needed Marcos in the troupe. Marcos would have to choose his own future.

And family loyalty would probably dictate that choice. His family had as much loyalty, and pride, as the Hamilton's.

"Well—let me know if I can help, Rosita, you know I want to. They are your family and mine, as my family belongs to both of us.''

She bent and kissed his lips gently. "Thank you, Zach. You are very kind and good.''

"And Madame Sonia thinks the sun rises and sets in you, my little darling! She scolded me for neglecting you.''

"She did? She should not worry you.''

He felt her reserve again, and turned and drew her down with him, putting her head on his shoulder. "She notices everything, little one!'' He yawned, he was very relaxed and sleepy now. "I think I could sleep a week,'' he muttered.

"Then sleep, Zach,'' she whispered, and began to rub his head again, very gently, turning so he could lie against her.

He went right off to sleep, and scarcely woke in the night. It was about ten in the morning when he wakened, blinking at the sunlight streaming in. Rosita lay quietly beside him, studying the patterns on the ceiling from the sun shining through the lace curtains.

"Gosh, I'm late to work,'' he groaned.

"It is Saturday,'' said Rosita, sounding severe. "And you promised me a picnic!''

"So I did—ummmm!'' He stretched and yawned. He felt so much better, so optimistic and lighthearted. It had been good to talk freely to Rosita again, and feel close to her. "Darling, we must talk again. I have neglected you, and you have neglected me!"

"I have neglected—I like that! You have been too busy for me!" She pretended outrage.

He chuckled, and pulled her closer, and began to nuzzle at her shoulder and ear. "I know I have been busy, but you should remind me that I have a wife!"

"So—it is all my fault!"

"That's the wife's job, to remind her husband that he is a married man!"

"Hah! This is a modern age, there is women's liberation—"

"Woman, you speak dangerous words!" He kissed her throat, and leaned up to run his lips over her curved breasts. It had been too long since he had held her intimately, and he was hungry for her.

He made love to her slowly that morning, moving luxuriously from her head to her heels, kissing her along the sweet breasts, the navel, the smooth, flat stomach, the hips so curved and rounded, the long pretty legs. His hands learned her again, his fingers pressed her soft flesh, his lips adored her. As he bent over her to take a nipple in his lips, he felt her fingers going over his head, down to his neck, pressing firmly, soothing and yet arousing him all at once.

He wanted her then. She was soft and ready for him, opening her long legs for his body to come over hers. He slid his hips between hers, and prepared to take her, smiling down dreamily at her half-closed eyes, the rapturous face. How lovely she was!

He brought them together, slowly, carefully, teasing a little because he felt her growing impatience. He waited so long that she pressed upward with her hips, toward him, moaning in her throat. "Zach, please—oh, darling—Zach—"

"Tell me," he said. "Tell me of your longing—"

"Oh, I want—I want—"

"Tell me, talk to me—"

"Oh—Zach—I want you—I want you—please—oh, I ache all over!"

He could not resist, he bent closer, and pressed firmly to her, and she moaned in satisfaction, falling back on the bed, so he could press tightly to her. They came together fully, he held it high, then drew back slowly, and plunged again, again. She seemed to explode in delight, little convulsions wracking her slim body, pressing him tightly and giving him great pleasure in turn. So he finally came quickly, also, and they rocked together back and forth on the bed.

They rested, holding together, and then he took her again. It was sweeter the second time, not so frantic, they could move gently, rubbing against each other, teasing, waiting, stopping and holding, then beginning again. He felt her begin to react to him again, and held high and tight in her, to enjoy the ecstasy with her. It was all the more delightful, that it had been so long.

They slept together, lazing away the day. Zach finally put on a robe, went down and asked for a tray of food and coffee. The cook tried not to grin, and prepared it for him quickly. He took it back upstairs again.

Rosita yawned, "We were going on a picnic, Zach!"

"So we are—right here in the bedroom," he laughed, and poured out coffee for her. They ate sandwiches, fruit, washed it down with coffee and drinks of rum and lime juice. And went back to bed again, to sleep, make love, hold each other. It was like their honeymoon all over again. He thought, this is the way I want to live, so close to Rosita, able to talk to her, and listen to her, and be one with her.

He resolved not to let differences part them again, coldness and doubts and family troubles. They were married, he adored her, and he thought she had matured enough to love him.

She had been a child yet when they had married, but she delighted him in how quickly she learned. Still, she was very young yet, not yet twenty. He could wait for her to grow up. Her young body was maturing with his love-making, she learned how to make love better all the time. And their hearts and minds would grow together as well.

He could wait. It was delightful to teach her new things all the time, about each other.

He knew the next weeks that Rosita was "managing" him, encouraging him to rest more, not to go in to the office on Sundays, enticing him on real picnics off in the car to be alone together.

When he worked too long in the study in the evenings, she came in and talked to him, rubbed his head, soothed away headaches, brought him rum drinks and drank with him. After that he could not work! And he felt better and more relaxed. He felt she really cared what happened to him, his depression lifted. And the family cared, Kevin confessed he had been worried about him. His mother scolded him gently, "You should not go so hard, remember your dear father, Zach!"

"And your Rosita should not be neglected, Zach," reminded Madame Sonia, smoothly. "A neglected wife is fair prey for rogues!"

They all laughed, and teased him and Rosita. Rosita never glanced at another man, and they knew it. Still, he took that lesson to heart also. He wanted to keep Rosita very happy, and all his own.

Rosita evidently liked dancing, and if a little ballet amused her, he would let her do what she liked. He wanted her happy, and contented, he wanted her to have everything she wanted.

And one day, they would have a child. He knew she wanted children, she loved babies, and sometimes spoke wistfully of her nieces and nephews. What a lovely mother she would be! The mother of his children, he glowed at that thought.

There was no hurry, they were both young. He would enjoy her, having her to himself. But one day, they would both be mature enough and adult enough, to want to start their family. He looked forward to that time, to a happy future with her.

Chapter 22

Rosita knew now that she loved Zach deeply. She wanted to be his wife completely, living with him, sharing not just his bed, but his thoughts, his worries and problems, his joys and pleasures. She wanted to belong completely to him, to know the great marvel of being the mother of his children.

Yet—did he truly love her, or did he still long for Melinda Valdes Oviedo? When she was spoken of, a deep hurt and anger came over Zach. He could not bring himself to speak of her, he pretended to shrug off the questions or remarks. But she sensed his deep hurt. Was it the betrayal only, or something that went much deeper into the core of him?

Rosita tried to forget it in her dancing. She could help him when he came home, at night when he was tired. During the day, if she did not have something to occupy her mind and tire her body, she would brood. So she danced all the more, practicing with Isolde and Dimitre and Delphine.

Delphine grumbled at all the rehearsals. "For what?" she exclaimed furiously to Rosita. "For nothing! We are not going to be dancing here! and I won't go to New York!"

One afternoon, Isolde and Dimitre had left the room, had gone downstairs to telephone about a possible engagement. Rosita went on warming-up, thinking about the ballet they were working on, the *pas de deux* from *Swan Lake,* of the white swan Odette and her Prince. She was going over and over it with Dimitre, he had endless patience in making the steps as nearly perfect as possible.

"Well, I'm tired," fumed Delphine. She slipped out of the room, went down the back patio stairs, and did not return. A little later, Rosita heard a strangely familiar sound, the sputtering of the Dominguez family car. Odd, she thought. Was Marcos coming?

She went to the window of the practice room in time to see the car stopping at the far intersection. And she saw the flutter of a blue sleeve in the window. She returned to her practicing thoughtfuly. So Delphine was still slipping out to meet Marcos—and growing more bold about it.

There would be trouble eventually. Rosita frowned over her step, tried it again. It was hard to concentrate on the movement when she was worried both about Delphine and about Marcos.

Isolde and Dimitre returned, bursting with excitement. Isolde's eyes glowed. "Where is Delphine?" she demanded at once.

Isolde frowned when Rosita said that Delphine was tired.

"Well, she can just wait to hear the news then! And it won't involve her anyway! Listen, Rosita, oh, stop working! Come and sit down!" she added impatiently.

Isolde sank into a chair, looked at the notes she held in her hand. Rosita obediently sank to the floor in front of her, moved her legs into a split, bent over her thighs and continued to exercise slowly and gently as Isolde spoke. Dimitre was striding about the room, his face flushed, his eyes sparkling also.

"What has happened, Isolde?" asked Rosita. "You have good news?"

"Marvelous news! A troupe from New York—the Melody of Broadway dancers—just toured the Caribbean, and half of them arrived in Puerto Rico sick!"

"Oh, the poor things! Diarrhea?" asked Rosita. "Or fevers?"

"Both, I guess." With magnificent indifference Isolde

tossed that off. "But what luck for us! They are scheduled for nine days at the theater, and don't have enough to make up the performances. They want some duets and solos to fill in. I have their numbers here—"

"Well, they are not doing anything like *Swan Lake*, we can do the *pas de deux*," said Dimitre. "You'll be ready, Rosita? The first performance is Saturday night. We have two performances on Sunday, matinee and evening. Monday off. Then every night, plus Wednesday afternoon. Then again Saturday afternoon and night, Sunday afternoon and night."

"You'll need more than one number," frowned Isolde.

Dimitre was silent. They had not been working long enough on *Sleeping Beauty*. He had not done *Giselle* for a year, neither had Rosita. And the troupe would be doing modern dance, they needed a contrast.

"What about *Spanish Reverie?*" he asked, coming to a halt before Rosita. "Do you remember that, Rosita?"

She nodded. "Yes. But we do not have anything but the record of that—can we use a record?"

Isolde said, "They have full orchestra traveling with them. The musicians won't stand for a record being played, and it would sound terrible."

"Oliverio," said Rosita, suddenly. "He learns very quickly. He could listen to the record, and then play it for me. Only the nightclub—" She bit her lips. Could she take Oliverio from the troupe for more than one week? The timing—maybe if she danced early, he could leave and go back to the nightclub for the second and third performances.

"Can he play well enough?" frowned Dimitre. Rosita felt shocked at his ignorance, but then he had not heard Oliverio play.

"He is counted one of the finest guitarists in Puerto Rico, indeed in all the islands," she said quietly.

"Well, then, call him, see if he can come tomorrow morning, and practice with us," said Dimitre, and turned back to Isolde. "Will that do, the two numbers? Or should we supply a third?"

"I think the two, and do them well," said Isolde. "There

341

will be different audiences for the performances. That should fill in nicely between their longer contemporary numbers. And be a good contrast. I'll bet they like our numbers better than those of the troupe!''

Dimitre laughed. Rosita ran downstairs to phone Oliverio, who promised to come if Pascual permitted. He went to consult, she could hear the rumble of voices, then Pascual came to the telephone, and asked her about it.

"Well, I give my consent, if Oliverio is paid well," he said. "The nightclub does not so well, now."

From that, she guessed it was not going well at all. "I'll see that he is paid well, papa."

Rosita returned upstairs, and said, "Oliverio will come, but papa is reluctant to let him leave the troupe for those hours. He will need good pay."

Dimitre waved his hand, "Of course, of course. We are receiving five hundred dollars per performance. When you perform only with Oliverio, the five hundred is yours and his, divide it as you will!"

Isolde looked as though she would object, Rosita held her breath. But she finally shrugged and agreed. Rosita was overjoyed, she would give all of it to Oliverio, for she needed no money. Zach was always generous to her.

She listened with more patience and interest now. Isolde ran downstairs to phone and tell the troupe about the two dances. Dimitre and Rosita practiced the *Swan Lake pas de deux* until five, and then quit for a time.

Zach looked grave when Isolde told him what they planned. But Dimitre said, "It is only for nine days," and his brow cleared and he nodded.

"Very well, then, if Rosita wishes to dance." He sounded cautious and reserved. Rosita kissed him quickly.

"Will you take time off from your work to come and watch me perform?" she teased him, sitting on the arm of his chair.

He smiled at her, and pinched her cheek, and drew her down on his knees. She blushed, and tried to get away, they were all sitting in the drawing room, and she was embarrassed at the intimate gesture before them all. He held her firmly.

"Yes, imp, I will come and watch my wife dance!" he said. "And we'll buy seats for us all, and for your family. They will want to come, won't they? What night? Saturday?"

"I'll ask them. Probably Sunday, they don't dance on Sundays."

So he bought tickets for them all, in the fourth and fifth rows center of the auditorium. Her family took up a row and a third, a neighbor would take care of all the little children so their parents could attend. Madame Sonia was terribly excited, and begged Rosita to come to her room.

There she showed her a frilly white dress, and a white headdress of down, soft and faded by the years to a gray white.

"This is the dress I wore in *Swan Lake,* many, many years ago. Is it too fragile? Can you wear it, darling? I was once about your size—"

Rosita took the dress in gentle hands, exclaiming in delight. "Oh, Madame Sonia, it is beautiful! What handiwork! The tutu is still stiff and lovely, and all that lace!"

"Try it on," Madame Sonia urged, her lovely face beaming with pleasure.

"Oh, I might damage it—what if it tears!" Rosita felt the garment cautiously, it was so fragile and old.

"No, no matter. The dress will be so happy to dance again! It has rested in my wardrobes these many years!"

Isolde approved it, after examining it critically. "That relieves my mind, we don't have any suitable tutus for you here. And what about *Spanish Reverie,* what do you have?"

"My new yellow dress," said Rosita promptly. Oliverio had brought it over for her that morning. She showed it to Isolde, she and Madame Sonia exclaimed over it.

"Beautiful, perfect, just right for the dance! How gorgeous—your sisters made it? Marvelous!" Isolde was all excited approval.

The announcements came out in the newspapers, and the tickets began to go swiftly. The dance troupe was rather

343

aggravated that news of Dimitre Kerenski and Rosita Dominguez should cause more ticket sales than their own troupe. But the manager soothed them. They are well known in Puerto Rico, he said disdainfully.

"That is not to say they will dance well!" he added, and Dimitre repeated it scowling when he heard.

On Saturday they did their first number, the *pas de deux* from *Swan Lake*. Rosita had not performed in ballet since her marriage. She felt different somehow, and Dimitre felt it as he partnered her.

Her hands fluttered like the swan's wings, her arms moved as though she would take off into the sky from his hold. She was shy, terrified of this man, until he reassured her, and she began to believe he could rescue her from the dread wicked magician. Then touchingly she responded to his tenderness, and began to dance with him. The love grew between them, and the audience held their breath as the two danced together. When it ended they applauded wildly.

Zach had been watching from the wings with Isolde. Rosita came off for the last time after the bows, and he held her gently for a moment. "You were so very beautiful, my darling," he said proudly.

She looked to Isolde. The girl nodded, smiling. "Better than ever, Rosita, there is more feeling and emotion, one knows it."

Rosita wondered as she changed back to her street clothes. Marriage had changed her, she thought. She felt—released—no longer holding back. Love, passion, desire, a new fire raced through her. She could express how she felt so much more.

On Sunday afternoon, they repeated the *pas de deux*. Then on Sunday evening, she was scheduled for the solo, *Spanish Reverie*.

Oliverio went with them to the theater, silent as ever, his guitar in his arms. He had never played at the vast theater, Rosita wondered if it troubled him. She kept glancing at her older brother, troubled. He met her look, smiled, shook his head. In Spanish, he said, "I do not have butterflies in my stomach, little sister!"

"Why should you?" said Zach unexpectedly. "You are the best guitarist in Puerto Rico, the best I have ever heard!"

Rosita was thrilled at his words. He never flattered, he was directly honest. Oliverio was well pleased, she could see.

Zach and the others left her after she had dressed, and she stood alone in the wings, waiting in the interval. Then Oliverio came, and they stood together, he with his guitar, she in the many-layered yellow flamenco dress.

"You may improvise?" Oliverio asked.

Rosita started. She had not thought of that, she thought only of following the choreography of Dimitre. "Maybe," she said thoughtfully. "We shall see how it goes, eh?" They spoke in Spanish, the other members of the Melody of Broadway troupe did not understand them.

The stage darkened for them, Oliverio led her out and sat down in the chair in the corner. Rosita went over to the far right corner, and stood in flamenco position, in profile to the audience, her head up, one hand on her hip, the other holding her fan.

The curtain came up, the lights slowly rose as Oliverio began to strum his guitar, his head bent over the shining dark red instrument. Rosita stirred, as though she felt the music moving her, like a butterfly in the wind. The fan snapped open, she moved, with Gypsy arrogance and pride, gliding smoothly across the stage. Then she began to dance, slowly, as though in deep thought, musing, in a mood of reverie.

The music went faster, she moved more quickly, and the melodies caught hold of her. She began to dance, swiftly, following the moves Dimitre had dictated for her. Yet she felt more fiery, impatient. It was not enough. She wanted to show how she felt inside, how demanding, how longing for love and adventure, the Gypsy in her striving to express her wild, free nature. Love, she danced, is like the wind, brushing over one. But freedom—ah, that is a goal, that is traveling to the ends of the earth—it is the wild dance around the campfire, to the lilting music of the guitar—it is leaping into the air—

The audience was aware of what she was doing when she left the fixed choreography. Oliverio was intensely aware of

Janet Louise Roberts

his young sister, on the stage, moving faster and faster. She left the floor in a split, landing softly on one foot, *en pointe*, held it for a heart-stopping pause, then moved on into wilder dancing. Her fan fluttered, and it became a flamenco ballet, improvised to the genius-plucking of the guitar of Oliverio, as he followed her, beckoned her, moved with her, and his music seemed to lift her to new heights.

Pascual sat there, watching his baby, tears of pride in his eyes, blinking away impatiently, for he could not miss a step. Margarita clasped her hands together so tightly they hurt after. Alejandra grinned in such pride, muttering "my *gitana*, my *gitana*," under her breath all the while. Her brothers and sisters watched in joy, and not much amazement, had they not seen her dance before, in nightclubs, and on the sands, freely, happily, the fire in her burning brightly before them?

Madame Sonia wanted to weep, but she wanted more to watch. Her little Rosita, her pride and joy! She had seen her blossoming, now the young Flamenco Rose was becoming a full-blown rose. She knew she was seeing something one could wait a lifetime to see. Dance genius married to deep feeling, expressed in the slight drifting figure of a beautiful girl. The face so sober, so enthralled, so absorbed in the dance.

Madame Isabeau was startled to her depths. The mother in her had resented it when Zach married a girl beneath himself. But she had reluctantly come to admire Rosita, to like her for her gentleness and womanliness with Zach. She judged the girl on how much she could help Zach, not for herself. But now—now she saw more clearly. The girl was a prima ballerina, she had more than talent, she had the star quality, the spark that one looked for in vain from more precise dancers. She almost jumped when Rosita soared in the air, her head back, her arms out joyously, landed *en pointe*, seemed to laugh, and spun about the stage in a dizzying whirl of *pirouettes*.

Someone cried, "*La Soledad!*" Others hushed him. One could hear someone breathing, it was otherwise so quiet.

Isolde glowed with pride, she had discovered this girl, Rosita was her puppet, she had created her. Dimitre sat quietly, a little envious, more dazed, that he had not realized what Rosita

346

could do. Before, she had followed him obediently. She danced well, he thought, especially when he partnered her and directed her. But now—tonight, she had escaped him, she had left the earth and his clear orders for the choreographic steps. He knew she improvised, and he had disliked it at first, angry that she had left the pure steps. But this—this was genius—this was inspiration, pure feeling . . .

Zach sat with his arms folded. He had seen his mother dance when he was a small boy, and been thrilled at his "mama" on the stage. He had been taken to ballets for years, he knew what was good, he knew when he saw someone brilliant, like Margot Fonteyn, Carla Fracci, Maya Plisetskaya. He had thought Rosita would be good, he had been pleased when he saw her in *Swan Lake*, and in the *Gypsy Wanderer*. But now—

Now he saw a woman transformed. Her fire and tempestuous performance was thrilling this whole audience. He saw her a magnificent dancer—and he was both excited and deeply troubled.

Rosita—his wife, this fiery creature on the stage! He had thought she wanted only to dance a little, to exercise. God, how could he have been so foolish? Here was a genius—and he thought to clip her wings and make her a wife and mother! He was so confused, bewildered, he did not know what to think. Did he have the right to make demands on her? Was it right to force her to remain home and stay with him? Yet—she was so sweet and fiery in bed with him—he adored her, he longed for her, he looked forward eagerly to being alone with her. Yet—he watched her on stage, torn between the delight of her magnificent performance, and the fear that with every step she raced away from him.

On stage, Rosita was following the music of Oliverio as he composed fugues on the melody she knew so well. She moved with the music, as they so often did; he led, she followed. When he played more and more rapidly, she spun across the stage in one chain after another of rapid-fire steps. *Pirouettes*, a racing step that went flying into the air, landing *en pointe*, then racing again, in delight and wild pleasure in poetic movement.

Finally she began to tire, and Oliverio saw it, and slowed down; slower, slower, she moved with him. Gentling to pausing, a contemplative pose, an arabesque, with arms out, pleading to the Muse of dance. Slower still, to a single step, a pause, then with head down in meditation, she moved from the stage into the wings.

The manager of the troupe was staring at her in sheer amazement, unable to speak. She heard them mutter, "Genius, sheer genius," and some of the dancers were applauding her.

The audience was applauding wildly, clapping in sharp high sounds, cheering, yelling. She heard them cry, *"La Soledad! La Soledad!* Flamenco Rosita! Rosita Dominguez! Rosita! Rosita!"

Oliverio had finished, he was leaving the stage. She caught at his arm, and made him come back with her. The curtain came up again, they bowed. Oliverio stood back, indicated her with his free hand, a slight smile of pride on his dark features.

She curtsyed, trying to pierce the shadows of the audience, the lights were not on, she could see her family and Zach only dimly. She saw her father, clapping. She knew him by his proud head held high.

The curtain came down again, she left the stage, and wiped her face quickly with the towel someone held to her. The applause went on, the stage manager gestured to her urgently.

She went back as the curtain came up again. This time they left it up. She curtsyed again, again. She gestured for Oliverio to join her, he did, standing behind her slightly, holding out his hand toward her, miming, "Is she not wonderful?"

A page brought out a huge bouquet of red roses. She knew before she found the card later that they were from Zach. His gesture; she knew he would send red roses, for his Rosita.

She held them, gave one to Oliverio, smiling. He kissed her hand, whispered, "My little sister, how well you did!"

They left the stage finally, the curtain came down. The applause went on, the troupe manager frowned. It was all right to applaud such a fine performance, but he wanted his troupe to go on stage! They began to change the backdrop. The audience was still clapping, still yelling, demanding Rosita.

The stage manager held the curtain open at the center, gesturing for Rosita to come. She did, stepping out before the golden curtain, dazzled by the lights that had come on. People were standing, yelling, screaming. Flowers were flung up before her at the footlights. She bent, gracefully, scooped them up, a yellow rose, red roses, hibiscus, jasmine, more roses. "Rosita!" they yelled. She saw a handsome young man gazing up at her, then he flung a bouquet toward her. It landed at her feet. She smiled, picked it up. He kissed his hand to her elaborately.

She went back, piled the flowers on the arms of the stage manager, went back out again to their calls. Again, again, she was stunned. They would not let her go. They kept yelling for her. She made fifteen curtain calls, sixteen, seventeen.

Finally the lights went up definitely, and she retired from the stage, not to go out again, though the clapping persisted for a little time, until reluctantly they gave up.

The troupe manager said, "You were magnificent, Miss Dominguez!" rather reluctantly.

"Thank you, sir," she said politely. She went to the dressing room, Isolde and Delphine were there. They hugged her.

Delphine said little, her smile told what she thought. So happy, so radiant for Rosita.

Isolde said, as Delphine unfastened the yellow dress carefully, "My God, you were magnificent! And how they liked you! But why did you change the steps, Dimitre will be furious, I know he will. Don't change them again, will you? You must stick to his choreography."

Rosita was silent as Isolde chattered at her. She had enjoyed dancing like that so very much. But had Dimitre been offended?

Zach came to the dressing room door, and waited for her. Rosita looked up at him anxiously, he smiled, but he seemed remote, brooding. "Did you like it?" she asked finally.

"You were—more than marvelous," he said seriously. "You stunned me. You were—brilliant, moving."

She smiled in relief, and squeezed his arm. Oliverio had left quietly, to go home with the others. She would not see her family again until tomorrow. Zach wanted her to come home and rest, Isolde wanted them to go out to dinner. Zach left it to her.

"Rest," she decided. "I am tired. And I am hungry!"

"You can eat in the restaurant," said Isolde impatiently.

Zach got angry with his sister. "Let her be! We'll go on home, see you tomorrow!" He hustled Rosita away.

She and Zach ate on trays in their room, he seemed quiet and a little depressed. She wondered if something was wrong at work, but she felt too weary to question him tonight. The high excitement was winding down. Now she could collapse.

At rehearsal the next day, Dimitre discussed the changes Rosita had made. "I was angry at first," he admitted. "But then I saw what you were doing. You were dancing as a flamenco dancer does, as the mood strikes you. Can you keep it up for the other performances?"

"If I cannot," she replied, "I will stick to what you choreographed. I always have that to fall back on. That is what we do in my family. We dance as instructed, then if we feel in the mood, we take off from there."

"I see," he said, staring at her, as though he had never seen her before. "And does Oliverio follow?"

She was puzzled. "He leads," she said finally. "He sees how I feel, and he leads me into the music."

Delphine brought up the newspapers in the afternoon. The English-language papers were lyrical. The Spanish ones went into rhapsodies. They praised Rosita and Oliverio to the skies, they knew what the couple had done. They went into great detail about their background, the great Dominguez family and their dancing, their heritage, and the movements Rosita had done. She had combined ballet and flamenco into one magnificent whole, they said.

She went over later, for a quick visit with her family. They hugged her, kissed her, praised her. When they had calmed down, she played with the babies, and talked to her mother and sisters, while the men discussed baseball.

The performances of the Melody of Broadway troupe sold out completely on Monday, there was not a single ticket left for those which included *Spanish Reverie*. The troupe was ecstatic, their reviews had been good, it would help them in New York.

"But of course, they come to see Rosita," said Dimitre at the news. "I do not blame them. She is marvelous."

"So are you, darling!" Isolde cried loyally.

He smiled. "I was good, as always," he said drily. "I am not inspired this week. I will try to do better. But I know it—they come to see Rosita. We are proud of her, yes?"

Isolde agreed. She looked thoughtful, she began to make plans.

The audiences were polite for the troupe, they did not all like modern contemporary dance. They applauded the spritely numbers which imitated the Broadway musical splashy numbers. But they saved their cheers and screams and flowers for Rosita Dominguez, their own Flamenco Rose. Every time she performed that number during the week the place was packed, standees insisted on clustering all down the sides and in the back of the theater, and they brought armloads of flowers with which they showered the stage at the end of every performance.

When they returned home from the Wednesday matinee at which *Spanish Reverie* had drawn cheers for fifteen minutes, hopelessly holding up the next number, Isolde had a telephone call from New York. She called them all to wait, in great excitement. Rosita collapsed on the couch beside Madame Sonia.

"The white dress is holding up, Madame Sonia," she murmured. "I am being so careful of it, so is Dimitre."

The old lady smiled, and patted her hand. "How lovely is my Rosita," she whispered. "It is like my youth again, to see the flowers and hear the applause."

"You were probably showered with all that in your dancing, madame!"

"You are kind to say so. I had my share!" She nodded her white head proudly. A maid came in, with vases in which to put some of the many flowers.

"You will send the others to the hospitals, as before, Angelica!" said Rosita.

"*Sí*, Señora Rosita! It is being done already." Rosita got up to help arrange the deep red roses which Zach had sent once more. She smelled them, loving the glorious fragrance.

Isolde returned, pale with suppressed excitement. "It was Eleanor Stanton herself!" she cried. "Just think, Dimitre. She begs us to come back to them! They want us all for the spring season! And a summer festival in Washington, and all over the Southwest!"

Rosita went numb with shock. Go away? From Zach? Mechanically she finished adjusting the red roses, unable to speak.

Delphine had no such inhibitions. She jumped up, shouting, "I won't go! I won't go! You cannot make me go! I won't leave San Juan!"

"Now, stop that, you spoiled child!" said Isolde crossly. "You'll do what you are told! Dimitre, we can fly back to New York as soon as this week is over. I'll phone for the Hamilton apartment to be aired and cleaned. We'll go right up, and be in on the rehearsals. Miss Stanton wants Rosita to be in *Sleeping Beauty* with you, and also they will do the *Gypsy Wanderer* again—it will be just right for their balance, she said—"

"I—am—not—going!" cried Delphine, and began to storm and cry. Madame Isabeau raised her voice to quiet her, Madame Sonia looked very distressed. Rosita sat down again, wearily. Was it all going to start again, that weary round of dancing, dancing? This week had been fun, she had enjoyed it. But after this week, she had wanted to relax again, and spend more time with Zach. She had scarcely seen him at all since they had begun their intensive rehearsals last week.

The door banged, Zach came in from the garage area through the patio. "What is going on?" he said, in the doorway to the drawing room. "I could hear Delphine screaming from halfway up the street!"

"I am not going back to New York!" yelled Delphine, her face a becoming pink, but the rage in her face not so becoming, her mouth was so distorted. "Isolde has no hold on

352

me! I won't dance again ever, if she acts like this! I will not leave San Juan!''

Zach looked tired, he sank down beside Rosita, and took her hand. "Will you please tell me, darling, just what is happening?" he said quietly.

"Miss Eleanor Stanton telephoned from New York," said Rosita. "She wants us back for the spring season, and all summer for a tour."

Isolde said quickly, "She saw the reviews, she was thrilled. I told her Rosita is dancing with more fire and perfection than before—beautifully! She said the reviews were raves, every one of them, and she wants us all to return. We can go as soon as this week is finished—open up the apartment—start rehearsals—be ready by March—"

Zach held up his hand. "Stop right there!" he said. "Now, you want to go back to New York, you and probably Dimitre. I have no wish to stop you. However, obviously Delphine does not wish to leave home, and why should she?"

"Because, otherwise the years of ballet are wasted!" yelled Isolde. "All those years of practice—"

"It is her life," he said flatly. "And so far as my wife is concerned—I do not wish to part with Rosita for months or even weeks. My wife stays with me."

"Zach, you are being unreasonable," said Isolde, taking a deep breath to control her rage. She eyed him cautiously. "You saw for yourself how magnificently she performed. She is a prima ballerina. Her best years are just ahead. As for your marriage, it can wait until she has performed for some years— maybe when she is thirty—"

Thirty! Rosita could have laid down and died. Separated from Zach until she was thirty?

"You must be out of your mind, Isolde," said Zach. "I did not marry Rosita to part with her for ten years! Rosita," and he turned to her, "do you long so to dance?"

She said, "I do not want to leave you, Zach. I like to dance, but I do not want to leave you."

He seemed to relax. "All right then. That settles it. She does not go. Make your own plans, Isolde, but leave out my wife. Why are you all sitting here and screaming? I thought Rosita should rest before the performance tonight. Have you eaten anything, darling?''

She shook her head, he scooped her up and took her upstairs with him, ordering a tray of light food and some tea. ''That Isolde, she has no consideration,'' he grumbled. He popped a piece of chicken into her mouth. ''There, darling, lie down, and relax. Do your legs ache?''

She shook her head, and leaned back against the pillows. His championship warmed her. She smiled. ''I did not ask you how your day went, Zach.''

''Oh, as usual, fighting, and bullying everybody to get them to do what I want,'' and he began to laugh. ''Just what I scold Isolde for doing! But you are not her employee,'' he said, and bent and kissed her nose lightly. ''Rest, darling, I'll waken you at seven.''

He went to the other room, humming, and she drifted off into a light sleep.

Chapter 23

Zach was finding it difficult to concentrate on work that morning. The Melody of Broadway troupe had left town, to return to New York and more engagements. He had thrown a party for them in El Convento, everyone had been very flattering about Rosita.

And his wife—how beautiful she had been, glowing in a golden designer dress with a black Spanish lace shawl about her shoulders, a Spanish comb in her hair. He felt rather awed by what he had seen that week, a brilliant star, a prima ballerina.

But what about their marriage? That was the question. Did she secretly resent his decision not to allow her to leave him for stardom? Rosita showed no signs of it, but Isolde fumed and fussed, Dimitre was soberly thoughtful.

Did he have the right to demand she remain with him in San Juan? Yes, they were married, and Rosita seemed content with him, loving and devoted. Yet—if she did not resent it now, would she one day feel cheated of her magnificent career?

How did she really feel about him? Did she love him? He thought she had not loved him when they married, she had been young, green, innocent, admiring him perhaps, but not in love, passionately in love. He thought she had found passion with him—but love, deep love? A lasting love for a lifetime?

He thought, if he did not keep guard, Isolde would take Rosita away from him. She and Dimitre ate, drank, slept, lived ballet. They had found a protégée; he admitted that Isolde had developed her potential very well. But Rosita was married to Zach!

He felt sadly torn. Much as he would like to see her in all the great parts—he felt she would do them magnificently—and he was a lover of ballet from many years of observation—yet he wanted Rosita as his wife, and eventually the mother of his children. If he felt this torn, how did Rosita feel? She must know she had an unusual talent, a genius burning in her.

The telephone rang, wrenching him from worries about Rosita. He answered, it was Kevin.

"Zach, the first cases of rum have come from Mexico."

Kevin sounded tense, Zach focused on that problem. "How do they look?"

"I'll bring up several bottles. Uncle Morgan is coming with me." He hung up.

Zach cleared a space on the desk, and took out from the cupboards some testing glasses and a pitcher, several test bottles to show the colors clearly. Kevin arrived with Uncle Morgan and Steve, Aunt Hortense arrived a minute later, then Uncle William hurried in from his office. "What's this, the rums from Oviedo already!" he grumbled. "He must have moved fast for once in his lazy good-for-nothing life!"

Zach did not bother to defend Jeronimo, his former friend. He felt very disillusioned, but already the scar was healing. One wiped him from the memory, he was not worthy of remembering.

When he saw the bottles Kevin and Morgan set out on the desk, a little mutter escaped him. "The devils—one would think on first glance they were ours!"

He picked up a bottle and examined it. The bottle was the same shape and size, not surprising. But the label—it had boldly copied the Hamilton label. Only on looking closely

356

could one see it was not the same. Both were oval in shape, a good, large size. On the Hamilton Rums, in a slight curve at the top were the words HAMILTON'S RUMS and beneath it in slightly smaller lettering PUERTO RICO. Beneath that was a line sketch of an island, Elysia, with two stylized palm trees and a plantation house. Below that was always the description of the rum, Hamilton's Dark, or Hamilton's Silver, and so on.

Oviedo had copied it almost exactly. He had altered it only slightly, enough, he probably hoped, to escape suit for copyright infringement. At the top of the oval label were the words HAMILTONIA RUMS and beneath that PUERTO RICO and then below that MEXICO in very small lettering. The line drawing was of a slightly smudgy island with two palm trees and a plantation house. Only below that was anything different, the words OVIEDO'S DARK RUMS.

"Hamiltonia Rums," said Zach in disgust, after examining the label in careful detail, with a magnifying glass. "Anyone will think at one look that it is ours! Damn him!"

Aunt Hortense was examining another bottle closely, her glasses up on her forehead so that her near-sighted eyes could read the inscription. She peered at it in disgust. "Hamiltonia! How did they get that? And Puerto Rico—in Mexico?"

"There is a small town on a river called the Rich Port, or Puerto Rico," said Kevin wryly. "So they have a right to use that. Only it is damn like ours!"

"The taste isn't," sighed Uncle Morgan. "I tasted two bottles, one is a one-year rum, the other a two-year, both dark. Poorly made, no proper balance. Any man who knows rums will know it is not ours."

"Let's see." Zach opened another couple of bottles, and poured out small amounts into glasses. All stood around and tasted it carefully. He finally shook his head in relief. "No, I cannot believe Jeronimo got hold of our formulas. There is no caramel in this, he must have depended on the sugar content of the molasses."

They tasted, discussed it, decided the rums did not match theirs. "But the label does," said Kevin. "What can we do about that?"

"Sue them," said Uncle William belligerently. "That is too damn close to our label!"

Zach was pouring out more rum into a flask, and holding it up to the daylight. He swirled the rum around in the flask, examining the color carefully. It was a poor color, and there was sediment in the liquor. It was a great relief to find that Jeronimo did not have the Hamilton formulas. He had never worked hard; he had not done a good job on this either. The reputation of the Mexican rums of Oviedo would never rival that of Hamilton's, Puerto Rico. Not unless they hired excellent chemists to come up with new formulas. And that would be a long time into the future.

He set down the flasks with relief. "Now for the labels," he said. "I think I'd better call in our lawyers and get them on the task of suing in court to have the labels stopped. That fortunately is always easier than proving a rum formula has been stolen. What a gall—to copy the labels so exactly! He must have taken some Hamilton labels with him, and ordered a Mexican printer to make up something just like it."

His fury showed in his voice, Kevin gave him a quick look. "Yes, Jeronimo would figure that was important, for the looks to be alike, even though the rums would be very inferior," he agreed soberly. "Jeronimo and Melinda also were very conscious of appearance for appearance's sake. The form, but not the substance."

"I feel as though I had never really known them," said Zach somberly. It hurt still, to think of their betrayal. "I feel very disillusioned, and disgusted. I wonder if I can trust any man again. Yet I know that I will. Jeronimo is not the man he was. He changed, I think. My mistake was thinking he would become the man that the boy promised to be."

"The seeds must have been there," said Uncle Morgan, frowning, as he set down the glass he had been holding to the light. "A man is—I forget the quotation—Steve?"

" 'The Child is father of the Man,' " said Steve, nodding. "I did not understand that Wordsworth poem in school, but now I do. What a child is dictates what sort of man he will become. Though he may hide it under some cloak, of pretense, or good humor, that which he is always comes out sooner or later. Jeronimo always laughed too much, he would poke fun, then apologize. He always liked to get the better of one. I suppose he thinks this is a very clever trick.''

They all went away, leaving Zach with his thoughts. He was glad the family was closer, but he hated the disillusionment over Jeronimo. Had he transferred to Jeronimo the qualities he wished a friend of his would have? He had seen the laziness, the promiscuousness, the gibing ways toward people he considered inferior—yet Zach had excused it all. Jeronimo had been unloved, unwanted, spoiled with too much money and too little love. But though that might be true, Zach could not see that it excused Jeronimo from becoming a fine man.

"Oh, well," he sighed, and telephoned the law firm. He said he would send over several of the bottles by messenger, and asked them to get on a legal suit at once.

Isolde had other things on her mind. The Melody of Broadway troupe had given her ideas. That troupe had combined many elements, and presented an enjoyable evening of dance, appealing to several tastes.

"I would have preferred a tighter theme running through," said Dimitre, lazily stretching out his long legs in the Hamilton drawing room. Isolde and her family were gathered around— all the lovely ladies, as Dimitre said with a smile.

Delphine and Rosita were seated across from Dimitre, sewing ballet ribbons on their dance shoes. Madame Sonia was pouring tea Russian style, Madame Isabeau was presiding at the coffee pot.

Isolde had called the conference. She and Dimitre had a grand idea, they wanted to test it on everyone, she said.

Her cheeks were pink with excitement, she looked softer these days, more feminine, in dresses more often than slacks. Today she wore her favorite soft green silk, with a ribbon threaded in her red gold coronet of hair. Her long legs were stretched out beside Dimitre's.

"Zach does not want Rosita to leave San Juan, not to be away from him so much. Well, I had this idea," said Isolde. "What if we formed a troupe based in San Juan, buy a building to have a school? We would need to train dancers for what we want—"

"What do you want, darling?" asked Madame Sonia, with interest, handing another cup of Russian tea and milk to Dimitre. He thanked her with a smile.

"A Puerto Rican troupe!" said Isolde, glowing. "We could combine ballet, flamenco dancing, and typical Puerto Rican folk dances. A real, authentic dancing typical of our island!"

Rosita was startled, thoughtful. She stared at Isolde, then Dimitre. "You could combine all three?"

He nodded, "Yes, your dancing convinced me. You combine ballet and flamenco so easily that it looks as though it was meant to be. We would probably not often do that. It would mean training our pupils, and the ones who eventually will make up our dance troupe in all three arts, difficult to do, yet possible with dancers drawn from Puerto Rico itself. It is a matter of finding the right pupils, and the right teachers."

"A school—here," said Delphine, her eyes beginning to sparkle. "Not go away for it! Do it here, in San Juan! That is a great idea!"

"I'm glad you finally like something that I do!" said Isolde with mock severity. She glowed with delight in her plans. "Dimitre and I will supervise the training of the ballet dancers, perhaps import some other teachers, and a ballet mistress. We would have to find someone to teach the folk dancing, but that will not be difficult. Rosita, Dimitre had the idea that your father and brothers could teach the flamenco!"

"What? Oh, Isolde!" gasped Rosita. "My father—my family—teach?" Visions began to open before her. Her family, safe and secure in teaching positions! Dancing evenings, happy, secure—secure! Some money always flowing in to them—and the prestige of being instructors in the school— "Oh, Isolde. It would be marvelous!"

"I understand they don't have good jobs in the nightclubs," said Isolde, with her usual lack of tact. "This would help them—"

"They cannot obtain girls for the act," said Rosita proudly. "If they did, it would go well. But my sisters—"

"Yes, yes, I understand! But the school would help them. We would recruit dancers from all over the Caribbean. Surely from among them we could find some who can learn flamenco, or even know it already and wish to learn ballet! Your father could use the students in his nightclub act, to draw an audience, and also to give the girls experience."

"Ohhh," breathed Rosita. It was almost too good to be true! But she had experience with Isolde and her domineering ways. If anyone could make a school go well, she could! "Oh, if we could only help the family."

Dimitre said gently, "I think this would help your family, Rosita, and it would help us. Your father can teach flamenco, can't he?"

"He is a marvelous teacher!" cried Delphine eagerly, without thinking of the consequences of her speech. "He taught me in a few weeks so I could dance—I mean—" She subsided, blushing. "I learned," she said weakly.

"Well, I think he could teach very well," said Dimitre, ignoring the curious looks of Madame Isabeau and Madame Sonia. "Oliverio and Jacinto can play for us, and also teach guitar for flamenco dancing. Pascual Dominguez, Tadeo and Marcos can instruct and be partners in the flamenco. We will have them to teach men also; in fact, that would be part of the contract. I visualize a school for ballet, flamenco and folk dance for persons beginning in their young teens."

Rosita listened to Isolde and Dimitre talking eagerly, adding to the ideas. She was numb, stunned by all the plans. What it could mean to her family! She had longed all her life to help make them secure, to help the money flow in. She loved her family so much. If they might be as secure, happy in their dancing and music, she would be so happy! It was the fulfillment of her ambitions of a lifetime.

Her family would work days, probably five days a week, in the school. They would teach, instruct, in the dancing they knew so well. Her father, so distinguished, so polished a dancer, would be looked up to, venerated as the magnificent flamenco dancer he was. And he could teach, he had taught them all, boys and girls in her family, and Delphine!

Her brothers would dance, and play the guitar, teach others to do so. Maybe even Marcos could be spared to go to the university, and continue his studies in chemistry! He might become a chemist! All their ambitions, all their hopes and dreams, to come true!

She could relax, and dance, and be a good wife and mother eventually—she could feel free to love Zach and be with him also! She would never again feel compelled to go away to be in ballet companies, in order to earn money to help her family! She could dance for the pleasure and delight in dancing, just as much as she wanted, or as little, and be free to be a woman in Zach's arms! If only he still wanted to keep her—but he must—he had said so—

It would solve all her problems, if this school was begun and went well in San Juan!

She was listening as well as thinking and dreaming, for she had heard what they said. Isolde and Dimitre were talking about a building to buy.

"Why not rent one first, and see how it goes?" asked Madame Isabeau dubiously.

"But it must go well! It must! It will," said Isolde, imperiously. "We will put such effort into it, that it will go beautifully!"

Dimitre exchanged a little smile with Madame Sonia. They were much alike in their thinking, Rosita thought. The two Russians, so molded by their experiences in Russia, yet eager to be a part of the new world of more freedom, and the excitement of doing what they wanted to do. The freedom to work as they wished and hoped.

"We shall look at buildings in the next days," said Dimitre. "We shall ask your brother's permission to proceed. After all, he is your brother—"

"Oh, Dimitre, this is not your Russia, or Europe!" scoffed Isolde. "I have my own money—"

"But he is Rosita's husband, and Rosita's family is important to our planning, I think he is the key to the success of the whole plan,'' Dimitre said practically. "We must ask him about this, and get his consent and advice.''

"He cannot object," said Isolde. "After all, we are doing as he wished, remaining in San Juan! He should be pleased!''

Rosita thought so also. Surely Zach would not object! He knew how she felt about her family, how devoted she was, and how she worried about them. He had offered them charity, this was so much better than charity. This was a chance for work they could do well, employment that would keep them in food and clothing for years, all going well. And pride—they would keep their pride, and their reputations would become stronger and more important. Everyone would come to see the Dominguez family dance!

She clasped her hands together in pleasure and excitement. "Oh, I cannot believe it will happen!" she breathed. "We will remain here in San Juan—"

"Except for engagements in the United States and Europe," said Isolde, complacently, her cheeks glowing pink. Her red gold hair seemed to stand up on her sleek head. "I can see it—performances in New York, Houston, San Francisco, London, Paris—"

Delphine moaned. "Oh, don't go on like that, Isolde!" she said, falling back in her armchair, her ballet slippers forgotten in her lap. "Don't talk about going away to perform! We can do that in San Juan!''

Isolde frowned. "Of course, we will perform elsewhere! But the school will be here, it will take several years to be sufficiently polished to perform in London!''

"I am glad you recognize that," said Madame Sonia drily. "Yes, it will take time to do this correctly! Haste will not make for a good school, and a good troupe. Patience! Do it right, and start slowly, build well. And by that time Rosita will have a child or two, to make Zach and herself happy!''

"Good heavens!" cried Isolde, sitting bolt upright. She looked positively horrified, as Rosita blushed and smiled happily. "A child! Never, it might ruin her figure!''

"Of course not," began Dimitre. "Many girls marry and have a child—"

"It is not your concern," began Rosita passionately.

"Honestly, Isolde, you are so crude and so—so mad for power!" cried Delphine.

"I think this is a vulgar conversation," said Madame Isabeau, severely, brought up in such fashion by her father. "The matter of children is between a woman and her husband, not a subject for the drawing room, with men present!"

"It is beside the point," said Isolde. "We are talking about a school of dance, and a magnificent dance troupe! What happens to one ballerina does not matter! We shall all learn, all teach, all perform—"

"Peace, peace!" cried Madame Sonia, and somehow her gentle voice vibrated through the room and calmed them. "I beg pardon for bringing up such a private subject! Yes, the school is the topic of conversation! Let us remain with it. You spoke of a building, Dimitre. Have you seen one for rent or for sale in San Juan?"

He relaxed, the others quieted. Rosita sat trembling, unable to sew any more stitches in the ballet slippers. She had the idea now, she was sure of it, Isolde for one did not want her to have Zach's children! What of the others, his mother, his grandmother? Did they think of her as a temporary wife? Did he?

Zach and Kevin returned home, Rosita heard the rumble of their voices. The two men came to the drawing room, both looked tired. She heard Kevin say, "Lawyers—labels—the rums were not good, but those damn labels—"

As soon as Zach stepped into the room, Isolde attacked. "Zach, I have a glorious idea!"

"What now?" he asked warily, his briefcase swinging from his hand. His shoulders sagged, he was deathly tired, thought Rosita, alarmed. Kevin eyed them all with a sort of cynical amusement. "I've had a rough day, must you present me with problems as soon as I walk in the door?"

"Not now, after dinner, perhaps," Dimitre said hastily.

Isolde ignored the storm signals. She rushed right in, tossing back her head like a fretful mare. "Zach, we have such a magnificent thought! A dance troupe, based here in San Juan! Rosita to dance for us, and Dimitre, and everybody involved in it! Dimitre and I are going to look for a building tomorrow, we can buy it—"

"I said no," said Zach, scowling. He turned to leave the room. "Rosita is not leaving—"

"But Zach, that is the beauty of the idea! Rosita won't have to leave! Her family will be involved. Her father can be an instructor, and her brothers, and they will train girls to dance with them, and Rosita can teach also—"

"My God, will you stop it!" he yelled. He was only half-listening, thought Rosita, in dismay. "I said no, and I mean no! Make your plans, go off to New York, get out of my hair! But leave me and my wife alone!"

"But, Zach, this is important!" wailed Isolde, persisting though Madame Sonia was shaking her white head at her. "Listen, this is the gem of the idea—a marvelous idea—it will mean living here, having a school here, and—"

"And my family will be instructors, they will be fully employed, Zach," added Rosita eagerly, unable to keep silent, "Don't you see how it will help them?"

Zach's eyes were tormented, but she saw only the furious anger in his strong face. "I told you no, I will not listen any longer!"

He turned to go out of the room, he took a step toward the door.

"You are not listening—" cried Isolde. "My troupe will be great! It is a terrific idea—don't close your ears—you are a bully, Zach Hamilton! Listen to me—" She was standing in the center of the room, under the chandelier, a tall fiery girl alight with hopes, the lights blazing on her red hair.

"I said—no—no!" he shouted back at her, and walked out. Rosita ran after him.

"Zach—listen—it means my family will have work— Zach—oh, Zach, please don't go away—please—"

He turned about to glare at her. "I have had enough!" he yelled at her. "Enough! This house is a nightmare! No peace and quiet anywhere!" And he went off down the hall.

"You are not listening to me," she cried. "It would be so good for my family—my father would not need to worry—"

"Hell and damnation!" yelled Zach, and she heard the study door slam after him.

"Oh, you—you don't listen to me!" Rosita cried, and began to weep, running up the stairs to her bedroom. Those in the drawing room heard her door slam after her.

Dimitre sighed deeply, his rueful gaze met that of Madame Sonia. "Red-haired people," he said.

"I suppose it is all my fault," gritted Isolde, her fists clenched. "You see what happens when I try to have a sane conversation with Zach!"

"He had a very bad day," said Kevin mildly. "You might have let him recover from the shock of seeing Oviedo come out with labels practically identical to ours! May cut into our sales by the thousands of bottles, maybe hundreds of thousands."

He might as well have saved his breath. They looked at him blankly, not listening, thoughts absorbed with the dance troupe. He sighed and went out alone to the study.

"It is all your fault, Isolde!" cried Delphine, her face white. "If you would not be so impulsive. But no, you have to push and push, you don't care what happens to people! Just you and your ideas, that is all that is important! You don't care really what happens to any of us! Now it won't work out! Well, I'll tell you this, I won't work in your beastly school—not if it means leaving San Juan!"

"What makes you think you will be asked?" flashed Isolde.

"Girls, girls," Madame Isabeau warned automatically.

Dimitre rose to leave. "I had best depart. I will come tomorrow for class, Isolde, if you permit," he added formally. He bowed to the ladies, started for the door.

"But you are remaining for dinner!" Isolde cried, alarmed.

She ran after him, to clutch his arm, she accompanied him into the hallway, still pleading.

They heard his deep voice, calming her, then the door opening.

"I wish he would marry her, and give her a baby, that would settle her nerves," said Madame Sonia.

"Mother, must you be so—so earthy?" sighed Madame Isabeau.

"Where do you think you came from? A cloud from heaven, my darling Isabeau?" Madame Sonia asked. "Thank God, your father did not think me too important a ballerina to have children! Or you would not be here. And Thomas Hamilton had sense enough to say no, when you begged for just one more year of dancing. Or you might not be the mother of four fine children of whom any mother would be proud!"

Delphine listened in fascination to this frank speaking. But Isolde returned, drooping. "Everything I suggest goes wrong," she mourned. "I'm going to my room!"

"You will remain here, like a sensible girl, and have a decent dinner, and quit nagging," said Madame Sonia, with unwanted severity. "You should have more sense than to start screaming at a man just as he returns home weary from work. I should think you would be ashamed. Look at your brother, how tired he is, with so many problems. And you did not give him time to catch his breath!"

"But it is a tremendous idea! And it would keep Dimitre here," said Isolde. Her face crumpled, she ran out of the room, and up the stairs.

"Tempers, tempers," muttered Madame Sonia. "And nobody in this generation really knows how to handle a man!"

"How do you?" demanded Delphine at once.

Madame Sonia chuckled, and looked more relaxed and happy. "My darling girl, I will tell you all about it!"

"Now, mother," said Madame Isabeau. "None of your advice for Delphine! She has been sheltered all her life."

"Too much," said Madame Sonia, with a wink at Delphine. She whispered, "After dinner, in my room, Delphine!"

Madame Isabeau was walking into the hall, unhearing. "I'll tell Zach and Kevin to wash for dinner, they all need food to calm them down. Dear me, what a fuss this has all become."

Chapter 24

Rosita sat silently at the head of the table for dinner the following evening. Zach and Kevin had phoned, they would not be home till midnight or so.

She had vaguely taken in that he was upset about the Oviedos in Mexico, something about labels on the rum. She thought he was also hurt again about Melinda Valdes Oviedo. And he had not listened to them about the dance troupe, he seemed to go up in smoke when Isolde tried to talk to him again. She felt so let down, so depressed.

Delphine had not come to dinner. Had she sneaked out again to meet Marcos? So far no one had said anything, but they were only on the first course.

Dimitre had come early for class and a short rehearsal. Then he had departed, leaving Isolde furious and desolate. She fears she is losing him, Rosita thought. And knew how she felt.

Dimitre could not afford to stay on and on. He must get employment, probably attach himself to some troupe in the States. It was mid-March. The rainy season was coming, and he would hate that. He would want to go back to New York, and join in some spring season. That meant leaving in a few days, mourned Isolde.

"Why does he insist on waiting for Zach to speak? I have my own money!"

They had gone over and over that. Madame Isabeau sighed, and tried to change the subject to a charity event to take place next week. Isolde was patiently not listening.

The fish course came. In the middle of it, Delphine slipped in, trying to appear unnoticed. Isolde turned on her. "And why did you leave rehearsal early?" she demanded.

Delphine pouted, guiltily. She wore a lovely blue silk dress with flounces, and looked radiant. "Dimitre left, I didn't think I had to stay—"

"You didn't ask to leave! I know you—I know where you went—you little sneak!"

Delphine went pale. "It is none of your concern."

Madame Isabeau said, "But darling, I thought you took a siesta!"

Isolde laughed, her eyes glittering. "She sneaked out to meet Marcos Dominguez—again! That is where she goes. She meets him almost every day!"

"Oh, Delphine! Without a chaperon?", cried Madame Isabeau, alarmed. "You are meeting a man, alone?"

Rosita had stiffened in dismay. Delphine tossed her red gold hair, tied back loosely in a blue ribbon. "I love Marcos," she said defiantly. "And he loves me. We are going to be married one day!"

"Married—to Marcos Dominguez! A dancer, in a night-club! No, you are not!" Isolde cried. "He is beneath you, far beneath you! Just wait till Zach hears this!"

Rosita gasped. "Beneath her! Now, Isolde, you go too far!" she cried. Delphine had started to cry, tears rolled down her cheeks. "Delphine has the right to marry where she chooses! And my brother is a fine man—he is good-hearted, a magnificent dancer—and he has a good brain."

"He is a Gypsy!" flashed Isolde, in spite of Madame Sonia's alarmed attempts to hush her. "She should marry well, with her money, looks, and family behind her! She should not throw herself away on—on a Gypsy!"

"But Zach married Rosita!" cried Delphine.

"Exactly, and he made a terrible mistake!" Isolde yelled, temper in her red face. "He was madly in love with Melinda Valdes! When she threw him over and married Jeronimo Oviedo, he married Rosita on the rebound! To spite me also! He knew I had plans for her as a ballerina!"

Rosita felt the blood draining from her head. To hear her doubts and fears put into words like this—! Madame Sonia was tut-tutting, shaking her head. Madame Isabeau said sternly, "Really, Isolde, you do go too far. Rosita has made a lovely wife for Zach, in spite of—I mean, she suits him very well. But Delphine, you must not go out without a *dueña*. And I do not approve of your dating behind our backs!"

"She should not see him at all!" Isolde said spitefully. "She will ruin her career. He will lead her astray—she will find herself pregnant by him, and you'll never make a good match for her!"

Rosita shoved back her chair. She could not remain and listen to this! Not about her friend, and her brother!

"You insult me, and my brother, my whole family," she said, wildly. "I cannot remain—my God, you go too far! I cannot endure this." She shook her head, unable to speak more. She turned and ran from the room, and up the stairs to her bedroom.

She heard the voices crying out behind her, Delphine weeping, Madame Sonia scolding, Madame Isabeau in bewilderment—and Isolde yelling at them all, such hateful words, such spite—

Rosita slammed the door of the bedroom, and stood there like a trapped creature. Now they had finally said aloud what they had all been thinking! They despised her and her family! They would forbid Delphine to see Marcos again—and they would do their best to rip her and Zach apart!

And Zach—she remembered in pain what Isolde had said. What they were all thinking. Zach had loved Melinda so deeply, that he had married Rosita, uncaring about anything in the world, on the rebound, trying to show Melinda he did not care—

She put her hands over her ears, as though that would shut

out the pain of those words, but they rang over and over in her head. "He made a terrible mistake—he made a terrible mistake—he married Rosita on the rebound—he married Rosita on the rebound—he was madly in love with Melinda Valdes—"

"Oh, God," she whispered, and shook her head again and again. She could not remain here, shut in the bedroom. She felt closed in, locked in, imprisoned with her fears and pain.

She found a shawl, flung it about her, took her pocketbook, and fled. She ran down the stairs, they were still arguing in the dining room. She went to the door, opened it, as the maid came forward, alarm in her face. Rosita shook her head, blindly, and went out into the evening.

She ran down the cobblestoned streets, ignoring the guards at the gates. She turned the corner, ran down toward the Cathedral, and down further into the shopping streets. Tourists crowded about the shops, talking, chattering, laughing. They turned to stare curiously at the running girl, in heels and silk dress, with the Spanish shawl about her shoulders.

In the next block, she found a taxi, and climbed in. She glanced at her watch, the family would not be home, but for someone with the children. She directed him to the nightclub where the family had a brief engagement. In dancing, she would find release and forgetfulness for a short time. Tonight, she would dance with them again!

After that, she must decide what to do. Could she endure remaining married to Zach, knowing he still loved Melinda, would always love her? Could she remain and work with Isolde, knowing the girl despised her and her family?

Pain rushed through her, making her feel half-sick. Her fist clenched against her heart, she stared blindly from the windows of the taxi.

"Here you are, Miss Dominguez!" smiled the Spanish driver, admiration in his eyes. "I saw you dance last week. You were magnificent!"

She managed a smile. "Thank you very much! You are most kind." She could not accustom herself to the fact that she was known by her face in San Juan.

"Shall I come back for you when you're through dancing, tonight, Miss Dominguez? I'll be glad to."

"Thank you, no, my brothers will take me home."

She gave him another nervous smile, he was kind. She slipped from the taxi after paying him, and walked to the alley beside the nightclub, and back to the stage door.

She went in, to the surprise of her family. They greeted her happily. "You have come, Rosita! How fine, how good! We were just speaking of you, wishing you had come!"

They crowded about, hugged her, her mother, her father, her brothers, Inez, Luisa. She blinked back the tears at their warmth and unquestioning welcome.

"I don't have my dress!" she cried, suddenly remembering.

"I'll race back home and get it," said Marcos cheerfully, and was gone in a minute. He returned breathless in twenty-five minutes with her dress and shoes, and the girls helped her dress. By the time the music started, she was ready to march out with them.

Yes, it was good to be with them again. In the rose red frilled dress, she pranced out on stage with them, smiling brightly in the lights. This could help her forget everything, Zach, his family, Isolde's cruel words—

In dancing, it was always necessary to concentrate, and this made all other thought just about impossible. She listened to the music of the guitars, glanced about the nightclub. Only half-full tonight, a smattering of men and a few women. But others drifted in from the street, peered curiously to see who was there.

She heard someone shout, *"La Soledad!"* on seeing her. She smiled brightly again, gave a little wave in the direction of the voice. The man ran out to spread the word. By the time she was into her dance, the room was filling.

She danced wildly tonight, to ease her pain. She flung herself into the movements, Oliverio directed her, watching her gravely as his hands strummed on the guitar. Faster, faster, until she stopped abruptly in a pose like an arabesque.

She was cheered and applauded. The music did not stop. Marcos came out, to their brisk clapping, and he outdid himself. Dear, good, handsome Marcos, so gallant and so loyal! Her heart burned to think how Isolde had spoken of him. Not good enough for Delphine Hamilton! Not good enough, only a Gypsy! Well, a damn good Gypsy! thought Rosita fiercely, and she bent her head to concentrate again. Clap-clap-clap, for Marcos, as his steps tapped on the boards of the stage floor. He stood proudly, side to the audience, so they could see his swift expert steps. Smiling, dancing, when he wanted to become a chemist, to study, to work—but too loyal to leave the family that needed him.

Later she danced a duet with Marcos, improvising with him, with the skill of long practice. They rumbaed, and danced in circles, he flung her about easily, up to his shoulder, sliding down again, then in bolero style, to finish elegantly in marvelous pose.

They were cheered and applauded wildly. The applause brought in more men from the street, who sat down and ordered drinks. When they heard that *La Soledad* was here, dancing, they remained, to order dinners, and wait out the evening for the next performance.

Backstage, Rosita laughed breathlessly, shaking her head over their praise.

"But I thought your husband did not wish you to dance!" said Inez, biting off the thread as she mended her husband's jacket. Her black eyes were full of curiosity. "And here you are, dancing!"

"Oh, I thought I would come, Zach is busy until midnight tonight," she said, with a shrug. "He has to work many nights."

Pascual eyed her gravely, then glanced at his wife. Margarita was troubled, and put her arm about Rosita. As the others chatted, and compared steps, and talked about the next numbers, she said quietly, "Rosita, my child, what is wrong?"

"Nada, gracias," said Rosita, avoiding her look.

Her mother squeezed her shoulders lightly, then patted her head before releasing her. "There are no problems between husband and wife that cannot be solved with love and speaking aloud of the problem," she said very gently.

Tears came to Rosita's eyes, she shook her head numbly. "Oh, mama," she choked, but could say no more. How could she speak to her mother of the terrible things Isolde had said? How could she tell her mother that her husband did not love her, that he regretted marrying her, and wished he had married a haughty aristocratic woman?

She accepted a cup of hot coffee from Luisa, and sat down at the dressing table to repair her makeup. She lined her eyes more carefully with dark mascara, studied her rouge and added a little more. The chatter was more subdued. Oliverio tuned his guitar, his dark head bent lovingly over it. Marcos hummed and tapped his foot, snapped his fingers lightly, a dreamy smile on his handsome mouth. Was he dreaming of the hours he had spent today with Delphine? Should she warn him that her family would break up their romance? No, she could not speak of that tonight, she felt too bitter.

Soon it was time to go on stage again. This time, the people had changed places in the nightclub, some had left, others had come. She noticed as she stood clapping at the first, that two men sat at a table near the side, staring at her intently. One was a very large stupid-looking man, the other was small and foxy. Both were very dark Spanish-looking men.

Rosita was accustomed to stares, but these were not admiring looks, they were hard, cunning looks. They did not talk to each other, they just sat and stared at her. They did not stare her up and down, they did not wet their lips and grin. They stared and stared, and she felt nervous and uncomfortable.

However, she was soon caught up in the dancing. One learned to ignore the audience most of the time, except after the performance to judge the sound of the applause, whether one was doing well.

She started forward, and began to dance. There was fire in her performance, she was still angry, furious at Isolde and Zach's family. That they should all despise her—!

Well, she was a Gypsy, a flamenco dancer. Flamenco Rose! That was who she was. A Gypsy girl, *La Soledad*, and her face took on the somber seriousness with which she always danced. She was caught up in the music, and she danced her heart out, her spinning feet, her rapid fingers, her snap of the skirts all showing her blazing feelings.

Marcos danced well, then Luisa danced quite well, her face bright and pretty now that she was married and beloved. Oliverio played a solo, and her mother sang after that. Then Rosita and Marcos danced a duet. That went well also, the family felt solidly together tonight, they encouraged each other with cries.

"Ay, gitana! Ay, gitana! Ay-ay-ay!"

"Bravissimo, Marcos, bravissimo! Gitano—gitano!"

"Ay-ay-ay—ayayaya—" That was Tadeo, caught in the spell of dancing, swooping across the stage with Inez caught in his husky arm.

The audience began to clap with them when four of them danced together, Rosita and Marcos, Tadeo and Inez, caught in the music, laughing, prancing in imitation of each other, improvising brilliantly.

Then it was Pascual, with his distinguished bearing, his serious, proud look, his feet dancing more and more rapidly, click-click-click-click! So fast one could scarcely hear the individual beats, only a blur of sharp sounds.

Much applause, then they ran off the stage to hearty applause. In the dressing room, there was laughter, and happiness. They had done well tonight.

Pascual came over to Rosita, his face worried. "You had best leave now, my baby," he said, gently. "Marcos will take you home before your husband returns. We will talk tomorrow, eh?"

She hesitated. She wanted to stay so late that Zach would come home before her, and be terribly worried! Would he worry, or be relieved?

Then some common sense came to her. She nodded. "Yes, I will go now. I will come tomorrow and talk, papa."

Perhaps tomorrow she would be more calm, and be able to talk to her parents about this terrible mess. Pain filled her now that she was released from dancing.

"Sí, tomorrow," said her father, and kissed her. Her

mother kissed and hugged her, then she wrapped the shawl about her Spanish dress. Marcos would just have time to take her home and come back again.

She picked up her other dress and shoes, wrapped them in a small bundle, picked up her pocketbook and smiled and waved at them all.

"*Mañana, todos,*" she said, and went out. They called after her.

"*Mañana,* Rosita! *Mañana! Buenos noches!*"

She walked out with Marcos, he had his hand cupped on her elbow lightly.

"That was a good evening," he was saying, as they entered the darkened alley, and he shut the door after them. "You dance better all the time—"

She was smiling, she heard nothing behind them. All she saw was a dark shadow beside Marcos. She then heard the thud as something came down on his head, and he crumpled up in the muddy alley without a sound.

She started to cry out. A hand clapped over her mouth, an arm caught her up. A big, powerful, hard arm, she realized, in her terror.

She was carried along the alleyway to a car. She could scarcely see around the huge hand, the man was choking her with his strength. She was thrust into the backseat, he followed her in, holding her roughly down in the seat so she could not be seen. She had dropped her dress and shoes, she still clutched her pocketbook, he had made no move to snatch that.

Rosita could not think, it had been so sudden. Another man got in the front, the car started up. She struggled, but the big man holding her tightened his grip, she was coughing, but unable to cough properly, he held her so tightly. She stopped struggling, she felt faint and weak. God, they were taking her away!

The man loosened his grip a little, and muttered to the man in front. They spoke a gutteral Spanish, an illiterate sound, with many curse words used as natural speech.

Who were they? Zach had worried about terrorists, about kidnappings because they were wealthy. Who were these men?

Fear was chilling her, though the car was warm. The night wind had swept over them, it was beginning to rain. She could hear the wind roaring, one man closed a window, cursing again.

They drove and drove, she thought it was hours, though it might not have been more than an hour. They pulled up with a jerk, and she blinked through the rain and dark trees. Where were they? It was not San Juan, she thought. They seemed to be out in the countryside, a few houses that were only small huts were nearby. The car had bumped through hard ruts to reach the tin-roofed garage area.

The man hauled her out, his hand once more clamped over her mouth. They said nothing as she was hauled across a rain-swept muddy area to the hut next to the garage. The small man opened the door. They had no lights on, the men stumbled into the house in darkness.

The small man lit a candle at a table. The big man set her down, his hand still clamped about her head.

She had no time to look around then. The big man pushed her over to a broken-down couch, with some metal springs sticking out. She sat down hard. He took a cloth, and gagged her. Then he bound her hands loosely, testing the cloth for firmness. The other man was roaming about the house restlessly.

Her feet were bound so she could not get up, she was fastened to one foot of the old couch.

The little man had found some paper and a pencil. He sat down in a chair, pulled up to the table that evidently served as a dining table; there were remnants of bread and cans of beer on the table.

He licked his tongue on the pencil end, scowled. He looked up, stared at Rosita.

"She's got to write it," he said gruffly. The big man nodded, and took the paper over to Rosita, and stuffed it under her face. "First untie her hands," the little man said impatiently.

The big man, a sort of shuffling giant of a man, like a gorilla, thought Rosita, fumbled at the bindings. He got her loose again, and put the paper in her hands. Seeing she could not write like that, he put her pocketbook on her lap. She rested the paper on the purse, and steadied the pencil in her fingers. She looked at them, with big dark eyes.

"Write it to your man, Señor Zach!" the little man commanded.

Rosita wrote, *Dear Zach*— and waited.

"Say, he got to leave money for us. Ten thousand dollars!" the little man said, his eyes gleaming.

"Yeah, ten thousand dollar," the big man repeated. He grinned, and stalked around the room, muttering to himself, "Ten thousand dollar. Ten thousand dollar."

"Shut up. Write. Leave ten thousand dollars for us at—at—at—the garage at the corner of—" He named two streets she did not know.

She wrote that obediently, her fingers shaking. This must be a nightmare. One minute, she had been safely with her family. The next—in a terrible dream—with two strange uncouth men—

"We got your wife, say that. We got Rosita Dominguez. We got *La Soledad*. If you don't come across with the money, we will kill her. Say that."

She gulped against the gag. She pulled loosely at the gag, her eyes pleading. The little man shook his head, but loosened the gag a little for her. She could breathe better again.

She wrote, *They have me, La Soledad. They say they will kill me if you do not pay. I love you, Zach. Be careful. Rosita.*

"What did you write?" The smaller man snatched the paper from her. She studied his face in the candlelight as he read slowly, mouthing the words. He was small of face, with a vicious foxy look to him. "Okay. I guess that is all right. I take the message now."

He went out, the big man sat down, and stared fixedly at Rosita. She would have screamed, but she could not. She folded her hands on the pocketbook, and hoped he would forget he had released her. He did not seem very bright, only very strong.

It was a couple of hours before the small man returned.

He grunted happily. "I slipped it in the mailbox," he said. "They were shouting at each other, and yelling around. I think they found that man you hit."

Rosita swallowed. Marcos! They had hit him. Was he dead? She pushed down the gag a little, dared to ask, "Did you kill him, my brother?"

They stared at her. "No, he ain't dead. Just a headache," said the little man.

Relieved, she leaned back. Then she realized they were going to bind her up again, as the big man started toward her. "I need to use the toilet," she said in Spanish. "May I go there, please?"

The toilet was a small windowless outhouse. She tried to ignore the filth and used it, and returned under the guardianship of the big man. He hustled her back into the house.

"You hungry?" growled the small man. "We got beer and pizza."

"Yes, thank you," she said politely. She would be very polite to them, very careful, and maybe they would not bind her again.

They ate and drank beer, she figured it was probably more safe than the water. By her watch it was past three in the morning. How long would it take? Would Zach pay them? Surely he would—oh, God, she prayed, keep me safe! And take care of Marcos, and of Zach—

She sat down on the couch, they tied her loosely but securely to the leg of the broken-down couch. They ignored her as a woman, she was very grateful for that. They gagged her again, she lay back against the end of the couch, and shut her eyes. She had pulled the Spanish shawl over her for warmth, the rain was coming down harder. She could hear it drumming on the tin roof, drowning out sounds of voices.

The men were quiet, playing cards now. They jerked up at any sound from outside, a car, a loud voice, laughter, a dog barking.

Some clicking metal sounds roused her as she was drifting off to sleep. She opened her eyes, and over the gag, she saw they were cleaning weapons. They had two rifles, and two small guns. And lots of ammunition. Horrified, she saw the piles of bullets.

It was then she realized this was very serious. They had laid wait for her, they knew who she was, and who her husband was, and how wealthy he was. She realized they were the men who had sat at the table in the nightclub and stared at her. This had been planned, it was no momentary impulse to kidnap her in the alley because they saw her with only one man to protect her.

She might die before Zach could rescue her. They were polite, but they were strong, and armed.

What if something went wrong, and they killed her?

Rosita closed her eyes. She could not stand to watch the men cleaning their weapons, drinking beer, playing cards. It was her life.

Never had life seemed sweeter to her. The quarrels at home, with Isolde and with Zach, seemed to fade to insignificance. What did it matter if Zach thought he still loved another man's wife? What did it matter if Isolde insulted her and her family?

Life mattered, and love, and passion, and peace. Lying in Zach's arms at night. Being with him, helping him, making him smile and forget his problems.

Love mattered. If only she could get out alive, she would love him and not count the cost and the price of it. Only to be allowed to love him again, to live with him—

How could she have been so spiteful to him? How could she have cried out to him when he was so tired and exhausted? How could she have neglected him, and been cold and rude to him? If only she might be with him now, and put her arms about his neck, and tell him she loved him, he might do with her what he chose, it did not matter.

In those hours of half-sleep and desperate thoughts, Rosita finally grew up. She realized what was important to her, what life meant to her. It meant Zach, and his family, and her family. Loving and being loved. That was what was important.

It was good to dance, but not that devastatingly important. She loved dancing, she loved being with her family more. She loved Zach most. He was the center of her universe. Anything else came second. And if she could only get out of here alive, she would tell him so.

Chapter 25

Zach and Kevin came in the back door, shoulders slumped, too tired to talk. "Good night," Zach said and he started up the steps.

Kevin nodded, went back to the study to leave his briefcase. Zach could hear voices from the drawing room, especially Isolde's shrill tones.

In the bedroom, he moved quietly, thinking Rosita must be asleep. He turned on the light in the smaller room, then hesitated. Was she asleep? He moved to the doorway and peered into the dimness. Then he turned on the light.

Rosita was not there. The bed was neatly turned back, her nightdress was laid out. He went quickly to the parlor, but there was no sign of her. Growing alarmed and unhappy, he went downstairs again to the drawing room. Entering, he saw the faces of his mother, grandmother and Isolde turned toward him. Guilt, he thought. What had happened? Alarm and guilt and weariness.

"Where is Rosita?" he demanded. "Did she go out to her family?"

They looked surprised. "Why no, she went up to her bedroom. She left dinner early," his mother said. She wet her lips. "We must confess what happened, Zach. I am very ashamed. We must make it right—"

"Where is Rosita?" he asked again. "She is not upstairs. Is she with Delphine?"

A maid hovered in the doorway. Madame Sonia asked, "What is it, Angelica?"

"Señora Rosita, she went out early, Madame Sonia," said the girl, her hands twisting together. "She is very *soledad*, her cheeks have the tears, she runs out, she does not stop. I watch, she run down the street, turn the corner into the street to the Cathedral."

"She should not go to church alone," said Zach. "And what upset her?"

Madame Isabeau signaled the maid to leave, she nodded, and closed the door after herself. "Zach, some terrible things were said at dinner," she confessed. "It is my fault, I should have stopped it—"

"What was said?" he asked sharply, fear growing in him. He glanced impatiently at his watch. "Quarter to twelve—my God, where is she? Where is the family dancing tonight?"

They all looked blank.

"I had better start phoning around," he said worriedly. "Maybe Delphine knows where they are dancing—"

"She probably does!" Isolde said, twin spots of color glowing in her cheeks, her blue eyes looked feverish. "She has been sneaking out to meet Marcos, evening after evening! That is what started it, I told mother, and Delphine yelled at me—"

"And Isolde said terrible things to Rosita," Madame Sonia said furiously. "She had no right! She said you still loved that dreadful Melinda Valdes and had married Rosita on the rebound. She called her a Gypsy, and said Delphine could not marry Marcos, it would be beneath her—and said Marcos would get her pregnant—"

Zach was speechless with fury and surprise.

"I did not say he would—I said he might!" sulked Isolde. "She is asking for trouble by going out with a hot-blooded dancer like Marcos. A Gypsy, a Spanish Gypsy, with no background—"

384

"His background is hundreds of years longer than yours," Zach said shortly. He was stunned by Isolde's spite. "And you dared—you dared to speak to my wife like that! You bitch! You cannot endure for people to be happy!"

Isolde did look shocked then. She jumped up; her hands held out in pleading. "But Zach, I only spoke the truth!" she cried virtuously. "You did marry her on the rebound from Melinda Valdes—"

He eyed her steadily, his lips tight. "I despised and detested Melinda Valdes. She was a greedy, heartless, spoiled child who practically begged me to make her my mistress! I was upset when she married my best friend, Jeronimo. I thought he deserved better. Now after finding out his true nature, I think they deserved each other! They will make each other miserable! And how dared you say that to Rosita? Who made you the guardian of my happiness?"

She did gulp and turn pale, at that speech. "But I thought—you seemed sad—we thought—"

"You might have asked me." He waved his hand impatiently. "All this is beside the point. I'll find Rosita, and tell her the truth. Surely she did not really believe you?"

"I think she did, Zach," Madame Sonia said. "Especially when Isolde told her you had married beneath yourself, and Delphine seemed in danger of doing the same—"

"Well, you seemed to put yourself out to make trouble!" Zach yelled at Isolde. "Delphine is going with a nice young man, I could not ask for a finer! Marcos is smart, brilliant even. I am thinking of asking his father to allow him to go back to the university to study chemistry, as he wished!"

"You knew Delphine was dating Marcos?" gasped Isolde.

Zach did not answer that. "I knew they were attracted, yes. Now, if you don't mind, I'll phone around and try to find Rosita."

He was just opening the door when the front doorbell rang, urgently. He went to the door himself, just as the guard was coming from the back hallway.

He blinked. A huge dark-haired policeman stood there.

"Mr. Hamilton? I am Sergeant Hernandez, San Juan

Police. I regret to inform you that your wife is missing.''

He heard a woman cry out, he did not turn. ''My wife—come in, sergeant.''

In the hallway the sergeant rapidly explained, as all began to crowd around, all the women, the maid, the guard, and Kevin from the study.

''She was leaving the nightclub where her family was dancing, she had evidently danced with them. At eleven-thirty, her brother Marcos escorted her from the club, into an alley-way which lies beside the club. They were going to his car. Someone struck Marcos Dominguez over the head, then knocked him out. Miss Dominguez—I mean Mrs. Hamilton then dropped the dress and shoes she had worn to the club, and evidently was carried off.''

Zach wiped his hand over his face. ''And where—no, I suppose you don't know where she is,'' he said dully.

''I'm sorry, Mr. Hamilton, I'm afraid not. We wish to ask you some questions.''

They went back to the drawing room. The sergeant remained standing, writing in his little notebook. Another policeman had entered, and was talking in low tones to the guard.

They went over the events of the evening, what time Rosita had left, what she was wearing. The maid identified the dress and shoes.

''She was wearing a rose-colored flamenco dress and black high-heeled shoes when she departed from the nightclub,'' said the sergeant, consulting his notes. ''She carried a pocket-book and the dress and shoes. The pocketbook was not recovered.''

''Was robbery the motive, then?'' asked Kevin.

''We are not sure. I think probably not. Mr. Hamilton is a well-known wealthy man.''

Stones seemed to sink in Zach, drawing him under the waters of despair. Such a development had been considered by him, he had hired guards, had warned the women. But it had happened anyway. Because Rosita had run off, hurt and dis-tressed, to her family.

"How is Marcos?" asked Madame Sonia. "Has he been able to tell you anything? Is he still unconscious?"

"He was just rousing when the police found him in the alley," said the sergeant. "His parents were notified, they took him to the hospital. I hope to receive a report soon. Mr. Hamilton," he turned to Zach, "may we take over your telephone? I wish to set up lines of communication. You may receive ransom demands, or some communication from the abductors."

It was Kevin who nodded, and took them back to the study. The police unhooked the telephones upstairs in Zach's bedroom and Isolde's, and added their own equipment to the telephones in the study, so they could record calls. The women were weeping in the drawing room, Madame Sonia seemed about to collapse. She was very fond of Rosita, thought Zach, it would hit her more than his mother, or certainly Isolde. A blazing anger against his sister had burned up in him. That she could have insulted his wife so! And told her that Zach did not love his wife!

He wondered if this might be part of the trouble between himself and Rosita. Had she worried also that she had been married on the rebound? Surely she did not think that he loved that little bitch Melinda! No time to think about that now. When he got Rosita back, he would tell her very clearly that Rosita was the only girl in the world he had ever loved or ever wanted to marry. He would make it very certain, so she never doubted it again.

Pascual, Margarita, and Oliverio arrived about two in the morning, from the hospital. Marcos was being forced to remain there in the emergency room. "He is recovering, and wished to come with us, but I urged him to remain. His head is injured, it is now bandaged," Pascual said, his face grave.

Evidently the police had informed Pascual and his family that Rosita had been carried off. They exchanged what other information they had.

The police had been questioning Zach and Kevin about what enemies they had. Zach had showed what letters they had

387

had to threaten them, a guard had brought the file from the Hamilton Rums office. They talked about who else might have something against them.

Then they sent everybody to bed. "Nothing more will probably happen tonight. We must wait for a ransom call or letter," the sergeant said.

Dominguez and his family were reluctant to go to bed, but Zach promised to keep them informed also. He went off to bed about three in the morning, unable to sleep much, but worrying about Rosita in the grip of some criminals. Would they harm her, rape her, even—even kill her?

He thought of her small, delicate body in the rough hands of a tough, callous man, and shuddered. Rosita, his Rosita, so gentle and innocent, so sweet and fine.

Fury rose in him again against Isolde. How dared she say such things, how dared she even think them! Yet even his mother had confessed, "I did not know you loved her so much, Zach. I thought you were fond of Melinda, and that you had married Rosita very suddenly after Melinda married. And really, Rosita was such a—a child! And from a Gypsy family!"

Zach had turned on them all, frantic with fear, and furiously angry with them. "I don't give a damn what her family is; if they came from the slums I would not care! Rosita is the woman I love! But you are wrong about her family. She is from a fine, distinguished family. Yes, they are Gypsies, yes, they are Spanish. Don't you realize, you snobs, that they were here before we were? Don't you realize that Spanish Gypsies are from long lines of famous people? Don't you realize that her ancestors danced before kings, long before Grandmother Sonia did? Our ancestor was a sailor! A Scottish sailor, held in contempt by the British! The English despised the Scots! And another ancestor was a tavern girl! At that time, Rosita's ancestors were dancing for kings and princes!"

That had silenced them, the words as much as his fury. The police had been listening with interest, and grave faces. Evidently there was more involved here than just a kidnapping. A family quarrel—umm, thought the sergeant, and questioned Isolde discreetly about her movements that evening.

Zach rose about seven, having slept uneasily. He showered and dressed. He wondered, did Rosita have any sleep last night? Had she eaten? Did she have water to drink?

He went downstairs, to find the police had taken over the house. Police guards were at front and back, and plainclothesmen wandered the streets.

Sergeant Hernandez met him gravely, with a letter in his hand. "This was found in the post box early this morning, Señor Hamilton," he said.

Zach read the brief note in pencil.

"Is this the writing of your wife?"

He nodded, unable to speak for a moment. He cleared his throat. "Yes, it is. When was it put in the box?"

"I regret to say we do not know. Someone must have come in the night. We are now guarding the house carefully, observing anyone who comes along."

The telephone was ringing constantly. A policeman came from the study, several notes in his hand. "Sergeant," he said sharply. "Several tips have come in. A girl in a rose flamenco dress was observed going out to the outhouse from a small house—"

The sergeant took the notes, then raised his head. "The house is one occupied by a man named Antonio Plácido, Señor Hamilton. Do you know that name?"

"Antonio Plácido!" said Zach, holding his head. "Yes, yes, I fired him—let me see— a couple of months ago. But he—yes, he was vicious, he could have—"

"Tell me about the incident."

Zach told him about the firing of Plácido and his brother-in-law, José Serrito. "One is very small and vicious, the brains of the two. José is big and stupid, he does the dirty work."

"Yes, that matches the observations of neighbors. Come, I think we had best go out there."

"What about the message?" Zach indicated the note in his hand.

The sergeant said, "We have already answered it. We put a dummy package at the garage, but nobody came to pick it up.

I'm afraid there were too many people milling around the garage. They may suspect by now we are after them, especially if they have a radio, or have gotten to see the newspapers.''

"You mean, it's all out—all over San Juan?" Zach was incredulous. Then he saw a newspaper lying on the hall table. Headlines blazed, **La Soledad missing. Rosita Dominguez kidnapped.** In smaller letters, it said, "Mrs. Zach Hamilton of Hamilton's Rums taken from alley near nightclub. Missing six hours. Believed kidnapped.''

He was just glancing over the story, frantically, as Delphine came down the stairs. Her eyes were red-rimmed.

"Any word?" she asked.

"They believe they may have located Rosita," Zach said, still reading the paper. "I'm going out there—just let me get my revolver.''

Sergeant Hernandez said sharply, "No weapons, Señor! You must let us handle this!''

Someone came in the door with a white bandage about his head. Delphine gave a little cry and flew into his arms. "Oh, Marcos! Marcos!" She held him closely to her, her hands tenderly at his head. "How are you?''

"I checked myself out of the hospital. Any word of Rosita?" He held Delphine closely, his face tense and pale.

Zach told him, added, "I'm going out there. There may be something I can do—''

Kevin had come from the study, he must have risen even earlier. "I'll go to the plant, oversee operations there, Zach. Phone calls are coming in there also, there may be other tips.''

Zach went toward the back patio door. "I'm going. I have to see what is happening to Rosita.''

Marcos said quickly, "Let us come with you, Zach. I'll call my parents first. Just wait one minute!''

"We'll use my car," Sergeant Hernandez said. "We have radio communications there, and a telephone in the car.''

When Marcos returned, and nodded, Zach and the others went out to the police car. In a minute, they were out on the busy streets, the siren clearing the way. They drove for more than an hour, at high speed, and Zach stared stonily from the window.

They were out in the country now. The siren was cut off, the sergeant was talking on the telephone.

"You have the house surrounded, what distance? Yes? *Sí*, he is with me—his wife—*sí*——Señor Dominguez—he has arrived—*Por Dios!* keep him away from the house—one block away—*sí*—*sí*—"

The sergeant lifted his head. "It seems your family, Marcos, has arrived at the site before us, they live nearer and arrived a few minutes ago. It is dangerous. When we get there, kindly try to get your family to leave, we cannot protect them all!"

"My mother, my sisters?" Marcos asked anxiously.

"*Sí*, and your grandmother, she is crying and making much noise!" said the sergeant grimly. "She is threatening to kill anybody who stops her from rescuing Rosita! Sounds hysterical—"

"She is very fond of Rosita, she always called her 'my baby, my Gypsy baby.' We all babied her," said Marcos, holding Delphine's hand. "She was so lovely, so sweet—"

"She still is!" said Zach sharply, stinging with the pain.

Delphine jerked in her seat between the two men. "Of course she is," she said bravely. "We must—must let the police handle this, Zach."

They arrived at a place where several police cars and a number of other cars were clustered. They all got out, and made their way through a curious crowd. On the edge in front they found the Dominguez family, also Uncle Morgan.

How he had found out, Zach did not know. He heard Alejandra Dominguez weeping and wailing, uttering Gypsy curses, in a loud voice, yelling at the small tin-roofed house.

"Is that it?" asked Zach, and started forward. Marcos caught his arm.

"Hey, wait, Zach!"

"Hold him back," said Sergeant Hernandez, alarmed. "He must not go closer!"

Zach strained against the grip of Marcos and of a policeman, his eyes yearned toward the small house that might hold Rosita. Then common sense prevailed. He nodded, and relaxed. "Yes, I'll wait," he said dully. "Do you—know if she is there?"

"We are not certain," said the sergeant curtly. He kept an anxious eye on Zach. Husbands could be unpredictable. "Our information is that a girl in a rose flamenco dress was seen going into the house early this morning. Two men are inside who refuse to come out."

A shot rang through the air, startling the crowd. Everyone jumped back, some ran, to return as the shot was not repeated. Zach felt as though the shot went through his heart. Had they shot Rosita?

A policeman came up to report to the sergeant. "They shot at random, sir, ordered us to move back. Ordered us to leave, sir."

"I'll send for a hostage team. Sounds as if we have the right men," said the sergeant.

Zach scarcely heard them. He was gazing at the house. His fists were clenched. A policeman got a bullhorn and shouted at the house. There was no answer.

The hours wore on. His mother and grandmother, and Isolde and Dimitre arrived, but Zach scarcely noticed them. What was happening to Rosita? How did she feel, were they cruel to her?

Madame Sonia was weeping into her handkerchief, Grandmother Alejandra was still crying and cursing, shaking her fist at the house. Pascual came to Zach.

"I am going to take my wife and my mother home, they are very upset, they will be ill," he said, his face strained. "Do you wish me to take anyone else?"

Zach turned reluctantly from staring at the house. Only shouts from the bullhorn, and murmurs of the crowd, radio calls on the police radios broke the noonday silence. Fortunately the rains had held off, but the skies were dark.

"I wish my mother would leave, and Madame Sonia," he said. "Why don't you take them all to my house? They can wait there for word, we have a telephone hookup from here to the house by way of the police.''

Pascual hesitated, Marcos urged him. "Yes, do that. It will only upset the small children if you take them home. Luisa and Elena are taking care of the children. Mama will wish to have word—''

"And I wish mother to go—'' said Zach. He went with them to his mother, where she stood in numb bewilderment deep in the crowd. Madame Sonia wept into her handkerchief, her small body shaking.

Pascual brought his wife and mother to them, they went to the cars. Zach persuaded his mother to go with them. "They will need you, maman, take care of them, for they are not well enough to stand this strain. See to it that they have hot tea, whatever they want.''

"Yes, my son,'' she murmured obediently, sounding more French than usual. She reached up and kissed him. "I am so sorry, dear Zach, for all this trouble. I feel it is my fault.''

"No, it is my fault,'' Isolde burst out, from where she stood with Dimitre's arm about her. "It is all my fault. I was so stupid!''

Zach's look warned her sternly to say no more. "We will straighten it all out later, Isolde. For now—all I care about is getting Rosita out safely.''

"Of course, I know, that is what I wish also,'' said Isolde, humbly for her.

Marcos urged them to one of the limousines, helped them inside. The white bandage on his head, the injury, did not seem to have taken away his strength and coolness. "Now, mama, look after granny, calm her,'' he said gently. "All will be well, stay together, say your prayers. We need your prayers, yes?''

"*Sí*, Marcos,'' said his mother, and sank back against the cushions weakly. The lines of strain made her seem older.

They saw the limousine depart, weaving slowly through the crowd of onlookers from the neighborhood, the police, others who had gathered from the radio, television and newspapers. Zach was conscious that someone was taking his picture on the television camera, someone blinked a flash in his eyes. He turned away impatiently.

He and Marcos and Delphine returned to the front of the crowd, near the policemen. The hostage team had taken charge. The bullhorn was being used to call the men inside. They knew their names.

"Serrito, you are inside, are you listening to us? Plácido, do you hear? Tell us about Mrs. Hamilton. Is she all right? Can she hear us?"

No answer yet. It would take a while for them to get a response from the uneasy men inside, said the sergeant. Meantime, they must wait and hope. And keep calm.

Oliverio prowled through the crowd uneasily, returning again and again, to listen. Tadio and Inez stood near Zach, waiting, silently. Jacinto went home, returned with some flasks of coffee and some sandwiches. They made Zach eat a sandwich, he ate mechanically, it tasted like nothing.

Marcos and Delphine stood next to him, watchfully. He thought they sensed his restlessness, his urge to jump away from the crowd, to make a dash for the house, to gather up Rosita in his arms and carry her to safety. He must not give in to the urge, he knew it with his mind, but his heart urged him on.

The afternoon wore on. How long would it last? It could last for days, said the sergeant, practically. They must be patient.

Zach folded his arms, and gazed intently at the house. Had there been a flash of rose at the window? He blinked, it was gone, if it had ever been there. Silence.

The crowd murmured. *La Soledad*, he heard. *La Soledad*. Murmurs of sympathy. It was *La Soledad* in there. It was Rosita Dominguez. Rarely did he hear them say, "Mrs. Hamilton."

They knew her, she was one of their own.

He thought of Rosita as his wife, his gentle girl. But to them, she was *La Soledad*, their own glorious dancer, one of them, beyond them in her rare talent, but Spanish, speaking their tongue, belonging to them.

He had failed to realize that fully, he thought. Oh, if she but came out alive and unharmed, things would be different. He would not be dominating and possessive, he would listen to her. He would let her do what she wanted.

What had they quarreled about? He had to make an effort to remember. Oh, yes, Isolde had wanted to start a Puerto Rican dance company, a troupe with a school to start. A building, she wanted to buy a building, she wanted to work in San Juan.

She wanted to hire Rosita's family as instructors. She wanted Rosita to dance here, in San Juan, and Rosita wanted to do this. She wanted her family to teach, as well as dance.

Well, why not?

"Why not?" he murmured to himself. It might work. Rosita was worried about her family, she had told him so, only he had not listened carefully.

Worry had been in her face, in her voice. She wanted work for them, the nightclub did not pay well. And Marcos wanted to go back to the university, to study chemistry. And why not? Marcos was a smart lad, he was mature, calm, intelligent. If he wanted to study chemistry—well, Zach could help him.

With the Dominguez family well settled in the dance school, Marcos could afford to go to the university and study. Zach would urge him to take postgraduate work in the States for a year or two. Then he could come back, if he wished, to San Juan and Hamilton's Rums, they could always use a good industrial chemist. Was that what Marcos would want? He would ask him soon.

Only first—Rosita must be rescued. He must have her again safely in his arms. That was what mattered the most. Oh, God, if they harmed her—had she been harmed already? He started forward a foot, Delphine's hand caught at him on one side, and Marcos caught at him on the other side.

"Patience!" Marcos said firmly.

"Wait, Zach, please wait," Delphine urged softly.

The sergeant gave him a worried look. "Sir, you must be most patient, the hostage team must have a chance to work well, Señor," he said.

"Yes, yes, I know. But the hours grow long."

He prayed for her. Holy Virgin Mary, he prayed, let her return safely. All the saints, pray for her, before the Holy Throne of God. Saint Anthony, and Saint Jude, pray for her. Help her. Holy Virgin, Mother of God, protect her. Protect your child, who worships you. Protect her, oh Infant Jesus, and His Holy Mother, and protect her now, and forever.

Delphine had a rosary in her free hand, holding it, her lips moved in silent prayer. Marcos stood silent, his legs apart, watching the house, keeping an eye on Zach.

All they could do was wait and pray their Rosita would be returned to them safely.

Chapter 26

Evening came and the television men wanted to turn on their lights. It was finally permitted. The hostage team turned on bright lights also, and called to the kidnappers inside the house.

They would keep the lights blazing brightly, and keep talking, so the men would be more easily worn out.

And what of Rosita? She would get no sleep either, thought Zach desolately.

A light rain came, then it grew heavier. The crowds of curious neighbors and friends drifted away, only a few women and some men remained.

Zach came to himself, seeing the haggard face of Pascual Dominguez as he was standing in the downpour. He went over to him, put his hand gently on the man's shoulder. Marcos and Delphine had followed him through the small crowd.

"Papa, you must go home, and get some rest. This rain is not good," he said.

Pascual looked at him intently, then a faint smile curved the hard, anxious mouth. "My son, it is not good for you either," he said gently. "Let us wait in the cars, we can see from there."

Tadeo nodded, and urged Inez with him to their large old

car, the roof was good, Zach saw. Oliverio hesitated, his head down.

Zach said to him, "Oliverio, you must go also. Protect yourself. It does no good for all of us to get soaked. There is room in all the cars—"

With his hand on Oliverio's arm, he led the way to the cars at the side. "She is so little, so young," the man muttered.

Zach felt himself shaking a little. "I know," he said, and his voice cracked. "If they harm her—"

"I will tear them limb from limb," Oliverio said wildly, his head flung up, his fists clenched to the skies.

Zach put his arm about his shoulders and hugged him. This man loved Rosita as only an older gentle brother could love a little sister, protectively, anxiously. "We must—wait—have patience, but oh, God, it is hard," he said, and Oliverio turned and put his arms about Zach, his face crumpling with grief. The two men stood there for a minute, drawing comfort from each other.

The other men stood in silence in the rain, and Delphine shivered in the shelter of Marcos's embrace. He opened the door of the next car, the silver Lincoln, and put her inside. "Come with me," she said, her voice shaking.

"Yes, get in, Marcos," said Zach, recovering. "Papa Pascual, come inside, get out of the rain," and he gently pushed the older man into the car next to Marcos.

Zach and Oliverio and Jacinto got into the next car, the amber Cadillac. Oliverio sat with his elbows on his knees, his face down, head propped on his fists. Jacinto lay back, gazing at the roof absently, hands on his knees. Zach sat as still as he could, he knew the other men were almost as disturbed as he was.

He could see Delphine in the other car, her head against Marcos's shoulder. The dear girl, she too had loved Rosita long.

Zach could not sleep, his eyes burned with weariness. He kept blaming himself. He should have talked more to Rosita, should have spent more time with her. He had neglected her for his work—as though that mattered so much! He was responsible for the factory, yes, but his marriage mattered terribly to him. When she returned—when, not if!—he would make sure it would be different. They would have more time together—he must never be too busy for his wife—

Tadeo got out of the car and went to speak to Pascual. Zach got out quietly, and went over to them. Tadeo turned to him naturally, hand on Zach's shoulder. "I think I will go for more hot coffee and sandwiches, it will be a long night," he said quietly. His firm hand was reassuring, his voice was calm, though his dark eyes burned.

"Yes, do this, please," Pascual said quietly. "It will help."

They stood closely, heads ducked to avoid the steady streaming rain. Zach put his arm around Pascual, felt the sturdy frame of his father-in-law. "Go to my house, if you will, Tadeo," he said. "Ask the women for the hot coffee and food, and reassure them. Tell them—" His voice faltered.

"*Sí*, tell them all is well," Tadeo said, his eyebrows quirked with resignation.

"All is well, my sons," Pascual said sternly. "God will be good to us, and to my beautiful baby, Rosita." His voice was a little choked, Zach gave him a hard hug.

"Ask them to pray for us all," Zach said. "And make sure the grannies go to bed and get some rest."

"*Sí*, I will do that," Tadeo said, and gave Zach a look of compassion as he got into the car beside Inez and turned on the ignition.

Zach stood talking to Pascual for a few minutes, he felt reassured by the man's calm strength. "I think nothing will happen until morning," Pascual said thoughtfully. "You will rest also, Zach, and be ready for what may come."

"*Sí*, papa," Zach said, and only when he had gone back to the car did he realize he had been thinking of Pascual as his own father, a gentle ruler, like his own father.

The night wore on so slowly. Zach left the car at intervals, getting soaked in the pouring rain. He would go to the front lines, crouch down near Sergeant Hernandez, and wait silently for any word.

"Nothing yet, Señor Hamilton!" would come the murmur.

He heard the radio men reporting. "We are still watching the Plácido house. No signs of life, but we know they are inside waiting a chance to escape. They have no chance of that, the house is surrounded by police, armored cars, plainclothesmen."

"One hears that there was fear of terrorists," he heard a voice say. "That fear seems to be settled now. The men worked for the Hamilton Rums plant. They were fired for making trouble. It seems Plácido has a history of making trouble in factories, he was in Ponce—"

Where did they find out those things, wondered Zach. They had their sources, they dug patiently, asked questions, put facts together— He listened absently to one man giving the early morning report in Spanish.

"*La Soledad* is still inside the house, yes, she is safe so far. Prayers are being said for her all over Puerto Rico. The churches in Ponce are filled with women praying for her, in San Juan—"

The rain was letting up. Tadeo and Inez returned about four in the morning with two huge picnic containers of hot coffee plus a number of thermoses. They must have scoured the Hamilton house and the neighbors' also, thought Zach, gratefully.

The men got out of the cars and came to talk and drink the welcome hot brew. "The women have finally gone to bed to rest," reported Tadeo. "I told them they could help more by resting now, and helping later."

Sergeant Hernandez came over to report, Zach offered him a mug of hot coffee. The policeman accepted gratefully, cupping his chilled red hands around the mug.

"When dawn comes we will talk to them again," said the sergeant gravely. "I think they must realize they cannot walk away from this."

Zach felt frozen, of a sudden. "What will you do?" he asked sharply. Pascual's face was drawn, anxious.

"We have to wait and see if they will be sensible," said the sergeant.

Dawn broke sullenly, a gray sky, with a streak of rose finally appearing. A good omen? Zach wondered, gazing up briefly at the sky. Inez and Delphine remained in the car, hands clasped. The men stood together, Zach, Pascual, Oliverio, Tadeo, Marcos, in a small group, waiting.

The bark of the bullhorn startled them all. Zach jerked, tensed, his fists clenched. Dawn had come, time for action, or more words?

The man on the bullhorn spoke in Spanish slowly, distinctly. "You will come out with your hands up," he said. "Throw out your weapons—throw out your weapons—"

No response from the house. Finally a hoarse voice cried out shrilly. It must be the small man, Antonio Plácido, Zach thought, straightening abruptly.

"We make this bargain with you!" he cried in Spanish.

"What bargain?" It was Sergeant Hernandez speaking now.

"We wish a car with the tank filled with gasoline! And everybody to go away!"

Zach's breath caught, Pascual touched his arm, held it carefully, next to him. Oliverio growled in his throat.

"That is not possible," said the sergeant, patiently. "You must give up, you cannot win this cause, Plácido!"

"We have the woman!" Antonio called, his voice shrill. "I have my knife at her throat!"

'Oh, God," whispered Zach. Marcos was taut and hard beside him, Oliverio groaned.

There was a pause, then they began to bargain. Finally a car was brought, filled with gasoline, motor running, and driven up about fifty feet from the house. Zach strained at Pascual's cautioning arm.

The men did not throw out their weapons. They ordered that the police should draw back. After a murmured consultation, the police and plainclothesmen drew back. The television and radio men were ordered back behind police barricades. Zach heard the television cameramen muttering to each other in excitement, the cameras were running.

Was this all it was to them, a show? God, Rosita was in

there, in the hands of those men, with a knife at her delicate throat!

Zach protested briefly to the sergeant. "They cannot take her with them—God, Hernandez, make them give her up first!"

"They cannot get far with her," said the man, gently, his brow furrowed with worry. "But we will have to attempt to capture them later. Roadblocks will be set up—"

Zach could see it now, the car dashing along roads in the winding hills, the roadblock, the flurry of gunfire, and Rosita slumped in death, blood on her slim body—

He went back to the Dominguez men, reported grimly. "They will let the men take her," he said in anguish. "My God, they must not leave."

Oliverio said softly, "We can stop them, eh?"

Zach looked at him, at the grim faces in the dawn light, the strained faces of his wife's brothers and father. *"Sí, por supuesto,"* he murmured, and the others nodded.

The police and cameramen and reporters had drawn back. Like shadows the Dominguez men and Zach moved slowly, until they were near the path where the men must walk to the car. Hernandez glanced at them nervously, shook his head warningly. He dared not yell out to them.

The tension was thick. The door slowly opened, and Rosita was pushed out first, a knife at her throat, held by the arms by the big man, José Serrito. Her slim body in the drooping flamenco dress looked so tiny next to his, like a doll.

She walked forward, impelled by his hard arm. He followed, then Antonio, small and foxy, revolver nervously in one hand, the other awkwardly holding two rifles.

Pascual was in front, somehow he was leading the little troupe. The others waited for him, silently, tense, ready to jump.

The two men watched nervously, glancing about, sighting the Dominguez men and Zach waiting. They jerked, they pushed Rosita forward, knife at her throat, glaring their warning.

They went past, Pascual did not move, he watched, tensely. His sense of timing had always been perfect. They were past, they were near the car, Antonio had to shift the revolver in one hand awkwardly to open the car door, José let go one of Rosita's arms to reach for the back door handle.

"Now!" muttered Pascual, and all five men ran. They raced to the car. Oliverio caught the big man, José, grabbed him by the hand holding the knife.

Oliverio wrestled the knife away from Rosita's vulnerable throat. Zach grabbed her, caught her in his arms, knocked down hard on the one arm still holding her, and José grunted in pain, and dropped her.

Tadeo had Antonio, he fought like a trapped weasel, and Pascual caught him from the back, and held him in a hard grip by both arms. Tadeo struck him a blow in the face, Antonio crumpled up, unconscious.

José was big and tough, for all his stupidity. Oliverio was wrestling with him, fighting him to the ground. Marcos jumped on José, helped his older brother with him. Zach moved Rosita quickly away from the tangle of long legs, rushed her to the police who moved to surround them. It was over in a minute.

"My God, you took a terrible chance!" said Sergeant Hernandez angrily, wiping his forehead with his hand. "The girl could have been killed."

"She could have been, but she was not," cried Zach, folding her tightly to him. "Oh, God, my darling, my darling . . ."

Rosita was shaking, she turned her face against his chest in silence. He folded his arms about her, she felt so small and slight.

The crowd began to yell and scream. *"La Soledad! La Soledad!"* She raised her head, in a daze, and gazed at them from the shelter of Zach's arms. Finally her hand lifted, she waved at them feebly. They yelled louder, Zach saw their smiles, tears pouring down the cheeks of some of the women.

The police had come up now, and had José and Antonio in their charge, were holding their arms behind their backs. Handcuffs were snapped briskly on their wrists. The weapons were gathered up, the revolvers, rifles and the deadly long knife that had been held at Rosita's throat.

The two kidnappers were pushed into a police car, the sirens whined as they were taken away. Now the radio men pressed closer, the television men came in close, calling out.

"How are you, Mrs. Hamilton? Will you say something—"

"How do you feel, how do you feel?"

"Rosita Dominguez, will you speak to our listeners—" Microphones were pushed in the faces of Zach and Rosita. A short distance away, Pascual was straightening his black rain-soaked jacket, Oliverio was brushing down his coat, Marcos held Delphine to him as they watched and listened, Tadeo and Inez were clasping hands and waiting, Jacinto had come from the car, relief on his face. He was slower-moving, and knew it, he had not joined the panther-quick Dominguez men in the attack, but had watched and prayed. He came to stand beside Oliverio.

Zach gave them a quick smile, so relieved he could have cried. My God, what men!

Rosita was speaking, in her shy young voice. "Thank you for your concern. I am—well. No, they did not harm me. They were—watching the windows—for the police— They gave me food."

"What food?" They wanted all the details.

"Beer and pizza," she said. "Warm beer and cold pizza."

"Did they hurt you?" one man persisted.

She shook her head. "No, they were listening and watching all the time for the police. I was tied loosely to a couch. I slept much of the time."

She was visibly weary and her hand shook as she brushed back her loosened hair.

They turned to Zach. "Are you happy your wife is recovered? What really happened? Were they terrorists? How do you feel? How do you feel?"

Zach finally spoke, and they quieted to listen and get it on their microphones. "I believe the men were two fired from the plant a couple of months ago. Not terrorists. No, they made a ransom demand. No, the ransom was not paid. Yes, thank you for your concern."

He saw the policemen, faces haggard, standing back. He saw Sergeant Hernandez turning away, his duty done, the girl rescued, the men sent to jail.

He thought of the people waiting beside their radios and televisions for news of the hostage crisis, the anxiety, the prayers of all in Puerto Rico.

Zach said quickly. "I would like to say something more. I wish to thank the wonderful police of San Juan for their patience, their concern. I am very grateful to them. And I wish to thank also, all the people of the island, for their prayers and thoughts. Our families are very grateful—my wife and I are most thankful—for your prayers and help in this difficult time—"

The reporters smiled, they were pleased, they had their human interest story, and they began to chatter on their microphones, reporting more of the final attack, as Zach led Rosita over to the car where Marcos and Delphine waited. Marcos hugged Rosita briefly, and so did Delphine, the two girls put their faces together, cheeks pressed tightly.

Zach heard a reporter nearest to them saying, "The five men sprang like pumas on their prey. The two kidnappers did not have a chance, with the men acting together. I never saw anything so quick as when the men sprang. They were determined not to let Rosita Dominguez leave with those killers— she was snatched away from the two men by her husband—"

Marcos put Delphine into the car tenderly, in the front. Zach put Rosita gently into the back, and slid in beside her.

Delphine turned from the front seat. "We have two thermoses here, coffee and tea, Rosita." She smiled lovingly at Rosita, her eyes shiny with tears.

"Coffee, please, that sounds marvelous—"

Delphine poured it out as Marcos drove slowly, and handed the hot cup to Rosita. She sipped at it, thirstily.

Rosita sank back against Zach's hard arm, and felt it close about her tightly. He put his head against her hair, and just held her. She felt safe, secure, after the nightmare. The drive did not seem long, she felt half-asleep.

At the house, she heard the stir, the crying, the calls. She paused briefly at the drawing room door, amazed to see her family there with Zach.

"Hello, everybody," she said shyly, smiling. "I am filthy dirty! Let me get a bath and change, then I'll come down."

"Oh, dear child," breathed her mother, her hand to her heart. Rosita's glance lingered on her, on the strange sight of Madame Sonia and Señora Alejandra sitting side by side on the silk sofa, of her mother next to Madame Isabeau with cups of coffee on tables beside them. Trays of food had been used, and set aside. Their families—together!

"I'll come back, and we will talk," promised Rosita. Zach had his arm about her, he led her up the stairs to their rooms.

"Can you manage by yourself?" asked Zach anxiously, as she stood in the middle of the bedroom.

"If you would unfasten my dress, please. It seems I have been wearing it for a week!" she tried to joke, as he clumsily worked at the intricate fastenings at the back of her dress.

He managed to get it open, and she slipped out of it, stepped free. Her shoes fell over on the floor, from her swollen ankles. She padded over to the wardrobe, and chose a gray skirt and rose cashmere sweater. She had been cold for so long, it had been chilly during the rainy night.

Zach left, to take a shower and change his clothes at one of the other bathrooms, leaving theirs to her. She stood under the shower, luxuriating in the warm water. She washed her hair, dried it a little, tied it back with a rose ribbon, before donning the skirt and sweater and some loose slippers.

Zach returned as she was pushing back her hair again. He looked weary, but calm, shaved, in gray shirt and sweater. His red hair stood up in peaks, he went to the mirror and brushed it back, in a familiar movement she had thought never to see again. How good the homey gesture looked. How good to be home, how good to see Zach standing near her, moving about their room.

He saw her in the mirror, watching him with love in her eyes. He turned about, held out his arms. She rushed into them, clung to him.

"Oh, my darling, my darling," he murmured, holding her tightly to him.

"Oh, Zach, I am so glad to be home!"

"Never, never do it again!" he said.

"Oh, never, never. I'll never run away again! I was so foolish!"

"Next time, talk to me!"

"I will, I will!"

"And I despise and detest, completely abhor, Melinda Valdes. I never loved her!"

"Oh—really?" she gasped. He nodded firmly.

"Isolde told me what she said. She was wicked, nasty, and completely wrong. I have not yet forgiven her for making such trouble. And Marcos shall go to the university and finish his chemistry work, his father permitting."

"Oh, Zach!" Her eyes began to shine. She put up her hand shyly to caress his smooth-shaven cheek. "I do—love you—so very much!"

"You had better, my girl! Because I love you more than anybody in the world. Hear me?"

She nodded shyly, glowing up at him. Their lips met, slowly, more deeply, and she rested against him, wishing she did not feel so tired. She would like to go to bed with him! But their families waited downstairs.

He released her slightly, to hold her back and look down into her face. "Oh, Rosita, so much trouble! If only we had talked honestly with each other! I was worried that you wanted to leave me and dance again, up in New York, and over so far in Europe!"

"Only if you did not want me! Only if you longed for that horribly beautiful Melinda!"

"She is ugly beside you!"

She chuckled, and hugged him, her arms about his neck. "I want to give you children, Zach," she said, blushing. "I want—I want to live with you always, comfort you, love you, help you—if I can—"

"My darling, just being you, that is what I want. If you want to dance, you shall, only don't leave me! You want that

407

dance school in Puerto Rico? You shall have it, only don't go away!" They kissed again, deeply, arms about each other.

"It would be so good for my family," she said simply. "That is why I want it. You would agree, then?"

He nodded, said reluctantly, "Let's go down and tell them, eh? Then we can go back to bed," and he laughed at the look she gave him, and hugged her frankly.

They went downstairs, slowly, arms about each other. Angelica beamed at them, said, "I will bring hot food, Señor, Señora! And fresh coffee, yes?"

"Yes, thank you, Angelica."

Jaime was in the hallway, again guarding. They smiled at him, he beamed, relief in his face.

In the drawing room, the talk stopped, all turned to see the couple walking in. Marcos was weary, unshaven, the bandage about his head dirty. But he looked blissfully happy, sitting with Delphine next to him on the arm of his chair.

Madame Sonia said, "Oh, my Rosita!" and held out her arms, tears in her eyes. Rosita went over to her, and knelt to put one arm about each of them, Madame Sonia and Señora Alejandra. Their faces were so weary, they each looked older this morning. They hugged her fiercely with frail arms.

"I'll bet you have been gossiping and bragging about your dancing," she said, with mock severity, smiling into the little wrinkled faces.

"I told her, I danced for the Czar of Russia!" said Madame Sonia.

"And I told her—I refused to dance for the Czar of Russia!" Alejandra said with a sharp satisfied nod.

Everyone in the room began to laugh. Honors were even.

Then they were all talking at once. Had Rosita been harmed? No? God be thanked! Had she eaten? Only beer and pizza? Horrors! Prayers had been said constantly. Nobody had slept much.

How was Marcos? Rosita had to hug him, and examine his face anxiously. "Your head—does it hurt?" she asked.

"Abominably!" he said, smiling. Delphine at once had to kiss his head. That made it better, he was sure, he said adoringly.

Rosita wondered, they were frankly sitting together, holding to each other, and nobody sent them so much as a bad look. Miracles!

Pascual hugged her, and her mother, and Madame Isabeau. Oliverio hugged her in silence, fiercely, it was not his way to speak his emotions. Tadeo and Inez. Isolde, even Dimitre all hugged her. Kevin grinned, and kissed her cheek. All the men looked so tired and unshaven. Zach looked the best, rested and cheerful, though he had not rested, she thought, not at all.

Two maids brought in trays of food for Rosita and Zach, another maid brought in hot coffee and tea, and began to fill the cups again.

"Well, we must go home now," said Pascual, more formally. "Now we know Rosita is safe and at home, thank God."

"You have telephoned Elena and Luisa?" asked Rosita.

"*Sí*, and Jacinto has gone to them, to reassure them in person. So, all is well, we are grateful to the Virgin."

"Before you go," said Zach, laying down his fork. He looked at Isolde. "I think my sister Isolde has something to ask you. About the school, Isolde. In San Juan. As you said."

She looked startled, then happy. "You agree, Zach? Really?"

He nodded. "Only don't get too many big ideas! And don't count on Rosita leaving San Juan! I want her here!"

She made a little face at him, happily, then turned to the politely questioning face of Pascual. She began to tell him about the school. He was bewildered.

"A school, in San Juan? To teach flamenco dancing?"

"And ballet, and folk dancing in the Caribbean styles," she said. "And I don't know anyone better than you for teaching flamenco. If you can succeed in teaching Delphine, you can teach anybody!"

"All right, Isolde!" said Delphine, laughing.

"But our work—in the nightclubs—" began Pascual, worried, glancing to Marcos and to Zach. "We must continue—"

Zach said quietly, "I think you could continue that. You would take whatever engagements you wish. Then in the daytime, for two or three hours, you and your sons and daughters would teach flamenco, and give demonstrations. You would rehearse the dancers, I believe. Programs would be made up, of combined dances, some flamenco, some ballet, some folk, for presentation in San Juan.''

"And later on, in New York, Miami, New Orleans—'' added Isolde.

"And perhaps in London, Paris, Rome,'' said Dimitre.

"When you are ready, in later years,'' added Zach firmly. "Begin small, do good careful work, build up. Then when you are ready, the dancers prepared well, that is the time to speak of going farther afield!''

Rosita added excitedly, "And Oliverio might teach some of them guitar! And he would play his own compositions for them to dance!''

Her older brother gave her a dazed look. She smiled at him, glowing, and nodded, pleading. He was so talented, surely he could do this!

"What name shall you use?'' asked Madame Sonia, entering into it with enthusiasm. "I think—the ballet of San Juan—no, that does not include it all. The dance company of San Juan, Puerto Rico—''

"Puerto Rican Dance,'' suggested Tadeo.

"San Juan Dance Company,'' suggested Zach, and that was what they finally decided on.

Kevin, ever practical, said, "I'll look it up, make sure nobody else is using the name. Then it should be advertised, to keep it. Something like copyright. Do they copyright names?''

Tadeo said, "Then we can get more girls for the act!''

"I don't see why!'' said Inez hotly, giving him a punch in the ribs.

"Because we need more girls,'' said Marcos. "The girls, in the dance company, the men also, could join the act from time to time, good experience.''

Rosita finished her eggs and bacon, drank the last coffee from her cup, and looked at Zach. He nodded. While everybody was still talking, they managed to slip from the room. Madame Sonia saw them go, so did Señora Alejandra, everybody else was busy talking and arguing, planning and adding to the ideas.

The two older women nodded to each other, and smiled, well pleased. They were the only sensible ones in the room, they thought. They knew what was important in life!

"The heritage goes on," murmured Alejandra. "My *gitana* is a fine dancer, she will have fine sons!"

"And Zach will protect her and cherish her," said Madame Sonia.

In their room, Rosita slipped off her shoes, and lay down, sighing. "I could sleep a week!" she murmured.

Zach nodded. He took off his shoes, yawned, was too tired to remove his clothes. He lay down beside her, put his arm over her.

He remembered the horror of the previous two nights, and held her closely. She was there now, in his arms, as he had longed to have her.

She turned her head, gazed into his eyes. "I vowed," she said, "if—when I got out, I would know what was the most important value of my life."

"What?" he asked, knowing.

"Having each other, loving, giving," she said.

He caressed her cheek with his fingers, gravely. He drew her even closer, kissed her lips. Their lips clung, they sighed with love, with weariness, with relief. Kissing, they closed their eyes, oblivious of the talking, arguing and laughing going on beneath them in the drawing room.

The families were united at last in love of Zach and Rosita, and would be even more so in love of dance. But they would not always agree!

Blissfully, Zach and Rosita were unaware that Isolde was already arguing with Tadeo about the first program, whether flamenco or ballet should be first on the numbers. And whether Rosita should dance one or the other.

Pascual raised his eyebrows resignedly at Madame Isabeau. She shook her lovely graying head, and said, "I really think there are other matters to plan first, Isolde!"

"We shall talk another time," said Pascual. And he managed to get his brood out of the house. Isolde accompanied them to the door.

"Come tomorrow!" she cried. "We must talk more!"

"But of course, it is our pleasure," said Pascual, bowing.

Isolde closed the door, and sighed. "Oh, there is so much to do!" she said dramatically. "I must get busy—oh, where is everybody going?"

"To bed!" said Delphine firmly, already halfway up the stairs, dreamy of gaze from Marcos's last kiss. "Like sensible people!"

Isolde finally gave up, everybody had departed. She went up to her room, and lay down, with pages in her hand, and a pen snatched up to write. She had so many people to work with now, she began to write down all the names—all the Hamiltons, all the Dominguez—and Dimitre—and she would hire more, and take in pupils at the school—all those people to manage—

First, they must rent a building, buy it if possible. Decorate the rooms, plan for a stage for practice and rehearsals. An auditorium? For small productions at first?

Pascual would help her, he knew how to choreograph. Dimitre—first dance with Rosita—a big number—with many dancers—

While everyone slept, Isolde wrote and wrote, until the pen dropped from her hand and rolled on the rug. And then she, too, slept, to dream of dancing, dancing across an endless blue heaven with thousands of men and girls—her own huge company, and music playing—and stars shining brightly down on both their proud, dancing families—

WARNER ROMANCE
BY DOROTHY DANIELS

THE LANIER RIDDLE
by Dorothy Daniels   (D84-806, $1.75)
Polly Lanier's testimony had once sent Stacy Bryant to prison for the murder of her sister. Now Stacy was free and Polly sees a glimmering through the windows of The Elms, which has been locked since her sister's death. From that moment on, Polly's life and sanity are in danger.

THE MAGIC RING
by Dorothy Daniels   (D82-789, $2.25)
It was a gift from the parents she had not seen since their return to Italy when she was eight. Angela slipped it on her finger and made a promise to herself. She would find her parents once again, even if she had to defy the secret societies that held Italy in terror, even if she must risk her life.

THE MARBLE HILLS
by Dorothy Daniels   (D84-807, $1.75)
For two months she lived in a world of unconsciousness. Then three strangers came to claim her and brought her to a village she didn't remember. Slowly, inexorably, the past begins to catch up, and she is forced to face the demonic facts of the village's existence.

A MIRROR OF SHADOWS
by Dorothy Daniels   (D92-149, $2.25)
Beautiful Maeve O'Hanlon cherished the ancient mirror which revealed images she could not disclose to anyone. Around her swirled the hatred and scheming of the Camerons—the rich and powerful family that had vowed to destroy the young Irish girl who had dared to marry Joel Cameron.